the GLASS TOWN game

Catherynne M. Valente

ILLUSTRATED BY REBECCA GREEN

MARGARET K. MCELDERRY BOOKS
New York London Toronto Sydney New Delhi

MARGARET K. McELDERRY BOOKS
An imprint of Simon & Schuster Children's Publishing Division
1230 Avenue of the Americas, New York, New York 10020
This book is a work of fiction. Any references to historical events, real
people, or real places are used fictitiously. Other names, characters,
places, and events are products of the author's imagination, and any
resemblance to actual events or places or persons, living or dead, is
entirely coincidental.
Text copyright © 2017 by Catherynne M. Valente
Illustrations copyright © 2017 by Rebecca Green
All rights reserved, including the right of reproduction in whole or in
part in any form.
MARGARET K. McELDERRY BOOKS is a trademark of Simon &
Schuster, Inc.
For information about special discounts for bulk purchases, please
contact Simon & Schuster Special Sales at 1-866-506-1949
or business@simonandschuster.com.
The Simon & Schuster Speakers Bureau can bring authors to your live
event. For more information or to book an event, contact the Simon
& Schuster Speakers Bureau at 1-866-248-3049 or visit our website at
www.simonspeakers.com.
Book design by Sonia Chaghatzbanian and Irene Metaxatos
The text for this book was set in Goudy Oldstyle Std.
The illustrations for this book were rendered in pencil.
Manufactured in the United States of America
0717 FFG
First Edition
10 9 8 7 6 5 4 3 2 1
CIP data for this book is available from the Library of Congress.
ISBN 978-1-4814-7696-6 (hardcover)
ISBN 978-1-4814-7698-0 (eBook)

FOR MY HEATH ON THE MOORS

AND, BEGGING THEIR FORGIVENESS,
FOR FOUR EXTRAORDINARY CHILDREN
I WISH I COULD HAVE KNOWN

It seemed as if I were a non-existent shadow—that I neither spoke, ate, imagined, or lived of myself, but I was the mere idea of some other creature's brain. The Glass Town seemed so likewise. My father . . . and everyone with whom I am acquainted, passed into a state of annihilation; but suddenly I thought again that I and my relatives did exist and yet, not us, but our minds, and our bodies without ourselves. Then this supposition—the oddest of any—followed the former quickly, namely, that WE without US were shadows; also, but at the end of a long vista, as it were, appeared dimly and indistinctly, beings that really lived in a tangible shape, that were called by our names and were US from whom WE had been copied by something—I could not tell what.

Another world formed part of this reverie . . . England was there but totally different in manners, customs, inhabitants.

—CHARLOTTE BRONTË
AGE 12

But surely you and everybody have a notion
that there is, or should be, an existence of
yours beyond you.

–EMILY BRONTË

And who can tell but Heaven, at last,
May answer all my thousand prayers,
And bid the future pay the past
With joy for anguish, smiles for tears?

—ANNE BRONTË

Forsooth, I'm the greatest man in the world
and these ladies the best judges!

—BRANWELL BRONTË,
AGE 13

PART I

A Sound Called Wuthering

ONE

The Bees

Once, four children called Charlotte, Emily, Anne, and Branwell lived all together in a village called Haworth in the very farthest, steepest, highest, northernest bit of England. Their house stood snugly at the very farthest, steepest, highest bit of the village, just behind the church and the crowded graveyard, for their father was the parson. Every Sunday he stood up in the chapel and told the tightly buttoned people of Haworth all about the wonders of a buttoned-up heaven and the dangers of this buttoned-down earth. The four of them were mostly looked after by their Aunt Elizabeth and their maidservant, Tabitha, for a parson has very little time for children, what with all that worrying about heaven and earth and buttoning, both up and down. But oftener and oftener, they looked after each other, which suited them very well.

Charlotte was the oldest. Her thick hair parted through the center of her skull like a dark sea. She had a round, pale face, a fearsome scowl, and a smile that was slow to come, but worth the wait. Branwell felt quite strongly that just because he was eleven and Charlotte was twelve didn't mean she could do anything he couldn't do, or know anything he didn't know. He had dark eyes and eyelashes and eyebrows and dark, curly hair. When he frowned, which he almost always did, he looked just like a storm cloud come to life. Emily, close behind her brother at ten years old, had ringlets the color of hazelnuts, soft gray eyes, and a wonderful memory. She could remember the tiniest details, like the color of the gloves she wore on the day their mother died. As for Anne, the youngest, she was very nearly the prettiest child in Haworth. Her hair shone almost the same blond as the girls in fancy paintings. Even though she'd only just turned eight, she watched everyone with her wide gray-violet eyes so intently that the whole house felt a little as though she were spying on them, making reports to some invisible spymaster.

There had been more of them, once. They used to be six. Maria and Lizzie, older than Charlotte, with matching fiery brown eyes and red cheeks and big, rolling voices. All the girls but Anne had gone merrily off to school together, but Lizzie and Maria caught matching fiery fevers and what came back in the carriage with poor Emily and poor Charlotte they'd buried in the churchyard. It was too big a thing to hold in their heads all at once, like the idea that the moon was actually a huge cold stone hanging in the lonely dark forever. They knew that *was* true, but if they tried to go outside and *see* how vast and empty it really was, they just couldn't make it *feel* true. They couldn't keep something that distant and frightening inside them for more than a minute. They had to go on with living, one foot in front of the other. How could anyone do that knowing something so unfathomably heavy and silent was just hanging above you all the time, with nothing to keep it from plummeting toward you without a bit of warning? All they could face in the night was a few soft beams of moonlight through the window, and the knowledge that they would never be six again.

Most days, the four of them were quite content to play indoors in the room at the top of the stairs. They tried not to cause much trouble for Aunt Elizabeth and

Tabitha and Papa. Causing trouble meant extra chores and early bedtimes with no candles. Still, they could never manage to be *completely* good. Each of them had a criminal specialty, a particular wickedness they could never resist.

Emily was an expert smuggler. She could burgle the stumps of candles up to their room before Tabitha even noticed they'd burned down low. The very second Papa finished reading an issue of one of his magazines, *Blackwood's Edinburgh Magazine*, the *Leeds Intelligencer*, or the *Quarterly Review*, it would vanish from his bedside table in Emily's hot little hands. She hid bits of seedcake and bread and boiled carrots away in her skirt at supper and fed them secretly to a little gang of birds through the playroom window.

Anne really did spy on nearly everyone. She could sneak and creep and vanish again like a fox in the hedgerows. Her ears were like little soft bear traps lying in wait for any scrap of whisper that floated through the house, and the village, too. She didn't understand exactly *every* word gruff grown-ups in brown coats and brown skirts mumbled under their breath. But she always remembered them anyhow so that she could ask Charlotte what *compound interest* or *tuberculosis* meant after supper. Secrets great and small stood no chance when Anne was about.

Charlotte could lie better and with a straighter face than any member of Parliament. She knew the truth was important, and honorable, and befitting the daughter of a parson. But whenever anyone asked her the simplest little question, a thousand terribly *un*-simple, magnificently *un*-little answers came flooding into her mind, and each of them shone far brighter than the tatty old truth. When Tabitha spoke sternly to her on the subject of stray salt left all over the kitchen and not tidied up in the least, she could have just apologized like a fine, upstanding girl. They'd snuck downstairs to play Polar Exploration and built up proper banks of snow crystals to conquer. But wasn't it just an awful lot more *interesting* to tell the maidservant that a star had fallen to earth last night, and walked all the way across the moors without touching the grass, and stars are just *beasts* for salt, don't you know? Even if Papa asked her something as tiny and silly as whether or not she had seen his pipe lying about, Charlotte would sometimes tell him she hadn't when she could see it resting just there, on the left-most bookshelf. She just wanted to see what sort of evening would unfold if she did the *unexpected* thing.

Branwell, however, had a true genius for badness. He was both a vandal *and* a brawler. He pinched his sisters whenever he could—it was so glorious to hear them shriek and see them squirm! He tussled with the neighbor boys, and should a dog ever bite him, he would bite back, every time, and *hard*. Branwell, when he was not hurling himself at things, had begun to furtively sketch the girls' faces on the plaster wall of the room at the top of the stairs. He desperately loved to draw, and he had no other models. He had no interest at all in becoming a parson like his father. Branwell would be a great painter. He hadn't told Papa yet, of course, but he knew it in his kneecaps. He practiced on his sisters because he didn't like to paint himself. After all, it was a boy's job to make things—furniture and machines and money and books and governments and art and such. It was a girl's job to sit still and let someone else make something out of *them*, and that was that.

Almost all their crimes went to furnish that room at the top of the stairs in high style. It was hardly more than a drafty white closet, nestled like a secret between Papa's room and Aunt Elizabeth's. But the four children ruled over it as their sovereign kingdom. They decreed, once and for all, that no person taller than a hat-stand could disturb their territory, on penalty of not being spoken to for a week. The geographical features of their empire were few: a woven green rug, a little matching desk and bookshelf, a slim bed against one wall, and a tall, narrow window that looked out on a splendid oak tree and down into the churchyard. Of course, none of them *slept* in that slim bed. The room at the top of the stairs was for better things than snoring. They kept it well-stocked with paper and inkwells and toys and watercolor paints. At the moment, they counted among the subjects of this small and tidy kingdom: Snowflake, Rainbow, and Diamond (a half-blind elderly raven, one-legged sparrow hawk, and motherless baby owl who visited at the window most nights), Jasper the pheasant who could not fly up into the tree but visited all the same, pecking among the roots, and two dusty dolls with lavender bonnets. But the three older children had ignored the dolls for months in favor of their prize possessions: twelve jointed wooden soldiers Papa had given as a Christmas present to his only son. The girls had made a quick end to *that*. No sooner had Branwell got the box open but his sisters had seized up his troops and named them outlandish things like Crashey and Bravey and Cracky and Sneaky and Gravey and Cheeky and the Duke of Wellington and Rogue and Goody and Naughty and Napoleon Bonaparte and Stumps, shouting with excitement while Bran fumed. Each quickly claimed their favorites for themselves and hoarded them close. Only Anne still loved her doll. Branwell could be bullied out of his soldiers, but Anne would not be moved on the subject of the ratty old thing with yellow horsehair and green glass eyes.

Charlotte and Branwell's favorite game was Welly and Boney. Charlotte adored the Duke of Wellington as fiercely as Branwell worshipped Bonaparte. The battle lines were drawn, the playroom nation divided. They knew all about the war with France from Papa's magazines. But whenever they tried to imagine what a war was actually *like*, it unfolded in their heads like a cross between a chess game, a horse race, a country dance, and a very racy night at the theater. What they felt absolutely certain about was that, some time ago, a French fellow named Napoleon Bonaparte had crowned himself King of Everything without asking Everything its thoughts on the subject. Then, another, *different* fellow called the Duke of Wellington, who was English like themselves, boldly, fearlessly, and possibly single-handedly, thumped Bonaparte and whumped him and jumped him until he was King of Nothing Much. Papa still didn't drink claret wine. He said it was too French to be any good for him. The whole world had once loved playing Welly and Boney, and Branwell and Charlotte did not want to be left out just because they'd gotten born a bit late.

Emily much preferred Polar Exploration, with her wooden men Captains Ross and Parry slashing the frozen sea in half to find treasure at the bottom. Whenever she touched Parry's wooden shoulders, ice filled Emily's mind, ice that went on and on forever and never stopped. It looked so clean to her, like a perfect lace tablecloth. Until her great wild roaring ships tore the lace to pieces, their sails clanging with icicles, their cannons full of fire.

Anne liked stories of Kings and Queens and Princes and Princesses best. In her hands, the wooden army became a glittering court full of schemes and intrigue and whispers behind curtains. She read through all of Papa's magazines very carefully for any smallest mention of the Royal Family. She wanted her games to be so near to real life that she could hear the bells of Westminster in her dreams. Finally, Anne found a perfect playmate, a minor, unimportant young Princess nearly her own age. She named the horsehair doll after the noble child and made her the star of all her imaginings. Of course she was always very respectful and never let Branwell torture or starve the Princess. You had to mind your manners, she knew, when telling unreal stories about real people. Anne did hope the girl wouldn't be cross at having fantastic tales told about her in Yorkshire. Victoria wasn't in any danger of inheriting the Crown in real life, after all, and London was so awfully far away. Surely the Princess wouldn't be bothered by Anne fibbing about her to make a nice story, as long as it was *very* nice.

But no matter the game, Branwell insisted on being at the center of it, whether he lurched around as Scurvy, the Vicious Prince of the Arctic Seals, or the wicked Marquis of Douro, out to steal Princess Victoria for his bride, or even as Napoleon himself. As the only boy, Bran knew the burden of being the hero of all their games, and indeed their lives, rested firmly with him. But somehow, his sisters were far too dense to understand this essential truth. He allowed them to touch his things only because he was magnanimous and very kind to those less excellent than himself.

Just lately, however, Crashey and Bravey and Welly and Boney and Ross and Parry and the boys had not fought quite so valiantly as they used to. Something about Gravey and Rogue's wooden caps and delicately carved rifles seemed to droop and sigh. The brave wooden lads lay in every which position, snoozing against the narrow windowsill, routed on the battlefield of the bed, hiding in terror behind a fortification of stacked books. Branwell's drawings suffered, as well. He could not get Anne's hair to curl the right way anymore, and Emily's nose simply would not *nose*. Now, whenever Emily tried to imagine the Arctic Circle, she could only see the flat, unbroken ice groaning on into forever, and no grand ship would come to shatter it. Anne's little wooden kingdom got rather stable and boring. She couldn't even coax Douro into sticking his dagger into one rival Lord. Even Charlotte's lovely handwriting melted into a sad little scrawl. Tabitha always said Charlotte wrote just as pretty as King George and twice as clear. But now, you could not tell her capitals from a chimney sweep's swipe.

"It's on account of the Beastliest Day," whispered Anne to her brother. Her eyes widened to hold the tears that trembled in her lashes. "It's so close now!"

"I know, Annie, I know," sighed Branwell, licking the tip of his best drawing pencil. "But if we say its name it'll only come faster. Now hold still. I've almost got your hands looking like hands again and not paws."

The Beastliest Day hung like gray, wet curtains over the Parsonage. Even the grown-ups couldn't pretend everything was perfectly all right, and it's practically a grown-up's job to pretend everything is perfectly all right. But Charlotte and Emily would not allow one word on the subject. If Branwell or Anne so much as took a breath to speak of it, Emily would only say: *Hush. We're together now and now is all that matters.* And Charlotte would say: *None of that. We've just got to stick as close as we can while we still have the chance, and soak up that close like a washcloth.*

One rare evening, Papa *and* Aunt Elizabeth *and* Tabitha sat in the red-rugged parlor by the fire, going about their mystifying old-people games: knitting, sewing, and tidying the books. Anne had only recently come to understand that *tidying the books* didn't mean Papa sat in his big cocoa-colored chair in the night dusting up the corners in Mr. Coleridge's poetry or soaping down the fairies in Mr. Shakespeare's plays, but something or other to do with money and making more of it come in than go out.

Aunt Elizabeth held up a lace shawl to the firelight. The pattern was so fine it looked like the flames themselves. Emily gave a strangled little sigh of envy. Aunt Elizabeth had such a clever hand with everything. She could make a dirty old piece of string into a ball gown if she had a mind to. Emily could hardly manage socks without help with the blasted heel. But she immediately regretted making any noise at all. The girls had become so sullen lately that Aunt Elizabeth seized upon her niece's sigh as a rare sign of life and ran off into the hedges with that sigh in her pocket. She patted Emily's head and dove straight into the Forbidden Topic without warning.

"It's for you to take with you, my darling. It really won't be so terrible, you know. . . ."

Emily froze. Charlotte's head snapped up from her book. The girls' glares burned so fiercely Branwell turned away, feeling his own cheeks go an unseemly red.

"Don't you *dare* say that," Charlotte hissed. "Or Maria and Lizzie will come up out of the ground and show you just how wrong you are."

Aunt Elizabeth's face drained of color. A tiny yelp escaped Anne's throat. They weren't to use those names in the house! Charlotte *said*. And if you didn't do what Charlotte said the sun would fall out of the sky and the river would turn black and the moors would catch on fire.

Tabitha folded her spectacles sternly and laid them in her lap as she usually did before telling one of her ripping stories of goblins on the Yorkshire moors. But this time, she didn't say anything about Ginny Greenteeth pulling wicked children down into her green dungeon under the River Nidd.

"We must all suffer through dreadful things in this wicked world, poor duckies. But . . ." The blue-eyed maid started to say: *when we come out the other end we're always the stronger for't,* but she couldn't quite believe in it. She started again: *but the good Lord never lets us draw a card we can't play,* but caught herself, and thought better of talking cards in front of the Master. Finally, she tried: *but now't's so beastly as we dream it in the dark,* but even that left a bad taste in her mouth. She couldn't lie to little ones. It was a weakness in her, she knew.

"But what, Miss Tabby?" chirped Anne. Tabitha felt certain, as she so often did, that the child knew her exact thoughts just as plain as a picture.

"Yes," Emily said coldly. "But what?"

The twisted, furious expression on Emily's dear face withered up her words. Tabitha flushed shamefully, put her glasses back on, and squinted at her embroidery.

Papa felt instinctively that he was losing control over his parlor. "I'll have none of this back-talking," he grumbled from behind a formidable mask of gray beard, spectacles, and soft evening cap. "You are my daughters and you will do as you are told. The books can't bear all four of you eating your way through Yorkshire and half of Scotland. And a country parson's daughters will tempt few husbands of real substance. If only we'd had more boys!" His craggy, half-handsome face softened. "I have prayed for a better fate than this, poppets. And I shall keep praying, every night and day. God gives us only a few choices in this life, but He always looks after us, in His way. Now, no more long faces! Mind your Bees and it'll all come out right enough. Do you remember your Bees?"

The children looked round at one another. Papa

never did the Bees. It was Mama's little saying she'd made up all by herself for her babies. She would tell them sternly to repeat after her and then make marvelous buzzing noises against their cheeks like a whole hive of bumblebees until they couldn't breathe for laughing. They kept saying it long after she was gone, when they couldn't sleep for worry or sorrow or cold. But there were fewer bees now. They'd retired Maria and Lizzie's parts. It seemed only right, after everything.

"Buck up," whispered Charlotte, weeping softly into her book.

"Be brave," whispered Emily, clutching her sister's hand.

This was where Maria would say: *button your coat!* And Lizzie would chime in: *buckle your soul!* But they didn't, because they couldn't.

"Busy hands," mumbled Branwell, pressing the sharp end of his pencil miserably into his thumb.

"Make bright hearts," finished Anne, as somber as the rest, even though she didn't remember Mama at all, except for a fuzzy, buzzy idea of something soft and warm and sweet and safe, with big dark eyes and hair as long as forever.

January came with an awful suddenness. All the holiday things had been put neatly away and the serious business of the year pressed hard against the house at the top of the hill. All the long week before, it had rained mercilessly, until the whole world seemed made of nothing but mud puddles and the only folk still living in it a few half-drowned field mice and badgers with stuffed-up noses. All week long, Charlotte and Emily had stared mournfully out the window of the room at the top of the stairs, hoping the whole world would just drown itself and leave them alone at the helm of their house, which they would steer and sail like Noah's old yacht. They had gotten quite a ways into a very sober listing of Which Animals They Should Like to Save and Which to Leave Owing to Being Crawly or Otherwise Horrid. All week long, Branwell and Anne had talked of nothing but What We Shall Do When the Rain Stops. For surely the rain couldn't last all the way up to the Beastliest Day. It just couldn't. The world wouldn't do that to them.

But when, at last, the rain ran away down to London to bother the bankers and the barons instead, their time had run out.

The Beastliest Day was upon them.

TWO

The Beastliest Day

There was every possibility of taking a walk that day. But not the walk they wished to take. However fine the air outside, however brilliant the sun, however inviting the winding paths through the moors, the air and the sun and the paths weren't theirs to explore. The only path they'd be allowed out of the garden and through the village would end in a lonely, dark town called Keighley and an even lonelier, darker carriage drawn by a lonely, dark horse. The carriage meant take Emily and Charlotte far away, to the Clergy Daughters' School in Cowan Bridge, the loneliest, darkest place of all.

The Beastliest Day had come.

When Emily heard anyone say the word *School*, she always flinched, as though it were the name of a horrible beast with black fur and vicious sickly eyes that she and her sister had just barely escaped. As far as Emily was concerned, that's just what it was. School always had a capital letter, just like all the most frightening things: God and the Devil and the King and the Empire. It was cold in the belly of the School-Beast. Cold and damp and there was never enough food. Children's coughs and the sounds of whippings hung in the air like lanterns. The only lesson was: *Shut your mouth, girl.* And School didn't like to let you leave its belly once it had you. Charlotte hadn't always been the oldest. She'd been stuck in the middle with Emily until only last year. Then, Maria, who was so tall, and Lizzie, who was so clever, got so cold and so damp and so hungry that their insides burned up trying to keep them warm. Every time Emily looked out the window of the room at the top of the stairs, these were the things she saw. The raven, the sparrow hawk, and the owl in the great yew tree. Mama, Maria, and Elizabeth in the ground. But though School had already devoured two of them, Papa was determined that his daughters should be educated. So that they could go into service, he said, so that they could become governesses, and produce an income of their own. Besides, he assured them, the place was much reformed since they left it.

Emily would rather have burned the whole village down than go back to that wicked, damp, cold, hungry School for one single instant. Of course, Papa would not dream of such a place for his only son. The parson instructed Branwell himself, in languages and history and figures, and they both got cake at teatime. Bran got all the good of the world as far as Emily could see it. Aunt Elizabeth insisted Little Anne was too young just yet, but in another year or two her time would come. Emily tried not to hate anything, but sometimes it crept up on her and pounced when she wasn't looking. Sometimes she found herself watching Anne comb her long hair and hating her, because Anne was allowed to be eight and still at home learning from the books in their lovely familiar parlor and eating Tabitha's puddings. Annie was eight already, but Emily had gone to Cowan Bridge when she was six. She'd braved the journey all alone, sitting in a gray carriage that bruised her as it clattered down a road that was barely a road. She'd disappeared into a gray classroom surrounded by gray girls, so frightened of the Headmaster and his punishments that she could feel the beating of her heart in her eyeballs. Maria and Lizzie had gone together, then Charlotte. They'd all had each other to cling to, like hens in a yard. Of course Charlotte hated School and wanted revenge upon it, but Emily felt certain her sister hadn't quite the blackened *terror* of the place crunching on her heart the way she did. It wasn't the same. Charlotte could survive anything. She'd out-last the moors out of sheer stubbornness.

Emily had no idea that Charlotte dreamt every night of that dank, pale place, with only the rain coming through the roof for company, and little girls coughing like their lungs meant to get free once and for all to sing her to sleep.

The Beastliest Day laughed in the face of January and dawned as brilliant and bright as June. The blue York-shire morning shone so crisp it seemed ready to snap in half at the slightest touch. Great scoops of vanilla sun-shine melted on the moors. The shadows of great, mis-chievous clouds cut the shaggy hills into a checkerboard of yellow and purple grasses. Little flocks of straggler sparrows pecked hopefully for worms in kitchen gardens, sleepy rabbits washed their whiskers in dry, cozy barns, and Charlotte and Emily sat alone in the room at the top of the stairs and cried.

Tabitha, to her credit, got a whole boiled egg, a wedge of bread, and a dab of her good plum jam into each of the four children, though no one felt much like eating. She and Aunt Elizabeth led them in one last whirlwind of household duties. On any other day, this would have been a pitched battle. Howls of injustice and declarations of the rights of children on one side, and on the other, promises, threats, bargains, appeals to heaven and all the angels. A double story tonight after supper if Charlotte would clear up the remains of breakfast. No sweets at all this week if Branwell didn't take the scraps out to the chickens and bring in the eggs. If only Anne would sort the mending into baskets, she might leave off her embroidery tonight and have the whole evening to read as she liked. And certainly Emily's soul would be saved forever by simply doing as she was told for once!

But none of that happened. Not on the Beastliest Day. Charlotte set one last kettle to boil as though she loved nothing so well in all the world. Emily lovingly put aside the evening bread to rise. Anne sweetly stirred the batter for a luncheon cake her sisters wouldn't even get to nibble. Branwell got the laundry water boiling without complaint. He even offered to cut potatoes for the mutton stew so Tabitha could rest her feet. But the old maidservant did not have it in her to rest so much as a toe. While everything bubbled (Aunt Elizabeth often said that bubbling was the main activity of a proper household between mealtimes: the bubbling of water, yeast, and one's own good mind) Tabitha set out their bonnets and caps and gloves and extra-thick woolen stockings.

All that remained was the room at the top of the stairs.

It needed constant minding, that perfect little white-washed country. And Charlotte made certain it always got it. Even if Emily, Anne, and Branwell had been born slovenly creatures with a stocking behind each ear, which they had not, really, Charlotte's heart was a clean, snug, and well-ordered place. With the iron jaw of a great Admiral before a grim battle at sea, she strove to match the world to her heart. Besides, she was the old-est. It was down to her to make the rules—at least this one last time. Under Charlotte's careful gaze, they put order to their upstairs universe. They straightened and swept and tidied and scrubbed off the ink stains on the floor. They stacked the newer editions of their beloved stolen magazines in alphabetical order. They said good-bye to the raven, the sparrow hawk, and the owl, and the birds seemed to nod soberly, as if they quite understood. Emily propped the threadbare dolls up where the two of them could see out into the churchyard and keep Mama, Maria, and Lizzie company. At last, they laid the wooden soldiers away neatly in their fine latched box.

"Take . . . take Crashey with you," urged Branwell, slipping his favorite of the brave lads into Charlotte's

suitcase. Charlotte felt her brother's forehead to see if he had caught some strange fever that made him *want* to share. He waved her off. "I don't expect I shall like playing Wellington and Bonaparte with only Anne to man the English side, anyway."

"I *can* man the English side!" cried Anne from the hallway, her pride quite, quite wounded. "I'll shoot the French right out of your mouth, you'll see!"

They all fell quiet. They knew very well that without Charlotte to dream up new adventures for her Duke and Emily to insist upon playing Polar Exploration instead, Branwell and Anne would settle on some other game of their own. By the time they all saw one another again, they would hardly remember where they'd left the Duke of Wellington and the Emperor of France, or why they'd ever fought so fiercely. In the end, Charlotte knew better than to refuse a gift from her brother, as she might never get one again. She folded a thick brown skirt round Crashey to keep him safe in her suitcase. Emily took Bravey, and thus ended the Napoleonic Wars. Finally, they could r think of any more ways to put off the beastliest part c Beastliest Day.

"Perhaps it *is* all different now," Emily w though she didn't believe it for a second. "W one came along while we weren't looking ?

over Cowan Bridge and now it's always summer there, and there's apples running down the rain spouts and fresh bread hanging on blue ribbons from every streetlamp and hot tea in the village well and a tiny dragon to keep every hearth lit all night long. And, and . . ." She faltered.

"And pixies in the pub," Charlotte jumped in, stroking her sister's hair, just as Lizzie had done to her whenever she was upset. This was part of the Eldest Child's Chores, as much as laundry or mending. Stroking Hair, Drying Tears, Never Showing How Afraid You Are, Disciplining the Naughty. Setting an Example. Charlotte wasn't at all sure she was doing them right. She never thought she'd have to do them at all. "And wheels of cheese in the fields instead of hay, and cider in the river, and books swimming around in it like fish, and you and me with miniature maypoles to fish with, and, and . . ."

Anne crept down the hall, listening to the older girls play the Game of And. Anne loved the Game of And almost as much as she loved toffee and Tabitha's stories, and not only because she'd thought, for the longest time, that it was the Game of Anne. They all played it whenever they had to do something boring or unpleasant, like mixing lye soap for laundry. *What if someone came along* *vhile we weren't looking and swapped the lye for powerful* *blin powders and the washing water for the Water of Life*

and . . . Then, one of them would catch on and pick it up and keep it going. *. . . AND made all our dresses and Branwell's Sunday suit come to life and take us away to the Kingdom of Clothes where they use thimbles for shillings and buttons for pounds . . .* Then, usually, Branwell would barrel in and spoil it by running off with the game and steering it straight into a cliff. *. . . and THEN all your dresses and my Sunday suit form up into an ace fighting battalion and convince the Millinery Ministers of the Kingdom of Clothes to declare WAR on the Kingdom of Soap and both kingdoms run RED with dye and blood!*

Anne crouched down like a cat on the stair just below the little white room where her sisters sat. She piped up:

". . . and you'll have red and golden evening gowns for uniforms and phoenix feathers for pens and the Duke of Wellington will invade the Headmaster's Office and beat the old man silly with a unicorn horn. . . ." She put that last one in specially. Anne thought Wellington was *rather* rubbish, but she liked imagining him walloping the Headmaster of that rotten school until he cried.

". . . and Maria and Lizzie will be there waiting, all well again and alive and only ever hiding all this while, like a pair of foxes in the fall," finished Branwell softly from the bottom of the staircase. Anne smiled at him gratefully. Sometimes, *sometimes* Bran could manage not to ruin things. For a minute. Here and there.

But then he wrecked it after all.

"Papa says it's time," Branwell whispered.

Papa and Aunt Elizabeth waited for them just beside the great, heavy, front door.

"No tears, now," their father said. He ran his hand over his mustache to keep his children from seeing the new worry lines he'd grown overnight. He looked his son over speculatively. "Eleven is old enough to taste a bit of manhood, eh? There's a lad. No daughters of mine will wander the countryside unchaperoned. Branwell, my boy, I'm trusting you to get your sisters safely to Keighley and see them *seated* in the Cowan Bridge carriage before you go running about gawping at city things. Protect them as I would, my boy."

Branwell's throat went tight. He straightened his shoulders under the responsibility, the authority, the *power*. He had better answer with something *very* grown-up. They were all looking at him expectantly.

"I shall prove your trust in me well-placed, Father," the boy said, and his voice didn't crack, though it very much wanted to.

"Take Annie along; you'll want company on the return." The youngest of them lit up as bright as butterflies. Bran rolled his eyes. Just when Papa had singled him out and given him a commission, he had to go and let everyone come along.

Aunt Elizabeth drew two small coins out of the wrist of her glove.

"You'll have to buy supper for you and your sister once the girls have gone," she said in her reedy, wobbly voice. "Here's a shilling and sixpence; give it to the man at the Lion and Rooster and he'll give you a pair of fish pies. You may have *one* hard toffee each at Mrs. Reed's shop on the high road. Bring the change safely home, agreed?"

Branwell took the money with a trembling hand. He felt unsteady on his feet, his head spinning, practically drunk. Finally, he had been given mastery over his sisters! He had the money; he had *position*! He was a man now, and the duty of a man was to care for soft, gentle girls and guide their soft, gentle minds. He would be their Lord, their general. But, Bran decided, a generous one. Mostly. His brain began working on wild plans at once. After the beastliest business was done, of course he would cry and feel terribly sorry, but he and Anne would still be in Keighley. And Keighley had a brand-new train station. And at a train station, you will almost always find *trains*. Lovely, filthy, smoking, booming, shrieking trains the size of dragons! The most incredible inventions ever devised! No one he knew had ever seen one. He would be the first. He and his sisters, of course. But mainly him. Bran's heart started to beat hard and fast in his chest like an engine chugging down the tracks.

Papa clapped his hand against his only son's shoulder, much as his own father had done, when he was Branwell's age. "Think you can do the day proudly, boy?"

"Yes, sir," said Bran stoically.

Aunt Elizabeth wept a great deal and kissed them all over. She hated this whole business. Even when they were safe at home, Elizabeth could hardly bear to leave the children alone, and rarely let them out of doors, lest they catch their death of damp. She watched them like little clocks, as though, if she turned her back even for a moment, one of them might wind down and stop just as her sister had, just as Maria and Lizzie and all the rest of the souls who were ever born into this vale of tears. But she must bear it now.

Emily tugged at her father's sleeve. Anne had already run out the door, holding up her arms to the sunshine they'd missed so. Charlotte called after her, dashing down the path.

"Papa," Emily whispered. But Papa was busy fussing with Branwell's coat and blaming himself silently for everything that had ever gone wrong in their lives. Finally, the boy untangled himself from all that paternal attention and strode out into the day like a peacock.

"Papa, listen," she whispered harder, almost a hiss, almost a groan.

"What is it, my dear?" the great, grown, gruff man said at last. He looked down into the lonely gray eyes of his daughter.

"Don't send Anne away to School," Emily begged. "Please, Papa. You can teach her here like you teach Bran, can't you?"

The parson sighed. His breath smelled of pipe tobacco. It fogged in the morning air. "Now, Emily, young ladies oughtn't to go about telling their fathers what to do, you know."

Emily watched Anne stand in the sun, soaking in the warmth and the gold and the light. Branwell pinched her, and the little girl screamed very satisfactorily. They could never understand, those two. They'd never *know*. Emily felt that little needle-stab of hate in her stomach. They couldn't even stay decently sad for five minutes, even on the Beastliest Day. She shut her eyes and said: "I know, Papa. I shall never do it again. But . . . cannot one of us be spared from that place? One of us should escape. One of us should have no . . . no horrors hanging on her heart.

Please, Father. If you will make me go, let her stay."

Emily kissed her father's bearded cheek and ran out of the Parsonage to join her sisters. He blinked after her, his own heart as heavy as a church bell, never to be rung again.

"Mind your Bees," Aunt Elizabeth called to them as they walked down the hill, away from home. And they did. *Buck up, be brave, busy hands make bright hearts.*

Good-bye, Aunt Elizabeth.

Good-bye, Tabby.

Good-bye, Papa.

Wild, stiff tangles of withered gorse and heather and wintergreen burst underfoot as the little tribe took to the day.

The wind had got up out of bed very early indeed to see them off. It blew busily all about the moors, catching at braids and coats and scarves and noses, making that peculiar howling, sighing, grumbling sound Tabitha called *wuthering*. The sunlight looked warm and delightful, but it was all a trick. Those fitful scraps of sunshine were hard and cold as a Headmaster's heart. They marched after the light all the same, up and out onto the little hills and hollows of the moorland, their cheeks whipped red and hot.

Charlotte trudged silently up a worn purple path through the January hills. Bran quickened his pace to keep up.

"I ought to walk in front, Charlotte!" he yelled after her. "Papa said I was your chaperone! I ought to lead the way! Charlotte? Charlotte! Are you listening? I am in *charge*!"

Charlotte was not listening. Bran's long curls whipped across the bridge of his great arched nose, his brow, as ever, furrowed and fuming. He would have been shocked if he knew how perfectly his face reflected his sister's own frown and grump. But he could only see the back of her, her woolen dress prickled with bits of twig and old, withered thistle burrs. Emily and Anne did not care who went first. They'd all get where they were going and no one could do a thing to stop it. Why rush? They hung back, holding hands and picking their path carefully so as not to crush any sweet plant that might wake up again in the spring. Emily looked up at the frozen sun, her brown ringlets crowding a narrow, sharp face that somehow looked already quite grown.

THREE

A Game of And

Down into the bruised, smoky valley they went. The carriage was to come to meet them at the hay market gate at a quarter of three in the afternoon. They would know it from the other black carriages drawn by black horses by the seal of the Cowan Bridge School on the side. It seemed the School had money to paint carriages, Emily thought darkly, but not to feed the students anything but watery porridge and a fortnightly slice of ox fat. Branwell had been preparing his farewell speech as they walked. He would take his sister's hands and tell her that he did love her, after all, and not to be frightened, because she was Charlotte, and Charlotte could take on anything and beat it until it turned into just what she wanted it to be. Even a whole School. Even him. Then, he'd tell Emily something nice as well. Perhaps: *If they give you one bit of pain, you just write to your brother and the men of the house shall ride out to protect you like a Lady with dragon troubles in a book.* He hadn't worked out Em's bit yet. He'd been too busy working on Charlotte's. Charlotte and Branwell were barely a year apart. Underneath all the shoving and jostling and rowing over who ruled over whom, he felt they understood each other. They liked the same things: war, stories, frowning, bossing others about. Em and Annie were so bafflingly *female*. If only Charlotte had been born a boy, there would only be understanding between them, and none of the shoving. He would have an older brother, and wouldn't have to lie awake at night worrying about how to wear the iron cap of being somebody's only son. He would say it all, except for the wishing she was a boy part, without crying or wobbling. The girls would look at him with such powerful love and gratitude that he would turn into a different person, a better person, the perfect person. All he needed was that one look and he could live forever.

Charlotte's furious pace had dragged them all across the moors and into the sooty Keighley streets early. The hay market gate clattered and echoed with horses and voices and smelled of many less wholesome things than hay, but no carriages waited there to collect two unhappy girls. Emily looked up to a bank's brassy clock tower. It wasn't near time for speeches yet.

"It's only half past one," she sighed.

"We'd have made it here by noon if Charlotte would be a proper Lady and let me lead on," groused Branwell, shoving his hands deep in his pockets. He still had Aunt Elizabeth's shilling and sixpence. In shillings and sixpences were the real power. Even Charlotte had to know *that*.

Charlotte rolled her eyes. What difference did it make who walked in front? Branwell could go *home* at the end of all this and she could not. Didn't that prove Papa loved him better? Didn't it show beyond a shadow of a doubt that the world was his and not hers? Shouldn't that make the little piker happy enough?

She gave up. "All right, Bran. I bow to your authority, my *Lord*." Charlotte spoke sourly and bowed grandly, sweeping one hand out to the side like she imagined the Duke of Wellington did. "You have the helm. What shall we do with our last hour and fifteen minutes of freedom?"

"I like the bowing," Branwell said brightly. "Though you oughtn't do it like a man. And when you call me 'my Lord,' you ought to at least *try* to mean it."

"Can we go to Mrs. Reed's shop?" asked Anne, who,

though very sad for her sisters, had distinctly heard her aunt promise *one* hard toffee, and she'd clung to that hard toffee all the way along. The toffee would fix her up. The toffee would make everything else all right.

"No, we can *not*," answered Bran imperiously. He couldn't help it. He knew he ought to just sit under a tree with his sisters and do a lot of hugging and blubbering and quoting dreadful soggy old poems or something, but he couldn't help it. The train was so *close*. He could almost taste the coal smoke. "We are going to do something amazing. We are going to do something fantastically exciting and modern. We are going to do something none of us has done before, something that will make us all so cheerful that we'll be thirty before we cry again! We are going to see the *train!*"

Branwell had imagined the train station would look just like a magazine illustration of a train station: full of bustle and industry and men in important-looking suits and even more important-looking hats, all running to catch the 7:15 or the 9:20 or waiting virtuously, all talking loudly at the same time about only the most important things. But *Blackwood's Edinburgh Magazine* only ever printed pictures of Piccadilly or Waverley Station. This was Keighley, and the three of them were as much alike as two wolves and a lapdog.

Branwell felt utterly cheated.

Though it had only just got built, somehow the station looked tired and worn down already. A single, rather shabby sign announcing KEIGHLEY STATION swung in the unhappy January wind. A few men and ladies wandered aimlessly along the roofed platform. Waiting, yes, but waiting without *purpose*, without that *energy*, without that *importance* Bran longed for. There was one with a small mustache cleaning his nails. Another had a big mustache, and he was picking his teeth. A Lady leaned on his arm in a dress duller than even Tabitha would be caught dead in, patting at her hair, as though anything could be done for her at this point. A great, round, dingy, white clock ticked down at them with all the sparkle and spirit of a dinner plate. Though the clock couldn't have been more than a year old, Branwell could already see a family of spiders, living undisturbed and undusted in the shadow of the numeral 6.

The grubby old stationmaster with muttonchops like angry squirrel tails glared at them from his booth with deep suspicion.

"I don't know what you expected, Bran," sniffed Charlotte. "It's only freight in Keighley. Though *Blackwood's* says that Liverpool is getting passenger service soon. The train's probably been and gone already."

Charlotte didn't think she'd ever hated anyone as much as she hated Keighley just then. Look at it! Just squatting in the moors, lording it over all the other nearby towns just because it had a train station and they did not. Trains only did one thing. They took you *away*. Ever so much quicker than a carriage, and you couldn't even turn around if you changed your mind. Why would anyone want such a thing?

No! Branwell simply would not accept it. He squeezed his eyes shut and clenched his fists against this *extremely* unsatisfactory reality. He whispered through clenched teeth: "What if someone came while we weren't looking and swapped the real Keighley for a false one and all the handsome, important people for a great lot of badgers groomed up to *look* like people and . . ."

Anne skipped along ahead and turned round so that she could practice walking backward while talking and not looking behind her once. "AND the newspaper shop for a monster who looks just *like* a newspaper shop and the bricks in the platform for bars of gold only painted to *look* like bricks, and . . ."

Emily smiled faintly. She had been seriously considering simply running away, across the platform and to . . . where? Nowhere, of course. Her stomach twisted over itself and threatened to bolt, but she couldn't help taking up the game. "AND the songbirds for miniature girls in songbird costumes and the moors for a patchwork quilt and the winter for summer and the sun for the moon and, and . . . and . . ."

"And the train for a pirate ship to sail us all away over the edge of the wild earth," finished Charlotte. A long, low whistle broke the fog into a hundred pieces. "Only no one did any swapping. This is Keighley, the real Keighley, and *that* is a real train come at last."

A deep, rhythmic thumping began in the distance. So deep that it seemed to growl up from inside their own chests. The platform roof began to tremble. The thump thumped again, and then again, picking up speed. All four of their hearts rattled in time with the strange sounds. None of them could move. Nothing in the world could sound like that. Like a monster and a parade and a thunderstorm and a lion and the end of the world all at once. Fear sizzled through their skin to the tips of their hair. Fear, and a wonderful, eager, starving curiosity.

Someone shouted behind them—a man's shout, the sort you had to listen to or else get a punishing. Charlotte startled out of her trance, expecting to be scolded for standing too close to the edge. Anne clutched her oldest sister's skirts as she hadn't done in years. Emily stood fast. Branwell puffed up his chest, determined not to be frightened for at least the next minute. After that, he told himself, he could crumple, if he really needed to.

But they were not to be scolded. The shout came from a hugely fat man running across the road to catch the train. His cheeks were quite flushed and he had his collar turned up against the cold. But his collar was not a collar: It was a fine, glossy page from *Blackwood's Edinburgh Magazine*, crisply creased. His waistcoat was fashioned from stacks of London newspapers. He had parchment for hair, pulled back into old-fashioned rolls, and a neat, small ponytail. His greatcoat was a special edition of the *Leeds Intelligencer* and his cravat was a penny dreadful folded over many times. The enormous belly that bulged beneath his coat was the carved ebony knob of an ancient scroll. Queerest of all, his enormous head was an open book longer than the Bible itself. A pair of glasses perched upon huge, decorated capital letters: two handsome Os that seemed to be his eyes, for they blinked furiously as he ran. The lower parts of the pages formed a mustache, and his nose crowned it all: a long, blood-scarlet ribbonmark, the sort used as a bookmark in old Bibles.

Branwell, Charlotte, Emily, and Anne looked around at the men with big and small mustaches and the Lady with the hopeless hair. None of them seemed to see the Magazine Man stumbling and jogging across the meadow on the other side of the platform. None of them seemed in the least concerned that a man made entirely of books was bearing down on Keighley Station with rather terrifying speed.

"I say," droned the one with the small mustache and very clean nails. "The train's running late today."

"It will happen," nodded the one with the big mustache and very clean teeth. "From time to time."

The Magazine Man hurled himself at the ledge of the platform. He didn't quite make it, grunting like a rhinoceros as he crashed into the thing. He hauled up his tremendous weight with beefy arms made from back issues of the *Quarterly Review*. Charlotte recognized it from Papa's subscriptions immediately. The man's cheeks flushed with red ink and great effort until, at last, the impossible fellow heaved himself over into the station and lay on his back, puffing mightily, exhausted.

"Quite the kind of a weather we're having," said the Lady in the dull dress to neither of the men particularly. The Magazine Man lay sprawled at her feet. She stepped daintily round his head.

"Don't they see him?" asked Anne wonderingly. "He's

right *there*." The train's mournful, owly whistle broke the fog once more.

After a moment of shock in which no one breathed and everyone clutched hands as tight as murder, all four children burst out of their stillness and tumbled toward the creature. They called out to him and demanded his name, his family, his business. He tried to scramble up and run from them, wheezy breaths whistling fearfully through the hundred thousand pages of his body. But the Magazine Man was as stuck as a turtle on his back, and forced to roll wretchedly from side to side in order to get on his feet. Once up, he towered over everyone, even the tallest of the Keighley businessmen.

"Go away!" the Magazine Man shouted finally, puffing and wheezing. He bent over with his paper hands on his newsprint knees. "Leave me be!"

All of them spoke at once:

"Who are you?" demanded Charlotte.

"Why did you climb over the ledge instead of coming through the station like a sensible fellow?" asked Emily.

"If you haven't got a ticket you can't get on the train, you know," scolded Anne.

"Where did you come from?" shouted Branwell, far too loudly. "Why do you look like a wastepaper bin?"

"Children ought to be seen and NOT HEARD,

ORRIGHT?" barked the stationmaster from his booth, showing no concern at all for the enormous *thing* right in front of him.

"Can't you see the paper man standing eight feet tall and coughing up both lungs in the middle of your station?" snapped Charlotte. She was unable to bear this total abandonment of adult responsibility one second longer.

"All I see are a pack of brats who ought to be in school!" the stationmaster snarled back, and slammed his little window shut. Emily flinched.

School.

The 2:00 train arrived in Keighley Station. None of them had ever seen one except in drawings. They'd heard the better-off folk in the village talk about the huge, noisy, smoky, rattley beasts. But here it came, in real life, barreling down the rails, a splendid engine, making that thumping, pounding sound they'd felt in their chests, puffing and whistling and thumping and clacking.

"They look so different in the newspapers," whispered Emily.

In fact, no train in any newspaper anywhere in any country looked anything at all like the one steaming into the station just then. It had a wicker engine made all of sticks and brambles, as though the dead winter moor itself had woken that morning and decided it wanted to see the world. The smokestack was a basket of spiky frozen gorse branches. The carriage doors were thatches of old heather and gooseberry thorns. Great hay wheels turned along the tracks as though they were wheels of iron, bound to a long, rough-hacked ruby axle. But not the pretty, polished rubies that you'd put in a ring. Ancient, glowering red stone still clotted up with black rock. The wicker engine drew impossible cars behind it, built out of apple skin and glass and pheasant feathers and even widow's lace that seemed somehow as sturdy as steel.

The train's headlamp was a star. A real, honest star, pulled right out of the night like a coin from behind your ear.

The children stared as the train came to a wheezing rest in the hollow, gleaming, its windows full of shadows. Emily's mouth dropped open. She simply couldn't make any sense of it, no matter which way she turned her head. Perhaps this was simply what trains looked like. They'd only just been invented, after all. Perhaps rubies and apple skin window curtains were so usual to the well-off folk in Haworth that it never occurred to them to bring such things up down at the pub. But surely, surely *Blackwood's* had never mentioned using *stars* to light the way.

"What if someone came while we weren't looking," Branwell whispered, "and swapped the *train?*"

Anne giggled madly. She felt as though the top of her head had come clean off. "We're dreaming!" she laughed. "It's all right, it's a dream and we're dreaming!"

Charlotte said nothing, but that smile that was so slow to come spread over her flushed and rosy face. Something was happening. Something straight out of a story. Something so astonishingly fantastic that no fanciful lie she'd ever told could top it.

The Magazine Man decided to make a run for it. But he was not a graceful sort of beast and they weren't about to let him get away. He was *magic*. It was all magic and they *knew* it was magic; they'd known it at once. Anyone would know! There had never been a train like that made in the London Yards, not ever in the whole history of the British Rail Service. And without saying a word to each other, they already knew that not a one of them wanted anything in the world at that moment but to get on board. Clearly, the Magazine Man wanted the same thing. He tripped and stumbled and the platform was only so big, so he ended up running somewhat pitiful circles *away* from his tormentors and more or less *toward* the tracks. He got so out of breath he couldn't even cry properly, but tried anyhow. Ink squeezed and sprayed out of his eyes. The train sighed and a great jet of steam belched out of its stack.

The four of them were going too fast round the cramped platform. They collided into the Magazine Man at full speed. Branwell took the scroll-knob of his belly to the nose. The fat man wheezed and pawed at them. "Leave me alone! Pirates! Brigands! *Librarians*! If the top brass hear of this I'll be remaindered for certain! I'll be punished! I wasn't to let anyone see!"

"We're awfully sorry," said Emily politely as she climbed off his back, which read in very large print: BONAPARTE STORMS GREENTEETH CASTLE! FORTY GIANTS DEAD! PANIC CONSUMES COUNTRYSIDE! "We only wanted to know about the train."

Charlotte straightened her wool coat, and added, only because she didn't quite know how else to put it, but felt very strongly that she *had* to say *something* on the subject or she'd just pop right there like a soap bubble. "You're made of *pages*, did you know?"

The Magazine Man shoved Charlotte aside with a bleat of terror. "Well, *you're* made out of *meat*," he snarled. His red ribbon nose coiled up as if it smelled something vile. "It's *disgusting*. I bet you've got . . . I bet you've got *bones* in there. And hair, too! Pah! How *grue*some!" Only the way he said *gruesome* was to stretch out the *grue* until it sounded very much like the train whistle. "No, don't touch me! I've a Horror! Next you'll tell me you've got *blood* and I just couldn't bear it, the *thought* of it, just under your skin, practically . . . practically *touching* me!"

"Nothing so wrong with blood," sniffed Branwell, brushing off his trousers. "Wonderful stuff!"

The Magazine Man shrieked and bolted once more. His bookend-boots echoed on the bricks. "I hate you!" he yelled behind him. "If you tell anyone you saw me I'll break in to your house at night and erase all your story-books! And . . . and tie knots in all your socks! Leave me alone!"

"I'm beginning to think there'll be no train at all today, old chap," sighed the man with the small mustache to the man with the large one. Charlotte and Emily rolled their eyes, Branwell and Anne laughed incredulously, and all four gave up on adults at once.

Finally, the Magazine Man stopped his mad dash. It wasn't his choice to stop. He couldn't help it. He skidded to a halt before two tall soldiers who were standing, quite suddenly, in front of the engine car. They held their rifles leaning smartly on their shoulders, their caps neat and crisp, their gazes clear and bold. Both of them were made entirely of rich brown wood, like jointed dolls. Anne frowned. They had *absolutely* not been there before. Not when the train arrived and not when they were playing merry-go-round with the Magazine Man. They were *new*.

The fat man looked up at the wooden soldiers in terror, then folded up his face, his collar, his cravat, his waistcoat, and his long newsprint legs. He folded up so completely that he turned, midair, into a great, fat, firmly shut book. The book fell with an indignant thump onto the platform between the children and the riflemen. One soldier, with painted black trousers, bent down and picked the poor fellow up, tucking the volume under his strong arm.

"Hullo," said the other soldier. This one had a wood-knot over his heart as though he had been shot there long ago. His mahogany mouth turned up in a sad little smile that seemed to say: *Well, what's done is done, and we had better make the best of things.*

"Good morning! Aren't you a noisy lot, and aren't there rather a lot of you! My name is Sergeant Branch, and this is my comrade Captain Leaf. But you may call us Crashey and Bravey. Tickets, please!"

FOUR

To Glass Town, My Girl!

Come on then, lovies. We haven't got all day. Gawping's free but seats cost. Tickets or run along!" Crashey barked with a businesslike snap in his voice.

"Oughtn't you be in school anyhow?" asked Bravey, bending precisely in half at the waist to stare Charlotte down. His big oak nose butted up against her small, pointed one.

Emily shuddered. Charlotte did not.

"To . . . to *hell* with School," Emily said softly, and got the very satisfying experience of hearing all her siblings gasp.

"Now, that's what I like to hear!" crowed Crashey. "I like a girl with a little swear in her. Barely gradtriculated stickth form myself. Too much sap in me, my teachers said! Hasn't got the smarts the good Lord gave a staircase. But I fooled them, didn't I? Got brains coming out me ears, nose, and throat, I have. Pluslike, I can shoot true as the day you were born and my right arm could hold back the ocean so's any one of you ladies could walk right through the world as dry as you please." He flexed his burly muscles, in case they doubted him.

Branwell resolved immediately never to set foot in a classroom again. He squeezed his own skinny arm and hoped no one saw him do it.

"'S'not a matter of sap, Crash. It's a matter of having nothing between your ears but squirrels."

"*Smart* squirrels," Crashey sniffed, cleaning out his ear with one stubby finger. "Genius squirrels! Nothing but the best!"

Bravey clapped his comrade's shoulders heartily. "Now, little masters," he said, "if you've got nothing in your hands, I'm afraid the Express is running late and we've got to get Brunty here back home where he belongs." Bravey patted the enormous book that had only recently been the Magazine Man.

"Where does he belong?" asked Branwell breathlessly.

Bravey winked one wooden eye. "In prison, of course! The P-House! The clink! Quite a naughty little pupper, is our Brunty."

"And where does the Express go?" said Emily, her voice high and strangled and tight, afraid of the answer and longing for it.

Crashey threw his brawny arms up into the air. "Why, to Glass Town, my girl! The grandest town from here to Saturn, the most glorious country ever invented, home of the daring and the demanding, favorite haunt of the lawless and the beautiful, the wild glass jungle, the crystal frontier! Where else would anyone *want* to go? Tickets, please! Tickets or NOTHING! Tickets or TOTAL DESPAIR! Tickets or BUST!"

Charlotte cleared her throat, and asked, in her most sensible voice, which she had copied from Aunt Elizabeth on her most sensible day: "How much does a ticket cost, sir?"

This brought Crashey and Bravey up short. They whispered to each other behind knotty pine hands, eyeballing the children through their huge fingers.

"A . . . million pounds?" offered Crashey uncertainly. "Each!" he blurted. Then, feeling a bit more confident, he smiled an enormous smile, showing outsized birchbark teeth.

"That's a respectable money number, so you have to salute it." Bravey sagely nodded.

The four of them hesitated. Finally, Branwell shrugged and touched his fingers to his mess of dark hair in a rather smart salute. His sisters did likewise.

"May we have a moment to . . . to . . . consult our accounts?" Emily asked, and curtsied, because it seemed they were doing silly things like that now, so she might as well get a head start on the next nonsense.

"Only a moment, miss!" warned Bravey. "We are quite, *quite* behind schedule, and Chuck here won't keep!"

The four of them huddled up behind a post.

Charlotte took the lead even though Bran stamped on her toes. *Let me do it for once! Father trusted me with the money!*

"Time for a Thump Parliament, I should say," she whispered.

Branwell crossed his arms over his chest. His dark eyes fumed beneath dark brows. The Thump Parliament had been *his* idea, and he especially liked its rhyming with *Rump Parliament*, which was a thing that happened ages ago and got a King named Charlie's head cut off. A Thump Parliament meant: *All three of you had better do as I say or I shall thump you like a bad, naughty King.* But as usual, the girls had taken it and run off and turned it into something much nicer and less fun, which was to say, any decision the four of them had to make together.

"I don't believe they've got the first idea about proper English money, really," Emily said, as quietly as she could.

"Of course they don't!" Branwell snapped. He rolled his eyes. "Aren't any of you going to say it?"

"Those are *our* soldiers!" cried Anne, too loud. They hushed her, and made a great deal more noise doing it than she had in the first place. "*Our* wooden soldiers! Crashey and Bravey! Ross and Perry will be hiding somewhere, and Gravey and Cheeky and Rogue and Goody and Naughty and Stumps! I can tell Crashey by the chunk knocked out of his leg from when Bran whacked him against the doorknob! But how *could* they be ours?"

"It might be a coincidence, Anne," said Charlotte, biting the inside of her cheek. "Lots of people could be called Crashey. And . . . made of wood."

Emily glared at her sister. "But it *isn't*. Oh, other people might be called Crashey and Bravey, but they said Glass Town! Glass Town isn't a real place. We made it up because you said it was 'tedious' to only set our games in countries that really existed. Stop being sensible! It's 'tedious' to be sensible at a magic train and wooden men! Sensible won't *stick*. Now, I say we have a very clear-cut moral problem in front of us. We can go to Cowan Bridge

School and learn a lot of rot we already know and freeze and starve and probably die of consumption, or we can get on a fairy train driven by our Christmas presents."

"My Christmas present," insisted Bran, but no one paid any attention.

"I wish we could ask Papa," fretted Anne. "Or Tabitha. She knows all manner of tales about the moors and pixies and kelpies and suchlike. She'll know if it's safe to ride a railway car with a tiger tail."

The other three glanced back toward the end of the line of train cars. They hadn't noticed. But Anne saw everything. A long, enormous, properly striped tiger's tail hung off the caboose, flipping lazily from side to side like a bored house cat.

"They'd think we'd gone mad and we'd all have to sleep with a doctor instead of a doll," Emily said.

Charlotte nodded. She kept nodding, as though she'd had a private conversation with herself and it had come out excellently. "It's no question at all. *I* am going. Maria and Lizzie would have gone. They'd have gone anywhere rather than back to those horrible cold dormitories where any day you might get death for tea. I won't let Cowan Bridge take me. Never. *Never.*"

Her words snagged on Emily's heart. Maybe Charlotte *did* understand. Their faces all went cold and serious.

"Never," whispered Emily.

"Never," Charlotte said again.

"Never," promised Anne.

"*I* want to take the train," said Branwell. He had no fear of School. Papa taught his only son himself in his musty, wonderful study, and always would, for he trusted no one else with the job. Bran felt terribly sorry for his sisters, but it was hardly his fault that the world was so determined to make girls suffer a great deal more than boys. He hadn't built the world. It had nothing to do with him. But the *train*. Branwell wanted the train to have *everything* to do with him.

Anne clasped and unclasped her hands. She whispered: "But won't Papa be worried if we don't come straight home? Won't Aunt Elizabeth cry and cry until she dries out completely like a kipper?" She couldn't bear to think of them waiting in the parlor, listening for footsteps that didn't come. That sort of thing happened in ghost stories, and ghost stories always made her shake and shiver and sob.

Branwell snapped at his sister, annoyed to the teeth at having to consider such boring things. "We'll just pop off for the day, Annie. We'll catch the evening train home from Glass Town just like proper businessmen and no one will be the wiser."

Emily and Charlotte would *not* catch the evening train. They would *not* just pop off for the day. Even if Glass Town was the Devil's own cowshed, it was better than School. They'd already told him that. But Branwell never listened. They twisted their littlest fingers together and held their tongues.

"But where will we get a million pounds?" whined Anne. "*Each?*"

Charlotte reached up under the wrist of her glove and ripped off one of the dove-gray little buttons sewn there in a neat row. She remembered the Game of And they'd played around the laundry tub. *And they'll take us away to the Kingdom of Clothes where they use thimbles for shillings and buttons for pounds. . . .*

"Come on now, all in," she said. "Hurry up! Everyone put in—you too, Bran. Oh, get the one off your coat, then, you great idiot! Stop arguing! I'll tell you what I'm doing once I've done it! Don't you trust me?"

"No," Bran grumbled. But he gave her one of his round black buttons anyway.

Charlotte marched back to the wooden soldiers and held out her hand: four buttons. One dove-gray, one burgundy, one round and black and shiny, one white and tiny as a seed. She took a deep breath and announced, in the voice she always used for her best and most outlandish lies: "There we are! One million pounds sterling for each of us!" She said it breezily, cheerfully, absentmindedly, as though it mattered so little she'd completely forgotten that she'd walked out of the washroom with four million pounds stuck to the bottom of her shoe. That's how you had to do it. No one ever believed you if you got all sweaty and trembly and nervous, even if you were telling the truth.

Crashey and Bravey exchanged glances. Crashey picked over the buttons. He counted them, lost count between two and three, and started over again several times.

"Sold!" cried Bravey, satisfied at last. "Sold to the young lady in the gray dress! And if we keep a wee bit of a tip for ourselves, no one has to hear about it, wouldn't you say? A little off the top keeps the bottom warm!"

Crashey reached under his red, rough-bark waistcoat and produced four shockingly large lemons with bits of branches and leaves still stuck onto them. He juggled them happily, and as the lemons came round, the wooden soldier tossed one to each of the children. The lemons smelled marvelous—fresh and sour and sweet and sharp and warm and so terribly, astonishingly bright! Charlotte hadn't known something could *smell* bright. But their tickets did. They smelled like what you imagine gold will smell like, before you find out that gold smells rather of nothing. Emily, Anne, Charlotte, and Branwell read what was written in gleaming, graceful, green ink on the peels:

> *Glass Town Royal Express Main Line*
> *South Angrian Loop*
> *One (1) Both-Ways Ticket*
> *Entitles the Bearer to Passage,*
> *Stashage, Gnashage, and Splashage*
> *Does Not Entitle Bearer to an*
> *On-Time Arrival, a Smooth Arrival,*
> *Any Arrival at All, or Pleasant*
> *Conversation with Staff*
> *Luggage Rights Strictly Observed*

"These aren't tickets!" spluttered Anne.

"Aren't they?" Crashey said, raising a twiggy eyebrow. "But you gave us a million pounds each! So these *must* be tickets! *Ipso facto quid pro quo ad hominem habeas porpoise* and all that."

"What does 'passage, stashage, gnashage, and splashage' mean?" Branwell said dubiously.

Bravey sighed. He felt around inside his coat and produced a hefty acorn cap, clicking it open like a pocket watch. He seemed very dissatisfied with what his watch told him. "A seat, one suitcase, a meal, and a drink, of course."

"And luggage rights?" ventured Charlotte, holding tighter to her suitcase.

Bravey glared. "You are *holding* up the *train*, young sirs."

"*I'm* a sir, *they're* misses," Bran insisted, quite horrified at the idea of his sisters being called by the noble, powerful name of *sir* when it did *not* belong to them.

"It's all sirs in Glass Town!" Bravey yelled in exasperation. "Sirs as far as the eye can see!"

"ALL ABOARD!" called Crashey, who clearly loved yelling best of all. "LAST CALL!"

For a moment, hesitation grabbed hold of them. If they got on that train, anything could happen to them. Anything at all.

Charlotte stepped forward first and climbed the silver carriage stairs with only a little shake in her breath. Bravey checked her lemon extremely thoroughly, which rather annoyed her, as he'd just given it to them.

One by one, Emily, Anne, and Branwell followed their sister onto the train to Glass Town. The door shut behind them just as the long, sweet, owl-song whistle filled up the gray Yorkshire sky.

FIVE

Passage, Stashage, Gnashage, and Splashage

Anne tried desperately to watch for the *exact* moment when Yorkshire stopped being Yorkshire and started being Somewhere Else. She pressed her nose to the fine glass of the dining car window, waiting for a bang or a flash or the bonging of a mystic bell. But somehow she missed it, even though she watched the whole time, holding her eyelids open with her fingers so she wouldn't blink and lose her chance. One minute the dear, familiar purple-gray moors rolled by beyond the train—and the next minute, the moors weren't moors anymore. The land outside the window had turned itself a thick patchwork quilt. It rose and fell gently, hills and valleys and seams, under threadbare clouds and a golden sun.

"Oh, it's not fair!" cried Anne. "It cheated!"

But she couldn't stay angry. It was too lovely to be angry at. The others crowded in to see. The patchwork fields flowed on and on, plaids, brocade, faded flower prints, blue satin, green silk, black velvet. Little ribbon rivers rippled through the lowlands. And wasn't that farm there growing turnips in one of Aunt Elizabeth's embroidered handkerchiefs? Every now and again, they spied the same tall gray standing stones they knew from home, casting shadows on the tweed thickets, the only things unchanged from there to here. It was such a pleasant, orderly countryside—nothing at all like the dining car of the Glass Town train.

Charlotte and Branwell sat on one side of a thick, scuffed, ancient walnut table, Emily and Anne on the other. They could hardly do more than sit. The dining car was an awful mess. As beautiful as the engraved silver car looked on the outside, it seemed no one had bothered to clear out the inside in years. Every other table and chair groaned underneath piles of cast-off hats: naval tricorns and bicornes, bonnets and boaters, army caps with golden braids, top hats and fearsome spiked helmets. Heaps of old swords and boots blocked the door into the next carriage. Dented stirrups from a thousand horses stacked up the corners to the ceiling. They'd had to kick over a small mountain of gold and silver and bronze and very nicely jeweled medals of valor and bravery just to clear enough space to crowd in round the table. Emily still felt quite guilty about it. Branwell did not. But then again, Branwell had not nimbly swiped a ruby-encrusted cross with FOR LAUGHTER IN THE FACE OF CERTAIN DEATH stamped on it and tucked it into his coat pocket. He had very much less to feel guilty about, on the whole. But not *nothing*—Bran had got his sketching pencil out of his coat and begun to draw out the pyramid of hats on the tablecloth.

A wooden soldier elbowed the dining car door open and wedged himself through with a great deal of grunting and swearing. Branwell hurried to hide his bit of tablecloth graffiti with one sleeve. It was not Crashey or Bravey. He had a completely different face, with a curly beard carved into his pinewood jaw and a splendidly tall black hat tied under his chin with balsam straps. His chest was covered with odd, lumpy burls and knots and craters of scabby, unsanded wood. He wore a waiter's apron over his uniform and carried a dish covered with a silver dome hoisted up in one strong hand. With the other hand, he blew a short blast on a tin whistle.

"Good afternoon, passengers!" the soldier bellowed. "I trust you and your luggage are comfortable?"

"I don't know why you're all so excited about luggage," sighed Emily. "We left ours in our seats."

The soldier blushed. It was the oddest thing! When the wooden man blushed, a thin, soft green moss sprang up over his cheekbones in the most handsome way. "I certainly do hope it will forgive you, young miss! My name, if it please you, is Leftenant Gravey—"

"Gravey!" yelped Branwell.

Gravey was his second favorite of all the toy soldiers in their latched box back home. That was why Bran always made sure he died gallantly in battle at the end of every game. Charlotte shushed him hurriedly. He didn't see why they couldn't just tell the lads they owned them! It would make everything so much easier. Branwell thought it would be terrifically pleasant to find out you were owned by such a splendid person as himself. But Charlotte had the most maddening way of making the rest of them do as she said without *saying* anything at all. He would have to study that more closely, now he was so near to being a man.

"As I was *saying*," Gravey continued with a pointed glare, "my name, if it please you, is Leftenant Gravey, and I have been charged with the honorable and hazardous duty of bringing you our finest luncheon service, compliments of the Glass Town Public Rail. Now, I must apologize straightaway. We have not had . . . *breathers* . . . on board in some time. Oh! You'll find that term offensive! I am a *stupid* stump! I shall hold my hand in the fire for a full minute when my watch ends, you have my word. Bleeders, then? Oh, no, that's worse! Meat sacks? What about weepers, that's *mostly* polite."

"Human beings," said Charlotte curtly, putting the poor man out of his misery. "Thank you."

"*Homo sapiens sapiens*, if you're fancy!" Anne piped up.

Gravey wrinkled his broad nose. "I'm only an enlisted man, miss. Fancy is above my pay grade. Human beings is *rather* an ugly phrase, but it's not for me to say, I suppose! Well then, we have not had any *humans* on board in some time, so the kitchen had a spot of trouble. More than a spot. A whole cup and a few tablespoons on top. But we've done our best, and we are *very* sensitive, so if you don't eat every crumb, we shall all take mortal offense and put our hands in the fire for *five* minutes." Gravey lifted the silver dome with a flourish. Steam rose from plates and bowls as he laid out a dizzying number of spoons and four puzzling dishes. "For the young *human* lady, we have a lovely *vol-au-vent*; for the gentleman, a delightful *pot au feu*; for the quiet lass, a sweet *éclair*, and for the littlest miss, a positively sinful *galette des rois*."

Leftenant Gravey set down a small, tightly lidded blue china pot like an unhatched robin's egg in front of Charlotte. He laid another pot before an astonished Branwell: a miniature black iron cauldron full of roaring blue flame. With a dramatic flourish, he produced a storm cloud crackling with violet lightning on a green glass saucer for Emily. Finally, he placed a red velvet cushion shaped like a cupcake into Anne's greedy, clasping hands. A magnificent silver crown set with black pearls floated ridiculously, in midair, above the pillow.

"And for your splashables, a round of champagne flutes for all!" cried Gravey.

He held one well-manicured wooden hand in front of his face like a magician and waggled his thorny eyebrows. Four crystal flutes sprang up behind his fingers. But they had no champagne in them. They couldn't possibly. These were the sort of flutes you played music with, not the sort you drank from. Any wine would just drip out through the finger holes.

"It's a fine vintage, a crisp, dry, publicly rambunctious, but privately confused '21 all the way from Acroofcroomb in the wicked wilds of Gondal!" The Leftenant waited for them to be impressed. He was disappointed. They only blinked a lot and opened their mouths and shut them again. Very unsatisfactory. "It's *absolutely* contraband," he pouted. "I swiped it myself at the Battle of Wehglon. All the other boys took jewels and paintings and silverware. But I knew what I wanted. I knew where to find the *real* Gondalier gold! I brought it out of my personal stash especially for you and you . . . you *humans* don't appreciate it one bit and I shall NEVER recover! Good day to you!"

Leftenant Gravey turned on one oaken heel and marched out of the dining car in a bitter fury. Branwell called after him, but no answer came. He could not bear the fine fighting man's looking at him with such contempt. Like he was no more than a little bug in a plaid scarf. He ought to have exclaimed at the soldier's tale of battle and looting, so that they could bond together as stalwart men and become comrades. *Stupid, stupid,* Bran cursed himself silently.

Charlotte, Emily, and Anne stared down at their lunch.

"It's all French!" Emily said with a hot little thrill in her voice. "Papa would make us throw it all out!"

But they could not quite sort out a plan of attack. They poked at their dishes with a few of the spoons, though the spoons didn't make much of a dent. One white crystal one melted halfway to the stump the minute it touched Emily's storm cloud. A rather brown, papery one started to smoke and smolder when Bran tried to get it up under a scoop of fire.

"Well, this is just the worst," snapped Branwell, throwing down his burnt spoon. "We can't eat this rot! They're trying to poison us. Or make fun of us. Or both at the same time."

Anne shrugged. She'd got the best out of the lot, if you asked her. She lifted her silver crown and put it on her head. If you had to miss lunch, better to get a new hat out of it! She giggled as it settled perfectly into her blond curls.

"Oh!" Anne shouted suddenly. "Oh! Em! Bran!"

She waved her hands frantically as the sensations of a wonderful meal filled her mouth and her belly, even though she hadn't eaten a bite. The talk tried to get out, but it stumbled over her excitement and the taste of almond cream cake. "It's marmalade and cheese on toast and a pigeon pie and almond sponge cake! I can taste it, I swear! As soon as I put the crown on! And I'm getting quite full. It's so *much!*"

"*Galette des rois,*" Charlotte said thoughtfully, and in a very nice accent, for Aunt Elizabeth insisted that all the children learn French, now that all that nasty business with the war was over. She looked down at her little china pot and said: "Let's see my *vol-au-vent*, shall we?"

Charlotte lifted the blue china lid, but the bowl was empty. A swift, noisy whirlwind spun up out of it, twisting like a miniature tornado straight into her curious face. "Oh!" Charlotte coughed, and smiled for the second time that day as she breathed in the wind. "I've got roast lamb and buttered artichokes and a strawberry soufflé!"

Emily and Bran peered doubtfully at their rather more alive and dangerous food. Almost at the same time, they each stuck a brave finger in. They yelped together as the lightning shocked her fingers and the blue flames scorched his. But in half a second they were laughing with their sisters and stepping all over each other's sentences.

"Mince pie and custard—" crowed Bran.

"Apple puffs and mushroom tart—" whooped Emily.

"And creamed lobster!"

"And oyster soup!"

"I've figured it out," Charlotte announced with triumph. She put her hands flat on the table. You could always tell when Charlotte was thinking as hard as she could. She'd stretch her fingers out like she was reaching for the truth and just about to grab hold of it. "*Galette des rois. Vol-au-vent. Pot au feu. Éclair.* Listen! Everything here is just what it is!"

"What are you on about?" Bran rolled his eyes, savoring the salty, creamy lobster and the rich mince pie. They only ever got mince pies at Christmas back home.

"Look!" Charlotte pointed at Anne in her crown. The silver prongs slowly began to disappear as the girl finished her meal. "Remember our lessons! *Galette des rois*! That's 'kings' cake.' *Vol-au-vent* means 'windblown.' *Pot au feu* means 'a pot of fire.' And *éclair* means 'a bolt of lightning.' I think . . . I think in Glass Town, everything does what it says on the tin." She pointed out the window at the blanket moors whipping by. "Doesn't everyone always talk about the patchwork fields? Well, there they are! I think they haven't got turns of phrase or colorful sayings or anything like that here, they've got the things *themselves*. Look!" She held up Bran's blackened spoon, a strange, brown, papery thing made with what looked like old leaves. "*Tea*spoon." She snatched another, a pale, fragile white one, then Emily's craggy crystal spoon, and yet another sticky yellow one. "*Egg* spoon. *Salt* spoon! *Mustard* spoon!"

"And champagne *flutes*!" Emily laughed. She blew a high, gentle note on hers and grinned as the bubbling, golden taste of real champagne filled her throat. Her first real champagne! Tabitha would be scandalized.

Charlotte started to laugh, too, helplessly, holding

on to her cheeks to keep her smile from flying away with her. She opened her arms to take in all the cluttered piles of old helmets and hats and medals and swords. "Don't you see? We're in the *Officers' Mess!*"

Branwell roared until his stomach hurt. Anne started to hiccup, she'd laughed so hard.

Emily's face went suddenly quite serious. "We must be very careful, then. We could run into a great deal of trouble if people think we mean just what we say."

"But what about our tickets?" interrupted Anne, holding up her calligraphed lemon. "A ticket's not a lemon and a lemon's not a ticket."

"Perhaps things get confused on the borderlands," mused Bran. "Perhaps they're only half what they mean. But I think . . . I *rather* think . . . every sailor needs to take lemons when he goes adventuring, or else he'll never get home with all his teeth still in his head. We'd best not lose them, anyhow. They're both-ways tickets. They're our way home."

A large wooden head popped through the door between carriages. It belonged to a wooden soldier with a wooden patch over one eye and several piratical earrings in his left ear. "Lads and Lasses, Officers and Enlisted, Lords and Laborers, Breathers and Bolters, Sweethearts and . . . and . . . oh, hang it all, I've run out. You lot! I am to inform you that the Glass Town Main Line is presently disembarking at the charming riverside destination of Port Ruby. Due to . . . er . . . local weather, you are also presently disembarking. Hold on to your luggage and do try not to get killed—it's an awful bother. Mind the gap!"

"But that's *Rogue*," whispered Anne. "How can that be Rogue? I made his patch out of a bit of kindling and pitch and it wasn't nearly so neat and tidy a job as he's got now."

None of her siblings heard her. While they had been busy translating their luncheon, the world outside the train had changed once again.

The patchwork moors had vanished. The train rocked from side to side as it steamed through a sea of red glass. A city rose up all around them. And not a city like Keighley. Not even a city like Leeds. A city like London. A city like Paris. A city like every metropolis the children had ever dreamed about visiting one day, all crammed together and forced to get along. Glittering towers and palaces and shops and pubs, sparkling statues and elegant houses and long, broad streets shaded by graceful trees, all shimmering brilliantly in the sun, all made entirely of scarlet stained glass. Branwell, even in his bloodiest dream, had never imagined so many shades of red existed in the universe. Scarlet, yes, but also crimson and vermilion and coral and maroon and fuchsia and garnet and pink and blush and burgundy and a million billion others he couldn't even think of names for. The glass streets shot prisms into the sky. Hot, molten blown glass cypress trees bulged up along the edges of handsome parks filled with cut-glass rosebushes. And through it all ran a river as wide as the Thames, as wide as the Amazon, frothing and roaring with deep red claret wine, all the way to the sea.

A deafening boom rocked the train. It careened up on its side, threatening to topple off the tracks and into the copper-colored stained-glass station house. All four of them lurched and tumbled and fell against the other end of the car, were instantly buried in officers' helmets and medals and Sergeant Major Rogue's extremely surprised wooden body, then hurtled back painfully against their table as the train righted itself, shattering the remains of their lunch and cracking the lovely wide carriage window straight down the middle.

Anne and Emily saw the creature sprinting toward them on one side of the crack. Charlotte and Branwell and Rogue saw it on the other.

It was a rooster.

A rooster the size of their village church in Haworth. A rooster made, not of rooster parts, but smashed, mismatched porcelain dishes spackled together into the shape of a demonic cockerel, with fiery, insane eyes and a tail of a thousand enraged shattered china feathers streaming behind it. It screeched and green flame vomited out of its teacup-beak. A young man no older than fourteen or fifteen rode the rooster down the scarlet streets of Port Ruby, screaming war cries fit to wake the Romans. His legs in the rooster's stirrups were long brass spyglasses. He wore a bicorne hat on his head like an awful black half-moon. His arms were two long muskets. With one he swung a great emerald hammer strapped onto the barrel, shattering crimson steeples and gates as he came. With the other he fired again and again, into the towers, into the palaces, into the tall, elegant houses of Port Ruby. But the face beneath that bicorne hat was bare, pure, white bone.

"What is *that?*" choked Branwell, terror eating up his heart. He reached for Charlotte's hand and squeezed it awfully, though he would never admit to such a thing later.

Sergeant Major Rogue stumbled to his feet and straightened his eye patch. He glared out the window with mixed irritation and admiration in his good eye.

"That, my lad, is the local weather. Napoleon bloody Bonaparte." The wooden soldier slammed open the door between carriages and shouted down the train. "Man positions! Form up! Sound the alarm! Oh, bugger, has Gravey died again already? Get him up! Give him a stiff drink! All hands on deck! Old Boney has come for us at last!"

PART II

In This Imperfect World

SIX

❧❦❧

Out of the Train and Into the Fire

Port Ruby exploded around them. Charlotte and Emily dashed down a red cut-glass alleyway after the squad of wooden soldiers in tight formation, clutching their suitcases and each other for dear life. Branwell and Anne scrambled close behind them. Anne held her hands over her ears as she ran. Napoleon's impossible arms and his rooster's jets of green flame thumped against the city like awful thundering drums. The demonic chicken scored a hit on a beautiful scarlet stained glass theater just ahead of them. It shattered with a terrible cry, as though it had been a living thing and not a building at all. Shards of broken windows fell into their hair.

One sliced through Branwell's ear, but he hardly felt it. It was finally happening, a real battle, all around him! He whooped in joy, twisting round to see if he could catch another glimpse of the great man astride his astonishing war-bird. Charlotte could feel the heat of that rooster-fire on her skin as she ran past the smoking ruin, scorching the hem of her dress, singeing her hair. She would never have confessed it to a grown-up person, but her heart burned with excitement, too. Only this morning her life seemed a gray, cold shroud. Now *she*, little Charlotte nobody, was running through ruby crystal streets after her old toys while a dead Emperor bore down on them like the devil come to life. It was just like a story. It was the most interesting the truth had ever been!

The lot of them burst into a wide plaza, paved in garnet looking glasses and ringed by smart vermilion cafés where giant overturned wineglasses served for tables. Loads of people huddled beneath the table stems and hid behind thick pink quartz trees, praying desperately for glass to stop being *quite* so easy to see through, if you please. The four children careened into a rather splendid maroon muffin cart just as a stray arrow of green fire crashed into the pretty pastry pyramid on display. They crouched down behind the toppled cart as currants and almonds and crumbly cake rained down all over them.

The wooden soldiers ignored them, taking up positions, barking orders, counting off their numbers and weapons. Charlotte and Emily shook off a little rain of exploded muffins and hauled up their suitcases in front of themselves and their siblings like a pair of knight's shields. Anne buried her face in Emily's back—but after a moment, she peered out between her fingers, so as not to miss anything. Branwell felt so extremely cross at being shown up in his duty by his sisters' old bags that he stopped being afraid at all. It's a very difficult job to be cross and terrified at the same time. One always wins out. He pinched Charlotte savagely and hissed: "Get over yourself! What are you going to do with those, throw your knickers at *Napoleon*?"

Charlotte gasped—but not because she'd been pinched or because her knickers were being discussed in public. The most extraordinary thing was happening to her suitcase. And not only hers, but Emily's as well. The girls clung on desperately as their bags cracked and unfolded and wriggled and unlatched and relatched themselves. The beaten-up, hand-me-down luggage groaned and stretched and grew until, impossibly, Charlotte was holding a fearsome, gargantuan sword in her small hands, and Emily had her fists clenched round a grand medieval mace big enough for a young ogre. The weapons did not gleam in the sun, for they were all of the same leather and brass and wood that the suitcases had been. Branwell gave a strangled, indignant cry just as the sisters cried out in delight.

"Look at that! I do wish *I'd* packed a bag!" Anne breathed in wonder.

Bran had gone quite red in the face. He matched the architecture of Port Ruby very nicely. "Give that sword to me at once! It's too big for you! And you don't know how to use it! It's not fair! Papa said *I* was to chaperone *you*! I am to see you safely to Keighley, he *said*! I'm to protect you, if protecting is to be done!"

"We're the same size, you donkey!" Charlotte laughed. "And we're not in Keighley anyway, so stand back and I shall defend thee, *milady*!"

Branwell's pride strangled him. He couldn't get a word out for his rage. He snarled wolfishly and shoved Charlotte to the ground rather more roughly than he meant. He instantly felt rotten about it and promised himself that he'd apologize just as soon as the danger was past. Bran took up the leather and brass blade himself. He tested its weight, feeling much better now he was in his proper place, despite Charlotte glaring daggers at him and rubbing her knees where they'd banged brutally into the street. He wasn't any *milady*, he was the knight, thank you ever so much! He would be *valiant*, and *dashing*, and keep his ladies *safe*, and Papa would be so pleased he'd just *burst* when he heard of it all!

"Form ranks, lads!" cried Captain Bravey.

The wooden soldiers instantly snapped to attention in the center of the square, unshouldering their musket rifles and snatching vials of gunpowder from their belts. They could hear the savage squawks of the beast catching up to them, cracking the road like an old mirror under its weight. Leftenant Gravey, who seemed perfectly all right, tossed a pair of long pinewood rifles just like his to Charlotte and Anne. Branwell frowned. His sword was bigger, and that was all right, but it wasn't a patch on an infantry rifle. Hang it all, if only he'd waited, he could have had a real weapon from a real soldier's own hand!

"I'll leave no comrade defenseless," Gravey bellowed, "be they breathers or bleeders or cows o' the field! Form up, girls, form up!"

Charlotte grabbed Anne's hand and started off across the plaza toward the squadron. But Anne wouldn't go. The little girl's eyes shone wild with fright and thrill and fright again.

"I don't expect we can be hurt in our own make-believe country, can we, Charlotte?" she yelled over the din.

Charlotte rolled her eyes impatiently. "Did you get hurt when we played Battle of Wehglon? Or Siege of Ascension Island?"

Anne considered. "No . . . only the teapot got dented and the kitchen drapes got singed along the bottom. Oh! And I tore my green dress taking the pantry for Glass Town."

"Right! Because nothing you make up in your head can hurt you, *really*." Charlotte's cheeks flamed red in the wind. Was that right? It sounded right to her. It *felt* right. She'd figured out the trick of their lunch and she'd figured this just as well. Back home, anything could hurt them. Anything could sweep in suddenly and take the whole of everything away. School, Papa, marriages, fevers. But somehow, *somehow*, they'd slipped the trap of the real world and found their own place, the place they'd dreamed into life. And in that place, *they* were the ones who got to say who went and who stayed and who married and who didn't and who lived and who died. No different now than in the playroom at the top of the stairs. "Think, Annie. Napoleon's been dead an *age*. This one's only a toy we named Napoleon! Can't you see? His rooster's got a bit of *our own dented teapot* for his wing! Come on, Annie, form up! Let's play! It's an adventure! We're having an adventure! Of *course* there's explosions and flames and all the good bits, or else it would be a *frightfully* dull game."

Anne took all this in, turned it over in her mind, and judged it as sensible as anything could be, under the circumstances. They dashed across the silence between barrages to join ranks with their wooden lads. The boys shuffled them into the rear, as they were so new to war and not in the least made of good, stout wood.

"Ugh," whispered Bran to Emily as he held his blade a little higher, trying to convince himself he'd gotten the best of the lot. He rolled his eyes. "They're only Brown Bess muskets, anyway! What a lot of rubbish. I rather thought they'd have something better here than our army back home. We used those stuffy old things against the Americans!"

Emily stared at her brother. She tightened her grip on her leather mace. "I don't *care* what kind of guns they are!" she hissed.

"Prime and load!" commanded Bravey as another volley of flame erupted against a stately tall bank and shivered it down to glass dust. The squad turned to face the narrow street leading into the plaza, ready to fire upon anyone who came through.

"Handle cartridge!" Bravey called. The men drew tight bronze-colored musket balls from their shoulder sashes, jammed them down the long barrels of their rifles, and poured their powder after. Charlotte and Anne scrambled to copy the soldiers. "About!"

Bran pouted. "Well, you ought to. Because I daresay they won't do as well against *this* Boney as they did against *ours*. Not when he's got a giant fire-breathing chicken! Oh, but I can't *wait* to see! Do you want to bet on it, Em? I bet you Aunt Elizabeth's shilling they don't even dent his *hat*. Just let him come in reach of my blade, though!"

"Draw ramrods! Ram down cartridge!" Bravey bellowed.

In went a long, thin mallet, crushing the powder against the ball. Charlotte could not quite believe how long it was all taking to fire a single shot. Somehow, she had always imagined soldiers firing quickly and surely, like archers, one volley after the other. Napoleon seemed to reload his arms in no time at all, which seemed a horribly unfair advantage. Just then, Old Boney wheeled into the red plaza. The rooster's claws scrabbled and careened on the glass. The Emperor of France pulled back his shoulder and fired his left gun-arm again. Gravey took it directly in the heart. He clutched his piney breast and keeled over like a King in a chess match, landing with a clatter on the glass cobblestones. Anne cried out and lurched toward the fallen soldier, but Charlotte held her back.

"Let me go! You said we couldn't be hurt!" The china rooster screeched and vomited green flame before him. The heat of it turned their cheeks pink.

Charlotte trembled. She was right. She was sure she was right. But the warmth blowing against her face felt *awfully* real. "J . . . just . . . just to be safe, Annie. We can't be fixed with glue if I'm wrong, after all."

"They'll all be killed before they get off one shot!" wept Emily, behind the pastry cart.

"Perhaps, if we wanted them to have better weapons, we should have imagined better weapons for them!" Bran snapped. Then, he felt a cold flush of guilt, for not dreaming up something spectacular for the lads. "Oh! If only we'd known they *could* come real, I'd have given them all cannons for eyeballs and swords for fingers!"

Bravey shouted his final commands. "Make ready! Present!" Anne and Charlotte hoped they'd done it all right and were not about to blow themselves up. They pulled up their barrels with the rest of the squad.

Branwell forgot his guilt in a moment. He was about to see *so many* guns go off all together, right in front of him! His eyes shone with a fierce delight. "Come on, Em, bet me! I bet they don't even hit him! Brown Besses fire wild all the time, you know."

"No! God, Bran, shut *up!*" Emily stomped her brother's toes, but the black-eyed boy only laughed as Old Boney reared up on his monstrous rooster, both of them crowing to the heavens, firing his great arm-guns at the cafés until they burst into rainbow showers of glass.

"*Bonjour, mes amis!*" howled Napoleon Bonaparte. "This can all stop, you know, my darlings, *mon chéries!* All you have to do is bow down and say I LOVE NAPO-LEON three times fast! And kiss my rooster on both cheeks; he likes that."

"FIRE!" bellowed Captain Bravey, and almost before the words left his birch-bark lips, a deafening rattling boom of muskets firing shook the cobblestones below their feet.

Emily turned her eyes away. Branwell stared, goggle-eyed. Charlotte's jaw dropped open as she pulled back the trigger. Anne started hiccuping, her nerves were jangled so!

"Is this really happening?" Anne cried as she wrapped both pointed fingers round the trigger to pull it hard enough to make any headway. "It can't be! Is it?"

Emily dared a look. A storm of musket balls exploded out of the phalanx of wooden rifles, soaring toward the giant bone-man on his horrible mount. Then, in midair, the bullets sprouted wings. And feet. And fat rosy cheeks.

They had never been bullets at all. Anne giggled helplessly as her shot flew from her rifle, somersaulted out of a tight brown ball, and became a sturdy, furious, tiny woman with broad brown wings, a brown dress and apron, brown hair flying wild, brandishing brown rolling pins with menacing glee. The head bullet in the volley of Brown Besses threw her head back and gave a piercing war cry, which all the other bullets took up at once. It sounded like a hundred piccolos broken over a hundred knees. As they hurtled through the air, the Brown Besses grabbed at snatches of wind and cloud and threw them under their rolling pins. Push, squish, crush! The ladies rolled out fearsome icy storm clouds like piecrust, and when the dough rose, it rose into a violent snowstorm about three feet wide, aimed at the heart of Napoleon and his war rooster. The porcelain bird took a breath to roast them all, sparks flaring between the broken plates of his body. The storm hit just as the flame poured out of his teapot-spout beak. The blizzard froze the stream of fire into a long green icicle, which promptly fell to the ground and shattered. Old Boney's rifle-arms seized up in the sudden cold, their flintlocks jamming, their powder turning to so much snow.

The wooden soldiers cheered and wept and embraced one another and clapped Charlotte and Anne's shoulders.

"*Cracking* shots, really!" Sergeant Crashey gushed. "I won't believe it's your first time, chaps, not for a minute!"

"Couldn't shoot straighter my own self," Sergeant Major Rogue marveled.

"I daresay a field commission is in order!" Captain Bravey allowed with a little bow at the waist.

Charlotte blushed and smiled and stood a full inch higher. No grown man had ever approved of her so *heartily* before, and without once calling her *sweetheart* or *dearest* or *girl*. And now eleven of them were doing it all together. She felt dizzy. It was too much all at once; she'd spoil her dinner with all this praise. Anne was saluting everyone madly, over and over, laughing and clapping her hands together between salutes. But when she went to salute Leftenant Gravey, her laughter withered up in her throat like old grass.

There was no time for grief. The Brown Besses gave their own salute with their rolling pins, brushed off their skirts, and flew off into the sunshine, their work done. The lads began all over again, priming and loaded and drawing ramrods for another go.

Branwell watched and scowled. "They oughtn't make such a fuss just because a couple of girls managed not to faint for five minutes at a go," he grumbled. "When I am right here and ready for real, proper combat! A real man fights with a sword, you know. Any old girl can fire a rifle."

"You're so utterly full of rubbish you ought to be fed to the hogs, Bran," Emily sniffed. "Joan of Arc fought with a sword, you know!"

"Doesn't count, she's French," Branwell scoffed. His shoulders relaxed a little. The plaza had gone a bit quiet. Perhaps it was done. He peered up over the top of the pastry cart.

Napoleon was not finished with them. Bran scolded himself. He wouldn't really have been Napoleon at all if one shot did him in. The sun fell on Old Boney's awful naked skull as his voice echoed through the empty glass streets of Port Ruby:

"Give him up, you stupid matchsticks! *Donnez-moi mon frère du coeur!* I'll have my Brunty or I'll have your heads! Hand over the book and I shall let you toddle back home to Papa, *non*? So few of you, so much of me! *Quelle tragique!*"

"Did you hear that?" Bran cried.

"He ambushed the train, the rotter!" Emily said.

"All this for that fat old Magazine Man?" Charlotte wondered.

"I'd be *very* cross if I lost any of *my* books," Anne shrugged. It made a good deal of sense to her.

"We've got a right *tragique* for you, Boney! Come and get it!" roared Captain Bravey, and knelt right down on top of the great book called Brunty as he primed his next shot.

Napoleon shrugged. "Is no matter to me! Either way I have what I want and I get to explode things!" He raised up the rifles of his arms as if to part the Red Sea. "Come to my side, my sweethearts! My strongtongues, my stoutlegs, my song in the twilight, my jumpkings, my greenskin glory!"

An army of mighty frogs leapt into the plaza from every corner, out of every fountain, down from every gutter. They twanged and bellowed and croaked mightily. They landed with crashes and clatters, for these bullfrogs were well-armored in plate and mail, like medieval knights. In fact, as Branwell peered closer, he saw that they were made all of greaves and breastplates and helmets and gauntlets, with no real fleshy frog inside, just like the rooster made of dishes and the Emperor made of bones and guns. Each of them was as tall as Emily and as burly as the old blacksmith back home in Haworth. They carried steel barrels on their broad backs, their fat arms bristling with poleaxes and swords and cruel, spiked maces, and they flew silken green flags with froggy crests blazing upon them. As one, the frog army whipped the air with fearful silver tongues and roared out the clanging tribal RIBBIT! RIBBIT! SNAPPANG! that was the song of their noble people.

"Well!" said Charlotte, and she meant to say something more, something clever, something brave, but she simply had not been prepared to stare down an army of frogs today. She opened her mouth and shut it again.

Just then, behind her lovely round head, the sun came up. Not a real sun, but an extraordinary golden-red-orange color wonderfully *like* sunrise, a molten smear of light surrounding Charlotte like a bonnet of lava.

"Oh, *Charlotte*," Anne breathed. "Look!"

An iron boy rode into the red plaza on a gargantuan lion made all of blue water. But he was not any sort of ordinary iron, nor any sort of ordinary boy, for that matter. He sat in his spectacular curving, curling sea-foam saddle with such a straight back and noble bearing that they all knew right away he was there to save them from the vicious frogs, even though he could only have been a year or two older than Charlotte. His features were carved in dark, finely forged and gleaming iron, but his hair was dusty, rusty red, his hat slick, oily green, his coat and buttons dark and glinting blue, his trousers and riding boots a brilliant violet, even his hands and his teeth shone with stripes of black cast-iron and sleek pyrite, the hundred thousand colors iron can become, given enough dirt and rain and impurities and time. But most splendid of all were his wings, which opened up at his back like the fiercest of all angels, made of molten, dripping, fiery liquid iron, orange and scarlet and white-hot oozing feathers, iron poured fresh from a forge. Beneath him, blue and white and green seawater swirled and crashed and bubbled in the shape of a magnificent lion, with a mane like a waterfall, a whiskered muzzle as blue as the North Sea, and a tail held aloft like a gushing fountain. Whenever a globby burning feather fell from the man's wings, it popped and sizzled and hissed against the lion's skin, sending up great clouds of steam, so that a warm, mysterious mist announced their arrival anywhere they went.

"Who is *that*?" gasped Emily behind the cart and Anne behind Sergeant Crashey, at the same moment.

"How should I know?" hissed Branwell.

But safe in her infantry ranks, Charlotte's secret smile had come out again, so wide it hurt her cheeks. "*I* know. I know! Everything in this place is like a riddle but I can solve it, I can! Sometimes! If it's not frogs! At least I can solve this one! That's *him*! Wellington! Sir Arthur Wellesley! The Iron Duke! That's what they called him, you know," she finished somewhat lamely.

"After the war. Because he was so strong."

A platoon of very serious-looking soldiers marched into the plaza behind the Iron Duke. Rank after rank appeared through the roiling mist of his burning wings and watery horse. They carried long green muskets tipped with green bayonets and wore tall green helmets. Fierce green sabers hung at their sides. And as the wind picked up over the roaring red river, the children caught an incredible scent in their noses. Their nostrils flared in the breeze to catch it. Armies were meant to smell dreadful, like old sweat and old socks and old wounds. But the Iron Duke's army smelled so wonderfully fresh and sharp and clean and sharp!

Branwell laughed. He didn't mean to. He was trying so very hard to be good at hiding. But he laughed anyway.

"They're made of limes!" The boy cackled. "Don't you get it, Em? They're *limeys*! Limeys and frogs! The English and the French!"

And Branwell was right. Their tall green helmets were rough, bumpy lime skins crowned with lime-pith plumes. Their rifles were long lime branches and their bayonets were made of pale ancient lime flesh, hardened and dried to a terrifying point. They wore fresh, wet, lime-flesh coats, lime-flower medals, and lime-leaf belts weighed down with vials of lime seeds, and lime juice where the wooden soldiers carried their Brown Bess bullets and powder. And beneath those dashing helmets they could see shadowy faces, faces carved out of whole limes like Greek statues out of marble.

"'Cause Frenchies eat frog legs and we eat limes so's not to get scurvy when we go to sea!" Branwell giggled. "Only I've never had a lime so no one ought to call *me* one of that. But they will anyway on account of how people are rotten. Glass Town isn't a riddle like Charlotte said. It's a joke! A marvelously weird, really drawn-out joke! The best one I ever heard!"

"Come, sourlads, come tarthearts, come ripetroops!" The Iron Duke shouted jovially, without the least worry in his voice. "My bitterboot berserkers, my jolly green-coats! Forward, MARCH!"

The limey lads stomped right up to the armored frogs and snapped to attention. As one, they saluted the exhausted squad of wooden soldiers, Crashey and Bravey and Rogue and the lot, relieving them of duty. The gang lifted poor Gravey from the field of battle and set him down behind the lines, near a bakery whose crimson windows had shattered all over its own steaming pies. They stood quite close to Bran and Emily, but didn't seem to notice them in the slightest, not even Charlotte and Anne, who knelt lovingly beside their beloved fallen toy.

"How do you like that?" Bran said. "Hullo! We're all right, if you were curious!"

It wasn't fair. It wasn't *right*. He was right *here*, just waiting to protect them, just *bursting* at the gut to defend their honor and defeat their enemies, and this stupid old place hadn't even given him a chance. Charlotte and Anne had hogged it all and Branwell had gotten nothing but a big leather sword and nothing to swing at. He'd have championed the *blazes* out of the girls; he would have!

Emily ignored her brother. She lowered her mace and ducked across the cobblestones to rejoin her sisters. She didn't look behind her once, but she didn't have to. She knew Bran would follow, furrowing his brow and dragging his feet and planning a cutting remark or two. He always had to plan them out well in advance.

"Prime and load!" thundered the Iron Duke, his molten wings flaring behind him. His oceanic lion roared to shake the sun from the sky.

"Ready tongues, my hoppers!" screeched Napoleon. His flaming rooster crowed green fire and green fury.

The limeys began shoving bullets and powder in while the frogs stamped their webbed steel feet and dipped their long, terrible tongues into the barrels of toadstones on their backs and coiled them back like catapults. Em scrambled into the shelter of the bakery awning just in time. Charlotte hugged her so hard she nearly strangled, even though it is very awkward to hug anyone holding a spiked mace while you've still got your rifle unslung.

"Where's Bran?" Anne asked.

"Oh, he'll be along," Emily said with confidence. She pretended to check an invisible pocket watch. "Right about . . . just precisely . . . *now*."

"Make ready!" Napoleon and Wellington screamed at the same instant, and Charlotte did wonder if they got tired of screaming every little thing, because her ears were certainly tired of it.

The sisters looked back over the little scarlet alley where Emily had come to see Branwell frowning furiously and stomping toward them, just as they knew he would be. It was wonderfully comforting to know a person so well.

"Oh, hurry up, Mr. Snail!" Anne called to him. Bran glared back at her—but he picked up his pace, trying to jog while hanging on to the massive sword. He needed both hands to carry the beast. It wasn't easy.

"FIRE!" howled Napoleon and Wellington together.

The air in Port Ruby detonated into a mist of red glass and lime skins and frog-tongues and gun smoke.

The earth itself shook. Anne fell against Emily, clawing at her throbbing ears. Charlotte stepped instinctively in front of them, even though her rifle wasn't half done with all that ridiculous loading and all she could have done was slap a frog with it. Emily stopped breathing. She shut her eyes. If she shut her eyes, she couldn't see it, and if she couldn't see it it, it wouldn't have happened.

Branwell stood stock still between the pastry cart and the bakery it belonged to. He didn't cry out. He didn't drop his sword. He looked down at his chest and said, very quietly: "Buck up." Blood tumbled out of his heart where the toadstone had struck him. The stain looked so beautiful, so perfect, like a rose growing out of him. Bran thought he would have to try drawing that someday. A lovely feeling spread over him. For once, he felt that he belonged just where he was, for his blood was as red as the glass cobblestones, as red as the claret river, as red as the roofs and gables and windows, as red as anything in Port Ruby could ever hope to be. But no one heard him, so no one could tell him to be brave.

Branwell collapsed into a heap of black woolen boy on the crimson ground, quite, quite dead.

SEVEN

Such a Little Thing

"What's the matter with you?" snarled Sergeant Major Rogue.

Emily, Anne, and Charlotte stood frozen. They stared at their brother's body as though it was a puzzle they could work out, and once they had it worked out, he would get up and laugh and pinch them and everything would be all right again.

"You said!" Anne burst out sobbing. "You said we couldn't be hurt! You said! You promised!"

Horror seeped up from Charlotte's stomach. A black, wet horror that would never leave her. She could see Bran's pale face lying against the glass road and it was

Maria's face. It was Lizzie's face. It was her mother's face. "I was wrong," she whispered.

"No, no, you're never *ever* wrong, you always *say* you're never wrong and if you're *never* wrong you couldn't be wrong about *being* wrong and you *can't* be wrong now!" Anne lurched toward Bran's body. Crashey caught her roughly and pushed her back against the bakery wall as the volley went on and on and on. Frogs bellowed and lime-boys beat their drums.

"What d'ya think you're doing, young sir?" snapped the Sergeant.

"Are you quite mad?" hissed Captain Bravey.

Tears ran down Emily's face, one after the other, helplessly, uselessly. *There's three of us now,* some awful grown-up, unfeeling voice said in her mind. *Only three.*

"I said he was rubbish," she said softly. "That was the last thing he heard in this world. You really ought never to call a *person* rubbish, and I did it all the time. Oh, Bran, Bran, I'm so *sorry.* I'm rubbish, I am, not you at all."

"You see this?" stormed Sergeant Major Rogue, pointing at the walls of the bakery. "This is shelter, you idiots! You're supposed to stay put when you hear the call to *make ready,* not run out into the ruddy *street* like a lost ball!"

"Bloody breathers," muttered the others, whose

names they did not yet know, but could guess. "Haven't got the sense the Genii gave squirrels."

"Excuse me," Emily cried suddenly, turning on the soldiers. "We followed *you*! This is your fault! We're only a parson's children! You're *soldiers*; you're meant to keep people safe! That's your *entire* job!"

No, thought Charlotte. *It was my job. My* entire *job. And I was wrong. And everything is over.* She thought she would certainly be sick.

"We are not mad," Emily kept on, shaking her finger directly in the Captain's wooden face. "It's *very* rude of you to say that to us when we've only just finished being shot at and our brother is *dead*! There is nothing the matter with any of the four of us, *sir*, and if we knew the rules, we'd have made a run for it at the proper time, but we didn't, and he . . . he . . . *couldn't*, so here we *'bloody'* are, with cake stuck in our ears and frogs *everywhere* and Branwell is *gone*! If anything around here is mad, that is!"

"Em! Don't let's get into the habit of swearing just because we're not at home," scolded Charlotte automatically, and a scolding from Charlotte, however mild her words, would wilt the heart of a wild rhinoceros and cause him to devote the rest of his life to keeping his horns sharp and his back straight. But her voice failed on the word *home*. What right had she to scold when she'd failed poor Branwell so? She wasn't ever the oldest to begin with. That was why it had all happened. Maria would have saved him. She was an imposter, and now everyone knew it. She had no right to tell anyone what to do anymore.

"What's Papa going to say?" Anne whispered.

"I don't know why you're making such a grand fuss over it," mumbled Sergeant Major Rogue sheepishly.

"Yes, you're being very *dramatic*," Crashey said. He rubbed his forehead under his helmet. "Very over-the-topsified."

"Embarrassing," agreed one of the soldiers they hadn't been introduced to yet.

"Our brother is DEAD! Of course we're being dramatic! Wouldn't you be?"

Captain Bravey and Sergeant Crashey looked at each other, then down at the corpse of Leftenant Gravey, then back to the girls.

"Nope," shrugged Crashey.

"Stiff upper and all that," Bravey said kindly. "Why trouble yourself over such a little thing?"

"It's not little, it's not," wept Anne. "It's *Bran*."

The gunfire went quiet at last with a rattle of armor and hammers falling on empty chambers. The girls tore away from the squad and stumbled out onto the road toward their brother. Charlotte and Emily got their hands up under him, slick with blood.

"I'm sorry, Bran," Charlotte said to his dear, sweet face. "I shouldn't have called you a donkey. I should have let you have the sword."

"A little help, Anne?" Emily groaned. But Anne did not answer, and when they got Branwell under the shelter of the stained glass walls, when they'd laid him out beside Leftenant Gravey and looked for her, the youngest of them was nowhere to be seen.

"FORM RANKS!" Napoleon and Wellington hollered again. "HANDLE CARTRIDGE!"

"Anne! Anne! Where's she gone?" Charlotte spun round, panicked. Her heart threatened to give the whole thing up and run off without her.

"PRIME AND LOAD!" came the cry from the English and the French.

Lime juice sprayed from a thousand rifle barrels. It stung their eyes, their skin, their teeth like acid. Emily rubbed at her eyes, her fingers covered in blood and the sour, vicious lime. She spied her sister first. Anne was creeping across the plaza toward one of the smaller bullfrogs. It had a catapult on its green back and a sleepy, friendly look in its eye—but then, all frogs have that look, and it doesn't mean they are sleepy or friendly.

"Pssst," Anne coaxed the frog, holding out her hand to it like it was a shy pony. "Nice frog. Brave frog. Handsome frog. Who's a nice, brave, handsome frog?"

The frog noticed Anne. It stared at her hand in disbelief.

"Er," the frog said uncertainly. "I suppose that I am, *mademoiselle?*"

"*Anne!*" hissed Emily. "Get back here this instant! What are you *doing?*" *Two, two,* the grown-up voice in her protested. *There can't be only two. We'll never make it on just two of us.*

"MAKE READY!" yelled the Duke and the Emperor.

"I'm going after her," Charlotte said firmly. "Hold my rifle, Em. I'll only be a moment."

"Hell on a *plate,* you ruddy fools!" screamed Rogue. "What did I clearly say about hearing anybody belch out *make ready?* Get inside, you *unfathomably* stupid breathers!"

Charlotte and Emily looked round the ruined red plaza. Not a single building still held roof and window together. Under the onslaught of Old Boney, everything that was once inside was now firmly outside, and mostly lying on the street in pieces.

"WHERE?" They shouted together as the armies bellowed commands they now knew too well, *handle car-*

tridge and *draw ramrods* and *ram down!* "HOW?"

"Yes you are a nice, brave, handsome frog!" Anne exclaimed warmly. She smiled the same smile she used on Rainbow and Diamond and Jasper back home, whenever a thunderstorm had made them nervous of eating from her hand.

The frog's whole body seemed to relax. He crouched down near her. "Thank you! You know, it feels so good to hear someone say all that. I always *thought* I was rather good-looking, and I do *try* to be kind to others whenever I can, and I have never shirked my duty to *roi ou pays*, king or country, don't you know, but no one ever seems to notice. I'm just one frog in a million, no matter what I do!"

"Oh, not to me!" Anne said winningly. "To me you are simply One Frog. One Perfect Frog!"

"Is that a bit of bacon you've got there?" Napoleon's foot soldier said hungrily. "We don't get meat rations anymore."

"Fresh from my breakfast," Anne nodded, for there never was a breakfast she didn't half-smuggle away for her animals. "All for you."

Sergeant Major Rogue rolled his good eye and made a disgusted sound. "Stupid *tourists*," he sighed. "You could be sitting on a mountain of books and still ask *where's the library?* Well, it's not my *entire* job to point the way to you splitwits, as I am neither a signpost nor a traffic police, but as you are about to get your adorable little meat sacks roasted and fried, I suppose I've got to go ahead and do every-bleeding-thing for you!"

The wooden soldier reached them in two short, businesslike steps. He snatched Charlotte's sword from Bran's cold, stiffening fingers and Emily's mace right out of her hand. He tossed them up onto the glittering scarlet pavement between a haberdashery and a redgrocer, whose beets and radishes and raspberries and rhubarb and grapes had already been half devoured by hungry warriors on both sides. Once away from their owners, the weapons shuddered and trembled and became suitcases again. Rogue yanked a little balsam-bound notebook from one breast pocket, a twiggy pencil from the other, and scribbled something down. He shoved the paper at Charlotte.

"Go say this to your luggage and say it NICELY, mind you. You've only got about ninety seconds before nothing you say will matter and we'll all be having tea together in Hades. Go on!"

Charlotte's bravery was starting to wilt. She looked down at the notebook uncertainly. What lovely writing Rogue had! Perhaps they could be friends one day, for Charlotte admired good handwriting almost as much as she admired good deeds and good intentions. She caught herself again, thinking of the future, of friendship, when Bran was dead and nothing *did* matter anymore. *Take charge,* she told herself. *You've still got to look after everyone that's left and keep them safe. You're still the oldest, for all the good it does. It is, as Em says, your entire job.* Charlotte gave the little notebook a squeeze against her chest and dashed over to their suitcases, trying to keep an eye on Anne inching toward her frog, feeling extremely silly and not at all sure what in the world this would accomplish.

Out of the corner of her eye, Charlotte saw her youngest sister do something awful. And wonderful. And *awful.* As the frog bent its great, wide head to nibble at the rind of bacon, Anne gave out a bloodcurdling savage war cry and leapt up on his back. She kicked his ribs brutally with her little feet and hauled back on the rope of his catapult with both arms. The frog burbled in pain and charged off wildly toward his own King, cursing Anne, cursing himself, cursing bacon and fate and the agony of war.

"For Branwell!" Anne shrieked. "For Bran and England and Bran all over again and forever!"

"Hurry *up!*" shouted the squad of wooden soldiers.

"You can't save her out here!" Bravey pleaded.

"O, Glorious Baggage!" Charlotte read out in her sweetest voice. "Blessed Childe of the Great Trunk! Scion of the Ancient House of Lug! I, while acknowledging Your Individual Right to Free Will, Self-Determination, Parliamentary Representation, and Bodily Autonomy, do Most Humbly Beg of You to stop mucking about and show me what you've got!" Charlotte glanced over her shoulder. "I say, this is long!" she whispered at the soldiers and her siblings.

Anne pointed the frog at Napoleon and slashed at the catapult's rope with the bayonet of her gun. It sprang; she dropped her rifle; she ducked as the basket hurled a beaten iron ball into the air.

"You're a rotten little goblin," the frog sighed as it flew.

"Keep going, for pine's sake!" Crashey hissed.

Charlotte tore her eyes away from Anne. A nimble frog-sniper was galloping clumsily toward her on webbed feet, lashing out with his tongue, trying to snatch at the handles of the suitcases with it. Charlotte cried out miserably, tears coming in earnest now. It wasn't supposed to be this way; it was supposed to be an adventure, a game, a joy! She cringed as she swung out the rifle's butt. Shooting was one thing, but to harm a poor creature right to its face was too horrid. A sickening crack echoed out over the plaza as she connected and the beast flopped flat. Charlotte's hands and her voice shook horribly as she held up the paper again and read.

"Carry me as I have Carried You, and in exchange, I solemnly swear never to Forget You in a Train Station and Condemn you to the Fiery Depths of the Left Luggage Office, nor Bash You Roughly when Lifting You into the Overhead Rack or forget to Pack My Toiletries Carefully and thereby Spill Unpleasant Unguents Upon, Throughout, and All Over You. You are the very Best and Prettiest and Strongest and Hardiest and Most Spacious of all Luggage, and I am awfully lucky to have purchased You, and not any of the Other Assorted Valises from the Shop. Valesium in excelsis, *keep me safe!*"

The two suitcases instantly unsnapped their lids and smacked them twice like teeth gnashing. Then, something began to happen. Something astonishing. Something enormous.

Anne's shot crashed directly into Napoleon's rooster. It stove in his wing, the one made out of an old dented teapot that looked so very like the one Aunt Elizabeth polished every month despite the dent. The chicken crooned pitifully and turned its blazing eyes toward its master, begging silently for help, for love, for forgiveness. Then, the rooster toppled over, clucking in misery and trying to reach the wound with his beak while Napoleon struggled to get out from under its fiery bulk. Anne cackled in vengeful delight. She turned the frog back toward her sisters and kicked and kicked his ribs until he was running at daredevil speed.

Charlotte and Emily's old, weather-beaten bags, the plain, familiar bags they'd used for years, since the first time they went off to the yawning cold prison called School, the bags that had been weapons a moment ago, outdid themselves. They unfolded and unpacked, joined together and grew—and grew and *grew*—until they became an enormous house wedged between the haberdasher and the redgrocer, yet taller by far than either of them, with two patched, threadbare leather and brass towers and dozens of windows made from their petticoats and bonnets and stockings and a great double door made from one of Emily's black dresses and one of Charlotte's.

It looked just exactly like Westminster Abbey. If only Westminster Abbey had a giant wooden handle at the top for easy carrying.

"FIRE!" howled Napoleon and Wellington.

Anne leapt off her frog as he barreled past the redgrocer and the haberdasher. She rolled and tumbled over herself and dove past the astonished throng of them all into the suitcase-abbey. Charlotte, Emily, and the wooden soldiers only just dragged the doors of the luggage closed behind them when the world exploded into a hurricane of frog fire and lime smoke.

EIGHT

A Refreshment of Spirits

Inside the luggage, they found a very pleasant lounge room waiting for them. Several long couches spread invitingly around a large table set with a whiskey and hardtack for the men and tea cake for the children. Vases of flowers were arranged elegantly around the room, the ceilings arched far above their heads like church buttresses, and several rich tapestries decorated the linen-lined walls, as well as stitched pockets meant for the securing of various smaller items within a suitcase. Charlotte and Emily felt somewhat embarrassed when they noticed that the couches were their old boots swelled up and stuffed till soft, the flowers were folded out of pages from the books they'd packed for School, and the rich tapestries were their shawls and gloves and chemises and hairpins and ribbons scrunched together, braided and twisted to look like hunting scenes and bowls of apples. The soldiers didn't seem to care one bit. They cleared off the whiskey and hardtack and cakes with businesslike quickness and laid out the bodies of Branwell and Leftenant Gravey on the table.

Sergeant Crashey drew a strange amber flask from his belt and tipped it into Gravey's mouth, then Bran's. Something the color of moonlight dripped out and splattered onto the corpses of the poor dead boys. In half a moment, the hole punched through Bran's heart and through the Leftenant's wooden head knotted up like two stitches knit together. Gravey groaned and rolled over onto his side. Crashey tucked his little bottle away again with a snort of satisfaction at a job well done. He relaxed, took off his helmet, letting an unkempt ruff of sawdusty curls free. Gravey managed to get himself sitting upright with the help of his men.

Branwell didn't stir.

Oh, thought Emily, without hope, *well, of course it won't work on our Bran, whatever it is. He's not made of anything fixable. We're not like them. We don't come back. We know that. We know it better than anyone.* Rogue watched the whole operation out of his one good eye. Anne thought she saw a sappy tear well up in his wooden lashes. *He must be such a very good man,* she thought, *to weep for his friend coming back to life. Most people only weep when somebody dies.*

"That was a good one, wasn't it, Sergeant?" Gravey coughed a leaf or two into his hand. "I spun right around like a top! Did you laugh? You know I always want to get a good laugh when I go."

"I chuckled," Crashey admitted. "But you'll never top Wehglon! Exploded seven times in one day!"

"Aw, I know, I know, Crash, my man," he sighed, grabbing his comrade's arm and hoisting himself upright again. "But a real artist never gives up trying to top himself!"

"I laughed," Branwell mumbled groggily, without opening his eyes. Three identical gasps rose up from the girls. Bran touched his heart. He stuck his finger through the bullet hole in his waistcoat. Finally, he winked one eye open, then the other. "I did. I laughed!" he said, though he hadn't really, but now that he knew he should, he resolved always to do it when something dreadful happened right in front of him. Or to him. But what had happened to him? He remembered the red, the lovely warm feeling and the *redness,* but that was all.

One moment, Charlotte, Emily, and Anne thought they'd never breathe again, and the next, they were hugging their brother with the ferociousness of a fistfight. They tackled him to the ground. He squirmed and protested, but, just for a second, toward the end, he shut his eyes and relaxed into his sisters' arms and enjoyed their love and their tears as much as he'd ever enjoyed plum jam or hot soup.

"You scared me," whispered Charlotte. "You scared me so." *But I wasn't wrong,* she thought to herself. *I wasn't, after all.*

"Did I?" said Bran, suddenly eager and keen. "Did you cry? Did you scream?"

"Well . . . yes, of course." Charlotte sat back from the pile of them. She drew all her fear and love and wonder and feeling back inside her. Perhaps you weren't meant to scream, if you were the oldest. If the oldest child screamed, how could the youngest be expected to hold herself together?

Branwell leapt up and peered at his sister with a dark, interested stare. "What did you scream?"

Emily stood up and brushed off her skirt. "What are you *talking* about, Bran?"

"Well, what I mean to say is, of course you screamed and cried, because I was dead and all. But *what* did you scream? How did it go? Did you scream my name? For God? For Papa? Any swear words? Did you fall down on the floor? When you screamed, was it like this?" Bran let out a little, helpless yelp. "Or like this?" He threw back his head and bellowed. The soldiers gawped at him. "Did all of you cry out for the loss of me or was it just Charlotte? Do it again, so I can hear you this time! I can mime it all over if that would help you get into character."

Emily and Charlotte rolled their eyes. Suddenly, the black knots of terror in their stomachs loosened and fell away. Branwell was Branwell again, as perfectly Branwell as ever a boy had been.

"We'll do no such thing," Charlotte snorted. "You are *bizarre*."

"You're such a little pig," Emily laughed. "Snuffling in the weeds for attention!"

"Well, I did *die*, you know," the lad grumbled.

"Dying's easy! *I* killed the rooster!" Anne announced, readying herself for a heaping serving of praise.

"No!" cried Bran. "How could you?"

Anne crossed her arms over her chest. "He was a monster! He's the enemy! They'd killed you!"

"Well, *yes*, but I'm fine now and he was such a *fantastic* monster! You didn't have to *kill* him! Before I could even get a good look!"

"Wounded, surely," Captain Bravey interrupted. "Not killed. Marengo is a tougher bird than that. Though I'm quite sure you've a medal of some sort coming your way, Private Anne."

Private! She had a rank! Anne beamed. Bran looked around, still a bit hungover from his recent death. He snorted nastily at a footstool fashioned out of Emily's bloomers. Without saying anything aloud, the girls silently agreed to pretend that they were not just now about to have tea in a house made out of all their personal belongings.

Outside, the volleys of the great battle of the frogs against the limeys boomed and crashed, but the thick leather walls muffled the noise until it sounded as though it were all happening ten miles away and no danger to them whatever. The wooden soldiers heaved a great sigh of relief and set to their lunch, uncorking the good stuff and passing round the tack. By now, Charlotte and Branwell were entirely unsurprised that the biscuits were actual nails and pins served on a dainty plate with orange roses painted round the edge. Crashey and Bravey and the rest crunched happily between their mighty teeth. But Emily and Anne could not help crying out in fearful delight when a pair of caramel-colored ghosts sprang out of the liquor bottle and rose whirling into the air, howling and moaning like the wind through a dead marshland. Their icy eyes glittered and its rags shone with the oily swirls of good whiskey. The ghosts rattled armfuls of liquid, frothing chains very convincingly before finally dissolving into a fine, wet mist that settled down onto the faces of the fighting men and left them quite satisfied and refreshed.

"Spirits," Branwell said, jostling his sister with an elbow, rather proud to have been the one to see it. "Get it? Oh, Charlotte, I could live here forever!"

"Not forever, though, Bran," whispered Anne, tugging his sleeve. "Not always and always. They've got whiskey at home, too, you know."

Branwell ignored her. They'd only just gotten here! He'd only just come back to life! He'd only just learned he *could* come back to life! Bran didn't want to hear the word home until six in the evening, at least. He practically leapt the table to crowd in with the fighting lads and get a bit of spritz on his cheeks. It did not leave him entirely satisfied or refreshed, rather more wet and dizzy, but in all his days Branwell had never felt so grown-up, and *that* satisfied him from his toenails to his earlobes.

"What was it like, when you were dead?" Emily asked. Her eyes gleamed with a curiosity like hunger. "Were you a spirit?"

"Dunno," Bran shrugged, eyeballing the soldiers' tea. Dying was *starving* work! "Wasn't like anything." But the question made him shudder. *Was* he a spirit for a moment? And if he had been, what was he now? No! He would not think of it. He would think of food. Food would set it right. Spirits didn't eat a hearty second lunch, and he meant to do just that.

"But how is it *possible?*" Charlotte said, with a little fear and a little awe—the kind of awe that wants to burrow right down into the wonderful thing and find out how it works. "What was that stuff Crashey had on his belt?"

Branwell scratched the back of his neck. "Tasted like some old lady's perfume. Vile stuff. Brrr."

The girls fell to their own rather odd tea, for grief, too, is a hungry thing. Their luggage had laid out two cups and two saucers for each of them, decorated with the same design of orange roses, a little too like the embroidery on Charlotte's summer dress for comfort, and four fine copper toffee hammers set neatly alongside with their names on the handles, bearing the same scuffs and scratches as the copper corner caps on their old suitcases. In one cup lay a large, elegant capital letter *T* done in red ink in a complicated medieval style; in the other, a typewritten lowercase *t* in sepia ink, as simple and honest as if it were printed in a novel. Bran much preferred the men's meal, for it looked terrifically dangerous to eat. He grabbed a piece of tack, a long, fierce, iron nail with an icing of rust. Gingerly, he bit the head off the end and found it, though very dry and crumbly, not at all vile. It tasted rather like cinnamon.

"You've always got to show off, haven't you?" Emily sighed, rolling her eyes. But she didn't want to look helpless and silly in front of the soldiers, either, anymore than they already had. They had to show that they could behave like locals or Crashey and Bravey and Gravey and Rogue would run off to find more interesting comrades. She took up the hammer marked *EMILY* with confidence, feeling nearly, almost entirely, positively halfway sure of herself. She tapped the lovely red capital *T* with the hammer just as she would do to break up a sheet of toffee. The letter instantly wriggled and wobbled and swelled up into a red frosted cake that bulged deliciously over the brim of the cup. When she whacked the lower-case *t*, it obediently dissolved into the most perfect cup of tea that had ever been poured. All four slipped their copper toffee hammers into one pocket or another as a souvenir, thinking no one saw, though everyone did.

Charlotte eyed the commander suspiciously. She knew the mystery ought to wait till after the tea, but she couldn't resist trying to get at it right away. She couldn't help it. She wanted the *story*. She needed it. Besides, the battle had got her blood up, and she was feeling awfully courageous.

"Captain Bravey," she asked by way of breaking the ice. "Won't you introduce us to your men?"

"By the Duke's left armpit, I am the most graceless grunt in Glass Town! Do forgive me, I am only a humble soldier, after all, and we are prone to sitting upon our manners rather than wearing them proper." Bravey blushed with true shame, that curious mossy blush creeping up his cheeks. "I am Captain Bravey, but you've met me, and this is Sergeant Crashey, but you know him. That's Corporal Cheeky there with the smart mustache; our recently revivified friend is Leftenant Gravey; that dashing fellow in the eye patch is Sergeant Major Rogue. Elbow deep in the snack tray you'll find Bombadier Cracky, Warrant Officers Goody and Baddy, and our company Quartermaster, Hay Man. Lance Sergeant Naughty, Lance Corporal Sneaky, and Private Tracky appear to have fallen asleep, poor lads."

There it was, laid out on the table like the whiskey and the tea, for them to make what they might of it. Those were the names, each and every one, of their toy soldiers back home, chosen carefully and with much yelling between the four of them. One or two or four might be coincidence. Perhaps names ending in *ey* were terrifically popular in this place. But twelve? Twelve meant something grand and mad and beefily *real*. Here sat their dolls, talking and eating biscuits like real grown men. It was magic, certainly, but what sort? Each of them felt their chests practically bursting to say something, but it seemed so awfully rude to blurt out: *I say, old chaps, did you know you're our toys? Isn't it funny how we've got a Napoleon and a Wellington in our world, too, only they're rather older, and also one's dead and the other's Prime Minister? What do you think of all that? Lovely weather we're having.* The soldiers would either laugh or take offense, and they loved them all too much already to bear either one. Besides, there was a war on. Intelligence was at a premium. They might be able to make some use of these strange secrets later, if they could keep mum now.

"Very pleased to meet you. I am Charlotte—" she began, but Branwell would not let her be the one who spoke for them. He was the one who'd come back to life not fifteen minutes ago. Whenever he got sick at home, Aunt Elizabeth and Tabitha made a tremendous fuss with hot water bottles and tinctures and sweets and kisses. It only stood to reason that they should all make an extra-tremendous fuss now. After all, when you rose from the grave in England, people tended to make whole religions out of you. He would do the talking. It was only logic.

"*I* am Branwell," he cut in, "and these are my sisters, Anne, Emily, and Charlotte. I'm *dash* honored to make your acquaintance, sirs, and, er, so're they."

Charlotte ignored him. She had questions, and when Charlotte had questions she could hardly bear to breathe until she got her answers. "And where were you born, Captain Bravey? Was your father a military man?"

"How kind of you to take an interest in little old blockheaded me, young lady!" the Captain said with a delighted blush. "But I'm afraid my story is rather dull. No different from any other soldier, really. My full name is Reader Rootstock Bravey. I was born in the village of Boxwickham, a little, dark place in the county of Shoppeshire. Do not feel in the least shamed if you've not heard of it! There's nothing to see there at all. A bit of velvet land, a pleasant enough river on the north side of town to keep brigands out, and the whole lot surrounded by sturdy, impenetrable woods that quite block out the sun. I never knew my father, only my eleven brothers, whom you see before you. Sometimes, I think I remember our old dad. In my dreams I see an aged fellow with a white mustache and spectacles, forever with a wood-chisel in one hand and a paintbrush in the other, with a Northern accent and a musty smell about him—wood oils and lacquer and sap. But then I wake up and think I am the silliest of Captains, dreaming about fathers and paintbrushes when there is work to be done!"

He means the toy shop in Leeds, Charlotte thought furiously. *And the wooden box they all came in, that Father gave to Bran at Christmas! He doesn't* know *that's what he means, but he means it anyhow.*

Emily caught on to Charlotte's game and played her turn. "And where did you get your marvelous name?" she asked brightly.

"And were you named after an uncle or a famous warrior?" Anne put in her *and.*

Bravey looked puzzled. He scratched the short, barky hair beneath his helmet. "Do you know, I never thought about it! I suppose I always thought it made plenty of sense, as I *am* quite brave. Perhaps the old man with the paintbrush gave it to me. Perhaps I am not so silly after all."

It was all Anne could do not to shout: *No, he didn't! No, he didn't! I named you that because you had such a stern look on your face when we took you out of the box! I named you! Me!*

"Dash splendid Valise you've got here," coughed Corporal Cheeky, feeling that the conversation had become a trifle too personal for his taste. He hoisted his ankle up on one knee and rested back on the sofa with a long nail wedged between his teeth like a toothpick. "So many of them don't bother to set a proper table these days. Labor disputes, you know."

Cheeky had a long burn across one cheek where Bran had left him too close to the candle.

Captain Bravey looked up round the walls and buttresses. "You'll have to excuse the Corporal; he's got a mouth like poison ivy." He slapped the lad's cockily crossed leg back onto the floor. "Do you want to cause a strike? Do try to behave like an oak and not a weed, boy!"

One of the tapestries began to shiver and quiver above the soap-brick mantel. The woven picture of spotted dogs chasing after a fox and a unicorn unfurled its ribbons and gloves and shawls and leather and wooden hairbrush handles and thimbles and knitting needles into an enormous face and neck and chest. It was the wise, old, beaked head of a turtle, only it had a snail's kindly, soft antennae, too. They could see half its shell poking out of the wall as well, pearly and spiraled like a snail, but plated and patchworked like a turtle. It stared down at them like the strangest hunting trophy. The two sorts of animals who carry their houses on their back like the loveliest of suitcases, crushed into one creature.

"It's my first day on the job," said the turtle-snail-beast. When he opened his mouth, they could see a soft, black, wool stocking-tongue moving. "I wanted to do well."

NINE

The Tragical Romance of Baggage and People, or the Romantical Tragedy of People and Grog

Emily blushed and looked down at her kneecaps. She couldn't meet the beast's eyes. They were made out of two pence she had hidden away long ago, so that no matter what happened in the unguessable future of School and Governessing and Being Grown, she could cling to the reassuring idea that she had some money of her own, however little. She'd never breathed a word, and now they would all know she had hoarded something for herself and not for them all. But no one seemed to notice, so Emily quickly stopped noticing, too.

"Noble luggage!" cried Leftenant Gravey to the

turtley snail on the wall. "May all the blessings of the Genii be upon you!"

The snail-turtle inclined his head politely, but did not reply.

"Not even one word for old Gravey; how do you like that?" The Leftenant grumbled quietly to himself. "I will hold a grudge, I will. I'm going to hold it and feed it and water it and pet it and tell it it's a good grudge. That'll show the old bag."

"The Genii?" Branwell scrunched up his nose.

Warrant Officer Goody grimaced. "It's like I always say, no one's got any respect for religion nowadays. The gods of Glass Town skip a few centuries between visits and suddenly everyone's an Anglican having a little picnic of a Sunday instead of repentin' like they ought. Now, me, I do six sets of repentin' every morning before chow. Twenty push-ups, repent. Twenty more, repent again. And look at me! Handsome, eh? That's the repentin'."

Crashey glared at Goody. He continued in a louder voice. "Most munificabulous bindles! We are most grateful for your . . . salvatervention? Intervupption?" Crashey was a brave sort, but he couldn't manage to keep his vocabulary any tidier than his closet. Long words were such naughty little hoodlums, always running away from him instead of staying put and making him look good like they were supposed to. "For thou hast-ed save-ed our trousers and hem-ed our bacon! It's a good job you did; the war will just ruin your afternoon, I tell you what."

"Why are you talking to it like that?" said Branwell, to paper over everything he wanted to say instead. "It's only Charlotte's and Em's old knockabout suitcases, *really*."

"I sat on one and popped its hinges last year," admitted Anne guiltily. She twisted her fingers together.

Bran pressed on, feeling bolder now that Anne had backed him up. "I daresay anything that got itself to Glass Town would grow some sort of magic! But they're just *bags* and you're talking to Em's *underthings* like they're the King of Spain!"

The wooden soldiers gasped and spluttered, covering their mouths and hearts and ears with their hands.

"He doesn't mean anything by it," pleaded Quartermaster Hay Man, quite the stoutest of them round the belly.

"Just a lad," cried Naughty and Baddy together. "You know how lads can be! Terrible inventions, lads!"

"The young'uns don't learn their history nowadays, that's the thing of it," Warrant Officer Goody moaned.

"Please don't pack us!" wept the Privates Tracky and Boaster, covering their heads with their arms as though the ceiling were about to crumble down and crush them dead.

Captain Bravey drew himself up to his full height. "My boy, a good soldier keeps both his wits and his powder dry at all times. A tongue is very like a gun, which is why they nearly rhyme. Both can be fired to devastating effect, for good or evil, and both can explode in your hands, wounding your comrades instead of your enemies."

Branwell flushed with a deep and burning shame. He never thought he could feel so poorly as he did just at that moment, under the oaken gaze of the brave Captain. All the wind of battle and whiskey and resurrection rushed out of him at once. He sat down with a heavy smack of trousers against sofa, and tried devilishly hard not to cry.

Goody mumbled on under his breath, but Anne heard him all the same. "You can't go blaming the youth for not studying! History's depressing! *And* boring. Like winter. One storm after another. Brrr. Why not stay inside your own head where it's cozy and tidy and the repentin's nice and hot? Nothing out there but the war and mad science and Princesses going missing and Boney bashing up the place nine times a week."

"What Princess?" Anne whispered to him. Her almost-violet eyes shone at the word.

"*The* Princess," Goody said with confusion. "*The!*"

"Can I say the story?" Crashey asked the snaily turtle. "If it please Your Excellejesties? Or is that meant to be Majellences . . . ?"

"Please." The head on the wall nodded. "One always likes to hear about oneself."

The Sergeant stood at attention, ramrod straight, arms stiff behind his back, and bellowed:

"THE TRAGICAL ROMANCE OF BAGGAGE AND PEOPLE, BY SERGEANT CRASHEY! See, as long as there's been people, there's been luggage, because it's practically the first thing you need besides fire and a cave and a mastopotamus to get rump steaks and trousers out of, on account of how you've just got to have something to carry all your other somethings in, right? So bags and people got right and proper civilized together, side by side. People got straight backs and high foreheads and agricusbandrilly inclined and . . ." Crashey felt his grip on his words loosening and hurried out in front of the mess he was making. "And we got *jolly* good at writing and building and inventeering stuff and goodsense, like moats and hats and pudding and the lot. But luggage got so *fantavulously* useful that we couldn't do without. You see what they can do, yeah? Carry us any which way! A house, a carriage, a balloon, a ship, a racing stallionocerosupine!

Is that a thing? It sounds like it ought to be, so let's say it is! *Plusly*, a good Valise can feed you and bed you and tell you all about the local customs and points of interest and, furtherditionally, keep out anything but the end of the world, and pack down to the size of a wee dog at the end of it all. All they asked was right and fair payment for their services—a sock or a mustache comb or a nice shoe every so once in a while, which is why oftener and oftening, when you get to the place you're going, you can't find that nice velvet coat you just knew you packed, right? It was payday, that's all, and your luggage took its salary; can't blame 'em. Er. Cap'n, they like to be called Valises, now, yeah? I think I said luggage. Curse my acorn-head! So hard to break old habits, you know!"

The turtle-snail interrupted Crashey's story, penny-eyes blinking sleepily. "All was well in the world and the wash," he said, and all the children thought his voice was wonderfully soothing and deep, like a big, soft pocket. "But you lot couldn't keep up your end. Charlotte, Emily, you must understand that *we* did not break the contract!" the Valise insisted. "The souls of people have so little carrying capacity! They got so angry at having to pay our wages, cursing and storming about and slamming us viciously. And it hurt, you know. It did hurt. Then, they began to treat us carelessly, tossing us into closets like we were no more than, no more than . . ." The snail-turtle trailed off sorrowfully. "No more than boxes," he finished. "No more than boxes, even though we'd spent weeks traveling together, talking, laughing, sharing meals and confidences, and us there with a hairbrush or a flask of wine or a bedtime story at the moment it was wanted! People dragged us through the mud, overstuffed us intolerably, bought new suitcases rather than caring for us in our old age, but, worst of all, they Lost us. Over and over, because they were drunk or sleepy or in a rush! Would you ever lose your dear aunt or your papa?"

"No!" cried Anne.

"Because you don't Lose family! And when a Valise is Lost, she ends up in the Left Luggage Office, which is a very naughty word among our kind." The luggage-beast shut its eyes in terror. "The LLO is a dreadful place." He shivered, shedding a single rosewater tear. "Ruled by the Handler, eternally cold, full of shadows and dust!"

Crashey, very put out by having had his thunder stolen by a couple of old bags, hollered: "SO! One day a hundrand years ago or summat, all the luggage—Valises!—everywhere went on strike together and that means on the count of three they all shut up tight with their people inside them and no one saw any of those citizenulation ever again, which is bloody horrifying, you know, and set civilizankind back an eon or nine, and this was called the Great Packing THE END."

He gave a little bow. The children clapped uncertainly. It wasn't a very nice story, but it was a story, so they felt they should clap. Probably.

"And that, my little man, is why we are unfailingly polite and kind and sweet to our baggage, and acknowledge their rights as free and intelligent creatures, because otherwise they might eat us, which sums up the whole of international politics," Captain Bravey finished sternly.

"Only *we* never did all that!" cried Charlotte's and Emily's luggage. "We've heard plenty about it, of course. Family gossip travels faster than any parcel. But we weren't born! And anyway, we never grew big enough to carry anyone till just now. Till us two suitcases put latch and hinge together and stopped being *Charlotte's* and *Emily's* and started being ME. One is . . . we are . . . I am . . . quite new to it. Terribly sorry, the pronouns get confused. We grew up in a tannery in Leeds, had our education in a shop in Keighley, and then lived happily with Miss Maria and Miss Elizabeth, and then with Miss Charlotte and Miss Emily. Who never mistreated us even a little." He cleared his boar-bristle throat. "Unlike Anne. But I'm not sore; you didn't mean a thing by it, poor poppet, and we were just sitting about where anyone could squash us. It was Haul O'Ween, is all, the only holiday of the Lug Year. We'd a right to congregate. But, dear Charlotte and kind Emily have hardly ever so much as sat on us to get us to shut or packed knives and such that might cut us. The only wrong you've done is not to know we were alive, and who could blame you? We never spoke up! But however you fold it, it's very pleasant to meet you properly at last." The turtle-snail pursed his leathery beak and bowed his head slightly. He waggled his antennae in distress. "I am so awfully sorry about your sisters. We wept and wept, but no one could hear us. That is the curse of being born an Object outside Glass Town."

Charlotte squeezed Emily's hand. Both of them looked under their lashes at Branwell, so strangely alive and sitting next to them.

The baggage-beast stretched out his neck hopefully. "We would very much like to introduce ourselves. It seems like the thing to do. But I haven't any names. Seeing as how we're foreign."

Emily thought of all the times they put things into their suitcases and took them out again, how the School carriage must have jostled the poor things, how the Headmaster had locked them with all the others in a dark room until it was time to go home for summer. Charlotte knuckled a tear out of her eye, for the baggage, for all that had happened in the last hour or two, for Branwell, for her sister's sleeping in the churchyard in Haworth. She felt suddenly quite tired and quite wretched.

"You look terribly like Westminster Abbey when you're all unpacked," Emily said shyly. "Only I like you a great deal more than Westminster Abbey, and Westminster Abbey can't do half of what you can do. So I shall call you Bestminster Abbey, if you don't mind it."

"We . . . I like it very much!" said Bestminster, and smiled a turtley smile. "I shall put it on the mantel where everyone can see it and praise us."

A long, deep horn sounded somewhere out in the battlefield of Port Ruby. Even inside the safe, thick walls of Bestminster Abbey, they could hear it clearly. The wooden soldiers all snapped to attention. Little leaves fell from the brim of Gravey's helmet.

"That's us, boys!" Captain Bravey said, with a twinge of sadness. "Now that the four of you are safe and sound inside your luggage, ah, *Valise*, I mean to say, we must report to the Duke and see to the washing up and the sweeping and the raising of the dead for tomorrow's fight. Duty is such a bother."

Anne could hardly believe they could say such a thing so easily, as though they were saying they'd have to see to milking the cow or reading the newspaper. But she'd seen it done to Gravey, twice now, and to Branwell once! She held her tongue, but only because she meant to learn to do it herself as soon as possible, and people don't give their toys to brats who beg and plead and moan. She hadn't known she wanted it until just then, but once she did know, it seemed like the only possible thing to want. She would get the little vial of moonlight from Sergeant Crashey, the one he'd given to Gravey and Bran to wake them up again, even if she had to steal it. She would get it and take it home and go to the church-yard and everything would be all right again forever and ever. It would be as easy as milking the cow or reading the newspaper.

"Cap'n," Crashey fretted, kicking at the carpet with his boot, "I don't mean to accusinag or nothing, but . . . well, I think you've forgotten about Brunty in all the hubbub and biscuits and suchlike. He's got to get to the P-House on the toot and the double sweet."

The soldiers groaned and pressed their fists to their foreheads.

Captain Bravey gritted his teeth. "Stuff it all to bits, Crash, but you're right. I only did it because our Brunt is such a nasty little grump, of course. I try to forget things like Brunty so that I can stay happy and on the upbeat."

The Captain reached into his coat and drew out the great book that had, not so very long ago, been a fat man running through the Keighley moors toward a train station. It seemed far too big to fit in his breast-pocket, but Captain Bravey kept pulling and pulling until the book popped free. The Duke's horn sounded again outside Bestminster, this time much louder, more urgent, and somehow, even a little annoyed.

"Nothing for it," said Sergeant Major Rogue, rubbing his wounded eye under the patch. "Brunt-o will have to wait, the stonking old tome." He kicked the book roughly. "We're wanted, and you know how the Duke is when we're late, Captain. I don't wanna bunk with Copenhagen tonight. Not again."

"Copenhagen?" Anne asked sweetly.

"The lion," answered all the men at once, in voices heavy with the knowledge of a lion's snores.

"They're very close," said Bombadier Cracky.

"Just like Boney and his rooster Marengo," Rogue sighed, rolling his eyes. "Great men and their pets, you know."

"Sir!" cried Branwell, snapping his hand to his brow in his best salute. "Private Branwell reporting for duty, sir!" He faltered then. He'd only gotten that far in his head, sure they'd shout him down for giving himself a rank. Anne got one. He didn't see why he shouldn't, having been killed in the line of duty and all. But they didn't shush him, which made Bran think he should have picked a higher one. But before he could show how gallant and brave he really was, Charlotte stepped all over his glory, just like she always did.

"We could deliver Mr. Brunty to his cell, if it would be a help to you," she said graciously. "It's the least we could do after all you've done for us." And perhaps, just perhaps, if they did well, they might get to meet the Duke. Even if he wasn't *the* Duke of Wellington, he was *a* Duke of Wellington, and the idea of shaking his hand shivered Charlotte down to her toes. And if they did really splendidly, *unreasonably* well, it was just possible that they'd rise high enough in the ranks to get a look at that moon-colored stuff that brought people back to life. A look or a swipe.

Rogue and Bravey looked quizzically at them, sizing them up. "Are you quite sure? He's a dangerous animal, our B, liable to bite and scratch and make you listen to his poetry at a moment's notice. And it's dash far to Ochreopolis."

"But we have Bestminster!" squealed Anne joyfully. The moment she'd heard the Valise could turn into a carriage or a balloon or a stallionocerosupine, whatever that was, she'd longed to try it out. "Only . . . will we be able to catch the Royal Express train home from Ocha . . . Ochi . . . ?"

"Ochreopolis," Crashey said helpfully, for he was very sympathetic toward anyone who had difficulties with pronunciation. "Most certaintively. The Main Line connecticates all the cities of Glass Town—at least it did, before Gondal invaded. Now it's only the GT hotspots on the big track. But you won't be going to disputed areas, nohow, so that's all right! Still, to leave a pack of breather children all alone with Brunty . . . Cap'n . . . is that wise or foolish? I can't decide."

"We're not *children*," Emily said indignantly, straightening her ten-year-old back as proudly as any soldier. "We're *us*! And we're clever and strong and *very* good with books." She longed to take the inexplicable mess of the story they were in and iron it all out neat and orderly, so that everything made as much sense as a pressed shirt, and the only way to do that was to keep moving through the thing.

"It's no trouble, sir." Branwell hurried in to reclaim his place at the front of the squad. "They make us quite tough in Yorkshire." It felt like something his father would say.

"Very well, then! We are most indebted to you all!"

Captain Bravey said. They could all see relief settle onto his wooden shoulders. "I shall have our Quartermaster deliver the appropriate maps to your Valise. Deposit Brunty with Mr. Bud at the P-House in Ochreopolis by sundown and he will reward you handsomely. Do not, under any circumstances, open him! He's a *dreadful* read, I promise you. Full of tricky devices."

Anne took a deep breath. Now was her chance. She tried to sound as casual as she could, but her heart stuck in her throat. She was too afraid they would say no to ask. But, out of nothing and nowhere, Emily stole her words out from under her.

"Perhaps," said Em, tucking her hazelnut hair humbly behind her ears, "seeing how it is so far, and we are only four, you ought to let us have a bit of that medicine you used to make our Bran and the Leftenant unshot and unkilled."

"Grog," Sergeant Major Rogue said uncertainly. His brow furrowed. He reached up under his eye patch to rub at the empty wooden socket there. "You mean grog."

"Why'dya have to call it that, Roguey," complained Crashey. "It has got a nice proper Latin name, you know. Scientific as bloody bromide in a bloody beaker."

"Everyone calls it that." Quartermaster Hay-Man

shrugged. "Latin's too many syllables. And the syllables are murder on the mouth!"

"Latin is the boiled jelly left over at the end of supper!" Corporal Cheeky laughed at his own joke before he'd finished it. "Yeah, it still *looks* nice, but that's only because no one wanted any!"

Private Tracky thumped his knee in agreement. "Here, here! Who has time to say *rhodinus secundi vitae*? I don't even know if that's right! It's GROG, man!"

"Grog, then," Emily said peaceably. Charlotte might have only just become the oldest, but Emily had been a middle child for ages, and she knew very well how to mend everyone else's tempers. "I only mean to say that it might be very *nice* and *useful* to have a bit of it in our back pockets. Just in case. Nice things are often useful, and useful things are the nicest to have."

Sergeant Crashey raised his eyebrow at her. He pursed his lips, shrugged, and reached for his belt— then thought better of it. "I . . . think perhapsbe *no*. It's powerful stuff, girl. State secret. Can't just go handing it out like ice crustard. Enemy's everywhere and all that."

Emily accepted her temporary defeat with grace. Anne squeezed her fists till they turned red. There was still plenty of time before the evening train, she told herself. They would have another chance. And with Emily on her side, stealing life in a bottle would be as easy as stealing seedcake for the birds in the garden.

"Oh, of course, sir!" Emily laughed as though it didn't matter at all. "It was nothing really, only a thought. I'm sure we won't need it."

"You're a gang of right toughies!" Leftenant Gravey assured them. "You'll be there and back before you can say 'Old Boney sucks eggs.' You have Bestminster, as you say!"

"We'll do you proud, sir!" Branwell crowed. "You'll be pinning medals on us like darts on a board, I swear!"

Charlotte and Emily set about securing the single-volume Brunty tightly against the sofa. It was easy, really, since the sofa was made out of their Sunday boots. All they had to do was pull the laces out and tie them down again in fast double-knots. Done and dusted. Now they could see Brunty up close, they could read his rather overwrought title, plain as postage, printed on the cover in little blue agate beads:

The Scurrilous Yet Stupendous
(but Primarily Scurrilous)
Chronicle of Brunty the Worst,
Who in Gondal Is Called Brunty the Best

TEN

Ochreopolis by Air

If you had been on holiday in Port Ruby on this particular day, and gone out for an excursion after the morning's excitement, you might have had the unique pleasure of seeing a towering leather stallionocerosupine canter gracefully down the Rubicund Road. His long, thin, splendid horse legs lifted up and clopped down with the perfect, practiced rhythm of dressage, and it had an extremely respectable tail, held at an angle any equestrian judge would admire. But his gigantic, rectangularish body rocked precariously from side to side, as though it might career right off those legs at any moment. The towers that looked so very like Westminster Abbey still tottered on his back like the plates of a stegosaurus. His rhinoceros head was an enormous origami of folded black cloth, brass nameplates, and brown and white leather-and-handkerchief horns. The beast nodded at passersby in such a way that you simply *knew* that, if he had a hat and a hand, he would tip his brim at every Lady and gentleman. And all over, the stallionocerosupine called Bestminster bristled with long defensive silver spikes, the points of overgrown pins and sewing needles glittering in the magenta Port Ruby sun. As he pranced down the Rubicund Road, the traveling Valise threw out muffled giggles and low voices like a normal horse and carriage throws out clods of mud.

Ochreopolis lay some twenty miles from Port Ruby. But the Rubicund Road, which led out of the city and through the fashionable suburbs, ended where the red ended, in a pool of mucky water. Bestminster Abbey pulled up short, leaping back to keep his copper hooves dry. Charlotte, Anne, Emily, and Branwell peered out a porthole in his belly made from an embroidery hoop. They itched in their muddy, grubby, sweaty clothes and longed to change. But, having used nearly everything to make itself, Bestminster had nothing left of Charlotte's and Emily's wardrobe to share. They didn't say a word, so as not to hurt the suitcase's feelings. Instead, they stared out the window at a great, wide swamp with no roads leading through it, only acres and acres of rolling wet black and white fur, dappled and mottled and spotted and streaked like fawns' pelts, dog-skins, cat-fuzz, badger-backs. Leafless, zebra-striped trees and tartan hedges crisscrossed with shades of gray rose up against a splotchy, cloudy sky. It smelled like puppies let in from the rain.

"'Tis the Plaidlands," said the turtley-snail head over the mantle of Bestminster Abbey. "They surround the cities of the world like a great furry sea. If folks aren't careful and tidy with their borders and trim the walls every Sunday, the Plaidlands will creep up and cover a town in moss and fur and wildness as fast as you can say mother nature. Thus, you must cross them to get anywhere at all."

Branwell squinted at the fields of sopping pelts. "It looks dreadful *open*. Nothing to hide behind out there. Which . . . which side are they on? Are we likely to get attacked out there? Not that I'm afraid of another battle, mind you!"

"Gondal and Glass Town both claim the Plaidlands, but they have no castles here and collect no taxes," Bestminster answered thoughtfully. "Just try to collect taxes from the Bluestockings! More likely to collect a thrashing."

Charlotte and Emily turned away from the porthole, startled by the word. "But . . . but we have Bluestockings! They're . . . clever ladies who gather together to . . . do literature instead of needlework," said Charlotte, who admired them terribly.

Bestminster Abbey shook its head. The suitcase scoffed: "Bluestockings are a race of one-legged, indigo silk-imps who rule the Plaidlands with a wild and rollicking hand, answering to no man, chanting their feelings in pentameter, and knitting fine new children whenever and if ever they want them. They average two and a half meters tall. Their capital is Montagu, and the current Queen of the Blues is called Wollstonecraft, aged seventeen and two-fifths. And she is *three* meters tall. Perhaps we shall see some as we make our way through the swamp. The proper collective noun is a *protest* of Bluestockings. Proper language is dreadfully important in these parts, you understand."

"I should say so!" Branwell cried. "All the words here think *very* much of themselves! Back home, a word just sits in a book and behaves. It doesn't *mean* anything like it does here. It doesn't *do* anything."

"We know," moaned Bestminster Abbey. "Wasn't it dreadful?"

"Bestminster," Emily said hesitantly, as she watched

the world race by below them. "You seem to know an awful lot about everything."

"It is a suitcase's job to carry anything a traveler needs to foreign lands," answered the turtle's head. "And no one's very careful with what they say around us. Who would ever think a bag was listening?"

Emily picked at her fingernails. Charlotte squeezed her hand. "It's all right, Em. Bestminster is more like us than them, really. He's a Yorkshireman just as much as we are."

Emily bounded down the staircase and stood on the footstool made from her bloomers so that she could whisper into the turtle's ear. She looked sideways at Brunty to make sure he wasn't spying, but it's very hard to tell if a book is listening to you, for they are very sneaky beasts. She took a quick, deep breath and whispered:

"Do you know why our toys have all come to life? Do you know how we can have come all the way to another world only to find Bluestockings and Brown Besses and a Napoleon and a Wellington our own age, still battling it out like there never was any such thing as Waterloo? Do you know what's happened to us? Do you know what Glass Town *is*? Did we invent it? Or did we just find it? Did we do something to make all this happen?"

The sun sunk unhappily through wispy clouds,

descending into the golden glow of Ochreopolis with a dejected sigh.

"We know a lot," Bestminster whimpered, crestfallen. "But not that."

"Don't cry, Bestminster!" said Anne, who could never bear anyone being sad if she could help it. "Just remember your Bees! Buck up!"

But the others weren't paying any attention, and they didn't run through the Bees for Bestminster. Across the black and white and green and tartan Plaidlands, they could see a dim golden glow: the lights of Ochreopolis, miles and miles away, but as bright as a second sun.

"Oh, but *how* shall we get there?" Anne sighed, disappointed. Once the Bees got started, she felt quite achey in the stomach if they didn't finish. "All that fur looks so sopping wet I'm sure we'll sink right in."

Bestminster coughed indignantly. "Young lady, do you mean to shame us? After all, no matter where you need to go, your luggage always arrives when you do."

It was a peculiar thing to be inside a suitcase while it changed shape. None of the children thought they would ever get used to it, even though they'd already suffered through the transformation from house to stallionocerosupine. The ceiling screeched, squeezed, and groaned with a terrible racket like workmen hammering away on iron scaffolding. The walls and sofas and tables and chairs and paintings and the snailey-turtle head crushed in on them at ghastly angles. Emily screamed, though she didn't want to, for she felt quite positive none of the wooden soldiers nor the regiment of limes nor any Bluestocking would have screamed. For a moment, they all thought of how awful the Great Packing must have been for the poor souls caught inside their cases, and then the racket shut off like an interrupted conversation. Everything in the lounge room and the upper floors stood much the same as they had before, if much more cramped and cozy. But now, halfway up from the floors and halfway down from the ceiling, the safe, thick leather bricks had disappeared, replaced by long, gauzy curtains made of Emily's and Charlotte's petticoats, billowing in the wind, showing slabs of sky through the spaces between them. Anne and Branwell raced to the left-hand petticoat, Emily and Charlotte to the right. They stuck their heads out into the open, twisting round to see what their suitcase had done now.

Bestminster Abbey began, smoothly, gently, almost lazily, to drift into the air. He had become a hot air balloon, and was trying valiantly not to let slip how proud he was of himself.

The balloon was still shaped like a grand old cathedral, all rose windows and gargoyles and spires. But the rich lounge room now hung down as a basket, secured by petticoats, looking out and down as the vast swamps and marshes of the Plaidlands raced by beneath them.

"We're *flying*," shouted Emily. Tears welled up in her eyes, and not only from the whipping wind.

Charlotte's stomach felt like it meant to float up through her chest and out through her mouth. She held her hands to her reddening cheeks. The sound of the wind was so loud and fierce! The cold on her skin felt so bright and sharp! "How many people do you think have flown, ever, in the history of everything?" she marveled. "Mr. de Rozier and Mr. Laurent in Paris, they were the first. . . ."

"Then Mr. Blanchard . . ." Branwell said softly, staring out into the clouds, down to the furry earth. He felt dizzy. "I can't think, I can't think. Where do we fall on the list of first humans to beat the birds at their own game? I'd bet we must be in the top ten! And to think, an hour ago I was stone dead!"

"I'm an owl," whispered Anne, stricken by the word *dead* bouncing around the room like an awful black ball. She hated being up too high. It made her dizzy and sick. And this was higher than anyone had any right to be. She tried to look out the way her brother and sisters did. Intrepid, like them. Brilliant, like them. *Out*, but not *down.* "A little baby owl like Diamond in the tree outside our playroom. And . . . and . . ."

"And I'm Snowflake, our poor raven," Bran said softly. "And . . . and . . ."

"And Em's Rainbow." Charlotte took up their game. All the birds and the tree and the playroom seemed so impossibly far away now. "The sparrow hawk with one leg. And . . . and . . ."

The sun fell on Emily's face, turning her hazel eyes to gold. "And Charlotte's Jasper the pheasant, who sneaks into the kitchen garden every night for bread and beans."

Anne finished the round for them, clutching her cold cheeks in her hands. "And we're all birds together in the clouds and nothing will ever be like this again, even if I live to be a *hundred* and eight."

And then, for a long while, they just flew, and stared, trying not to blink and miss a flock of passing loons or a shaft of cold sunlight, thinking each to themselves that no one would ever believe a word of this in Haworth, and how that didn't really matter to them one bit.

Branwell broke their thrilled silence, as he usually did.

"Can we talk about it *now?* We're finally alone, just the four of us! Can we finally talk about the soldiers? I can practically *feel* it burning me up! I've got blisters on the inside of my mouth from not saying anything! Did you hear them say Gondal on the train? And the Battle of Wehglon? And Acroofcroomb! I thought we were playing all that time, but it couldn't have been *only* pretend, it just *couldn't* have, because here we are! Only it's not *exactly* like we played it, really. It's all jumbled up and upside down, thrown in with a lot of other stuff and nonsense *I* never thought of. But we must have known somehow. Known this place existed. Heard about it . . . someway . . . and then forgot? Or do you think we're secretly magicians and we were casting spells but nobody ever guessed it all this time? But . . . but don't you have to *mean* to do magic? Doesn't it have to be on purpose, with a wand and that? Wouldn't you have to *know* you were doing it?"

"Wouldn't you feel it happening, if you made a whole world?" Emily said softly.

Branwell ended feeling a bit confused, for it didn't seem they could ever forget such a thing. But it was just as impossible that a battle they'd waged in the sitting room on Boxing Day and given a silly name, with teapots for cannons and magazines for barricades and overturned soup bowls and napkins for command tents, could turn into something so real that poor Leftenant Gravey had died there. But on the other hand, they'd never imagined a place called Port Ruby, and all that red glass, or the Iron Duke being really and truly actual iron. Bran *did* know he couldn't leave off sounding wobbly on the subject, so he tried again.

"Did you see the burn on Cheeky's face where I scorched him? It looks jolly good in real life! I did that! That's mine! I wonder what else is mine round here?"

"Grog," said Anne, without looking up.

"I don't *think* so," Bran said, rubbing the spot between his eyebrows. "I don't remember inventing anything *that* good."

Anne rolled her eyes. "I meant that *we* made grog, not *you*. If you think about it, it makes heaps of sense! Didn't we always bring everyone back to life once the game was over? Can't play again tomorrow with a heap of dead toys. So of course everyone here pops right back up! No one dies in a game. Not really. Not forever."

The four of them were very quiet for a moment.

"I think it's time for a Thump Parliament," Emily said. "Because if it worked on Bran, it might . . . it might . . ." She could not finish, the idea of it was so big and so awful and so wonderful and so impossible all at once.

"We need to get some," Anne said. She clenched her fists so hard they went pale. "If we could take it home with us, everything would be as it was! Everyone would be as they were! And Mummy would hold me so tight and I would know her so well and bring her tea and nobody would have to miss her or Maria or Lizzie . . . nobody would have to be sad anymore. . . ." Anne's half-violet eyes filled up with tears.

"It couldn't work, Annie," Charlotte said gently. "It just couldn't. Any more than you could eat a pot of fire back home. If such a thing were possible, cleverer and crueler fellows than us would have dragged it back home to England long ago, like coffee or tomatoes or chocolate."

Anne went pink. "It worked on Bran! It does work on people! On breathers! On us!"

"Just the chance of it . . ." Emily whispered. "It's worth anything. Anything, if the house could be full again. If we could be *six* again." Even going back. Even School. Even a lifetime of nothing but School.

Branwell wiped his palm on his trouser leg. He reached out and stroked Emily's hair, even though he felt rather stupid doing it, and Emily looked at him like he'd thrown a fish in her lap. Papa stroked their hair. Touching people was part of protecting them. He had to learn how. Below Bestminster's balloon, something dark and blue bolted across the spotted streams and islands: a protest of Bluestockings, riding mares made of iron gates and silk banners and turquoise fire.

THE GLASS TOWN GAME

"I feel completely fine," he said finally. "I was dead. I was deader than most people, even, because I was bleeding all over everywhere and not just very still and cold in a bed. You saw it. You screamed, even if you won't tell me how. And I feel completely fine now. It does work, somehow. Maybe, just maybe . . ." Branwell bit the inside of his cheek savagely so he would not cry. He missed his mother so much it sometimes felt as though he were missing his own head. And he missed the way his father had been before Mummy died. He missed everything the way it had been before Mummy died.

"Maybe indeed," a low, thrilling, secretive, seductive voice said.

It was not Bestminster. It was not Branwell. It was not a wild Bluestocking far below.

"Oh, God!" said Charlotte sharply. "Quiet! All of you!"

"All of *us*? You were talking, too!" said Anne.

"Fine. All of us. And *we've* made a fine job of it now!"

"What? Who?" Branwell looked about for the voice, but it had come from nowhere.

"We're not alone!" snapped Emily guiltily. She cursed herself. She should have spoken up sooner.

"*Brunty*," cried Anne, and pointed toward the heavy

book with its long, mysterious title lying propped up on the couch and tied down with hair ribbons and wool yarn. "It says 'scurrilous' right on the cover! That means he's a *sneak*. He's *in* there . . . *waiting*. I don't want a sneak to know our business, do you?"

"But I do know it," the book said smugly. "I know it all, now. Whisper, whisper, who likes the whispering game? Why, I do! I do so *awfully*."

The book of Brunty began to unfold. But it could not quite manage it. Charlotte and Emily had tied it too tight for that. He settled for getting his wide face and his ribbon nose out of the top of the great tome and stared them all down as though they were in his house, and not the other way round.

"Perhaps I might even be of some help, if you mean to start your careers as thieves. I have rather an interest in grog myself. And I do love a good heist."

"But you're wicked!" sneered Anne. "Everyone says so—even you say so, on your own cover! You're going to prison, and only the very worst go to prison."

"You mustn't believe everything you read, my dear. And anyway, it's terrifically freeing to be wicked. There's only one way to be good—the straight and the narrow! But there's a thousand and four ways to be wicked, each longer and wider than the last. And if you want to do something wicked to Glass Town, why then, I am your servant!"

Branwell's eyes sparkled. "What did you do, then? It must have been something top drawer."

Brunty shrugged silkily. "Stole. Spied. Lied. Brawled. The usual bits of fun. Don't tell me you've never heard something you oughtn't, or said something you shouldn't, or pinched someone you needn't, or taken something you wanted while no one was looking." The children blushed like four guilty roses. "Well, little ones, when you do these things at home and get yourself caught, you get sent to bed without supper. But when you get nabbed doing them for your country, they serve you up for supper and go to their beds with full consciences. It's no different to swipe a bit of cheese from your father's table than to swipe a bit of cheese from the enemy's table. Better, actually, since your father never did a thing to harm you, and you took his cheese anyhow. I'm just the same as you. I was you before *you* were you."

"But you're very sorry? And you won't do it again?" asked Anne hopefully.

"Not particularly. And I shall certainly do it again, and worse, and better, and more, and oftener. My story is written—why apologize for the plot? Now, let us return to *our* plot."

"We haven't got any plot with you, sir," sniffed Charlotte.

"Oh, yes you have, young lady. I know your secret, after all. Never whisper in the presence of a master spy, you giggling dolls."

Branwell squared his shoulders. Finally, the truth was loose. The Magazine Man had heard them say they invented the world. That's why he was being so nice all of a sudden. The only people who invent worlds are gods, and you had to be nice to gods. He prepared himself for worship. "And what's our secret, then?"

Brunty unfolded one newspaper-leg out from the bottom of his book body and stretched it luxuriously. They heard a knee pop. "You're mad. Every one of you. Mad as mutton. Mad as mittens. Mad as a mink in a straightjacket."

"We are NOT," hissed Emily. She could feel the blood beating in her fists.

"I don't mind mad! Not in the least! What would the world be without the mad? Tedious and tawdry and plodding without a cliffhanger or a twist to its name. Oh, Glass Town is full of prejudice and snobbery, but in Gondal, we do not make a fuss about whether one's head is on straight, or whether one has a head at all. But even we would call children who think the whole universe is made up of their toys and dreams and games quite barmy. Let me go and I will be your dog, your sweet little Gondalier hound, bringing you grog in a barrel round his neck for the price of a pat and a treat."

"W . . . what treat?" Anne said softly.

"Anne!" cried a shocked Charlotte. "We do *not* make bargains with villains!"

"But he's *our* villain! He can't be all bad if we made him! We made *wonderful* creatures."

"I don't remember making a Brunty at all! Unless he's one of Bran's," mused Emily.

Charlotte kept mum. She had dreamed once of a man made of books. She had thought then how lovely it would be to know a person who could be read like a story, known and loved like a perfect ending. She had not thought how books can hide their meaning, withhold their secrets, lie better and longer than any human person. Brunty was not Bran's. He was hers. And he was a beast.

Branwell smiled tightly. He made a smart little bow. "We shall never do anything that makes Napoleon's man happy," he announced loyally.

"Oh, Bran!" exclaimed Emily. And she looked at him with such admiration and surprise that Branwell felt quite out of breath with it. *Yes, that,* that! His heart crowed.

That's respect, that is. He wanted to gobble it up like hot cake. He cleared his throat and deepened his voice a bit. "It's all well and good to *play* Welly and Boney, Em, but we are still Englishmen, in the end."

"Are you now?" crooned Brunty. "Pray tell, what matters that in Glass Town? Come on, boy, we'll make you a Prince in Gondal. You and I want the same thing, after all. Just a bit of grog to keep our bellies warm."

Bran and his sisters shook their heads.

"It's . . . it's no good if we have to be villains to get it. We'd never be able to look our mother in the eye," whispered Anne.

"Fine," sneered Brunty. His face changed in an instant, from friendly and coaxing and open to furious and cruel and hard. "Then I needn't bother keeping up the niceties. I've had to listen to you swooning and sighing for hours! I thought it would be the death of me. Oh, isn't Glass Town *grand*! Oh, isn't the Duke *handsome*! Look at all the pretty red houses! Aren't they precious? NO! Glass Town is hell, those pretty houses shelter demons, the Duke is the devil himself, and if, somehow, beyond all reason, you really brought all them to life, then you are the cause of all my misfortunes and I hate you like brimstone. Once I am free, I shall have you all chucked, pulped, and remaindered for the glory of Gondal and Bonaparte. Or perhaps I'll just feed you to Marengo. I do so *hate* loose plotlines. And a gaggle of violent little madmen in shabby clothes and shabbier accents has no place in any respectable tale. I shall enjoy seeing you—"

Suddenly, Charlotte had a notion, and as soon as she had it, she'd done it, and as soon as she'd done it, her mind caught up with her heart and she told herself it was too ridiculous to ever work, so sit down Charlotte, for God's sake. But done it was. Charlotte dashed over to the sofa where Brunty sat bound and tied, bent over, and screamed in his pale face full of pages:

"THE END!"

Brunty promptly sucked his head back down between his covers and snapped shut. His brass lock clicked firmly.

"That was wonderful!" Anne squealed.

"That's dash useful." Emily grinned.

"What'd you have to go and do that for?" Branwell protested. "He was going to say something really dreadful and now I've missed it."

"We can't go listening to villains when they want to make their grand speeches and devil's bargains," Charlotte said, as though she'd always known it would work, never doubted it for a moment. "Best to end the story before they get their side in. Now, no more Thump

Parliaments in the presence of strange books. We'll . . . we'll find our moment. We'll find a way. Our way. After all, we invented Glass Town. The least they could do would be to spare us a cup of—"

Charlotte did not get a chance to finish, for just then, they landed with a jolt, a tumble, and a vicious thump on the brilliant, bright earth of a new city.

ELEVEN

The Problem of Primarily Scurrilous Brunty

Ochreopolis sprawled and towered and twisted in as many shades of yellow as Port Ruby had done in red. But this city had got rather bored of glass halfway through the building of it and decided to haul in a lot of other stuff to fancy up the place. From up above, it looked like pictures of Oxford that they'd pored over in Father's books, if Oxford had run off with Vienna and got itself in trouble. Golden glass bridges arched over a branching river of bubbling champagne. Lemon and banana and golden apple and quince trees shaded slender alleys that wound through patches of saffron shadows and bright sunshine. The people walking here and there wore yellow rain slickers and ivory wigs. Burly amber glass walls closed it all in like York or Chester. Three butter-colored crystal gates let folk out and in.

But of course, balloons need no gates.

The towers beyond the walls were not straight and tall and proud like Port Ruby's. They sagged tiredly, and leaned woozily, and bowed like old, old trees until their pointed roofs almost touched the ground. The buildings of Ochreopolis were only partly mortared out of good, strong yellow glass. Mostly, they were much softer stuff: great swathes of yellowed and yellowing paper, ripped from novels that must have been published in the land of giants, for any one page stood as high as a shire horse. Those same giants had folded and creased and wrapped their pages around slabs of glass to make spindly ochre belfries and squat chartreuse shops and dog-eared daffodil chapels with round topaz windows.

Bestminster Abbey set them down in the middle of a cobble-glass square the color of honey. Two lion statues, both presumably of Copenhagen, glared down as they wheeled round and round, trying to look in every direction at once. The city was far too beautiful to have one single wicked soul living in it. But the balloon assured them that this was the right place, the P-District, where all the criminals and villains and misbehavers of Glass Town ended up sooner or later. Bestminster then promptly folded his giant balloon-body back into two ordinary suitcases, and so fast Charlotte actually felt her head spin.

They could not see anything like a prison, no matter which direction they looked. One fat tower, bent over almost in the shape of a lowercase *n*, had a sign out front that read: NORTH & NOUGHT EDITING SERVICES. The round stained glass (and stained page) building next to it, shaped rather like a pineapple, advertised itself as HUME & HALFORD PRESS. Another tower, whose top leaned one way, while its middle leaned the other, to make a sort of sloppy lightning bolt, had a handsome blond-wood post that announced the owners as COOPER & LOCKHART PURVEYORS OF FINE BINDINGS. The biggest of them all was a clutch of shorter towers all bursting out of the ground in the same spot like sticks of dynamite crammed into a golden pail. The towers twisted and bulged and doddered and slumped in every which direction. The writing on their page-and-glass walls all ran together, creasing sharply or tearing gently. Someone had circled several of the larger letters in dark tawny ink so that, from the left-most tower to the right, they could read: BUD & TREE PUBLISHING HOUSE.

"Look!" cried Emily, laughing and pointing. "It's *Romeo and Juliet!*"

"The people?" asked Branwell, who at this point was quite willing to believe anything from any story could get up in Glass Town and walk about and swoon from a balcony.

"No, the *play!*" said Charlotte. She pointed just where Emily had: at the folded, mortared pages that wound round and round the glass buildings of Ochreopolis. The circled R in BUD & TREE and the O in PUBLISHING HOUSE were the first letters on the title page of some enormous edition of *Romeo and Juliet.* The scenes and speeches chased each other up the height of the tower, stopping at odd angles where the paper jackknifed and split to make corners, and starting up again beneath banks of windows. Suddenly, without meaning to, the children found themselves running toward Bud & Tree Publishing House. It felt so good to run after all that crouching and hiding and flying and dying. They called out all the titles they could find in the brickwork as they ran:

"*A Midsummer Night's Dream!*" Anne giggled.

"*Much Ado About Nothing!*" Branwell whooped.

"*Hamlet!*" said Emily as she spotted the telltale H in HOUSE. "And that's . . . well, that bit's a cookbook, I think!"

"But it's all wrong." Charlotte frowned, standing at the base of the tower built out of *Romeo and Juliet.* She clutched Brunty tightly in her arms. "That's not how it goes. Look closer!"

And on the winding half-glass walls they read in letters two feet high:

Two households, both alike in dignity

In fair Angria where we lay our scene . . .

Charlotte bit her lip. "It ought to be Verona! 'In fair Verona where we lay our scene'!"

Branwell pointed at the pages bent back to make a pretty curtained window. "There, too, see? That should be Capulet and Montague!"

But the famous family names were nowhere to be found. Instead, Shakespeare's speech now read:

Three civil brawls, bred of an airy word-o,

By thee, old Elrington and proud Douro . . .

"Now, that makes no sense at all!" Emily grumbled. She loved her Shakespeare and did not enjoy seeing it mangled in the least. They'd done *Romeo and Juliet* Easter last for Papa and Aunt Elizabeth and Tabitha in the front parlor. Charlotte had made such a marvelous, cruel Romeo, and Emily thought she'd died as Juliet rather well. Near the pointed crystal cap of the tower, the last lines of the play flowed in golden ink:

For never was a story of more woe

Than this of Bertha and the Marquis of Douro.

"Why's it even called *Romeo and Juliet* if it's about somebody named Bertha?" Emily grumbled.

But the Marquis of Douro . . . she did know that name. It was the name they'd given to the dashing and dastardly villain of their games. It sounded dreadfully exciting, with all those vowels. But she would not say so, not in front of Brunty. "What an ugly name anyhow! Anyone called Bertha's got no place in a romance!"

"P'raps Juliet was only ever her middle name." Bran-well shrugged, unconcerned, when it came right down to it, about the fates of Capulets in Glass Town. He'd never much cared for *Romeo and Juliet*, really. He preferred *Henry V* or *Richard III*, the plays where people fought fabulous battles and died all bloody and afraid and yelling about horses.

"This one says *The Glass Town English Dictionary, Fourth Edition*," mused Anne, peering at the next tower over. "It's the *Oxford English Dictionary*, everyone knows that. How can there be a Wellington here if there's no Oxford?" She squinted in the sun. "*Parson: any one of the million male offspring of Parr, the Salmon King, who ruled the Kingdom of Roe Head with a silver fin during the Sea Age.* But that's not even a little bit what it means! *Papa's* a parson! That means he leads Sunday services at the chapel and . . . and . . . you know, Tabitha always says he's the man to see for the marrying and the burying. It's nothing to do with whose son he is. And he's obviously not a *fish*!"

A voice came whipping toward them, quite cross and quite yellowed. How a voice could have gotten yellowed, none of them could have exactly explained, but it was, and so it could be.

"Oy! You! For Gutenberg's sake! NO LOITERING! I've had enough of you inkin' gangs of youths and hoodlums footnoting about on my property! If you've got no business here, kindly erase yourselves immediately!"

A rather short, strange man came running out of Bud & Tree Publishing House. His body was made up all of book bindings, the fancy, old-fashioned kind you found on very ancient or very precious books, the kind that had lovely, mysterious names like Coptic and Bradel and Girdle and Sammelband. Leather, silk, and flaxen bindings crisscrossed, looped, knotted, and stitched themselves into the shape of a long-nosed, high-cheeked fellow in a suit with long tails and buckled shoes. That dashing suit coat was fastened with row after row after row of brass book-clasps. His long leather hair was lashed back handsomely with a Coptic knot and he wore a long, fierce page-cutter with a bone hilt at his hip like a saber.

"But we *do* have business!" protested Branwell. "Only

we're meant to do it at a prison, and all you've got here are publishers!"

"But we're just lost, not loitering, thank you very much," said Anne huffily, for she only liked to be accused of things she'd actually done.

The binding man narrowed his eyes at them. "What business is that, then?"

"Brunty!" Charlotte and Emily said together, and Charlotte gave the book in her arms a not-too-gentle thump.

"We're to hand him over to Mr. Bud at the P-House," Branwell explained, trying to sound as local and as gruff as he could. "So mind your own business, sir!"

"Well, I *am* Mr. Bud, all right, and this is my house, and it *is* where we keep the baddies. You know, the typos and the misprints, the damaged copies and the rough drafts and the *rude little boys like you*, Mr. Mouth!"

Branwell opened that very mouth and shut it again.

"Don't mind him, Mr. Bud," Charlotte sighed. "He's not a baddy, he just acts like one for fun sometimes. Is this the prison, then? Are you the warden? Mr. Brunty is rather heavy, and rather unpleasant. We'd be glad to be rid of him."

Mr. Bud straightened his ropy sheep-hide shoulders. "It is a *publishing house*, madam, and I am an *editor*. But for wicked, dirty, nasty books like your Brunt-Brunt there, it's much the same difference. All right, ink it all to hell! Bring him in and we'll get him sorted on the double sharp and the triple quick."

Charlotte shifted Brunty's unabridged bulk into Emily's arms so that she could carry both suitcases. Being the oldest sometimes meant being everyone's boss, but mostly, it meant being everyone's pack mule. Branwell and Anne ran on ahead, still calling out half-familiar bits of the mismatched writing on the walls. They all followed Mr. Bud into the many towers of Bud & Tree Publishing House, where they found a very pleasant lobby with a large brass desk on one end, a tall golden hat-rack on the other. Between the two spread a wide, elegant floor tiled with pages from *The Canterbury Tales*, only this *Canterbury Tales* seemed not to have been satisfied with *The Knight's Tale* and *The Miller's Tale*. It also had a story called *The Governess's Tale*, and another called *The Bluestocking's Tale*, and still another called *The Case of the Missing Princess*, which all four of them knew wasn't even the right sort of thing to be in *The Canterbury Tales* in the first place. The walls were lined with massive, ancient printing presses like doors, their wood so old and strong it had almost turned to stone. But they could only see the backs of the great machines—the rest of their hulking bodies disappeared into thick, frosted, amber glass.

A stout man stood behind the desk, watching them with a raised eyebrow. His body, like everyone's in Glass Town, it seemed, contained not one bit of flesh or skin. He looked like someone had stacked up all their spare bookends until they were as tall as a man and then given it two bronze magnifying glasses for spectacles. The handles of those detective's glasses stuck out from the sides of his head at wild angles. Carved wooden hawks, fairies, griffins, trees, even miniature stacks of ceramic books made up his whole self: big ones for his ribs and his neck and his arms, thin, delicate ones for his fingers. His face was a huge, proud, jowly silver bust of a man with leafy hair and a mossy cravat etched into the metal. What held it all together? Charlotte wondered. The bookends, Napoleon's bones and rifle-arms, his rooster's pottery, the frogs' armor, Mr. Bud's leather string? What was inside? The idea made her skin prickle.

"Ready the presses, Mr. Tree!" cried Mr. Bud with gusto, unclasping his coat and hanging it up on the rack. "We've got a *right* rough drafter here! Just *riddled* with errors! I don't know how he gets up in the morning!"

"Is that who I think it is?" said Mr. Tree, peering over his glasses at the still-closed volume of Brunty. He did not seem like the sort of fellow who worried much over anything, no matter how alarming that anything might be to everyone else.

"Dunno," answered Mr. Bud. "Do you think it's Brunty the Inking *Liar*? Brunty of Godforsaken Gondalier, Can't-Take-Him-Anywhere Brunty, Brunty the Spying Sack of Slime? Brunty the Miserable Fat Folio?"

Even Charlotte was taken aback by such mean names for their prisoner. He hadn't seemed *that* altogether horrible. Well, until he got to the part about feeding them to the rooster.

"I do," answered the bookend-man. "I do indeed."

Mr. Bud laughed and whacked the front desk with his leather-bound fist. "Then a happy inking birthday to you, Mr. Tree!"

"Well, this is *very* exciting," said Mr. Tree in the same calm, friendly voice. "A banner day for Bud and Tree! *Four* real live breathers as sure as I'm standing, a glorious victory for Glass Town, and here's us wasting paper chatting with each other! Miss . . . ?" He indicated the book's guardian with his silver eyebrows.

She tried to curtsy, but Brunty was incredibly heavy. It came off much more like a stumble. She wondered how long Charlotte's clever trick would last. Or perhaps Brunty only wanted them to *think* they had gotten the goods on him and was only waiting like a horrid old snake in the hedges. She squeezed the Magazine Man tighter. She was beginning to lose feeling in her arms. "I'm Emily. And this is Charlotte, Anne, and Branwell."

"I say, what exotic names! Next you'll be telling me your mother's called Leopard and your father's Toffee Pie! Miss Emily, if you'll follow me to Press Number seventeen—seventeen is free, isn't it, Mr. Bud? Excellent. Don't let go of Master Brunty there, now, not until I say. Manuscript transmission is terribly easy to stuff up, you know. Here we are."

The lot of them hurried along behind Mr. Tree, who took frightfully long steps for a man with such strange legs. He stopped at one of the dozens of backward-facing printing presses that lined the lobby walls. It was made of dark, stained wood gone ashen with age, shaped like an enormous heavy door frame with ponderous wooden screws and plates and blocks inside it instead of a room. The number seventeen glittered on the right plank of the frame in gilded letters. Mr. Bud and Mr. Tree took up positions on either side of the press. On the count of three, they each pulled a lever that wound a screw thicker than Anne's whole body. The screw ground around and around until the gigantic machine groaned, rattled, creaked, and finally pulled out away from the wall. It just kept coming and coming, further and further, until it finally lodged against the glass wall like a desk drawer and stuck there. They could see all the mechanisms of the press now: the frame for holding pages, the copper plates, the boxes full of letter blocks, the ink jugs, the levers and chains and straight edges for keeping lines of print tidy. All the children were thrilled to stand so close to the impossibly marvelous machine that made books, that could make book after book, as many as you wanted, as many as you could think of! But each of them thought to themselves that, honestly, it looked rather sinister when you got close up to the thing. All those racks and screws. But they didn't say a word of it. Mr. Bud and Mr. Tree were obviously very proud.

Mr. Bud whipped out a golden ruler and began to measure Brunty, still clutched deathly tight in Emily's arms. He talked cheerfully while he worked.

"You see, my little felt bookmarks, Glass Town is a fabulously *fair* sort of place. We put our justice on one law at a time like anybody. Why, when a fellow goes bad, you can't just throw him in the nearest dungeon and call it a day! Heavens, no! Barbaric! You gotta consider his backstory, his conflict, his motivations, his genre, his foreshadowing! Maybe he just got a bad draft. Not his fault. Maybe he fell into a plot hole, poor chap. Saddled with lazy clichés or an unlucky twist ending—could be any one of us, really. You can't blame a book for its story. It's only done what it was written to do. If the thing's set in a cold and loveless house and it grows up to be cold and loveless, that's just plot! If the poor scrapper began in a war-torn city with thirteen brothers and no bread or warm kindness for itself, you can't expect it to end the way it would if it started out in a fine manor house in peacetime with songs round the piano every night! That's just *genre*, and it's a rare bird who can escape their genre. Everyone has to get from the Page One to The End one way or another. That's just life!"

"But not everyone's a book like Brunty is," Branwell frowned. It sounded like no way to run a criminal justice system.

Mr. Bud and Mr. Tree frowned right back.

"'*Course* they are," said Mr. Tree.

"Can't say I like your tone," said Mr. Bud. "It's a bit offensive."

"How else do you explain people?" Mr. Tree exclaimed, stroking his silver etched muttonchops. "The way they are born into a variety of interesting situations and grow up and set out to make their fortune and fall in love and get married and lose everything and discover secrets and fall ill and get tangled up in plots that go nowhere and have long boring stretches where nothing much happens and children and motifs and colorful imagery, the way they start at the beginning and the way they stop at the end? Sounds *just* like a book to me. Sounds like every book I've ever read! How is anyone *not* a book like Brunty is? Just because old Brunter looks like one and you don't? Very prejudiced thinking, young sir. If you continue that sort of thing in my presence, I shall have to ask you to leave."

Branwell didn't think this made much sense, but he didn't want to leave. He thought something dreadful might happen to the godforsaken Gondalier, and he wouldn't want to miss it. No one talked this much before doing his job if it wasn't going to be a little dreadful.

"But!" Mr. Bud shook his knotty head to clear his mood and pressed on. "*We* have no prejudices against the slings and arrows of outrageous plot! Bad writing happens, what can you do? I'll tell you what you can do! You can correct your paper, young man! You can revise it. You can edit it *until* it's good. You can take up the very reddest of pens and mark up the whole mess. Deduct points for improper spelling, faulty logic, profanities, dangling punctuation! And that's just what we're going to do today. We're going to correct Brunty! Rewrite his rough and ugly bits, cut out his quick temper and his violent tendencies, cross out his crimes, tighten up his themes, reorder his scenes, start him over nice and fresh and proper. When we're done with him, he'll be as harmless as a nursery rhyme."

The four children exchanged fretful glances.

"But . . ." Anne whispered, nearly faint with the fear of contradicting constables, which was what they were, even if they didn't say so.

"Yes?" said Mr. Tree sharply. "Some problem?"

"Well, it's rather awful, isn't it?" Anne breathed. "It's rather the awfullest thing I can think of!"

"No, it isn't," Mr. Bud snorted. "You're only saying that because you don't know what old Brunty did."

"We do so!" Branwell snapped.

Mr. Bud crossed his arms over his chest. "Well?"

"He stole something or another and told a few lies and got in fights and spied on people but *everyone* does all that when there's a war on! I don't see why Brunty should be treated specially rough."

"Sweet lad," sighed Mr. Tree. "Sweet and innocent and dumb as a Christmas card. You haven't the first idea. Bruntus there would eat you whole if he could, and not even list it among his crimes. Is it awful when your teachers fix up a composition you've written? Is it awful when your governess tells you to change one word for another in your dear clumsy little poem about love or souls or the moors or what have you, even if it's a better word? Even if it's the word you should have used all along? Or do you learn something from all that red?"

Charlotte stood up for her sister, which meant standing up for Brunty. "Yes, it *is* awful. You're going to go in with that red pen and make him not Brunty anymore. You're killing him, really."

"Nonsensical! Don't be so dramatic. He'll still be alive! How can it be killing if he's still alive? He'll still be wretched old Brunter." Mr. Tree waved his wooden hand in the air. "Just corrected. Edited. *Fixed.* He'll be a better Brunty! A critically acclaimed Brunty! A Brunty for the whole family! Approved for all ages Brunty! Perhaps we'll give him a new name, so as not to muddle his marketing. Something gentle and pretty. Heathcliff, perhaps. Or Edward. Or Leopard, after your mother."

"Mum's not called Leopard," mumbled Anne. How splendid it would be if she had been, though! The whole world was all over Marias and Elizabeths, but *Leopard* was someone special. Anne imagined her mother lying on the sofa in the parlor, curling and uncurling a long, spotted tail beneath her petticoats.

Emily twisted her fingers together till her knuckles turned red. "But he *needs* all those rough and ugly bits.

He'd be lost without them. He wouldn't even know who he was. If you . . . if you rewrote *us* so that nothing bad ever happened, so that Papa was always smiling and we never had to go to School and it was never cold in Haworth and there never was a war and . . . and mother and our sisters never . . . never died . . . if you took all that away just because it makes us prickly and untidy and depressing and unwieldy characters . . . well, then Emily and Charlotte and Anne and Branwell wouldn't exist anymore. Some other people would, people we wouldn't even want to have tea with, whose shoes were always new and who never learned how to cry. We, *us*, would be gone. I know Brunty isn't the *very* best person, but you can't, you just can't. He'll never be good if he can't choose to be nasty. It's the choice that makes the good."

"Aw, well said, Em," Branwell said, and gave her a pinch, but not a painful one. He could admit that the girls turned out a nice phrase now and again. He was gallant, after all. He *chose* to be gallant.

"And what do *you* do to criminals in Breathertown?" Mr. Bud sniffed. He was rather upset at seeing his job so disrespected, but he tried to hide it.

"Hang them," Branwell said immediately.

"We do give them a trial first!" Charlotte protested.

"It's all on the up and up! Everyone wears a wig and everything."

"Or we lock them up till they're sorry," Anne added quickly.

"Or we send them to Australia." Emily chewed the inside of her cheek thoughtfully. She readjusted her grip on Brunty. He was so *intolerably* heavy.

Mr. Bud and Mr. Tree reeled backward in horror.

"How dare you call us awful when you *kill* your baddies?" Mr. Bud huffed.

Mr. Tree fanned himself to keep from fainting. "I'd wager this 'Australia' is just your fancy name for burying a criminal up to his neck in sand and waiting for him to die of his own accord, and/or vicious biting fire ants!"

"It isn't!" Charlotte insisted. "It's a place on the other side of everything! It has kangaroos and a kind of an otter-thing with a duck's face." Between the kangaroos and the wigs, Charlotte began to feel that she was not helping their world to sound particularly upstanding or superior or even sensical.

"Correcting is *worse* than killing," whispered Branwell, half-terrified and half-impressed. "A fellow still lived, even if he died badly. An edited man never *was*." If he'd stopped there, it would have sounded a very regal and moral statement. But he couldn't stop himself. Words poured out. "I'm sure Papa and Aunt Elizabeth have wanted to edit me plenty of times since I was born. I'm sure everybody would rather I be much better than I am. Older and stronger and nicer and cheerfuller and hand-somer and cleverer and abler, oh, ever so much abler!"

"Branwell, no . . ." Charlotte said softly. She put a hand on his arm but he shoved her off.

"Branwell, yes! You know it's true. You'd all rather a new and improved edition of a brother! You were probably hoping for it when I woke up on that table in Bestminster, but I'm still me. I can never get away from being me and neither can you! Don't try to be sweet. Papa would roll up his sleeves and get right into me if he could. He'd cross out all the painterly bits and paste in parsony bits instead. He'd make me obedient and ambi-tious and fix it so I never cried or screamed or kicked walls ever again." He was blubbering now and he knew it, but he couldn't stop. It's very hard to squash your feel-ings down deep inside when you only came back to life at lunchtime. Resurrection brings the truth out in a person. "But he can't fix me, he *can't*, and Charlotte can't make me brilliant and Emily can't make me friendly and Anne can't make me patient because I'm just *Branwell*, only Branwell, and if you subtract Branwell from Branwell you're left with *nothing*."

"Hold fast, there, lad, no one is suggesting you get your pages clipped," said Mr. Tree. Displays of emotion gave him rashes. He scratched his palm.

"How many people have you corrected?" Branwell seethed.

"More than a few," Mr. Bud shrugged.

"Less than a lot," Mr. Tree demurred. "Really, if the idea gets you so worked up, I daresay you've never seen a hanging."

Mr. Bud grabbed the book of Brunty out of Emily's arms. She struggled a bit, but the editor was frightfully strong. "You've no right to look down your inkin' noses at our ways," he sneered. "Nobody asked for your opinion. Do you argue with judges and suchlike where you come from?"

"No," all four of them mumbled. A tear dripped onto Branwell's shoe.

"Then what makes you think you can tell us off? How bloody like a breather, barging in and blathering on! I suppose you'd rather just let the unedited, unabridged, *unexpurgated* Brunty run wild? Or maybe you'd like to just *kill* him. That seems nicer, doesn't it?"

"Well, what *has* he done, specifically?" Branwell protested, his face red with shame. "Maybe just Australia . . ."

Mr. Bud and Mr. Tree grimaced at them, shaking

their heads. Ignoring the children's protests, they hoisted Brunty up onto the frame of the printing press. They slotted him right into the spot where fresh new pages were meant to lie and wait to be inked. They bent down to unlatch one cover from the other. Of course, Brunty didn't want to be opened just now. They pulled and pried, but the brass latches wouldn't come free. Finally, Mr. Bud pulled his page-cutter from his waist. He stepped back, took a mighty swing meant to slice through the locks with one fierce stroke.

"Wait!" pleaded Emily. It was too gruesome, to watch somebody get hacked open, even if that someone was mostly a book. That only made it worse, somehow. Emily would rather have hacked off her own arm than maim any of their books back home.

"What for?" said Mr. Bud, his page-cutter still held high.

Emily thought quickly. She was better at quick thinking than perfect thinking, if she was honest, but perfect thinking only got you good marks in School and good marks in School got you nothing but cold paper in the end. She took a deep breath and said, quite grandly:

"The Scurrilous Yet Stupendous (but Primarily Scurrilous) Chronicle of Brunty the Worst, Who in Gondal Is Called Brunty the Best. CHAPTER ONE!"

Brunty's ornate cover sprang open. As quickly as they'd seen him fold up into a book on the Keighley train platform, he unfolded his pages into arms and legs and a great round belly and a neck and a huge head. He was the Magazine Man again, with his newspaper collar and newsprint waistcoat and glossy illustrated great coat and his red ribbon nose. He twisted and bucked in Mr. Bud's and Mr. Tree's grip, hollering and groaning. But though they could hold on to his arms, the editors could not wrestle all of Primarily Scurrilous Brunty at once. He heaved up his long, fat paper legs and kicked them both soundly in the head. Mr. Bud and Mr. Tree let go instantly, streaming ink from their brows, cursing and shouting.

Brunty breathed heavily, staring at the children. His black eyes glittered with malice behind his spectacles.

"What did I do, you little brats? *I won the war for Gondal.* They just don't know it yet!"

"We don't care about your silly war," Anne said, turning up her chin.

Brunty turned the great book of his head to one side. "Now, that is what society folks call a *lie*, Miss Gum-flapper. I think you care quite a lot." He turned his glare to Emily. His voice turned high and mocking. "Ask them who invented grog, Mr. Bud. Ask them who invented the

Iron Duke. Ask them about their toys. And then once you've returned from the asylum with the keys to their cell safely in hand, you can see to me. Go on, I'll wait."

Brunty's inky eyes gleamed. He wiggled his ribbon nose. Then he drew something out of his newsprint waistcoat. It was just the most curious object Emily had ever seen. It looked as though someone had poked out all the glass in a fancy copper hourglass, dumped out the sand, filled it up again with a great stack of milk saucers wrapped in linen, and hung two clock pendulums off it on copper ribbons. The whole business oozed with greenish acid and crackled with tiny, bluish white arcs of lightning. Wet, sickly gunk bubbled out between the saucers, oozed down the ribbons, and crusted up the metal rods holding it all together like salt brine on a ship's hull. It smelled vile, like rotting pennies. Brunty the Liar, Brunty the Godforsaken Gondalier, Primarily Scurrilous Brunty gave his contraption a good shake. The thing sprayed glittering, boiling, green-gray acid in a neat circle on the floor before him, that lovely floor so carefully painted with the words of *The Canterbury Tales*. Charlotte and Emily jumped and scrambled backward into the nearest printing press, barely missing having their toes sizzled off by the spreading muck.

Branwell and Anne were left on their own, on the

other side of the puddle of poison, with a furious book-man brandishing his alien weapon.

"Change *my* tune, will you? Take my youth in the slums of Spleenpool, on the shores of Lake Elderna? Will you take my sisters, too? Stanza and Strophie huddling under the eaves in gloves with no fingers and only their brother to protect them?" Bran's heart lurched toward the savage spy. "Is that too dark and cruel a first chapter to make a good man in the end? You want to look inside me and erase my pain, cross out our father casting us away in favor of our stepmother's handsomer, merrier, uglier, and stupider children? And then I suppose you'll cut my education with the Spyglaziers' Guild? What about my doomed love affair with Indica, my beautiful Thesaurus, back in snowy Almadore where I dueled my usurping brother to the death with an icicle? You want to take her memory, her ghost? Will you redact everything, *everything* Brunty and replace it with your neat and tidy Glass Town daisy-man idea of goodness? You won't! I AM FOREVER BRUNTY AND YOU CAN'T STOP ME."

With a gurgling groan, the golden floor sagged, and rippled, and crumbled in wherever Brunty's slime touched it. A sudden, yawning hole opened up at their feet, its edges hissing and smoking and crackling with that blu-ish lightning, and nothing inside but darkness. Brunty whooped joyfully and lunged like a terrible lion. He seized Anne's arm in one newspaper-hand and Branwell's neck in the other, the crook of the arm still hanging on to that monstrous acid-fountain. Everyone began screaming at once. Mr. Bud and Mr. Tree bellowed in rage and made ready to jump the gap. Emily and Charlotte started inching round the seething edge, cursing and hollering and calling their brother and sister's names.

Brunty's burning glare bored into Branwell and Anne. His grip on their bones crushed down, as unstoppable as stone. He smelled like new books, and the perfect capital O's of his eyes narrowed until they were shaped like bitter, bitter almonds.

"Are you mad?" he snarled. He stared like he could blow open their skulls if he only looked hard and hateful enough. "Are you? Can four together catch the same madness?"

"Are you?" snapped Bran defiantly. "Go set yourself on fire."

"No," whispered Anne, who could not convince her chest to breathe.

The hulking book nodded, the way a man nods when he is looking over a job nearly done. He squeezed Bran and Anne to his massive chest and bellowed: "You filth of Glass Town! You deserve this! You deserve every single thing that is about to happen! You have killed yourselves!"

"Now, that's just uncalled for," Mr. Tree sputtered, deeply hurt.

Emily was so close. She was almost there. She could almost touch Anne's sleeve.

But Brunty just grinned. He grinned, and laughed, and howled, and with Branwell, Anne, and his dread machine firmly in hand, hopped straight down into the poisonous pit he'd made and vanished. Inside half a second, the acid had writhed and wriggled and seared itself back together, leaving nothing but a long, ugly, green scar down the middle of *The Governess's Tale*.

Charlotte and Emily stood horribly still, stunned silent and quite alone, apart from two very furious-looking editors, in the lobby of Bud & Tree Publishing House.

PART III

I Am No Bird

TWELVE

Gone, Gone, Gone

ot us! Not our fault!" cried Mr. Bud, holding out
his leather arms in the air. "Don't you go blaming
us—I can see you want to! Stop that right now, right this
instant. Stop *looking* like that! It's distressing Mr. Tree,
can't you see?"

Emily had gone white as paper. She pressed her hands
over her mouth, digging her fingernails into her jaw, trying to shove a scream back inside. But it was no good.
The scream wanted out. Tears tumbled down her cheeks,
soaking her knuckles, dripping off her wrists. She could
feel the weight of the lemon in her dress-pocket, suddenly as heavy as her heart. Their ticket home. *They're*

gone. Gone, gone, gone. Two more of us gone. And no grog can help 'gone.' How could they ever go home again without Branwell and Anne? What would they tell Papa?

"We're only editors!" Mr. Tree shouted, far too loudly. The pair of them stood pressed together, trembling, like two flamingos who have sighted an alligator. "We don't make things happen; we just clean up the mess when it's done! *You* brought that book in here. We're innocent! And if you'll follow me, I've got some papers for you to sign saying just that. And a few other unimportant little clauses. Be a good girl and we'll have no trouble here."

Charlotte stared at the mangled, ropy, yellow scar on the floor where her brother and sister had been standing only a moment ago. It looked like a century's worth of candle wax. She knew she *ought* to cry. She *wanted* to cry. If there was ever a time to cry, now was surely it. But when she reached into herself, into the place where her most terrible fears hung up their coats, she found only a bright, tidy room with dry white walls, furnished with her own sturdy Will. And quite a bit of righteous indignation. She turned her dark gaze on Mr. Bud and Mr. Tree. The pair of them tried valiantly, but they could not meet the eyes of a twelve-year-old girl.

"Open that floor up at once," Charlotte demanded.

"You can't mean to go after them, miss." Mr. Bud

tugged fretfully at the leather cords that made up his beard. "Be reasonable, now!"

"They'll be long gone by now, my dear," tutted Mr. Tree mournfully. "Best take it on the chin, eh?"

Charlotte rolled her eyes. She marched up to Mr. Bud so forcefully that the poor editor truly thought, for a moment, that this breather child meant to hit him, which would leave him with the severe moral dilemma of whether to hit her back. Instead, she snatched his page-cutter saber from its sheath, glared at him so hard that it felt every bit as painful as a slap, and began trying her hardest to wedge the blade into the twisted, waxy ruin of the floor.

"They'll only be long gone if you two keep standing there doing nothing like a couple of bricks in a silly old wall! What's the matter with you? They might be killed! Crashey might spend his grog on us, but Brunty never would spare a drop, and you know it."

"Oh, no," Mr. Tree assured them. "Don't say that. They wouldn't *kill* them. Not even Can't-Take-Him-Anywhere Brunty."

Mr. Bud nodded. "They're very good about that sort of thing over in Gondal. Sensitive, don't you know."

Charlotte wanted to feel relieved, but she'd no real reason to believe the editors. So she ignored them. She softened her voice a little. "Come on, Em, help me."

Emily's tears dried up at once. Charlotte always knew what to do when the worst thing possible actually happened. It was like a magic spell only her sister could cast. If Charlotte started bossing her about, then all was still right with the world. She fell to her knees and began trying to wedge her nails into the golden wound Brunty had left behind.

"You don't understand!" Mr. Bud wailed. "They are *gone*. Remaindered! Departed. Decamped! Skipped town! Flown the nest! Hit the road! They've taken their leave! They've exited, stage left! Not at all due to any action or inaction by myself or good Mr. Tree, I'll remind you. But their print run has been well and truly *pulped*."

"You'll never catch them, even if you could get that bit of our floor open again," sighed Mr. Tree pointedly. "It is *our* floor you're vandalizing, you know. I don't know who you think you are. If they couldn't get Victoria back with the whole limey army, I daresay you won't find more than half a bootlace."

"And she was the Crown Princess of Glass Town and Angria *plus* heir to the throne," Mr. Bud whined. "If one of those can up and vanish like my office keys of a morning, you won't find a couple of nobodies stuck down the cushions."

Charlotte pushed her hair back away from her face. It had become quite a situation, after everything. She locked eyes with her sister. *Victoria?* she mouthed. *Anne's Victoria?* Emily shook her head. She didn't know. Anne never shared her secret Princess with the rest of them. She played the Victoria game after they'd all fallen asleep, whispering under the blankets to herself so that Branwell could not hear and drag her perfect girl into the bigger story and murder her for the drama of seeing Anne cry.

"Well, of *course* we will!" Emily said, breaking off curls of the horrid tallowy stuff with both hands. Then, she had the marvelous idea of going at it with the toffee hammer she'd swiped from Bestminster's tea service. The melted parquet did look rather like toffee. But her hammer had no more effect than asking the wreckage nicely to let her through, thank you kindly. Still, the problem, the *puzzle* of it, put Emily in a much brighter mood. What couldn't they sort out together? Nothing, that's what. "I don't think Brunty's much of a runner, you know. And Anne's only little; she'll slow them up. She always makes *us* late to wherever *we're* going."

Mr. Bud and Mr. Tree shook their heads.

"Nothing travels faster than bad news," Mr. Tree said. His silver muttonchops quivered in sympathy. "And

Brunty's is the baddest news there is. Bad news hasn't got to obey the usual laws of velocity and inertia and traffic police. It just . . . *phewwwt!* Arrives. Before you do. Might as well try to catch up to the sunrise."

Mr. Bud patted Emily's head awkwardly. He meant to be comforting, but it came out more like tapping a bell at a bank desk. "Gondal's got tunnels and vaults and all sorts of wormy passages running under the city. It's like old cheese down there, pet."

"And he had that . . . that *thing* . . . the . . . the *Thingy!*" Mr. Tree shuddered, his bookend-shoulders rattling.

Charlotte stopped stabbing at the floor with Mr. Bud's saber. "What *was* it? Don't you know?"

The editors stared at their shoes, quite unaccustomed to not knowing. "I've never seen anything like it! It's dash good at wrecking floors, that's clear! Who knows what else it does? P'raps Brunts can just give it a tap and they'll all come tumbling out into Old Boney's privy in Regina!"

"Boney!" cried Charlotte and Emily.

"What's Regina?" Emily added in after.

Mr. Bud and Mr. Tree frowned into their chests. "Well . . . yes?" Mr. Tree shrugged. "The capital of Gondal. That's where old Brunty will be headed. Unless he beelines it to Verdopolis. It *would* be faster, I suppose."

"But Verdopolis is in Glass Town," Emily protested. Verdopolis was their greatest city. The one they'd planned out over and over. Anything wonderful they read about from any other city they put into Verdopolis. The pyramids of Egypt, Balmoral Castle in Edinburgh, the Alhambra in Spain, the Great Wall of China, even the Colosseum in Rome. Branwell had drawn them over and over until they really did almost look like the real ones. She knew exactly where Verdopolis lay on the map and it wasn't in Gondal. "It's our . . . *your* capital!"

"Verdopolis is . . . disputed," Mr. Tree said darkly. "After he overran Northangerland and Zamorna and besieged the Isle of Dreams, Napoleon claimed the new border between Glass Town and Gondal ran right through Ascension Island. Right through the city of cities, the jewel in Glass Town's glass crown!"

Mr. Bud clenched his braided jaw. "Then Wellington said: *It inkin' well does not, it runs right where it always ran, through the Calabar Wood down the Mountains of the Moon to the sea. Kindly stay on your side of it, yeah?* Old Boney stuck his nose in the air and nobly replied: *nuh uh.* Then Wellington stuck *his* up there and said: *does so.* So then that sack of kneecaps took half the city by force, right up to the river and the Great Wall. Started building fortresses and fashionable housing down the left bank and sticking his tongue out at our limey boys on the other side, hollering: *I'm building on it, aren't I? That means c'est mine according to the ancient law entitled: You Can't Stop Me, Ha Ha!*"

"Glass Town still holds half of Verdopolis. Napoleon lords it over the other half. It's much closer than Regina. And they've just finished turning the airy ancient corridors of our most sacred palace into some hulking brute of a dungeon called the Bastille. Now we've put our thoughts in the pot, it seems the likeliest place for Brunty to stash the little ones."

"Caught himself some plump fishes, hasn't he?" Mr. Bud nodded. "He'll want to get them weighed and gutted and sold. Oh! Sorry. Not *really* gutted. Gutted for information, see? There's a war on, you know!"

"But we've only just arrived. We don't know anything useful. So they'll have to let Bran and Annie go. Right, Charlotte?"

Charlotte looked as though she might be sick. Of course they did know quite a lot. They probably knew just about everything. If they could only figure out which game, which campaign, which rainy day in the room at the top of the stairs was happening on *this* day in Glass Town, there really was nothing Branwell and

Anne *couldn't* tell Brunty or Bonaparte or that demonic screaming chicken about the war. And what did men at war do to get the information they wanted? Hadn't Branwell loved to play interrogation with the wooden soldiers?

Mr. Bud groaned. "Stop *looking* at me like that! I've told you! It's no use trying to shame us! *Nothing* travels faster than bad news. It's best if you just forget you ever had a brother or a sister and get on with whatever it is you're doing with your lives. If they turn up—fantastic! Cake and gin all round. If not? Well, more cake for you, yes?"

Charlotte clenched her teeth. "This *is* your fault, Mr. Bud."

"Isn't!" cried the men at once.

"*Is*," Emily hissed. "And yours, Mr. Tree. You were showing off, punishing Brunty right away so we could see it and tell you how brave and clever and excellent you are. You might have waited till we'd gone and all was safe, but then you wouldn't get to hear the tourists *ooh* and *ahh*."

The proprietors of Bud & Tree Publishing House blushed and found several rather fascinating things to stare at on the ceiling.

"You're editors," said Charlotte carefully, narrowing

her eyes as she thought it all through. "You clean up the mess. So, the way I see it, you've got to clean up *this* mess. Take us to Gondal. Fix the story. It's all gone wrong now; you must see that. Branwell and Anne were meant to be home on the evening express. It was a nice little fairy tale wrapped up with a bow and now you've got loose children running all over it and a fat spy with some kind of hideous acid-and-lightning machine and the government's involved. It won't do at all. So . . . so . . . make it right! Cut something or add something or move it all round until it's a nice, tidy story again. Take us to Gondal, load us up with grog in case the worst has happened, and we'll call it good."

"Not us." Mr. Bud held up his leather-braided hands again. "We're a specialty press, lovey. Strictly criminals and criminality, in small batches. Spies and machines and Gondal? That's too big for our blood. And we haven't even got any grog. They don't let just anyone handle the strong stuff. You gotta put in a request. There's forms. Signatures."

Mr. Tree fiddled shamefacedly with the buttons on his waistcoat. "We can't just totter on over to enemy territory and say: *So sorry for the trouble, lads, but would you mind if we just popped off with a couple of prisoners of war? Perhaps a biscuit or two for the road? Won't be a moment!*

My dear girls, you may think we're powerful, glorified men, and who could blame you? Look at us! But we're not anybody! We're just working class Angrians! Salt of the earth and . . . that. We'd be shot!"

Mr. Bud tugged on the Coptic bindings of his jacket. "No, we can't do a thing for you, I'm afraid. We feel terrible about it, of course. Miserable. Desolate."

"Of course!" Mr. Tree gushed. "Just *tormented.*"

"You need better friends than us. Braver friends. Grander friends. More . . . more famous friends."

"What's famous got to do with anything?" Emily asked.

"Fame means money, money means power, power means getting to do whatever you want. A couple of poor editors can't mount a rescue mission to Gondal in dead of night. But the Duke of Wellington can. The Marquis of Douro can. Lord Byron can."

"We don't know any of those people," protested Charlotte.

"Lord *Byron?*" Emily gasped.

A great sigh of relief rippled through the bookends and bindings of Mr. Bud and Mr. Tree.

"Well, I suppose I *can* do you a decent turn, then." Mr. Bud smiled and reached behind the reception desk to fiddle with something. "I'll send word to our Ginny right away. She's dressing maid to Miss Mary Percy—the missus and me are terrifically proud! It'll be no trouble at all. Ochreopolis has the fastest ghost in Glass Town."

"Ghost?" Charlotte repeated, sure she'd heard it wrong.

"Ghost," Mr. Tree repeated, sure the child was deaf.

"Post?" said Emily hopefully.

"Ghost," answered Mr. Bud firmly. "The Ghost Office. How else do you get your messages into the hands what want them? I can't think how a post could deliver letters. It hasn't got hands, you know. If a body dies along the highway, sometimes their spirit keeps walking or riding or driving a cart up and down the same patch of lane, back and forth, as ghosts will do. Well, back in the timey mists, the first Marquis of Douro, may the Genii bless his soul, got the inking *gorgeous* idea to give those poor wights a job. Every man's happier on the gainful, yeah? As long as they were haunting this and that, why not take a sack of letters and parcels and suchlike while they're moping on their way? A ghost doesn't have to obey the laws of the mortal world. They can find anybody, anywhere, so long as you've got a name and a stamp. They just listen to the earth or the heavenly spheres or something. Can't say I've ever understood it. Now, Glass Town has regular routes all up and down the county! Wonder of the modern world!"

"Ah, but even patriots like ourselves must admit Glass Town is nothing to Gondal on that score. For"—the tall bookend-man cleared his throat politely—"obvious reasons. A Gondalier can get a letter from Elseraden to Zedora before the ink is dry."

"Wait! What reasons? They're not obvious to us," interrupted Emily, wiping the sweat from her forehead.

The editors glanced at one another knowingly, then away guiltily, then at their hands furtively, then toward heaven at last. "There are . . . ahem . . . many more ghosts in Gondal than in Glass Town, my dear," Mr. Tree mumbled shamefacedly. "War is such a very dreadful thing, when the singing and the marching and the hurrahs are all done."

"Don't you go feeling sorry for them! Gondal attacked *us*! They're getting their just desserts, and I hope there's a fat cherry on top for each of them." Mr. Bud stomped his foot. "Why shouldn't there be more of them dead than us? Why have we got to feel guilty for winning? Well, I won't! We weren't doing a thing but minding our own business when Napoleon decided he just *had* to be Napoleon and shoot up the place of a Sunday. Old Boney could end it all in an instant, if he'd only inking well go home."

"But he won't," Mr. Tree sighed. "Not now. None of them will. We're in it till the end, I'm afraid." And he would say no more.

"We know a man called Napoleon as well," Charlotte said very carefully. "He was . . . much the same. Perhaps it's the name that does it."

Emily wanted to tell them not to worry, that it would be all right. Their war was only a bit behind hers, you see, and once events caught up, Napoleon would die alone on a rock in the middle of the ocean like he did back home, and everyone would be able to speak French and be happy and eat *vol-au-vent* again. But she couldn't be sure of that rock, not *completely* sure. Would there still be battles called Trafalgar and Waterloo in a place where Leftenant Gravey could come back to life a hundred times and Old Boney really *was* a lot of old bones with guns for arms?

Mr. Bud waved his braided hand. "Yes, well, I hope you drowned him so thoroughly even his grandchildren never got dry. Bah! Enough of the war! I was bragging, and you shouldn't interrupt a fellow bragging unless you want to cause a stroke." He cleared his throat to praise the Glass Town post again. "If you think a horse can shake a leg, you've never seen a ghost gallop. Our local'll be along presently. I've already rung the bell."

And indeed, down from the highest windows of the towers came a pale mustard-colored shade, all smoke and sunlight. They could see straight through him as he circled down to where they stood, especially as he had several holes through him made by some sword or other. The ghost left a trail of frost in the air like skate scratches in an ice pond. His clothes were beautiful velvet tatters, his face long and sad and noble, with a tidy beard, but his back and shoulder were oddly twisted. He wore a white rose on his tunic and tall crown on his head.

"Em," whispered Charlotte. Her breath fogged, though it had been warm a moment before. But Emily just stared. Her mouth hung open. She clasped her hands together in delight. She didn't seem to notice the sudden cold at all.

"Em!" Charlotte whispered harder, and jabbed her sister in the ribs with her thumb.

"A ghost, Charlotte! A real ghost, do you see him? He's *amazing!*"

"*Emily!*" Charlotte hissed. The spirit was almost upon them. "I think that's Richard the Third!"

"What? Don't be silly. He died on Bosworth Field! I don't even think there is a Bosworth Field here!"

"I think there's everything here we've got back home, only turned around and shaken up till it doesn't know its own name," Charlotte sighed, but though everything was as dire as any war for any roses, she couldn't help smiling all the same. It *was* Richard. She knew that face, from the woodcuts and paintings in their history books, from the illustration beside the list of characters in their collection of Mr. Shakespeare's plays. If they had a Napoleon in Gondal, and a Duke of Wellington in Glass Town, why not Richard and the Princes in the tower and all the rest? She *knew* it was him, she was so sure! Dick the Bad, as big as life and twice as dead!

Suddenly Emily knew it, too. The hunchback, the put-upon expression, the crown! She clapped her hands like they'd just seen a magician pull an English monarch out of his hat. Both girls quickly remembered themselves as subjects to the Crown, even if the Crown was in another world and stone dead. They knelt before the last Plantagenet.

"I suppose there are roads enough through Bosworth now," Emily said thoughtfully.

"There you are, Dickie, my lad, there's you set," Mr. Bud chirped bossily. He handed a note card to the King of England as though it wasn't the most remarkable thing that had ever happened. Richard took it without complaint. He inclined his head toward the kneeling girls, touched, perhaps, that someone would still think to do such a thing. He laid his misty amber hands upon their heads and looked down with love and a sadness as deep as the grave. When he spoke, no more than a whisper, his voice was misty and amber, too:

"So wise, so young, they say, do never live long."

King Richard pressed the card to his wounded breast, and melted away like butter in summer. Warmth returned to the lobby of Bud & Tree Publishing House.

"Rude," Charlotte said when the King had gone.

"What a morbid thing to say to a person you've just met!" Emily scoffed. "Just because you're a ghost doesn't mean you have to go around saying creepy things all the time. What's the matter with *how do you do, happy to take your letter, isn't it a bit of weather we're having?* I suppose nobody raps a King's knuckles for bad manners, even if they clearly should." The color drained from her cheeks. "You don't think he's cursed us, do you? Richard is meant to be a villain, after all!"

Mr. Bud chatted away at them, too fast and too loud, trying to outrace and outshout both his guilty conscience and any mention of ghostly curses. But Charlotte and Emily kept staring after Richard's ghost, trying to memorize forever the vision of a King delivering their post.

"What Mr. Bud means to say," interrupted Mr. Tree, "and what he is not saying very well at all, is that the

Wildfell Ball's on tonight, up at Lavendry-on-Puce."

"Good gracious, we haven't got time for a ball," Charlotte scoffed. "My brother and sister have been kidnapped by a book! I'm not going to *dance* while they're tied to some horrid chair in Verdopolis getting that vicious acid dripped on them till they give up everything they know." Charlotte had begun to wobble. It started in her legs and moved everywhere, all through her, till she thought she might come apart. All she could see was poor Branwell lying on that red glass street, bleeding and bleeding and bleeding. . . .

"I can't be wrong again," Charlotte whispered. No one bothered to hear.

"Ugh, I'll tell you twice for free and three times for a penny, I'd trade that whole town for a pair of wool socks." Mr. Bud grumbled on as though Charlotte hadn't said a word. "They've got a ball or a festival or a holiday or a feast for every day of the calendar. You'd think they'd get sick of it! Too much pastry spoils the beef!"

"It's to benefit the war hospital, Mr. Bud! Don't be ungracious. We must all do our part."

"Oh, they always say it's to benefit St. Tosh's Home for Poncery and Blatherall. But really, it's only ever to benefit their bellies with donations of champagne and cakes!"

Emily clapped her hands to get the editors' attention. "This is ridiculous! Mr. Bud, Mr. Tree, we are *not* going to a party. We are going to Gondal. We are going to save Annie and Branwell! What kind of person could drink champagne at a time like this? There's no time for rouge and fans and all that nonsense. They're getting farther away with every second and all you want to talk about is cake!"

Mr. Bud shook his leather-lashed head. "My dearies, you misunderstand. It'll be an inking *battlefield* for the likes of you. Rouge? Fans? Champagne? Yes, you will, for their sake. With all that frippery you must arm and armor yourselves. They'll all be there, every one of those high-class ponies with silk for snot. Wellington, Douro, Byron, Elrington, the Duke and Duchess, the Queen of the Blues. You've got half a clever tongue between the two of you and a ripping sob story in your pockets. *So play your hand.* Mind you, you look like a couple of spaniels who've been at the mud again, but Ginevra will get you sorted out. Be big, be bright, tell your tale! Go about with hat in hand and hand on heart and make the ball benefit *you.*"

Emily let the book-binding man natter. She glanced sidelong over the ledge of Mr. Tree's desk. Her burglar's instincts pricked up. She couldn't help herself. They needed to press on and Mr. Bud simply insisted on talking and talking and talking. He liked talking and Mr. Tree liked listening so much neither of them saw Emily's quick fingers disappear into the desk and then into her pockets without a sound.

Charlotte desperately wanted to run, all the way to Gondal if she had to. Running seemed far more useful than dancing. But perhaps the publishers were right. Perhaps they needed friends. Perhaps two young girls from Yorkshire could not invade a country entirely by themselves. And perhaps, if the highest of the high were all together in one place, they would have brought enough grog with them to revive all the elephants in the Alps. The rich and the political were very partial to their own skin, after all.

I can't be wrong again.

For once, Charlotte did not know what to do. She had failed. Half her family was gone. Maria and Lizzie had been the oldest their whole lives and never lost even one of them. She had been wrong when she said they couldn't be hurt. What if she was about to be wrong again? The Wildfell Ball sounded like the right sort of thing for a girl in a story to do, and they were in a story, in a manner of speaking. But people made the wrong choices all the time in stories. Wrong choices were what made stories *go*. But making one for a doll was ever so much different than making one for Bran and Anne. What if the only thing to do was get into Bestminster and run for Gondal, run and never stop, no matter who shot at them, no matter whether she had any idea what to do when they got there? *Someone else be oldest*, Charlotte wept in her heart, without a single tear showing on her face. *Someone else.*

Emily reached out and tucked a strand of loose brown hair behind her sister's ear. She smiled into Charlotte's frantic eyes. Emily tried to give her back a bit of that magic spell of bossiness she doled out so freely to the rest of them.

"We will attend the ball, Mr. Bud, Mr. Tree," Emily said with a hard brightness in her voice.

Mr. Tree laid a hand over his bookend-heart. "Poor innocent lambs fed to Gondal's fattest lion! Woe betide these unfortunate maidens! You know the song. Get a Duke or two on your side and I daresay you'll have your brother and sister back by the crack of the Sunday church bell."

Mr. Bud and Mr. Tree beamed eagerly at them, and for a moment, Charlotte and Emily almost believed everything would be all right.

THIRTEEN

Sir Rotter and Lady Rubbish

Deep down in the earth beneath Ochreopolis, an awful buzzing sound filled the dark.

"Lay off it, you dog-ears," grunted Brunty, the Magazine Man, Master Spy of Gondal. Inky beads of sweat stood out on his papery brow. "I'm not afraid to smack you one if you keep pulling and shoving and *biting*. . . . ow! You little splitter! If I drop you, you won't land in Mummy's lap, you know. You'll land in a broken neck on wet black nothing, so *hold* bloody *still*!"

"Our mother's dead, you great glocky beast!" Anne snarled and bit their captor again savagely, though she couldn't see where her teeth landed. "Let us go!"

"You'll get worse than a bite when Charlotte finds us," Branwell scoffed with confidence. No one could beat his older sister for punishments when a game got spoiled. He couldn't help it. His sister drove him sideways, but when he was in trouble, he turned to her as toward the sun. That's what came of being the oldest, he suspected. Nothing more than that. All the same, Branwell wondered what it would be like to be that sun instead. "Believe me. She once sentenced a doll to vivisection. I almost feel sorry for you."

The Magazine Man chuckled softly. "She won't find us, young master Lackbrains. Haven't you heard about bad news? It travels fast and it travels invisible. And just look at me! Have you ever seen worse?"

But they couldn't see a thing beyond blackness. They hadn't seen a thing but blackness since the Magazine Man dragged them underground and shoved that horrible machine with its green and blue lights back into his seemingly bottomless waistcoat pocket. At first, it was a very thick, hot blackness, a blackness you could taste on your tongue and swallow and feel very sick over, like bad treacle. Then, as Brunty plowed through lightless tunnels and caverns and catacombs at the speed of wickedness, scrambling down ladders of shadow and shade, it changed into a cool, slick blackness that ran all up and down their arms and legs like midnight rainwater. Now, wherever they were, so deep beneath the city they could no longer hear the distant, muffled, comforting sounds of their sisters arguing with somebody or other, trying to save them, surely, trying to get to them, the blackness froze them to the bones of their thumbs. It chewed at their fingertips and slashed at their noses. And this new blackness had a sound, too. It *buzzed* and *thrummed* and *whirred*. The buzz came from everywhere at once and nowhere at all. It bounced and echoed off invisible walls. Branwell thought Brunty was making it when it first began. Then he thought perhaps somehow he himself was doing it. Then, he was quite sure Anne was playing some silly game to annoy him. But he couldn't tell one idiot thing in the dark, really. It might be the buzzing of a bee in South America for all he or Anne knew about their situation. All together the buzzing and the cold and the dark ground against them like the spinning gears of some terrible factory where winter and despair were made and it would not stop; it just would *not*.

Brunty wheezed in the shadows. They could feel the beating of his gluey heart. His breath smelled like a burnt-down library.

"Now listen, you little rotters," the Magazine Man whispered, though there was no one to hear them in the deeps of the earth, "I'm going to set you down for half a tock and you *might* think it's a swell idea to run off, but I promise you, you'll get nowhere fast but dead if you do. I know these twisty-turnies like my own covers, front and back, but *you* can't see in the dark any better than a blind, drunk hedgehog. Understand your old Brunto?" The creature sniffed the air. He turned right. "Postscript! There's a chasm three inches to your left that bottoms out in a subterranean ocean just teeming with ravenous wormsharks and at least one immortal three-eyed leviathan, so root your stupid feet to the ground, right?"

Branwell trembled, and was glad Anne couldn't see it. Anne. Why couldn't old Brunty have grabbed Charlotte instead? Anne was little and slow and any time he had a really good slaughter going among the soldiers in the room at the top of the stairs, she gave them all sweet, tender burials and resurrections in Tabitha's butter dishes. What could he do with an Anne?

Anne looked up at him in the dark. He couldn't see her, not really, but he could see a sliver of the shine in her big eyes.

"Don't leave me," she whispered. "Don't you run off."

She didn't think he would. But she couldn't be sure. If only the Magazine Man had snatched Emily instead, Anne would have felt much safer. At any minute, Branwell might get the idea that he could save her better by dashing off to do some foolish thing with a trebuchet, a bucket of nails, and a bloodsucking bat, or whatever other savagery came into his head. She grabbed his hand and squeezed so tight his knuckles popped.

"Right, Mr. Brunty. We'll be good." But Bran felt rather small and childish saying that, and he hated that feeling more than old porridge or new shirt collars. So he added: "For now."

Brunty clapped his illustrated hands. Anne could hear it in the dark, dry and raspy and sneering. "Oh, *very* brave, Little Lord Backtalk!"

The buzzing grew louder and more pointed while their kidnapper rummaged and rustled with some bit of presumably frightful business Bran and Anne strained to see. Finally there was a popping, sucking noise and the blackness fizzled away in a gout of greenish-blue light. Brunty had got his uncanny contraption working again, that strange and sickly hourglass frame full of weeping saucers. It glowed on an outcropping of shining obsidian stone, bubbling with acid and sizzling with tiny forks of lightning. The ghostly lantern-light flickered over the pages of Brunty's brutal face, his scroll knob belly, his glossy evening-edition hands. It turned his spectacles to spectral green lamps. And they could see, now, that

Brunty *was* all bad news. The newspapers on his waist-coat announced WAR! and MURDER! and ALL-DESTROY-ING FLOOD CONSUMES PLANET in giant headlines. The magazines that formed his meaty hands showed terrible woodcuts of famine and mayhem. The master spy raised the capital O's of his eyes to heaven and patted his waistcoat for something—what had he forgotten? Ah! A tiny glass vial of sand, which in any other light, would have shone red.

"What *is* that thing?" Bran asked. He could hardly take his eyes off it. The seething, venomous green danced deep in his pupils.

"None of your bloody business, Quentin Q. Questions! Hasn't anyone taught you anything? The first rule of spying is Do Not Ask Plainly for What You Seek or Nobody Will Tell You Nothing. You'd get strangled on your first day. Oh, the Great Encyclopedia tests me so! He *knows* I hate children. What a better world we'd have if we were all born grown!"

"That's a nasty thing to say and you're a nasty man," Anne said matter-of-factly.

"What's the second rule?" Branwell piped up.

"Eh?"

"Of spying. You said the first rule already. What's the second?"

"Ah. Er. Never Use Your Real Name."

"Is Brunty not—"

"Third rule of spying is No Backtalk!" yelled the Magazine Man.

Anne glanced to her left. There really was a vicious cliff dropping down into mist and shadows. She hadn't believed him at all, but the wind blew up from the depths of the chasm like the breath of the earth.

"You were little once, too," she hissed. "And I'd bet anything I've got you bit somebody fierce and then went back for seconds and I *know* you backtalked everyone you ever met."

Brunty tapped the vial of sand, licked his finger, and held it up to test the wind. "Well, that just shows what you know, Little Lady Whinebag! I never was little. Never. The Great Encyclopedia made me as I am, from page to spine. You don't buy a book when it's tiny and watch it grow on your shelf, do you? Nonsense. On my day of publication, I was every inch the Brunty you see before you. Childhood is ruddy inefficient, I tell you what. I don't know why your lot bothers with it."

"The Great Encyclopedia?" Bran asked, shuffling his feet away from the chasm's edge, though he really desperately wanted to know what a wormshark looked like. "Do you mean . . . God?"

The Magazine Man grunted. He unstoppered the vial and poured it out in a neat little pool on the floor of the cavern. "Who else would I mean?"

Anne laughed. "God's not an encyclopedia! That's the funniest thing I've ever heard!"

Brunty's eyes grew rounder and softer and gentler. The headlines on his waistcoat ran like water. Now they read things like CANDLELIGHT VIGIL HELD AT MIDNIGHT and MIRACLE IN LAVENDRY in modest type. "The Encyclopedia is the *Son* of the Gods, sent to redeem us from disorder." Brunty lifted up his O-eyes. "In the beginning were the Genii, blessed be their crowns of lightning! The Genii dwelt together in the void and fashioned out of nothing Heaven and Earth and Participles and Fate and Gravy Without Lumps and the Great Encyclopedia. The Encyclopedia contains everything in the world, from first to last, top to bottom, A to Zed. He protects the world, and organizes it, and explains it to any with the patience to listen. We all begin in the Nest of Knowledge, and from thence we learn to fly. I am of strong Bookish stock. We are an ancient race, possessed of great secrets and great strength. No Bookman could exist without some sacred spark of the Encyclopedia inside him." Brunty seemed to remember himself. His face snapped back into its usual irritated expression. He whacked his chest until the headlines went boldface and angry again. INFIDEL HORDES AFOOT IN OCHREOPOLIS! "Oh, I suppose you think God is shaped more or less like you, only bigger and burlier and beardier and boomier?"

"Well . . . yes?" Branwell ventured.

Brunty snorted. His ribbon nose fluttered up and down again. "Disgusting."

The buzzing sound suddenly sharpened itself into a long, wet scream. A huge shape came barreling down the tunnel toward them, something black and massive and shrieking and humming, something that reflected the light of Brunty's horrible acid-lantern and exploded it into green and blue fireworks.

It was a fly. A fly the size of a small whale.

The fly descended on the little pile of red sand and devoured it, raising its head every once in a bit to chortle and thrum with delight. Beneath a rich, carved onyx saddle, its body rippled with shimmering black muscles and veins and long gray wings. Its huge, faceted eyes drank up the dark. It flicked its proboscis and rubbed its feelers together, gloating over its feast.

"Oh!" shrieked Anne. "It's *hideous!*"

"Oh!" breathed Bran. "It's *brilliant.*"

Despite himself, Primarily Scurrilous Brunty felt rather proud. He puffed up his chest. "One of the little secrets of my trade. Didn't you ever wonder how bad news travels so fast? Time Flies! *Musca Tempus Fugicus*, to be precise. I do *so* love to be precise! And only the bearers of bad news can command them."

"With that stuff you poured on the ground?" asked Anne shyly. She supposed insects were animals and she ought to love them equally to a dog or a bird, but she couldn't quite manage it.

Brunty grinned. "The Sands of Time, Duchess Disappointment! They can't resist."

Bran stuck his finger in what was left of the red sand and tasted it. The Time Fly hissed at him and hurried to suck up the rest before he could steal anymore.

"It's sugar!" he said.

The fly buzzed, velvet and kind. "Time past is sweet, boy," she said. "And time to come is sweeter still." Her voice echoed like a little thin flute in the stone caves.

Brunty patted the jet-black, wrinkled hide of the beast. Her wings quivered. "They're terrible gluttons, the Time Flies. Overeaters of time and space. No restraint at all. They gobble up all the time it would take us to get where we're going and excrete the space between us and our destination. Not bad, wouldn't you say?"

"Not bad," agreed Bran and Anne. They were in such terrible trouble, yes, of course they were, but they could not help marveling at the creature.

And then the most peculiar thing happened. Brunty the Liar, Brunty the Spying Sack of Slime, Can't-Take-Him-Anywhere Brunty gave the deepest, most graceful, humblest bow anyone has ever bowed.

"Madam," he said, in the most elegant, courtly, grandest of accents, "might I, your lowly servant, inquire after your name?"

"It's Ryecote, sir!" chirped the fly. "Ryecote, daughter of Applemeal, daughter of Spillwine, daughter of Horseye, daughter of Dunglace—"

Brunty interrupted her, but he did it so sleekly and smoothly that it seemed as though Ryecote had quite finished her sentence. "What a noble and august lineage! How fortunate I feel to have found myself in the care of the scion of such a queenly and ancient house!"

"Goodness, that's perfectly all right," the fly demurred, but anyone could tell she was pleased. "Very pleased to meet you and all."

Brunty pressed on, his voice growing ever more adoring and kind. The headlines on his waistcoat shimmered and read: MERCY AND CHARITY RUN WILD IN THE STREETS and PRINCESS TRAVELS ABROAD TO HELP THE POOR. "And I, Lady Ryecote, am called Brunty Errata-Huntingdon, of the Elseraden Errata-Huntingdons, lately made Lord after the untimely death of my stepbrother. May I also present . . . these . . . people." He gestured halfheartedly at Branwell and Anne. "Sir Rotter and Lady Rubbish."

"Oh my! Of the *Middenheap* Rubbishes?" exclaimed Ryecote in insect awe.

Brunty bowed deeper. "Indubitably, your loveliness. Now, Lady Ryecote, if you will excuse the intolerable imposition, my companions and I have great and pressing need to journey swiftly to the Bastille in the fair and glittering city of the Lefthand Verdopolis, far and far from here. Will you, Princess among flies, Gloriana in her highest, consent to carry myself, my wards, and my excellent and *entirely* safe technological cargo upon your sublime back and bear us to the welcoming arms of Mother Gondal?"

"What is he *on* about?" whispered Bran. "It's only a fly!"

The Time Fly rubbed her ashen wings together in joy. "Oh, Lord Brunty, I would just *love* to give you a lift! I don't think I'd like anything in the world half so well, unless it was a bit more of that yummy sand you've got, but who can say no to a lick of time? Not me, and I've got the thorax to prove it! That's all right, Mr. Ryecote loves my thorax best of all the thoraxes that ever were! What a lucky bug I am! Just wait till I tell my sisters! Pithpip is always going on and on about how our grandmum snatched away the Jewel of Glass Town to Gondal so fast no one knew little Vickie'd gone! I'll finally get to show her up, the old tailflicker. Said I'd never amount to much when we were larvae—well, look at plain little Ryecote now! And such a handsome, well-spoken man asking for me. My, my, Mr. Ryecote will be jealous! But I don't care a bit. I'm pleased as a pony! A fine, powerful, *beautiful* pony that no one would ever call *hideous*."

Anne blushed with shame. Now that she'd met the fly properly, she rather thought she'd like to take her home to Haworth with her and feed her through the kitchen window every night forever and ever. And yet, through her blushing, her clever, hungry ears caught a word that meant nothing and everything to her. *Vickie?*

"Can't I take it back?" Anne begged shyly. "I think you're wonderful. Just wonderful. The prettiest fly I ever saw."

Ryecote lifted her huge cut-glass eyes and chortled gleefully. "Of course you can! I was only teasing. Teasing is the most fun you can have on the ground, I think. I don't hold a grudge; it's not in my nature! Got a heart like a sugar lump, me. Hop on, darlings! I can't wait, I'm starving! It's a long way to Gondal, a nice big tuck-in with dollops of dessert. Don't mind the weight, now. I'm a strong girl; everyone says so. That Ryecote, she could carry the whole world on her back, our pa used to say!"

Branwell and Anne grabbed at each other's hands. It was their last chance to run. Run to Charlotte, run to Emily, run to Bestminster, run to Crashey and Bravey and Gravey and Rogue, run back to the light. But before they could decide to brave the black labyrinth underneath Ochreopolis and cross their fingers that they'd not starve to death before finding the way in the shadows, Lord Brunty Errata-Huntingdon of the Elseraden Errata-Huntingdons seized them by the waists. He shoved them up onto Ryecote's gleaming onyx saddle, a saddle so big it could have held a second Magazine Man, a second Bran, and a second Anne, even a second horrible acid machine, and still had room for a lunch basket.

Brunty punched his chest viciously a few times. "Come on, don't go soft on me, lads, or we'll never go a mile," he mumbled.

The kindly headlines on his breast faded out and bled black until they read bad and worst once more. WAR! DEVASTATION! REVENGE! VICTORY AT ALL COSTS! The Magazine Man squeezed Anne and her brother painfully tight against his gut and held the Thing out before him like a ferryman's lamp.

Ryecote trumpeted into the stony darkness ahead

of them. Had the sun ever reached down this far? Anne thought it might have tried, but gotten scared and run back up to the sky and never told anyone about it. The Time Fly wiggled her hindquarters like a cat about to dash after a mouse. "Everyone safe? Everyone cozy? Everyone snug as a bug in a wine jug? I got caught in a wine jug once when I was wee. It was the best half-minute of my life—"

The caverns wobbled. The tunnels shuddered. The chasm full of wormsharks and at least one immortal three-eyed leviathan groaned. The underside of the city seemed to, somehow, and only once, *tick*. Like a minute hand juddering into place. And then, everything was buzzing and nothing was not buzzing and the buzzing was inside them and outside them and they had always been buzzing, their whole lives; they would never stop buzzing for buzz was the whole of the universe from star to moon to dust—

And

then

—they were tumbling out onto thick, sharp grass drenched in frost, into wintergreen and dead clover and a forest full of empty bare trees and high, tight clouds that promised snow by sundown, into a clearing that held nothing but an old road, a broad stone house with round windows, a fresh thatch roof, and rosy lights inside, a man shaped like a book, two children, and a giant fly lying motionless on the cold, cold earth.

"Ryecote!" screamed Anne, rushing to the creature's side. She didn't even notice the pool of ichor spreading into the grass until her knees were soaking with it.

"It's no use blubbering," Brunty sniffed. "She's dead. Flies only live a day, and she ate up that and more getting us here. Thought you'd know that sort of thing, being such a Clever Cathy."

"You knew all this while she'd die? And you used her anyway?" Bran's voice shook, though even he couldn't quite tell if it shook with anger or awe.

The Magazine Man patted Ryecote's dull, lifeless eyes. "Why else would I treat her so nice? Poor bugger."

Anne seethed. Her lips drew back from her teeth like a wild fox. Anne had never really hated anything before. She didn't recognize it when it happened to her. Hatred felt like the terrible burning lye soap they used for laundry splashing up onto her heart instead of onto her hands. It tasted like hot dirt in her mouth. She wanted to tear out Brunty's pages one by one and eat them. He'd taken them away from Charlotte and Emily. He'd called them names and dragged them around by their hair. They were going to miss the train home because of him.

And he'd killed poor Ryecote and he wasn't even sorry. He didn't even *care*.

"THE END!" Anne cried hoarsely. "THE END THE END THE END!" It had worked when Charlotte had done it. She should have remembered sooner, but it had all happened so fast, and there had been the matter of the three-eyed leviathan and the chasm. . . .

But Brunty did not fold his covers up with a pop and plop to the ground as a neat and tidily shut book. He glanced back over his newsprint shoulder.

"Oh, no, no, no, my love," he scolded silkily. "That won't be working, not a bit. In the comfort of your own parlor, you may end a book and stop a tale anytime you don't like where it's headed, but we are in the *wild* now, I'm afraid. The story is quite, *quite* out of your hands."

The Magazine Man looked up toward the thatched house. Voices tumbled out of the windows and doors like washing-water. The most marvelous smell Bran and Anne could imagine came puffing out of the place along with chimney smoke and candlelight: beef stew and brown beer. It was a pub! Branwell's stomach growled. But Brunty rolled his great eyes and made a disgusted noise in his throat. "Fat lot of good it did, either. She didn't even get us all the way to Gondal. Thanks for that, you old nag." And he gave her a resentful little kick.

Ryecote wobbled and shuddered and groaned just as the black caverns had done. Her body vanished, back into the great trash heap of time that birthed her. Tears began to freeze on Anne's flushed cheeks.

"Halloo!" came a deep, booming, oaky voice from a big round window in the public house. A handsome, finely carved face stuck itself out into the cold, still wearing a proud soldier's helmet. "I say, is that you, Master Branwell? And Miss Anne! How extraordinary! What a bit of a thing this is! Come in, come in! This is my place, built it myself! And for my comrades, everything is on the house! Oh! Erm. Oh dear . . . who *have* you got there with you? No, you wouldn't. You couldn't. Oh, it *is*. Tsk, tsk, Brunty! Have you been a naughty little pupper again?"

It was Captain Bravey.

FOURTEEN

A Bath, a Bit of Paint, and a Pile of Cloth

Bestminster Abbey seemed very empty indeed without Branwell and Anne. It had turned itself back into a stallionocerosupine, hoping to make the girls smile, to share in a good memory. But Charlotte and Emily only sat together in the lounge, staring into nothing. Each wandered wild on the moors of their own thoughts as the gentle-hearted suitcase padded, as softly as it could, through the chic topaz streets of Ochreopolis, past the golden banks of Canary Wharf, beneath the shadows of a thousand amber spires. Bestminster crept so quietly, in fact, that they'd fallen fast asleep by the time it climbed up through the brilliant jeweled hardscrabble

Kaleideslopes that separate the learned folk of Ochreopolis from the eternal wild party of Lavendry, where no one ever sleeps for fear of missing the next dance. They did not even wake when the suitcase re-un-packed itself into a slim town house. Nor when it settled down like a roosting hen on the fragrant purplish-pink banks of the mighty Puce River, sandwiched between a hat shop and a perfume-maker's studio. Bestminster steadfastly refused to disturb them. Emily and Charlotte had meant to finally hash it all out between their good brains—the why and the wherefore, the how and the what exactly, the which and the whether. The grog and the game. But it was all too much for a single day, the running and the shooting and the Brunty-ing and the screaming and the digging in a publishers' floor with a letter-opener. Sleep ran them down like a gray tiger before one word could escape its claws.

When the knock came at Bestminster's door, it startled them both awake so harshly they nearly fell off the long sofas onto the floor. For a moment, still sticky with afternoon dreams, Charlotte thought she was back at the Cowan Bridge School. She could not breathe; her heart rattled in her chest, and she reached out for her sisters—not Emily, but Maria and Elizabeth, who were so much older and wiser. Who would protect her from the

Headmaster. Who could make everything all right so she didn't have to all by herself. But then, Charlotte's eyes scraped over the leather suitcase walls, the half-snail, half-turtle over the mantel, the petticoat windowpanes. Cowan Bridge School was very far away. Maria and Elizabeth were dead. Branwell and Anne had been kidnapped by a book. Charlotte was the oldest and the wisest one left. But she feared she was not at all old or wise enough.

The knock at the door rapped again.

"Charlotte, I dreamed we were back at School," choked Emily, her mouth horribly dry.

"Don't worry, Em," Charlotte said, smiling as hard as she could while she smoothed her dress and tucked her hair back in place. "We're only in an insane, upside-down world populated by our toys, our stories, and Napoleon riding a giant chicken on fire. Nothing so bad as School."

The knock grew annoyed.

"Please." Bestminster Abbey's mighty plea. "You're embarrassing me. Someone is being kept waiting on our account. It's . . . it's *unbearable*."

The two of them apologized over and over to their suitcase and hurried to open the door. They peered together out into the warm, syrupy afternoon sunlight. A young lady not much older than they stood there with a large steamer trunk in her arms. She was very young and very pretty and she wore a lilac-colored dress with bits of indigo lace and real violets along the neckline. She was also made entirely of powder. Clouds of talcum powder, rouge, charcoal powder, cinnabar, snuff, and pearl powder floated in the shape of a girl with red curls and big brown eyes and cheekbones like birds' wings.

"Oh," the powder-girl clucked in a terribly refined voice, looking them up, down, and over. "Richard was right. That won't do at *all*. Poor kittens! Who left you out in the rain? What a jolly thing you've got Ginny to let you in the back way and fill up your saucers with milk!"

Ginevra Bud swept into Bestminster Abbey in a mist of flowery scents and set her trunk down with a loud *thwack* in the center of the lounge. She left little glowing footprints of pearl dust wherever she walked. Charlotte and Emily felt suddenly like a pair of warty bridge trolls next to Mr. Bud's daughter. No dress or paint in the world could make them look like that. Ginny was a girl from a fairy book. They were girls from Haworth. And her only a dressing maid! What would the Lords and Ladies at the Wildfell Ball look like, then? They'd stand a better chance of blending in with a pack of leopards.

Ginevra winked at them. She lowered her voice, and suddenly it wasn't near so fancy. "I know just what you're thinking, 'cause I thought it too, first time I clapped lash on Lady Percy. Oh, Ginny, I said to meself, you just clip-clop on home to Custardside 'cause you're never'n nothing but a rumpy horse with flies in her hair and a bray in her mouth. You ain't the same kind as those Lavendry Ladies. Not even the same species. As much like 'em as a badger to an angel. But lookie now!" She twirled around and her lilac dress flared out and when she finished twirling, her voice was all shine and silver again. "Miss Mary taught me proper and I'll teach you better than that. Have you ever played a scene, girls? Swanned over a stage, even if it was only the boards of your bedroom? Recited lines as a grand old Emperor or a fairy in the wood?"

Emily and Charlotte nodded shyly. Ginevra popped open her steamer trunk.

"Well, half-done, then! The difference between the likes of us and the likes of them is nothing but a bath, a bit of paint, a pile of cloth, and a funny voice. And do you want to know the deepest, darkest secret of all? *They're* playing scenes, too, each and every one. It's the most marvelous and terrible thing in the world. Everyone, but *everyone*, is pretending to be someone else. Tumbling and tripping along, writing their own little play as they go. Look at your Ginny. Isn't she fine in her gown? Lovies, this is my *only* dress! When washing day comes I wear an old plaid blanket with a belt round my middle. Very well!" She clapped her powdery hands together. A little cloud of scented dust puffed out from between her palms. Bestminster very helpfully made two bathtubs out of gravy boats leftover from their tea with the wooden soldiers, swelled up like flour sacks filling at a mill. He pumped them full of hot water. Bestminster had spoken with the city pipes while the girls slept and come to a very fine arrangement. Ginny politely turned around while Charlotte and Emily peeled off their gray and black school dresses. They climbed into the gravy-tubs and began to scrub all the grime of traveling between worlds away till their skin turned raw and pink.

Ginevra busied herself in the depths of her steamer trunk. Every once in a while, she tossed a little vial of oil or a cake of soap or a sachet of mysterious powders over her shoulder for the girls to catch. They applied whatever it was to whatever bit of body or bathwater the picture on the packets showed and hoped for the best. Ginny talked like Tabitha did—as though, if she stopped, she'd just wind down completely like a pocket watch and never spin up again.

"You've auditioned, and I've cast you as two Angrian Ladies visiting from your country estates. Just Ladies, I think. Any higher in rank and we'll run right into trouble. They expect Baronesses to be rather the life of the party, you know. But a Lady can just flutter her fan in the corner. Of course, you'll have to have new names! The wild foxes at the Wildfell Ball know all the noble families down to half-cousins and lesser hunting hounds." She looked at them appraisingly over her shoulder, her charcoal-dust eyebrows furrowing. "Best to put you far away from the action. So . . . let's see. I think you grew up on family lands in Smokeshire, in the wild counties north of Verdopolis, our fair capital. Before the occupation, naturally. Lord Linton Bell runs those counties from his estate at Thrushcross Grange. He's got more grandchildren than grapes on his vines. What's another two, more or less? You'll be Bell girls, just introduced to society. You've got inheritances, but nothing so posh that the boys would come tripping over themselves to dance with you. A word to the wise: *May I have this dance?* never means *may I have this dance.* It means: *May I scheme with, for, against, or, at least, near you?* Whether that's scheming for marriage or money or a ride home in your carriage so the fellow doesn't have to walk, you'll have to snuffle out for yourselves." Ginevra began to lay out hairbrushes, combs, bottles of mysterious somethings, scissors, puffs, and pots all in neat rows on the luncheon table. All laid out together, it looked like an armory full of rifles and swords. Ginevra twittered on. "Of course, we must give you good, Angrian names. I've never met a Charlotte or an Emily in my life, and no one would believe Linton Bell would allow such modern-sounding names to land on any of his little grapes. Something strong and heavy and fashionable about a thousand years ago, that's his speed! I think . . . Lady Currer and Lady Ellis Bell will hang very nicely on you both." She clapped her talcum hands together. "Now for the best part! The best mask is fitted precisely to the wearer's face!" Ginevra Bud rocked back on her heels between the two gravy-tubs and sparkled at them. Her eyes shone with interest and merriment. "Tell me about yourselves. What do you like best in the world? What do you dream of having for your own that you cannot touch just yet? And I don't mean having your brother and sister back safe. That's too easy."

Emily clasped and unclasped her hands in the foaming bathwater. She felt like she was standing under a waterfall, getting her head soaked by Ginny's gushing talk and her new history and her new name. How could you think in a waterfall?

"I like dogs with white ears, and half-blind old ravens, and extremely tidy rooms, the opposite of arguments, and thunderstorms on the moors, and . . . and ghosts," Emily breathed out all at once, adding the last without quite meaning to. "I . . . I suppose . . . I should like to love someone who makes me feel the way I feel when the thunder storms on the moors. And to not be a governess ever."

Charlotte dunked her head in the bath and bobbed up again. "I like books, and—"

"Books!" protested Emily from her gravy boat. "Well, I would have said books, too, you know, but books are just *obvious*. That's like saying you like air!"

"*Books*," Charlotte repeated firmly, "and pheasants at the kitchen window, winning arguments, plum cake, and the room at the top of the stairs. I want . . . I want everyone to be all right, to know they're all right, forever and ever. And . . . oh, I suppose I should like to love someone, too, but not someone who will be a storm on a moor, for he would put out all my fires with his nasty wet downpours." She paused and flicked at the water and then whispered: "Fire is so fragile, sometimes, you know."

Ginevra Bud narrowed her cinnamon-dust eyes. "Is that really what you want most of all, my girls? Come now, a dressing room's as good as a confessional. Just love, and all that rot about fires and storms? Even kittens want more than that."

Charlotte and Emily blushed and looked down into the water and until it started happening, they'd no idea really that they were about to say much the same thing.

"I want to write down—"

"All the things in my head—"

"All the stories and poems from the room at the top of the stairs—"

"The way Mr. Shakespeare or Mr. Chaucer or Lord Byron did—"

"Or Mrs. Shelley or Miss Austen—"

"And know people have read them—"

"Other than Papa and Tabitha and Aunt Elizabeth—"

"To know *everyone's* read them—"

"So that everything *inside* me is *outside* me at last."

The sisters looked sidelong at each other. Their ambitions hung in the air like Christmas garlands. They had said the most true thing in their hearts, and it had been the same thing, which is very nearly a miracle between sisters. There was nothing for it but to dry off and slip into their shifts and get after the future as fast as they could.

"Excellent!" said Ginevra. "These things are crucial. No Lady would wear a dress to a ball that she did not love, and no Lady could love a dress that did not speak to some secret desire she daren't reveal any other way. The secret language of gowns is the language of the soul, my darlings! I think I've got something for both of you. Don't tell anyone, but I raided Miss Mary's third wardrobe for the occasion. She has so many dresses she'll never notice, believe me. Now . . . dogs with white ears and ravens and moors and thunderstorms and no governesses, yes?"

Ginny pulled a gown out of her trunk and laid it on the sofa. It was so lovely Emily gasped out loud—and so did Bestminster. He blushed above the mantel, all the way back under his shell.

"I never thought in all my life I'd get to carry a garment so fine," Bestminster confessed, and bashfully drew his head back into his half-shell and even the wall itself. But his eyes still glinted in the shadows as Ginny held the dress up to Em's shoulders. "I'm so proud," the suitcase whispered. "I could *die*."

The gown was pure white silk with a long ruffling black train. Wild whips of heather blossoms ran all round the neckline and down the skirt, and the lace was knotted up out of the tiniest, most delicate thunderclouds, as thin and wispy as the rags of ghosts. Emily reached out her fingers to touch it, sure that it would curl up and turn brown like a lily if she did.

Ginevra turned to Charlotte. "And pheasants and plum cake and un-put-out-able fire and books?"

This time Ginny lifted a dress so bright it hurt to

look at. The bodice was all the colors of pheasant feathers *except* the plain brown bits. The skirt was deep, deep violet with a red petticoat, like plum skin and plum fruit, like a fire burning underneath a night sky. Charlotte's lace crackled orange and black around her neckline, tatted from real, burning embers that did not burn her skin, which was impossible, but happening all the same.

The dresses were windows into a world they had never known in Haworth, in the little house above the churchyard, in the orbits of Papa's universe, where there wasn't enough money to save all four of them at once from cold and hunger and the long life ahead. They didn't even know how to put them on. You'd need an instruction manual—or a Ginevra. The powder-girl moved like Tabitha in the kitchen, every step perfectly placed for the task. Step in here, button up there, tuck in and smooth out and lace tight and bind down. Finally, Ginny put belts round their waists, swiped from Bud & Tree Publishing, no doubt: two sturdy leather book spines, stitched in gold and stripped from some poor lost novels. The gowns were so tight Emily and Charlotte felt as though their hearts would explode or they'd throw up or both. But somehow, the clothes felt very like the arms and armor Mr. Bud said they'd want.

Ginny was frowning. She pursed her powdery lips.

"I was putting off this bit," she admitted. "I knew it was coming, but the dresses were ever so much more fun. It's only that I wanted to see you two happy. Miss Mary is never happy with her dresses. She's too rich for anything so simple as a dress to make her smile. And it's a sad lady's maid who never gets one single joyful gasp for her efforts. But . . . you must see, don't you. They'd never let a pair of . . . of . . . *breather* girls into a Lavendry ball. Oh, I know that's a dreadful way to put it, but it's just not *done*. Wildfell Ball is for loyalists, and you're the foreignest of the foreign."

"Well, if it helps any, I think I've stopped breathing." Emily laughed. The laugh turned into a cough partway through.

Ginevra fidgeted. "It's not that, it's . . . it's your skin, you see."

Charlotte ran her fingers over the purple silk of her skirt. It felt like water. "What about our skin?"

"Well . . . erm . . . you *have* it. It's all *over* you. There's little hairs on it, and moles, and it's awfully *warm* and squooshy." Ginevra's pink-powder mouth wrinkled in distaste. "I don't know how you stand it, honestly. But I've got a solution! I thought and thought and short of gluing pottery all over you, it's the best we can do. Only please don't be offended and please be willing to stand very still and not blink for quite a while?"

Ginevra Bud plunged her talcum hands into her trunk and came out with two large lavender pots and two long, wide brushes.

One was full of gold paint. The other was full of silver.

"I would imagine," Ginny said apologetically, "that this is going to itch like the devil."

FIFTEEN

Me and Mine and Bonaparte

"Come any closer, Bravey, you bloody stump, and I'll jug these two like hares and serve them to your customers," Brunty snarled. He held out his long newsprint arm toward the unflappable Captain.

Branwell stared curiously at the Magazine Man. Beads of inky sweat trickled down the pages of his head. His voice was high and tight and bitter and brittle. Brunty was getting desperate now. Things were not going to plan. Somehow, that made Bran love him a little, despite everything with the acid and the pits under Ochreopolis and the dead fly back there and him presently threatening to boil them up in a pitcher for supper. Nothing ever went to plan for *him*, after all. It was wonderful to know that Bran wasn't alone in mucking up even something as little as getting home at the end of the day. And at the same time, it wasn't wonderful at all, because he could feel in his own chest how rotten Brunty must have felt just then. Branwell didn't like empathy. It made him itch. It was a real busted cog in the design of people, is what it was. What use was there in feeling wretched just because someone else did? If only it were possible to file a complaint.

Anne's hate and fury burned so hot she hardly noticed the frost or the patchy snow. It filled her up as sure as cider and twice as spiced. She was certain that if Brunty tried to touch her one more time, just at that moment, his pages would go up in smoke.

They might have run then. Brunty was trying to get his hands round their collars again, but they dodged him easily, ducking and rolling in the frozen grass as he lunged for them like an old fat nanny puffing after a pair of runaway cats. If they had been watching it all happen to another boy and another girl, they'd have laughed themselves breathless. But Brunty was not happening to another boy and another girl. They didn't laugh at his girth swinging toward them like an exhausted boxer. They didn't laugh and they didn't run. Bran couldn't help it. He wanted to comfort the great spy.

Anne wanted revenge. For Ryecote and for herself and for Branwell and jolly well for anyone else who felt like queuing up and putting their name in.

There would be no running for a good while yet.

"Now, now, you big dumb Bruntersaurus, such language!" Captain Bravey tutted. "I'm going to have to take you over my knee and dog-ear every one of your pasty pages. You almost got away! I'll bet that felt jolly fantastic, hm? It's so close! If you're a good wee pupper I'll let you look at the border from my attic window while you wait for the constables. You Gondaliers haven't got the sense the Genii gave a hole in the ground. What happened, Time Fly sputter out on you? Aw, poor poppet. They'd last if you wouldn't ride them like the devil after a Sunday roast. You've no respect for the working class and that's the truth."

"It won't matter, once I've got back to Verdopolis. Nothing you blithering, snot-blooded Glass Towners ever say again will matter."

Captain Bravey made a mocking face. "So dramatic! Such tragedy for our Brunty! I shall play the saddest of shanties for you tonight on my saddest bagpipe. Frankly, Christmas is going to get to Verdopolis before you do, and New Year's, too." The Captain laughed, such a warm, unafraid, fatherly laugh! "My dear, stupid doorstop, you really have no luck at all. You've managed to tip yourself out at Bravey's Inn, and Bravey's Inn caters exclusively to veterans of the armed services. I assure you, all the old bears hip-deep in beer and the same stories they've told a hundred times are still *very* armed. And very drunk. And very belligerent. And very keen to get a few new war stories under their belts. All I've got to do is yell."

Brunty stopped groping for Bran and Anne. He stood up very still and very straight. He grinned.

"No, Cap'n Bravey, wait!" cried Anne.

"You don't know what he's got in his waistcoat!" shouted Bran, whose sympathy for Brunty stopped flat at Captain Bravey's noble feet.

"Go on then," sneered the Magazine Man. "Yell."

Captain Bravey did. He threw back his wooden head and bellowed two words that would bring every man inside running before their ears could even finish hearing them: "FORM UP!"

A flood of wooden wounded lads poured instantly out of the doors of Bravey's Inn. They wore eye patches where they'd taken Gondal's musket balls, and slings round their arms where they'd been crushed against their comrades, and hobbled on peg-legs where cannon fire had shredded their knees, and leaned on crutches where

Old Boney's frogs had sliced off their legs with their sabers. But each one came running with their scuffed and ancient rifles resting ready on their broken shoulders all the same. Each one would grow new arms and legs and even hearts if their Captain Bravey so much as hinted that he'd like to see it.

But Brunty paid no attention to the ramshackle squadron taking a knee and pouring powder into barrels, all for him. He reached into his waistcoat just as Bran and Anne knew he would. He yanked out his dreadful device, still oozing green acid over its strange stack of saucers and spitting blue lightning. But this time, the two of them did not watch in horror with their toes frozen to the ground. They leapt at him, tearing and pulling at his paper limbs, tearing at his parchment hair, biting wherever they could get their teeth in, screaming and scratching at their captor. Anne, in particular, said some *very* ungraceful words Branwell hadn't even known she knew. Brunty could do all he liked to them, but not Captain Bravey! Not their dear wooden soldier! He had only just come to life; they would not let him go now! But the Magazine Man paid them no mind. He was so ferociously *strong*. He flung Anne aside like she weighed no more than a hat. She slammed into a twisted black yew tree and slumped to the chilly earth with her eyes shut, just as Lord Brunty

Errata-Huntingdon struck Branwell hard across the face with his thick, illustrated fist.

Bran dropped to the ground. His blood burned bright in the white air. He was too surprised to cry. The pain soaked his mind like spilled paint and turned him the color of being *alive*. It was too big a feeling for Bran. He didn't know what to do with it any more than he'd know what to do with a dragon. The feeling bound him to the grass as well as any rope. He'd been angry before. He'd been ashamed. He'd been hurt and he'd wanted to get his own back plenty of times. But the sharpness of the pain and the brightness of the blood and the coldness of the wind and the desperation of the danger he was in made everything *shine* in a way it had never done when he was sitting at home studying French. The edges of everything shimmered brilliantly. The shadows and light were suddenly so astonishingly vivid. His jellied mind thought wildly that if only he could paint *this*, he would be the greatest artist who ever lived. And over and under all of it came the indignant fury that had always been his closest friend, closer even than Charlotte. Branwell had never wanted to utterly *erase* someone he'd felt so soft toward only a moment before. Brunty had *betrayed* his softness, even though he'd never known it existed. *Never again,* Bran swore to the blood pouring out of his nose. *Never soft again*. But even as he thought it, he knew that he liked this new, big feeling, liked it better than anything.

Brunty raised his painted eyes to heaven—was he praying? Was he laughing? Was he looking for help on its way? Captain Bravey called for ramrods to be drawn and cartridges to be rammed down. The Magazine Man just reached round to the left side of the carved ebony scroll-knob that was his belly and flicked a brass latch hidden under his ribs. His stomach creaked open like a rusty, round door. Bran thought he was going to be sick. Then, quick as a page turning, he was fascinated. *I'm going to see what's inside them. What's inside all these people made of things! Or at least, what's inside Brunty.*

Inside Brunty was a dark, empty bookshelf. It was very clean, with no cobwebs or dust or spiders.

The Master Spy of Gondal placed his oozing, spitting machine on the shelf within him, shut his gut, and locked it fast. He looked triumphantly at Branwell, his only audience.

"What is it, young master Nobody? You wanted to know, didn't you?"

Bran nodded mutely, helplessly. Brunty waved his device in the frosted air.

"It's a Voltaic Pyle! I stole it from Mr. Volta's laboratory in Switzerland. Just swiped it—right out of your world and into mine. I think he called it a *battery* when I broke his fingers getting it free. Very stubborn, your Swiss. That's what your wooden friends are so cross about. Not supposed to go hopping the fence into Breathertown. But why not, I say? You can trip on your own faces and get up in Glass Town. Why shouldn't I see Switzerland?"

Branwell blinked. He shrugged uncertainly. "What's a bat-tree?" he asked.

"It's what'll make Glass Town and Gondal equal at last, that's what it is!" the Magazine Man snapped. He seemed very put out that Branwell had not gasped or shown other signs of awe. "It gives me power."

Suddenly, the capital O's of Brunty's eyes looked terribly young and afraid.

"I . . . I actually don't know exactly what's going to happen next," Brunty whispered. "If it all goes pear-shaped, tell my sisters I tried—"

But Branwell never heard what the poor man wanted his sisters to know. Brunty the Inking Liar, Brunty the Godforsaken Gondalier, Can't-Take-Him-Anywhere Brunty, Brunty the Spying Sack of Slime, Brunty the Miserable Fat Folio, went rigid as a streetlamp. His arms shot straight up to the cloudy sky. His jaw hung slack. Inside his mouth, his wood-pulp teeth began to glow green and smoke.

"Make ready!" cried Captain Bravey.

His raggedy regiment thumped their oaken chests in the jumbled joy and terror and regret and blind red rapture all soldiers feel in the moment before the fight begins. Whatever happened next, they would have a new story to tell round the hearth of Bravey's Inn. Some of them would, anyhow.

"Fire!" roared the Captain, and they did, but so did Brunty.

The volley of loyal Glass Town musket balls banged across the frosted meadow in an arc so perfect military historians would have fallen to their knees in awe. Anne moaned and began to stir against her knotty yew tree. She only just managed to convince her eyes to open as the bullets began to unfurl into the stout Brown Besses they'd seen in Port Ruby, with their brown aprons and brown rolling pins and their stout brown hearts. Anne's vision blurred and wriggled and through a groggy silver film of pain she saw the musket girls explode in gouts of ultramarine flame. She tried to scream for them, but nothing came out. Her head lolled round, trying to find someone she knew in the smoke.

Brunty was gone. Or, at least, he wasn't Brunty anymore. The thick, soapy green acid of his machine foamed out of his mouth. It rimmed the scrolls of his

perfectly arranged hair. It seeped through the joints of
his elbows and knees. It overflowed the capital O's of his
eyes like moss climbing out of two broken windows. The
blue lightning no longer snapped or spit or crackled. It
exploded from the tips of his fingers and boomed out of
the middle of his chest and even dribbled horribly out of
his nostrils. Wherever the lightning hit a musket ball,

it detonated, and the half-uncurled little warrior inside vanished into half a thimble full of ash. The headlines on Brunty's waistcoat shivered. They broke open into new print: HEAR YE HEAR YE, READ ALL ABOUT IT! THE TRI- UMPH OF BRUNTY'S AMAZING BATTERY! VICTORY ASSURED! V-GT DAY HAS COME AT LAST! The lightning kept coming and coming, firing at crazy angles, seeming to suck more strength from the heavy clouds above. Bravey's men scat- tered and took cover behind stumps, woodpiles, inside the thick wooden door of the pub. Someone inside began passing buckets of water out down the line, to put out the flames before they could creep toward the inn with its thatched and naked roof and its rooms full of wooden men.

The Captain did not flinch. He just shouted:

"Form ranks, lads, form ranks! Prime and load! He's just one man! Not even a man, he's just Brunty! *Naughty. Little. Pupper!*"

The air smelled of old coins and ozone and lamp oil and a house still burning to the ground. Anne tried to stand, but she was so dizzy. The tree felt real and true against her back. Everything in front of her felt mad and gruesome and wrong and she wanted it to turn right back around and go back where it came from.

Brunty began to laugh. Then, his laughter boiled

into a scream. A howl, really. And once he started, he couldn't stop. Green smoke hissed up from his body. Burning holes opened up in the text that covered his clothes and his face and his hair and his hands, the text that *was* Brunty. The block-print headlines on his waistcoat sizzled together into a wet black mass of nothing. Acid ate up whole chapters of him as Bran and Anne watched, wanting it to stop, wanting to be free of him, wanting no one else to get hurt. Under all that great pile of wanting they could not twitch the smallest muscle. The Magazine Man groaned and screeched and wept. And slowly, slowly, while his fingers flung lightning at the world, he dragged his hand toward the latch on the side of his scroll-knob belly. The hand did not want to obey. It wanted to keep living the life electric. Brunty the Godforsaken Gondalier lifted his eyes to Anne. Green foam poured like moldy tears out of the once-elegant printed O's of his eyes.

"Please," he rasped through dissolving teeth. "I can't turn it off. I don't know how. It hurts. Wasn't supposed to hurt."

Anne found her feet. Her head throbbed and her spine ached, but she stood up all the same. She stood and looked at the sorry man writhing in pain and reaching out to her for help, reaching out for Anne, who could not even bear for one solitary field mouse to go hungry in the garden if she could help it. She stood, and watched him burn, and did nothing.

"Poor bugger," Anne said, and the smile on her face was cold and cruel.

Branwell took a step away from his sister. She was only eight years old. She wasn't supposed to know how to be cold yet. Had they taught her that, the three of them? He remembered suddenly a night years ago, when Anne had been so small and so quiet. It had been deep night, and the fire burned in the parlor, and they had still been six, then. Maria and Elizabeth had been tatting lace by candlelight. Papa had asked Anne what she wanted most in all the world. Just a silly thing papas ask sometimes. But Anne had looked at him with huge, serious, willful eyes and said: *age and experience*. What kind of girl said that, and not: *I'd very much like a pony, thank you*. It had made him shudder then and it made him shudder now. And in that eerie winter light all shadowed with acid flames, Anne looked quite, quite grown.

Branwell ran. He ran up the hill, toward Bravey's Inn, away from that old, knowing look on his little sister's face, away from the book burning to death on the grass. He felt as though his heart were crying and his eyes were beating. He snatched one of the fire-buckets from a retired corporal's hands and dashed back down the hill, trying not to slosh all the water out as his legs thumped against the half-frozen ground. Finally, Bran stopped, his breath hitching with sobs and hiccups and misery and the brightness of battle.

"Everyone mucks up sometimes!" he screamed at Brunty. The Magazine Man looked at him like Branwell had just turned into a camel. A sputtering bolt of sickly flame shot past Bran's head, missing him by the space of a fly's wing. Branwell scowled. Well, of course it made no sense *now*, but it had seemed just the perfect thing to say ten minutes ago, when the Gondalier had looked so beaten. Branwell sighed and dumped out the bucket of water onto Brunty's smoking, boiling chest. The beastly ultramarine light went out of Brunty and he crumpled to the ground, his burnt fingers still working, grasping, twitching.

"If you'd have stopped hollering so loud, I might have gotten a word before now," Branwell complained.

Anne's heart sank down into the icy pit of her stomach as a horrible cry bashed through the woods behind her. The spine that had hardened into diamond in her went wobbly as water. The cold, cruel expression vanished from her dear face. Anne knew that cry. She'd made it herself enough times when they were playing soldiers and Bran killed Captain Bravey *again* and forced Anne to act out a noble death for him and give him a state funeral in the butter dish. She turned and bolted up the hill.

Branwell was already running at a dead sprint across the hoarfrost to the fallen warrior in the grass.

Please don't let it be Bravey, he thought, and Anne did, too. *Please don't let it be Bravey. Let it be someone we don't know, someone we never named and slept with and made to march across the parlor in formation.*

But it was. It was Bravey. Half his body was charred black where the last fork of Brunty's unnatural lightning had struck him. Bran had not thought a wooden eye would look any different dead than alive, but Captain Bravey's did. They had been such a nice walnut-wood color before. Now they were white as birch-bark. Anne flung herself onto Bravey's scorched, stiff chest. Branwell let her. She was a girl, after all, and girls could fling themselves and cry and that. Sometimes he envied them, but not often. He wiped dried blood off his upper lip. The danger past, Bravey's loyal men crowded round. They took off their caps and held them to their hearts. One old Quartermaster, with splendid muttonchops carved into his rowan-wood face and a long bandolier full of vials and capsules and cartridges round his barrel-chest, began to weep golden sap onto the Captain's gentle forehead.

"Stop it!" snapped Anne.

Branwell recoiled. His lips curled up into a snarl as he got ready to scold her stupid for being so callous in the face of tragedy. What was *wrong* with her?

"Stop it right this instant!" the girl cried. "What are you blubbering about? Go back inside at once and get that moony stuff Crashey gave Leftenant Gravey that fixed him up and made him all alive again! What's it called? Grog! I know one of you has some, you bunch of matchsticks! What are you waiting for?" Anne was crying now. Tears dripped off her chin and her nose was running and she felt quite silly and quite desperate. Through her tears, Captain Bravey's body looked no different than Maria's and Lizzie's had before they buried them. The stillness of them, the ghastly *stillness* that meant nothing and everything. But this time, it would be different. It *could* be different. It *had* to be different. It would be different now and different forever. Yet through all her grief and bashed-up head, Anne had remembered the first rule of spying. Do Not Ask Plainly for What You Seek or Nobody Will Tell You Nothing. She'd pretended grog meant nothing to her, that she couldn't remember its name. Why *not* give it to a poor defenseless little girl who couldn't scheme against a dust-bunny, and certainly was not planning to do anything extra with it? *What a funny thing it is that I can think so sensibly and feel so frantically at the same time,* Anne thought. And then the feeling took over again. "What's the matter with you?" she wept. "He's your Captain! Do it and everything will be all right! Make everything all right! Please! This is the place where everything can be all right! Even if it can't back home, it can here, and you're just *standing* there!" The wooden soldiers looked at one another uncomfortably. They shuffled their heavy feet. Anne rubbed her eyes and glared up at them. Grief turned its cards face down inside her and a sneering rage dealt itself in. "Oh, I see how it is! You want to hold out and give it to him once the *breathers* have gone. Well, go and get splintered because my brother's already drunk that mishmash! If Crashey and Bravey and Gravey and all the rest trusted us, I daresay you might get a bloody move on!" A chilly terror crept through Anne. It was only an inn in the woods, after all. What if no one had thought to bring any? It wasn't too likely to die of singing bad drinking songs off-key or eating too many fried potatoes. What if there was nothing up there in that stone house but beer and memories?

What was left of Brunty gave a last strangled, bubbling sigh in the distance. The wooden soldiers knew that sound as well as a bugle. They saluted downfield. The enemy was dead, but that was no reason not to honor him. Branwell did not salute. He stared at Anne, impressed despite himself. Perhaps she was not so little and useless as all that. Perhaps she was not so harmless as all that.

"Orright, Orright," the muttonchopped Quarter-master grumbled. "There's no need to carry on like that, young lady. It ain't about nobody *breathing* or nothing. We don't like to break out the grog this close to the bor-der. S'dangerous. Gondal's got eyes and ears and noses *and* sticky fingers; I'd think you'd know that'n all. Loose stoppers will come a-cropper, that's what the Duke says."

Anne's tears came roaring back, only this time she was just relieved, relieved to have been right, relieved for Captain Bravey, relieved that at least someone was prepared. She did wish she didn't cry so easily. But she decided to forgive herself just now, since the circum-stances were rather out of the ordinary.

"There, there," said the Quartermaster awkwardly, and patted Anne's hair as though she were a strange and irritable dog.

Muttonchops (whose real name was Quartermaster Stumps, as he was missing one leg at the knee and one arm at the elbow) reached round the back of his bandolier and pulled out a vial wrapped up with leather and bits of speckled fur. He knelt on his good knee, even though the cold pained all his parts frightfully. Stumps knocked his wooden head fondly against the skull of his dear Captain, with whom he'd served and supped all those many years. He worked at the stopper with old, creaky fingers.

"Don't spill it, greasy-paws," said one of the Sergeants. "That's the lot. Boaster used up the rest wrestling bears. There won't be time to send for more."

Finally, the cork popped free with a happy little gasp.

"How *dare* you," a flat, furious voice hissed.

Branwell, Anne, Quartermaster Stumps, and the raggedy regiment turned as one.

Brunty stood behind them.

The ruins of Brunty, at least. He was no longer a jolly fat villain. He looked as though all the air had gone out of him and left only a newsstand fluttering in a frigid wind. The pages of his face hung down in long rags, torn and smeared and streaked with brackish burns. His hair lay unrolled and unpinned down his back. His ribbon nose was full of tiny holes where sprays of acid had hit his face, and the glasses teetering there were shattered and twisted. His greatcoat was soaked in bat-tree acid and the ink that is the blood of a book, so sopping wet you couldn't tell that it had ever been so finely sewn from copies of the *Leeds Intelligencer*. His belly hung open on its hinge. He had somehow managed to drag the machine back onto the shelf of his heart. Its saucers no longer burned green and blue. It just dripped sour water. No lightning howled out of him. The headlines on his waistcoat said nothing at all. But the foaming muck still bubbled behind his eyes, and he still had strength enough in him to kick the crutch out from beneath a hapless infantryman and crush his good leg beneath a heavy leather-bound foot. The rest of the men roared and lunged as one toward the Gondalier—but Brunty moved one broken hand back toward the bat-tree in his chest. The machine looked dead and drowned. But if it was not . . . if it was not all those wounded wooden boys would go up like kindling. They shrank away.

"You unbelievable *cheats*. I knew Glass Towners had no shame. But I never thought you'd do it *right in front of me*. Rubbing it in my face like a pack of rich boys in the schoolyard! Boney was right about you. All of you. Glass Town is a scourge. All you do is take and take and take and use and waste and laugh at the rest of us. You have no *right*. It's not yours. You bloody villains. You horrid *thieves*." Brunty leaned toward them. He smelled like rot and bile. "Give it to me. Give it to me now. It's mine."

"Well, it's not yours, Brunt-o," wheezed Quartermaster Stumps. "That's sort of the whole point, my lad. Grog belongs to Glass Town. We invented it. We had to, didn't we? Or else we'd all be speaking Gondalish and where would that get us?"

"You'd never *have* it if it weren't for Gondal!" screeched Brunty. He reached out his scorched fingers toward the flask of grog, but didn't take it. The Magazine Man seemed almost afraid to touch it at all.

"We'd never have *needed* it if it weren't for Gondal!" Quartermaster Stumps bellowed.

Brunty turned to Bran and Anne as though they were judges on a high bench, and if he could convince them, the war might never have happened and no one might ever have died. "They make it out of stuff that only grows in Gondal," he whined. "They've got a secret recipe we can't crack, and we've sent more souls after it than you can possibly imagine. But Glass Town? They disassemble our best boys and then send raiding parties to do their bloody shopping in the Gondal wilds every month. If they didn't, they'd all die when we shoot them, like they're *supposed* to. Like *we* do. Grog is *ours*." He dropped his head like whatever barely held him up had been cut in two. When Brunty raised it again, his eyes bulged with hate and agony and they were fixed on Quartermaster

Stumps and his bandolier. "My mother died, you piece of blighted driftwood. My mother died and everything in the world went wrong and my sisters and me starved and I had to do such terrible things to live, just to live, until I could claw my way to my stepbrother and take back one tiny shred of a future for us, and if you Glassers weren't such a ruddy pack of gangsters with rotten onions for souls, it never would have happened because I could have . . . I could have just made her a pretty cup of groggy tea and she'd have got up again right as a new edition, but I couldn't, and she *died*. She was perfect and beautiful and kind and she died anyway, you horrors, you mockers, you *wolves*; she died and you just keep coming back."

The creature collapsed sobbing on top of the ancient Quartermaster.

Anne covered her mouth with her hands. *Poor, poor Brunty!* she thought. *Only he's not poor Brunty, he's awful! But poor, poor Brunty.*

"Our mother died, too," whispered Branwell. The softness was coming back, no matter how he told it to stay where it was and mind its own business.

Brunty growled into the soggy earth. Stumps tried to push him off, but Brunty weighed more than the moon. "Yeah? Jolly good thing for you! I don't care! You're with *them*. You don't even know what death *is*."

"Yes, we do," Anne whispered. "It's you who doesn't know."

"Death is a churchyard so full of people the earth towers over the street," Branwell said softly. "Death is your mother and your sisters down there under all the others."

Anne squeezed her brother's hand. "Death is cold and blue and it doesn't move and it doesn't care about anything. But at least *you* live in a place where *some* people come back, sometimes. Only one person ever came back where we were born, and He didn't get to stay. Our mother died and our sisters died and the only people who came back were *us*. We came back to the house and it was so quiet, so quiet . . . !"

The Magazine Man had enough shame left in him not to answer. He got up and jabbed the toe of his boot into the Quartermaster's ribs. He straightened his ruined back. He latched his scroll-knob belly shut.

"Well. There it is, then. Something between us. Like a chain. Soon enough, Lady Sorrowful, no one will have to know what we know. Not in Glass Town, not in Gondal. It's all *their* fault, don't you see? If only they could share, the world would already be as it should!"

"You mean Old Boney would already have conquered the world and we'd already be kissing his boney feet."

The Quartermaster coughed. His men helped him up, gave him his crutch again.

"Even a child knows how to share!" Brunty shot back. He turned to Branwell and Anne. "You're better off with me. *I* will share with you. Every good thing. Me and mine and Bonaparte. You can have everything you want. And when we are done, who will not call us heroes, while they live forever and a day?"

Branwell and Anne looked down at poor dead Captain Bravey, scorched as black as a gentle-hearted fly.

"You won't 'share' a single all-fired thing with them on my watch, pupper. You'll go straight to—" Stumps began.

But he did not finish.

Godforsaken Brunty bellowed at the ranks of broken toys. He shoved his fist into the remains of his pockets and drew out a handful of the red and glinting sands of time—glinting because the shards of their bottle stuck up out of his palm like an awful garden. He threw the sand in the soldiers' faces and roared:

"DROP. DEAD."

A great thrum and buzz filled the cold winter wilds of the Calabar Woods. Far faster than Ryecote had managed to find them in the bowels of Ochreopolis, another elephantine Time Fly skittered toward them across the blasted heath. The soldiers shouted and scrambled to their feet, to their rifles, to their powder. Quartermaster Stumps reached his arms out to Branwell and Anne. But the fly skidded in between them, blocking their rescue with his fat, black, iridescent body.

"Hullo, sirs and ladies!" chortled the fly merrily. "Isn't it a loverly day we're having! Air's crisp as old bread! The name's Boarham, son of Peachmuck, son of Scraphole, son of Ol' Cowskin—"

The Magazine Man seized Bran and Anne again, and his arms were no less strong for having been tortured till they'd nearly fallen off. This time, the children just went slack, resigned.

As she fell back against Brunty's tattered, wheezing chest, Anne could feel the Quartermaster's flask hidden there. It pressed up against her spine. She glanced over the hump of Boarham's thorax. None of the soldiers had even realized it was gone yet. But they would, of course. They would know the minute they tried to bring Captain Bravey back. Tears blurred her eyes. *The only difference between a thief and a spy is what you steal,* Anne thought drowsily. *And Brunty's stolen everything that matters. Poor Captain Bravey. He really was. So marvelously brave.*

"Shut your cursed mouth, bug," Brunty snapped. "You'll be dead in an hour and no one cares who spat you out. Gondal. Verdopolis. The Bastille. Now, now, now!"

The woods wobbled. Bravey's Inn shuddered. Anne began to slide her fingers behind her, ever so gently. The silver, frozen, ruined meadow groaned. The whole wintry world seemed to, somehow, and only once, *tick*. Like a minute hand juddering into place.

And

then

—they were in Gondal. But Branwell and Anne never saw the hills or the blue houses all in tidy rows or the silvery sunlight on Lake Elseraden or the meadows of Zedora or the spires of Regina. They simply disappeared from the meadow and the woods and Bravey's Inn and reappeared within the walls of a great prison, with the door already locked fast behind them.

SIXTEEN

The Wildfell Ball

Charlotte and Emily stood at the top of a long, curling staircase made of jewels so scuffed and ancient they had faded to the color of milk. Vines of heather and bilberry and lobelia flowers raced up one banister. Wine-grapes and wild lavender tumbled down the other. A man slapped together out of broken brandy snifters looked them up and down with one frosted eyebrow raised disdainfully. Charlotte straightened her back and placed the little card Ginevra had given them into his outstretched hand. Candlelight glanced off her perfectly pinned and curled hair, her skin, her eyelashes, her lips: all painted as gold as a goose's egg. Not one square inch of plain skin-and-bones Charlotte was left. She was nothing but gold. Emily raised her own eyebrow at the same angle as the snifter-man, but somehow, on her new silver face it came out less *disdainful* and more *furious and prone to violence*. He looked suddenly alarmed and turned away from this terrifying metal girl immediately.

"May I present Lady Currer Bell and Lady Ellis Bell of Thrushcross Grange!" roared the herald to the shimmering throng spread out below the staircase.

No one paid him the least attention.

But Charlotte and Emily could not make themselves move. Now was the time to descend the stairs gracefully and melt into the crowds. That was what was meant to happen next. But they could not force themselves to do it. The great hall dazzled them so completely that they just stood there like two bathers at the edge of a swimming hole where everyone else has already jumped in.

The vast mansion that hosted the Wildfell Ball had no roof. The buttresses and garlands were the wheeling silver stars of Glass Town and a warm evening wind conducted the music. Huge thistle blossoms hung like chandeliers from nothing at all. Their spiky petals burned with blue fire. Indigo couches lined walls sheathed in magenta wallpaper; but the walls ended cleanly twenty feet in the air. Bronze candlesticks as tall as two men stood everywhere like sunflowers, boasting fifty candles each. On a little velvet stage, a quartet in lavender wigs played a maddeningly fast waltz on a violet harpsichord, a plum cello, a bassoon the color of raisins, and a drum hollowed out of mulberry stump. The ballroom floor was checkered amethyst and black marble, reflecting hundreds of feet spinning in steps so complicated Emily thought she could practice till she was eighty and never learn them. The Wildfell Ball was a blur of people. Tall, handsome limeskin soldiers lounged in their uniforms, Lords and Ladies danced in their finery, servants rushed here and there with platters and goblets and armfuls of new shoes in case anyone wore theirs out. And there, there in the middle of it all like a cake topper, stood the Duke of Wellington, his burning iron wings lighting up the dance floor as a laughing young maiden made of playing cards pulled and prodded him to join in the fun.

Each Lord, each Lady, each soldier, each servant was terribly young, just like Wellington, just like Bonaparte, just like Charlotte and Emily. Even the oldest reveler they saw wheel by could not have been much more than sixteen or seventeen.

Strangest of all, a woman made of roses hung miserably in a cage above the party. Below her, Copenhagen, the great blue water-lion, stared up intently, his sea-foam whiskers twitching, batting at the bottom of the cage with one huge, salty paw. The cage rocked back and forth. The rose-lady hissed. The lion purred and chortled in feline glee and whacked it again.

"Come on, Charlotte," Emily whispered. "Er. Currer. Lady Bell. We can do this. It's just like playing with dolls and wooden soldiers at home. We know their names and their histories better than they do—we made them up in the room at the top of the stairs! I don't know how that can be, but it is. We'd better stop marveling at it and start using it to our advantage. This should be as easy as one of our games."

"I'm more worried about the things we didn't make up, Ellis," Charlotte said smoothly. A new name was nothing to a liar as practiced as she. "Wehglon, Acroofc-roomb, Captain Bravey, Verdopolis? Those feel good and safe to me. Old friends. But we never imagined Port Ruby or Bestminster or . . . or . . . *this*. Our games have gone on without us and I don't think we're all such good friends anymore." Charlotte took a deep breath. She put it all in a neat stack underneath her heart to worry at later. "Buck up," she said.

"Be brave," Emily answered her.

But there was no one to do the other parts. Two was nothing. What good were two bees out of four?

A voice bellowed out above the noisy throng. Someone was coming toward them, making his apologies as he dodged dance-traffic. Someone made of wood.

"Well, cut my rations and wet my powder! Never thoughtmagined I'd see you girls in a place like this! I hardly recognized you! What's that all over your face-parts? Did you change your hair?" Sergeant Crashey was panting by the time he got to the bottom of the jeweled staircase. The wood of his face had gone from ash to cherry. "You surely do look grandnificent, if you'll take a compliment from an old army-man! What're ya standing up there for? It's boring up there! Much better down here. Down here there's me!"

Charlotte and Emily found their feet at last and bolted down the steps toward the one familiar thing in all the world and hugged it fiercely. Sergeant Crashey cleared his throat to rid himself of the embarrassment of this sudden outpouring of breather affection. The song changed to something slower and kinder to tired feet. Dancers drifted toward the wallpaper to rest their nerves.

Charlotte wiped her eyes, careful not to disturb her golden paint. Emily shook his hand vigorously, hardly able to stop herself, so the handshake went on, really, far too long. "What are you doing here, Crashey? I thought Wildfell was only for the richies! Is Cap'n Bravey with you? And Gravey? And Cheeky and Rogue?"

The wooden soldier looked terrifically offended. He clutched his heart. "How do you know I'm not a richie? I could be. Could be sitting my arse-end on a fortune the size of Mount Pavonine! You've never asked me my busindustry. I could be the Crown Prince for all the knowledge you've got in your block about the House o' Crashey. And even if I was broke as a bloody wheel, Her Majesty's armed forces are welcome at any society to-doering. 'S only fair, as we put our skins on the line so this lot can have their canapés. Gravey and Rogue will be around here someeverwhere. As for the Cap'n, he's off indulging himself. Can't soldier all the time! And didn't we all have dreams before we heard the drum? He's got an inn out in the wirralywilds of Calabar Wood. Dunno why he likes it up there in the freeze. Too close to the border for the tastes of me. Practically dumps his rub-bish out the back window into Gondal! Mostly he puts up grizzlelimp old army boys, the shot up and the sawn off and the slumped over. Bravey's an unforgivlievable softie. I expect sooner or later, we all end up at Bravey's Inn." The oaken Sergeant stopped and looked about. He lifted up one of Emily's arms, then one of Charlotte's. "Hold on. I could've sworn there used to be more of you! Where's the little monster and the wee moppet?"

"We did *try* to get Brunty safely to the P-House," Emily moaned. A silver curl of hair slid out of her bun and lay gracefully against her collarbone. "But he sprang himself and kidnapped Bran and Anne and they've run away to Gondal and we've got to get them back, we've just *got* to, even though we're far past catching the evening express train home now. He's our brother and she's our sister and he's a beastly little beetle sometimes but he's *our* beastly little beetle. We've come to rouse up a gang to go after them. You'll help us, won't you, Crashey? You'll come. You must. It's a real military operation! Under cover of darkness! Search and rescue! Espionage in the black of night!"

"I don't reckonoitter many of the peacocks round here will be too keen on buckling up to a couple of breathers and crossing borders with ill intent, I'm sorry to say it."

"That's why we're in disguise, sir." Charlotte curtsied a little. "Incognito. We're Lady Currer and Lady Ellis Bell, in from Thrushcross to enrich ourselves culturally. Lord Bell is *such* a country boor, you know." She winked and batted her eyelashes as she imagined an upper-class girl might. She pulled it off rather well. Emily touched her silver fringe with a nervous hand. She didn't think she looked that winning when she fluttered her eyelashes.

She mostly looked like she had something stuck in them. "Now, if you don't want to lead our rescue party, that's perfectly understandable, but you mustn't give us up."

"Wouldn't dream of it, my lamb kabobs!" Sergeant Crashey nicked a flute of champagne off a passing butler's platter and blew a little golden note on it, smacking his lips. "Now, if you mean to rattle hearts and rustle minds, you'll need more than a new paint jobbie. If you want to raise an army, however small, you've got to have *intelliconaissance*. The slope of the high ground! The lay of the land! Look around, my girls! Who do you recognize?"

"That's the Duke of Wellington," Charlotte said at once, pointing her gloved finger at the Iron Duke, his many-metaled handsome face laughing over a mug of something hot and heady. Emily rolled her eyes. She couldn't think of anything more boring than the Duke of Wellington. *I'd wager he sleeps with a stick jammed in his teeth so he doesn't lose that stiff upper lip to a stray dream,* she thought. *His lion is ever so much better! If I had my way I'd roll out a ball of yarn for him right this second.*

"That's Copenhagen under the Lady in the cage, though I've no idea who she is," Emily ventured. "And you're Sergeant Crashey. That's all, really."

The wooden soldier clapped his birch hands. "Oh, *brilliorgeous*! I do so love to say a story! Gather round me pant-legs, Misses Bell, I present to you: THE COMICAL FARCE OF EVERYBODY WHO'S ANYBODY AND HOW THEY GOT THAT WAY, BY SERGEANT CRASH C. CRASHEY ESQUIRE, WHO MIGHT BE RICH, YOU DON'T KNOW DO YOU, THAT'S RIGHT YOU DON'T. Let's start with the Lady in the cage, shall we? Hullo, Copey. She's not a mousie, leave her be, there's a pussycat."

Copenhagen purred loudly and nuzzled Crashey's head. His seawater mane sloshed over the soldier's uniform, soaking him through. The woman in the cage stared down at them with two purple primrose eyes blooming in a white tea-rose face. Her hair was a river of plump red roses so brilliant and dark and thick they seemed to suck the light and life from everything around them so that they could glow all the brighter. Her limbs were thin, green, and sharp. Thorny vines twisted together into fingers and arms. She wore a black gown whose skirt was one single, stupendous black tulip. The bodice was a charcoal fleur-de-lis wrapped round her petaled chest. *That's the flower on all the French flags*, Charlotte thought. *I wonder if it's Gondal's flower, too?*

Crashey let the oceanic lion gnaw on one wooden hand a bit. He knocked on the bottom of the cage with the other. "That there is what you call spoils of war. Our most precious prize-oner—Old Boney's own wife, Josephine! We nicked her right out of Reversailles while she was sleeping! Capital operatiomission. Had her locked up ten years now, and don't plan to spring her any time soonlike."

"Drop dead, *mes chers diables!*" Josephine said cheerfully, and waggled her pink fingers at them.

"Now, Josey, you'll prickle my feelings if you're not careful," Crashey said solemnly.

"Don't be silly," Emily said. "She couldn't be a day over sixteen. You couldn't possibly have kept her in there since she was six!"

The wooden soldier scratched his head. He counted on his fingers. Then, he got lost, shook out his hands, and counted again. "Dunno, kittens. Maybossibly when you say a year and I say a year we don't meandicate the same thing. Sometimes a day in my own room thinking my own thoughts feels just like a year. Sometimes, when I tell a long, complicatory story, years go by in a word or two. If I had the right fork I could probably spear one to the plate, but they're slippery as oysternails, the little snots. I don't like numbers. Not good for me waistline. Don't feel too badly for her, mind you. We only went Josey-fishing after Boney's spies snatched our Victoria and locked her up in the Bastille when she weren't nothing but a baby! 'Course it wasn't the Bastille then. Those're her parents, there, the Duke and Duchess of Can't." He pointed to a tall, slim couple standing in a corner. He was made of soft ermine; she, mother-of-pearl. "Come on, then, I'll intropresent you! Strap your best curtsy on and scrub up your vowels. We're going in headfirst!"

The Duchess of Can't wept softly when she saw Charlotte and Emily.

"Forgive me," she said in a weak, high, breathy voice. "I can't help but see my own lost daughter in every grown-up girl. Perhaps she would have looked like you. Perhaps she would have danced. . . ." Shimmering tears poured down her delicate, pearly face. Her husband patted her shoulder absentmindedly, staring off into the distance at nothing.

"May I presentroduce to you Misses Currer and Ellis Bell of Thrushcross Grange?" Crashey said, and very prettily.

The Duke of Can't bowed stiffly, his ermine face yellowed and spotted with grief. His wife held a lace handkerchief to her silvery mouth.

Sergeant Crashey bowed grandly and kissed the Duke's hand. "Perhaps you two could show the young folk how real dancing's done? I'm told they've been very well brought-upducated, despite living in the dullery of the countruralside, but there's no substitute for watching the masters at work!"

"Terribly sorry," whispered the Duke, too deep in his sorrow to speak up. "We can't."

Crashey bowed low. "Then, mayhappenation the Duchess is picking over the market stalls for a new Lady in waiting or two?"

"Oh, darlings," sighed the Duchess, feeling horribly faint, "I *would* like to take you on, ever so much. You seem perfectly exquisite. Truly, as lovely as my Victoria would be if she were here before me as you are. But I simply *can't*."

Charlotte tried to remember something about Anne's Victoria. She'd never much cared about her youngest sister's tiny little story of a Princess no one had ever heard of. Let Annie have something of her own. Something that didn't get blown up in glorious sieges of the pantry every other afternoon. Every girl needed a story of her own.

"Doesn't your daughter have a second name?" Charlotte asked innocently.

"Why, yes!" sniffed the Duchess of Can't. "But I can't bear to say it. It burns my tongue like ice."

Emily combed back through every night she'd heard

Annie whispering to her doll under the blankets. "Alexandrina?" The Duchess nodded in mute misery. "And she had a spaniel or something, didn't she? Dash?"

The Duke clamped down on Emily's silver arm like a sword-blow. "Do you mean to say you've seen her? I can't believe it. Darling, I can't feel my cheeks. Who are you, child?"

"No, no, not at all, sir, you're hurting me!" What could Emily say? My sister named one of her dolls Alexandrina Victoria and after we've all gone to bed she makes her dance with all the wooden soldiers, one after the other? They'd put her away and all would be lost.

"We've only heard the stories, like everyone else in Glass Town who mourns the loss of her most precious jewel," Charlotte said without the slightest hesitation, in a voice like cool water. She even lifted the Duke's hand from Emily's elbow, which was frightfully familiar.

"Oh," sighed the Duke and Duchess. They sagged together, their fine clothes wrinkling. "We can't thank you enough for your kind words. Carry on, sally forth . . . whatever the young folk say nowadays."

Emily stared. She'd only ever seen Charlotte lie to Tabitha about stars falling to earth and spilled salt and the occasional tear in her stockings. But now Charlotte's lies spooled out like perfect, silken thread, and whatever they touched stuck together fast.

The Sergeant swept them away, rolling his eyes once the royals couldn't see him do it. "There you have it!" he laughed, shaking his head. "Does what it says on the tin. Just the most *dreadppalling* people! I don't care what rank they've pasted on. You'd think it might be different if they hadn't lost their girl? Nope! Goes with the Duchy and the ring and the rest. They *can't* do a bloody thing. Well, *I* can't imagine them trying to order supper. Now! This here is Dr. Home, physician to the Crown and damnably fine vivisectionist. You know what that meanifies?"

"An anatomist. Someone who studies the human body by examining the dead," Charlotte said eagerly.

"And a smashing chemist, and naturalist, and cricketer. As well as a personal friend to yours trulyself. See? You wouldn't think a lowly Sergeant in the lowly old army would know such fine people, but I do. So what else don't you know, hm?"

Charlotte and Emily laughed a little and admitted that their old toy soldier could be the Sultan of the Moon and they wouldn't have the foggiest idea. *Only wouldn't we know?* thought Emily. *We never played Sultans on the Moon, so he oughtn't be one. Then again, we never played Wildfell Ball, either.*

A tall, thin man folded out of the sort of black leather that doctor's satchels are made of straightened up and looked them over. He had been feeling the forehead of a lovely young lady whose skin was patterned over with a thousand bronze coins. A fountain of penny-curls crowned her head and tumbled down her slender back.

"I hope you're both *very* well?" the doctor said in a voice like stitches sliding neatly through a needle. But somehow, when he said it, Dr. Home sounded more excited at the prospect of what might happen if they were *not* well, rather than anxious that they should be in good health.

"And here we have Miss Mary Percy." Crashey kissed the penny-girl's hand. "Heiress of Angria and paramour of the Marquis of Douro."

"That's not a very nice word," Emily said, embarrassed for the beautiful Mary. "You shouldn't call people things in French without their permission." Her heart beat faster. Ginevra Bud was lady's maid to this gleaming copper woman. Emily and Charlotte were wearing her gowns. She felt terribly exposed. Mary Percy raked her gaze up and down the pair of them. She narrowed her eyes and started to say one thing, but ended on another.

"Oh, don't be silly, dearheart, I don't mind a bit." Mary Percy laughed and patted Emily's gloved hand.

When the heiress touched her, Em felt the weight of real metal on her painted silver arm, and shivered. "Truth in advertising! I prefer everyone to know everything. That way, no one has to suffer any nasty whispers in the powder room. Don't you agree?"

Crashey shrugged and took Mary at her word. He plowed on within earshot of everyone. "They say Douro explained it all patientsweet to his wife Marian. How he loved Miss Mary and couldn't live without her, how if she held him back he'd only grow to hate her, that sort of rubbishnrot. And after he'd said his piece, being the obliging sort Marian always was, the Marchioness up and killed herself dead so as not to be a bother."

"Marian always was such a lamb." Mary smiled humbly. Everything she said sounded careless and free, yet taut as a violin string, all at once. "A true Lady always knows when to make her exit. Though I prefer to focus on the entrance." She turned her pretty bronze head to one side like a bird. She lifted one coppery eyebrow half an inch. "What utterly charming dresses you both have! You *must* give me the name of your girl."

Emily coughed.

Charlotte did not miss her cue. "Geraldine Branch," she said distractedly, as though a mere dressmaker was far beneath her notice. "Out of Smokeshire."

"My stars! I don't know her," said Mary in that same careless-but-careful tone. "I do believe I know the name of every seamstress in Angria and I have never heard those syllables together in all my days!"

Emily dove in with both feet. She would not be shown up. "I daresay you don't adventure out to our part of the world very often! Poor Geraldine is well and good for us, but she'd lose her wits trying to make anything fit for you, my lady." Her voice wobbled a little and Charlotte's never did—yes, but not much, not much at all.

"Douro was supposed to be here tonight, the cad," Crashey said loudly, veering the conversation off its cliff. "I don't see his deviliandsome face anywhere—no! There he is, over by the dice tables, wouldn't you know it? He's a dash hand at just about everything, but I could swear the dice are all in love with him, the way they carry on when he turns up. S'not fair, if you ask me. I always say you can be rich or talented or handsome but all three's just obnoxious." Crashey pointed out a boy of fourteen or fifteen, made all of blackened wood and ash. Ancient flame glinted under his cheekbones. Mary beckoned lovingly to him with one long bronze arm. Her bicep and elbow were stamped with a victorious griffin rampant and rather a lot of roman numerals. The Marquis of Douro swept across the hall, straight through the line of dance, ignored Mary entirely, caught up Charlotte's hand, and kissed it all in one smooth motion, without breaking stride.

"Madam," he said in the deepest and most charming voice Charlotte had ever heard.

"The Marquis of Douro," Crashey announced with a flourish of his hand that told both sisters he really didn't think too terribly much of the man he was about to praise. "Conqueror of the Realm, Father of Glass Town, King of the Pioneers! Ladies Currer and Ellis Bell, of Thurshcross Whereverandever."

"Don't be a cow, Sergeant," purred Douro without taking his burning eyes from Charlotte's. "All that was my grandfather, eons ago and good riddance, and you know it. I must insist you call me Adrian, young lady. The glory's all gone, but the money's left, as they say. Which emboldens lesser men to try to pull at my tails, but in the end forces them to be satisfied with holding my coat. What a world we live in, wouldn't *you* say, Miss Bell?"

Charlotte did not like the way the Marquis—the way *Adrian*—was looking at her. It felt as though he were watching her through a window, like the raven in the tree outside the room at the top of the stairs. Only she had never fed this bird a single crumb, and didn't think she'd dare. The way he said her false name made her think he knew quite well that it was false. She tried to imagine him talking his wife into killing herself to set him free, and found she could, quite easily. Charlotte shuddered, but she did not let it show. She smiled instead. It seemed a good trade. Shuddering rarely got you anywhere. But behind her smile she was thinking furiously: *I invented you. It was autumn and it was sunny when I had the idea of you. I know every little thing you are because I thought every little one of them up. Except the parts Bran did. Which rather makes me your mother, and you really oughtn't look at your mother that way.*

Charlotte's imaginary Douro always respected a little defiance, so she did not hold back her annoyance. "I think everyone ought to stop asking me if I agree and *isn't it just* and *wouldn't I say*. Isn't it enough that *you've* said it? Or don't you believe much in yourself, Adrian?"

Emily dug her nails into Charlotte's wrist. *Too far, too far!* But Douro just chuckled in that infuriating way that grown-ups did whenever they thought Charlotte was being precocious. It was the same way she chuckled when one of their birds did something particularly sweet. *I am not a bird,* she thought angrily. *I am Charlotte. No one here has any right to talk to me like an amusing child up past bedtime. We're all the same age, for God's sake!*

She opened her mouth to say so. But Crashey felt the storm coming and quickly dragged Emily and Charlotte out of the shadow of Douro's stare toward merrier folk. He steered them right into a crowd milling round a card-table. A pair of boisterous young men were calling bets. The one made of crushed green peppercorns choked on his brandy and hurried to shake their hands. Then he seemed to remember that one ought not to shake young ladies' hands as if they were friends at a pub, even if they were from the middle of nowhere. He blushed, wiped his hands on his suit jacket, and bowed properly, though not half so prettily as Sergeant Crashey. The other kept chatting to a girl all of bluebells.

The Sergeant took in the crowd at a little velvet-covered table with a grand arm. "This jumpedupstart boy is Young Soult the Rhymer, who fancies himself the greatest poet of the age, though he's more than a bit rubbish. He'll be performing tonight, the Genii save us all. And *this* is my preferfavorite soul in the Glasser, excepting Captain B, of courseviously, Georgie Gordon, Lord Byron, who actually *is* the greatest poet of the age."

Charlotte and Emily startled, nearly jumped out of their skins, for they knew that name. They *loved* that name. The most famous poet in England! Though surely the one whose poems they read so eagerly back in Haworth was much older than this Lord Byron, and much more, well, dead, not to put too fine a point on it. Time and history as they knew them seemed to have never so much as nodded to Glass Town as they passed on the street. This Byron was very much alive, and smiling, and pretending to laugh at Young Soult's joke. And surely the poet *they* knew wasn't made of a hundred different animal pelts flowing smoothly and beautifully together into one glossy coat.

"Aw, Crash, you might let them think well of me for a *minute*," Young Soult pouted.

Lord Byron took in Charlotte and Emily with sloping, sleepy, wolfish eyes.

"She walks in beauty like the night, of cloudless climes and starry skies—"

Emily and Charlotte burst out laughing. Byron looked quite hurt, and quite like a kicked dog.

"Oh, I *am* sorry," Charlotte said, wheezing a little as she tried to laugh in her corset. "But it's too good! It's *perfect!*"

Emily remembered to put up her fan at the last moment and hide that she was mocking the great man. She wondered suddenly if that's what fans were always used for. "It's only that you *would* quote yourself, you know," she giggled helplessly. "It's just all over *you*. But thank you kindly, we *are* rather nice-looking!"

Crashey hurried them away from the stricken look on Lord Byron's face. After a moment, the poet called after them:

"You know my work?"

But they were already on to a new throng.

"Now the short bluestone fellowman tilting at the punch bowl is King George, but he's only King George *today*, you see. On other days of the week he fancies himself a crawfish, an oyster, a heather flower, a blue flame, and a soldier called Captain Flower. Mad as a *carpet*, that one. But best call him His Majesty King George or else he'll bite you. No use judging! I once had an uncle who thought he was a cricket bat, and I've got the paddlemarks to prove it."

"Who *is* King if not him?" Charlotte said suddenly. It seemed such a logical thing to ask that it had completely escaped her mind until now.

Crashey stroked the faint beard lines etched into his pine chin. "Well, that is the questionorium, wouldn't you know it. See, it *ought* to be Douro, if you go strictly by bloodgeniture. But after the first Boneyonic War, Adrian's Papa got himself slapped down. Kicked out. Deposdicated."

"The first Boneyonic . . . *Napoleonic* War?" Emily

interrupted. Of course there had been two of them at home, as well, she supposed.

Sergeant Crashey nicked a biscuit from a passing maidservant and popped it into his mouth, talking around the crumbs. "Yeah, love, look, it's been a fiery mess around here for an eon and a half, but that's history, innit? I daresay yours don't look any better after a rough night. So *then* we had Parliament running the place from Greenhall in Verdopolis, until all the badtacular business with Gondal started up again. That's when Miss Zenobia's brother, Lord Elrington, rode in on a rhinoceros and told them all to go get hung. Lucky Rogue! When he marries her, he'll be the richest man in Glass Town. If he ever gets around to it. But *then* Elrington diedinated himself with no babies, so, this, that, and the other far too complicated thing to do with half-cousaunts marrying barn doors or summat: It's meant to be little Victoria now. She had brothers, but they all got killed by frogs back in the Ugly Ages before we inventixperimented up the *rhodinus secundi vitae*, which the boys call grog and Gravey calls morning tea. But no one's had a peep out of Vicks since she were 'napped in her nappies. Anyway, it'd be dash hard to rule from a prison in enemy territorizones even if she hadn't got reared up by who-knows-who. So *technicalliwise*, it's Vickie's Papa, the Duke of

Can't, but he's only a Regent. I'll bet you can imagine how *that's* going." Crashey put on a reedy, aristocratic voice. "Terribly sorry, I just *can't* run the kingdom. I just *can't* decide which troops go where! I just *can't* wipe myself of a morning ho, ho, ho!"

The Sergeant stopped them, and his history lesson, beside a tall lady with only one leg, clad all in the brightest blue damask. "But here's a monarch with none of that baggageosity! This fetching young maidcreature is Wollstonecraft, Queen of the Bluestockings." Crashey seemed to have an idea. "Perhaps, your Graceroyal Highmajesty, we might have a word with you later, regarding . . . er . . . a sensitive matter?"

"Charmed," said the Queen, who did not bow or curtsy, for she bent knee to no one. "And perhaps, indeed. I am always on the lookout for new conspiracies, and the beginning is always today, after all. Find me after the entertainments, Sergeant."

"Is there any end to the people you know?" Emily marveled.

"Haven't found it yet!" shrugged their man.

The Queen hurried behind her fan and away, leaving them face-to-face with a most extraordinary pair—a young man nailed together out of the parts of a shattered ship and a young girl all of crackling electricity and steel.

"Mary and Percy Shelley, may I present Misses Currer and Ellis Bell?" The wooden soldier leaned down and whispered in their ears: "I know, I know, the names can get brutally contwixting! Would it kill this lot to have a few less Marys and lads what start with the letter A?"

When Charlotte touched Mary Shelley's hand, the electricity of the other girl burned her golden fingertips within her glove. "I . . . I am honored. I . . . I read your book. Papa said I oughtn't. But I did anyhow and it was so awfully splendid and Frankenstein is the most terrifying creature I could ever think of until . . ." She thought of Brunty grinning horribly over the top of his acid machine and shuddered. "Until quite recently, actually." Then, it occurred to her that perhaps Frankenstein was not called Frankenstein here, just as Juliet wasn't Juliet. Maybe in Glass Town, Shelley had named her wicked scientist Edward or Mason or Rochester or something.

"Frankenstein is the creator, you know," Mary said, her lips firing off sparks when they met. "Not the monster."

"I know," Charlotte squeaked. "But . . ." She thought she might fall to the ground or lift up through the air. These dresses wouldn't let your heart beat more than once an hour. *Don't say another thing, Charlotte, don't you do it!* "But he . . . he is, you know. He is a *bit*. The monster."

Mary Shelley quirked one sizzling blue eyebrow.

"Your poems are very nice as well, Mr. Shelley," Emily hurried to add, as it was clear the other felt slighted.

Sergeant Crashey guessed that his young charge was about to faint with the excitement of meeting the Shelleys. He pushed them further in and farther on through the crowds, pointing here and there and everywhere. "The fellow who's all over lace handkerchiefs is our own Mr. Keats. You look awful cold, Johnny! Put some mittens on before you catch your death! Right, where was I? That pile of pine-branches swiping purses 'cause he thinks I can't see him is Robin Hood, the tall drink of mulled wine dancing by herself is Lady Guinevere, that plaid wool scamp is Sir Walter Scott, aaaaand he's making off with a bit of silverware, good for him! Ah, and the girl with the black walnut cheeks playing with the little babies in the corner is Miss Katie Crackernuts. Thought I was to marry her once upon a time, but she got cursed by a fairy and we just drifted apart after that. Oh, well! Ooh, there! The ice-lads playing dice at the green table are Captains Ross and Parry, the gallant explorequistadors of Ascension Island and the frigid wastes of Parrysland, which, obviclearly he named for himself, but that's the paybackoff for having to eat your sails and getting were-scurvy twice. And lo! Here we are, here we land, here we anchormoor our barking barques! Good gravy in a leaky boat, I am parched from all this naming and shaming! Where's that butler?"

Crashey pulled them along after a tuxedoed boy carrying goblets on a tray and nearly ran right over into two wooden soldiers with dear, familiar faces. One with a knotty burl on his forehead where he'd been wounded earlier that afternoon, and one with an eye patch Anne had made out of pitch on a rainy afternoon back home in Haworth. But now they had two handsome ladies on their arms instead of rifles. One was made of teacup handles and quill pens. She wore a pale, plain dress the color of a real, deep, proper blush, the kind that flood's a girl's face when society has offended her. The other had long green leaves for skin and wore a lovely delicate gray, the color of ash in an attic. Crashey greeted them with embraces and slaps on the back. "Of course, you know Sergeant Major Rogue and Leftenant Gravey!"

Gravey and Rogue exclaimed and kissed their cheeks and were informed by a wide variety of eyebrow-waggles and nose-tappings from Sergeant Crashey that they were not to spill any flavor of beans about the girls' new names and faces. Rogue looked tremendously dashing in his eye patch and formal coat. Leftenant Gravey had worn a splendid lime-green sash for the occasion, the only way to display all his medals at once. The sash sagged with the weight of hundreds of crosses and coins and bars and stars. Emily caught her breath. *One for each time he's died on the field. Oh, poor, poor Leftenant Gravey!*

But Gravey did not seem to feel himself poor at all. He kissed their cheeks and proudly displayed his newest: a brilliant red sunburst with *The Battle of Port Ruby* engraved on one side and *Distinguished Service Above and Beyond the Call* on the other.

"They do make those up rather quick, don't they!" said Charlotte.

"Command's got a special press for Gravey in the big tent," Sergeant Major Rogue laughed. "He gets cross if he doesn't get his praise on time."

"Well, I did *die*, didn't I? Deserves a bit of jewelry!" Gravey laughed along with his men and snuck a sip of something from a flask on his belt.

The lady in the gray dress cleared her throat politely. "Ah!" Sergeant Major Rogue cried, slapping his beechwood forehead. "I would forget my own King if he weren't on the money! Miss Currer, Miss Ellis, this is my betrothed, Lady Zenobia Elrington of Verdopolis."

Gravey put his arm round the shoulders of the girl in

blush. "And this is most emphatically *not* my betrothed, Miss Jane Austen of . . . well, anywhere she likes, I expect. Jane is *far* too fine for the likes of me. Says I'm morbid and rude. Well, I only squired her up because I am an excellent and long-suffering friend. Roguey told me to scrub it and get my arm under this one so Miss Z wouldn't feel lonely, and here we all are! You must try to hear one of Janey's storyables while you're here; they're better than any of the desserts."

Charlotte and Emily stared all over again, dumb-founded once more, delighted once more to meet some-body so famous she shone. But this time Charlotte didn't gush about the lady's novels. She had never much cared for them. Too prim and neat and breakable. Nobody could ever really be that polite when their lives burst open like rotten dams. Emily liked them just fine, and said so. But more importantly, Leftenant Gravey just called Jane Austen "Janey." And he was still alive. Jane's pale eyes shot daggers at the Leftenant. Crashey hurried to skewer the awkward silence.

"All rightnough! Moving on to the lessminor gentry!"

"Oh wait, please! That's quite enough for a first course!" pleaded Emily. "I'm already full!"

Gravey and Rogue and their dates made affectionate farewells and promises to find them all again later, but

Charlotte and Emily scarcely heard a thing.

The dancing floor of the Wildfell Ball was half-filled with their toys and half-filled with the greatest men and women in Britain. Either of them could recite all those names back with hardly a breath between, but they could not *understand* it. It made them dizzy, trying to untangle the mess. Charlotte and Branwell had invented Adrian, the sly and wicked Marquis of Douro! And Emily had dreamed up Mary Percy after Branwell killed Douro's first wife "to make love more interesting." Branwell signed all his dreadful poems as Young Soult the Rhymer. And of course Anne had her Victoria. But Victoria, and Ross and Perry and John Keats and Jane Austen were quite real, and so was Lord Byron and Mary Shelley and Napoleon's poor wife, Josephine. They'd never played Byron and Josephine of an afternoon, not once. Yet right at that very moment, Charlotte was staring into the black eyes of Lady Zenobia Elrington, a name she had spent hours thinking up while the Headmaster droned on about the Norman invasion.

"Look at what we made," Charlotte whispered to her sister.

She could not doubt any longer that they *had* made it. Not with Douro and Zenobia and Mary Percy slurping brandy not ten steps away. It was impossible, of course, and no one would ever believe it, and she hadn't the first guess as to how or why or when they'd done it. Only it was all so much grander and bigger than just the four of them huddled together in the playroom at the top of the stairs. So much thicker, so much wilder. She was, against all logic, walking through the insides of their four heads, and the wine there tasted *wonderful*.

SEVENTEEN

The Only Onions in the World

Branwell and Anne slept and slept and slept.

They had a few dim, unpleasant dreams. When they hashed everything out later, they discovered they'd dreamt the same murky, echoing stuff. Very clumsy ogres with cold, sticky hands moved them about. They pinched and sniffed and prodded roughly, shoved them here and there, ordered them to take one or another thing off or to put this or that thing on, marched them down halls and up staircases that never seemed to end, the way they never do in dreams. And the whispering! Those stupid ogres were always whispering, and at the most maddening volume: just softly enough so that they couldn't hear, but too loud to ignore. Their whispering breath smelled like water in a still, scummy pond.

Anne woke first, but she pretended she was still asleep, just in case the ogres weren't dreams. The pond smell still wriggled around in her nostrils. She pretended for so long that Bran woke up as well, and she lost the chance to scold him for being lazy. Her hand flew to her chest—was it safe there? Was it hers? She breathed a shaky sigh of relief.

"I can tell you're faking, Anne," Branwell said, and poked her in the ribs. "You always scrunch up your eyes when you're faking. Come on, up you get! Prison's not bad, really. Though I'm hungry as *Hades*. Oh, and don't look out the windows. It's a ghastly long way down. You know how you get."

Anne opened one eye. Clear, cool sunlight drifted through six tall windows shaped like church candles. She was lying in a bed in a little round room. Bran sat on the edge of his own bed, swinging his feet impatiently. Their sheets and blankets were blue and red. So was Anne's nightgown and Bran's pajamas.

"Gondal's colors," Bran said. The idea of it excited him a little. He picked at the white buttons on his night-clothes.

"And France's," Anne said. "And England's, come to

think of it. *And* America. And Russia as well!"

Bran shook his head. "Good grief, didn't anyone think that might get confusing? What's the matter with a bit of black?"

"Or purple! Purple is much nicer than black. Oh!" Anne exclaimed, clutching her rough-spun nightgown. "Bran, where're our clothes? My dress and my shoes and my *lemon*? That's our ticket home!"

"I haven't the foggiest," Branwell answered gloomily.

Anne climbed out from under the covers to have a look round. The polished flagstone floor was cold under her bare feet.

There was a hearth down one end of the room with a fire going about its business inside. A pot of something that smelled oaty and milky bubbled over the flames.

"It's vile," Branwell assured her. "Turns out gruel is gruel wherever you go."

Over the hearth hung an obnoxiously large portrait of Bonaparte and a lady made of roses wearing crowns the size of rain barrels. They looked smugly pleased to be having their portrait painted. The lady's rose-hair had lost a few petals, and where they lay, they shone the most peculiar color, like moonlight. Anne chewed her lip. Down the other end was a thick, heavy door hacked out of wood so old it might have started out as the gangplank on Noah's Ark. It had one little square window in it, too high for either of them to look out of, and full of iron bars anyway, even if they tried.

"Prison, you said?" Anne said to her brother.

"Well, it's locked, if that's what you mean. I don't expect they lock you in if they mean to throw you a birthday party." Branwell clasped his hands behind his back and began to pace up and down the cell with his best hardened warrior expression on. "Best face up to it, Anne. We're prisoners of war, now. It's to be interrogations and meager rations for us. We shall have to be strong. We shall have to be resolute!"

Anne rolled her eyes.

"You sound like you're counting Christmas presents! I don't know why you have to be so *odd* all the time."

"But, Anne! We *are* prisoners of war! And that means we're important. If we weren't, they'd just drop us out the window and wave at us while our heads splattered on the rocks. I *like* being important. Don't you? It's important to be important! Why, it's the most important thing!"

"*I* like being Anne," she sniffed. "That's quite important enough."

Finally, she could put it off no longer. Bran was right. She *did* know how she got when she found herself too high up in a tree or the bell tower of Papa's church or

Bestminster's balloon basket. She *wanted* to like it up there as the others did. But it made her stomach turn inside out. The trouble was, Branwell had said not to look, which meant Anne *had* to look. She *needed* to look. She *would* look. Anne hadn't disobeyed anyone in ages. It made her itch.

The windows were thin and graceful and went almost from the floor to the pointed roof of their cell. Anne peered over the sill. It *was* a ghastly long way down. Miles and miles. Probably not miles, she corrected herself. But taller than any tree or chapel or even the palaces of Europe in their beloved magazines. They were in a great, grand house, greater and grander than any English house could ever dream of growing up to be. The walls were neither brick nor stone but pure diamond, billions of them, perfectly cut and dazzling in the cold sunshine, sweeping off to the left and right into endless banks of windows and gables. They were on the top floor, or very nearly. Glittering crystal walls plunged down toward a craggy, jagged cliff, which plunged down into a rocky, barren valley, which plunged down until it ended in an icy river that raged and frothed itself into a pure white scream of water. Anne yelped softly, then tried to pretend she hadn't. She couldn't be scared. Not now. Not here. She had too many other feelings for stupid old *scared*. Scared would have to queue up.

Anne dashed to the opposite wall. This was better. No cliff or valley or river. Just a vast, busy courtyard full of those wonderful, terrifying frogs slapped together out of steel armor. Other folk had joined the elite fighters: tall and short and fat and thin and made out of every which thing. But many of them were Ascension Islanders: walking, talking ninepins and chess pieces and checker-stacks and dice and dominos. Gondal's soldiers stood in row after row, rank after rank. They turned sharply, left, right, all in perfect unison. They exercised and drilled and marched and practiced their stabbing skills on straw dummies with Wellington's face painted on them. Bonaparte's army was mustering. It wasn't a better view at all, really.

But above the courtyard of the Bastille soared spires and towers and roofs and gables that Anne knew as well as she knew the kitchen garden and the tracks through the moors beyond. The glorious skyline of Verdopolis filled her eyes and her whole heart. The Tower of All Nations rose in a column of green glass and smoky crystal and wrought iron pillars. The crumbling pyramids looked like green mountains in the distance. The guard houses of the Great Wall of China stretched on forever over the hills and plains, a wall so impossible to believe that the moment they read about it in Papa's magazine, they knew they had to build it in their ideal city and man it with their wooden soldiers. The Hall of the Fountain pierced the clouds with its pale jade steeples. The rose window of the Grand Inn of the Genii, which they'd decided sounded ever so much more inviting than "cathedral," caught the sun, so far away but still, just barely, shining.

"We're in Verdopolis," she whispered. "We really, *really* are!" The frogs bellowed orders and turned on their green, three-toed heels. "What's this place, then? We never put a prison in!"

Branwell liked being asked. At least Anne acknowledged that he was an authority. Charlotte would never. But Charlotte wasn't here. He was finally the oldest. Finally the smartest. Bran was, without argument, in charge. It felt warm and bright in his chest, like Brunty's amazing bat-tree. "I think this is the Hall of Justice. Or at least, it used to be. That's where we always put prisoners awaiting trial when we played Verdopolis. But if we *are* in Verdopolis, courtesy of Brunty, that means we're in Gondal territory, which means Napoleon must have taken the city. And he wouldn't keep calling it that. I think it's the Bastille now. Do you remember? Brunty said something about a Bastille a thousand years ago when all this started. That's where the Frenchies keep their baddies in our world, anyhow. It only makes sense."

Anne turned away from the window before she was sick all over the thick, bubbled glass. "We've got to break out, obviously."

Bran blinked at her. "Why?"

"Well, we're not anyone's baddies, for one! But, Bran . . . Charlotte and Emily will never find us in here! They can't storm the Bastille! What are they meant to do, throw their shoes at it? Do up a Trojan Bestminster and hope those frogs fall for the really, actually oldest trick in the oldest book?"

"But we'll miss the interrogation!" Branwell furrowed his brow. He hated the little whine creeping into his voice, but he couldn't help it. "I've never been interrogated! It was ripping fun back home when I had Crashey interrogate Douro in the kitchen garden and pull out all his fingernails! I want to be strong and resolute! Don't you want to see who they'll send to question us? Brunty is a *bit* worse for wear at the moment. I'd wager it'll be Boney himself!"

"I don't want my fingernails pulled out!" Anne cried. "Pull out your own! I'm going to find a way out of here and back to Em and Charlotte and Glass Town and the train home!"

She started to march toward the heavy door, but

Bran stopped her. He got down on one knee so he could look his sister in the eye.

"All right, all right, Annie. I wouldn't let them do anything awful to *your* fingernails. I say, girls frighten so easily!"

"I'm not frightened! I'm angry, because you're being . . . you're being . . . oh, you're just being *Branwell* all over yourself! I'm hungry and cold and we're *far too high up* and I want to go home!"

"Yes, but, Anne . . . do you really want to go back to Glass Town? You heard what Brunty said! This whole beastly war is their fault! They steal all the stuff to make their grog from Gondal and they don't let them have a drop. I don't call that fair and I don't call that right. If Mrs. Reed down the way popped over the garden wall in Haworth and swiped all our onions, Papa'd go bashing on her door, wouldn't he?"

"I suppose . . ."

"And what if they were the only onions in the world? And what if they were magic onions that you could make medicine out of, medicine that should go to anyone who needs it, only Mrs. Reed was hoarding it just for herself and her million horrid children who always pull the washing down whenever we've got it pinned up nice? Well, then *everyone* would go bashing on her door!"

"Oh, the Reeds aren't so bad as all that! Well, John's a brute. But Georgiana gave me a crabapple out of her pocket once and *you* never have. I'm on the side of the crabapples! You shouldn't talk nasty behind people's backs, Bran."

"They aren't the goodies, Anne! Just because Glass Town has a Wellington doesn't make them England. And even if it did, England isn't so jolly nice to anybody not called England anyhow."

"Bran! *We're* English!"

"So's Prince John and Morgan le Fay and Mrs. Reed and Macbeth and the Headmaster at Charlotte and Em's school and Richard the Third and Henry 'Dunno, What'dya Think, I'll Just Cut All My Wives' Heads Off, Shall I?' the bloody Eighth! No one's good just from being born any place." He tugged on the sleeve of Anne's red and blue nightgown. "All the same colors, like you said! Glass Town isn't any safer or sweeter than Gondal, Annie. Perhaps we should break out of prison. Perhaps you're right and I'm wrong. But if we do spring ourselves . . . perhaps we should think about rescuing Charlotte and Emily, not the other way round."

"But Brunty isn't sweet at *all*. He's a Master Spy! That means he lies for fun! You haven't heard one word of what anyone in Glass Town has to say about it!"

"I don't need to! They've got the magic onions from Gondal's garden. Gondal just wants its own back. And isn't that what we want, too? Why not throw in with those who see the world our way? We could use a frog army right about now, that's for certain."

"But that's just it, Bran." Anne twisted her fingers and stared down at her bare, frozen toes. "They *do* have the magic onions."

Anne hadn't wanted to say. She'd wanted to sneak her prize home while no one was looking, and then when they got there everyone would say how astonishingly clever and brave and nimble she was. And her mother, whom she couldn't remember, not really, would love her best of all. Of all of them. But now, Bran had gone and spoilt everything, like he always did.

A soft, sidelong smile crossed Anne's face. No matter how it came out in the end, she'd done it. Not Bran or Emily or even Charlotte. No one could argue with that. No one could best her. She reached into her dressing gown.

The door of their cell swung inward with a horrid scrape and crunch of wood against flagstone. Anne's hand froze. She put it back at her side. A tall girl entered with a smile on her face like a birthday candle—merry, but oh, how it burned. She was made all of cake from top to bottom. Cake and whirls of icing, swirls of icing, rosettes and pipettes and ribbons and twirls of vanilla, strawberry, pistachio, lemon, and lavender icing. She wore a great buttercream gown with a hoop skirt that barely fit through the door. Her hair rose up from her head in clouds of meringue, toasted at the tips. Her eyes were bright blue, her mouth bright pink, and she moved like a nervous ballerina. She was carrying a silver tray that steamed with lovely, hot smells Branwell had almost forgotten existed. She closed the door behind her with a sweet, creamy foot. She looked fifteen at the outside, but carried herself very proudly.

"*Bonjour*, children!" she said, and very sweetly. "You will be Monsieur Branwell and Mademoiselle Anne, and I? *Je m'appelle Marie, d'accord!*"

Branwell looked at Anne. Anne looked at Branwell. An awkward silence ticked by.

"G . . . good morning, Miss Marie," Anne stammered. She knew that face. She *knew* her. But it was too impossible. She couldn't force herself to ask.

"Terribly sorry, but would that be Marie Antoinette?" Bran cut in.

"But of course, my darling! I am the one and the only, all other Maries are stealing from me, yes? It is a *sin* to call a shop girl by the same name as someone as marvelous as myself!"

"But . . ." Anne sunk her chin into her chest. She raised it again. She lowered it. "But aren't you quite dead?"

"Deader than the Sunday roast, I'd say," Branwell scoffed. "You can't have Napoleon and Marie Antoinette in the same city, it's just . . . it's just wrong! They killed you! Long before Boney got his crown! They cut your head off!"

Marie Antoinette stroked her vanilla throat with a frosted hand. Beneath the thin frosting they could see the red velvet cake of her famous neck. "Pssh! Is nothing a little icing cannot fix! My *cherie*, Monsieur Bonaparte, allows me to stay on as maidservant so long as I never, never touch the crowns in the cupboard, or even think about them."

Branwell goggled. "*Maidservant?* You were Queen of France!"

"Is not so different as you think, young man," the Queen said ruefully. "At least a maidservant only uses the guillotine to chop carrots, no?"

Something slid into place in Anne's mind. "Are you our interrogator?"

"I said maidservant, did I not? You heard me, loud and clear and loud again? I am here to clean up after M. Brunty's *petite* mess. But first, you must eat! Eat bread,

bread, all the bread you can stuff in your adorable faces. You see? Enough bread for all. I learn my lessons."

Marie Antoinette had brought a silver tray piled high with food. Branwell blinked, confused. He saw no pots of fire or flutes of champagne or dishes full of hardtacks, just simple brown bread and brown soup and brown tea, no different than if Tabitha herself had served them up. Where had they gotten all this?

"There is nothing for the heart like the taste of home," Marie said in a singsong voice. "That's what I always say."

A moment later it was all gone, and Anne had no memory at all of eating. She just opened her starving mouth and then Branwell was licking his fingers like a wolfy pig.

"I thought Boney would come." Bran pouted through the crumbs. "I thought he'd want to meet us. Very well, then!"

Branwell sat up straight. He stuck out his chin. He could feel himself getting courageous. He *would* be courageous.

"Do your worst!" he shouted.

"Please don't!" cried Anne. "I like my fingernails!"

Marie turned her head to one side. Her meringue curls tottered. "And how do you imagine that you are at all important enough for the Emperor to trouble his time with? Are you Wellington's son? Douro's heir? Silly me, I thought you were the two wee little mad children Brunty brought in! With two mad sisters running whizz and wild out there, scheming with bad elements, stirring up trouble?"

"Charlotte and Em!" Anne cried.

"At least they are not locked up tight, yes? I think they are maybe cleverer than you, Monsieur Branwell. If you had not put out Brunty with your wonderful bucket, he would have died—*kack!*—and you would not be here with me! But no! What a fool am I! That is not you! You are someone *important.* I am so absent of mind! Why, I'd lose my head if it weren't attached. Who are you then, my darlings? You have my full attention."

"We . . . we are . . . I mean that Brunty did bring us in, and I am Anne and he is Branwell, but we're not mad. And we're not little."

Marie Antoinette made a mocking pout with her pretty iced mouth. "Oh, you are just precious. Precious like a lost earring! Did you not babble in the presence of the Brunty and say something about having made us all up like Cinderella? Did you not call Wellington and Napoleon your toys and make wild claims about having gotten them from a shop in *Leeedz?*"

"It's the truth," mumbled Branwell. She was so beautiful. He hated her beautiful mocking mouth. He wanted it to smile for him.

"Well, that is rather *awfully* mad, *non?* Insane. Crazy as cake! You did not make me up! If anyone made me up, it was myself! You said I was the Queen of France. How can I be Queen of France and a little boy's toy all at the same once?"

Anne blushed. "Sometimes we . . . sometimes we used real people in our games. To make them more exciting. Because sometimes the real people were terribly interesting or beautiful and . . . and we wanted to meet them and show them the moors behind our house and feed them eggs from our chickens, but we couldn't, you see, because they were very dead or very famous, so we called our toys by their names and invented stories for them, stories that brought them to us."

Marie Antoinette wrinkled her delicate powdered-sugar nose. "Disgusting. Rude. You ought to be spanked. But, then how do you know I am your toy-Marie, and not the real-Marie?"

Bran and Anne exchanged glances, and Anne spoke. "You're made of cake."

"And alive," Branwell added.

"And Napoleon's maid," Anne put in.

"But of course. And who else have you invented?"

Bran blew air out of his cheeks. "Well, just . . . everyone, really! Crashey and Bravey and Gravey and Napoleon and Wellington and Rogue and—oh! You said Douro! The Marquis of Douro? He's one of ours! And Mr. Bud and Mr. Tree and Tracky and Boaster . . ."

"Not Brunty, though," Anne said softly. "Not Bestminster. Not lots of them, when you think about it."

Marie Antoinette sparkled at Bran. She put her frosting-face in her delicate hands and smiled. "Did you do all that by yourself? What a talent you must be!"

"Well, Charlotte did Douro mostly. And Wellington. And Gravey and Crashey and Zenobia. But I did Dr. Home. His backstory, anyway; she ran off with him a bit over the winter. . . . And Emily did Ross and Parry and a jolly lot of ladies I can't remember the names of because she won't let me hold them hostage in my castles. . . . Rogue is mine, though! And Napoleon!"

Marie leaned closer. He could smell the warm baking pastry of her heart. "Fascinating! Tell me more! Who else?"

Branwell warmed under the sun of Marie's interest. He wracked his mind. "Oh! Anne has some sad little dolly called Victoria, but we haven't met her yet. She's Anne's *secret*."

"*Bran!* You . . . you *worm!*"

"She talks to her doll all night long. There's a million stories and she won't tell us one," Branwell confided in his new friend. Anne went white with rage.

Marie patted Anne's hand. She smelled like warm, rich chocolate and cool lemon cake. "Do not be upset at your brother, *mon fille!* It is not beautiful on you. Why would you keep secrets from him? He seems very nice! You should never keep secrets from your family."

"He wouldn't *understand,*" pleaded Anne, her eyes full of tears. "He'll be angry. He gets very angry, miss."

"Don't we all, *petite* Anne? Ah, but you see, there is no proof! How can I believe such a thing?"

Branwell went red. "You don't know anything! I can prove it!"

"Can you?" The former Queen of France said curiously.

"Can you?" said Anne. "How?"

He would turn that mocking expression into admiration. He would.

"I know all about Glass Town. And Gondal, too. I know every plan Wellington's ever had, every siege, every defense. I can tell you—"

Marie leaned forward eagerly. "Yes, *mon amour?* What can you tell me?"

Anne pinched him more viciously than he had ever been pinched in his life. Branwell went slack with horror. In another moment, he would have told that perfect icing-girl everything he could think of, just so that she would believe him and think he was important enough to meet Napoleon and smile. Just for her smile.

"No," he croaked. "Nothing. I am mad. Mad as mittens. You can't invent a person. You can't invent a world. It's preposterous. Like you said."

Marie clapped her coconut-cream hands and giggled. "Oh, do you know I am so good at interrogating! Brunty is always telling me *fingernails, fingernails, and if that doesn't work, why not try cutting off a toe?* But is only me to tidy up all that drippety-slop. Why bother with any of that when you can wink and flutter and gasp at a boy who is so dreadfully afraid that he is not so good as anyone else? A sad little sour-faced baby punching his sisters because he knows he's the least of them? Is easy as eating cake."

"You knew we were telling the truth?" Anne asked miserably.

"Brunty always knows. Is the fourth rule of spying. When Someone Tells You Something Impossible, Listen."

"But I didn't," Bran rasped. Oh, he was wretched.

He was just what they all said. He was small and vicious and useless. "I didn't give them up. And I won't. I won't ever. I am a locked chest buried in a well in the ground."

Marie Antoinette shrugged. She rubbed her finger round the rim of one of the empty bowls of brown soup and tasted it. "C'est la vie! It would be much better for you if you did. There are worse things than me in this place. And if you don't spill your delicate English innards, then we'll bury all of you in a chest in a well in the ground, trouble-stirring sisters and all. Brunty is home, and the world is about to change. Soon grog won't matter any more than madness. Maybe you should be on the better side of that world, non? We have the most delicious cake here."

With that, Marie Antoinette swept out of the room and shut the door fast. A long, horrible quiet fell onto Branwell and Anne. He could not bear to look at her. She could not bear to speak to him. Finally, when the sun began to get low and golden outside their windows, Anne sighed and said:

"Don't listen to her. Didn't you hear the frogs in the courtyard?"

"No, of course not. It's a hundred feet down and I had other things to think about!"

Anne, who always heard everything, the little spy without rules, shrugged. "I did. They moan and complain so, and when they march, their knees creak. Don't listen to Marie. They're losing the war."

EIGHTEEN
❧✦❧

The High Ground

M ight I trouble you for a dance, Miss . . . ?"
Emily coughed, glanced round, and found
herself standing far, far too close to the boy Crashey
had said quite confidently was Lord Byron. All his wild
animal pelts didn't frighten her. He looked rather like a
calico cat—sleek panther fur along his jaw, snow leopard on his high cheekbones, bear on his throat, fox on
his forehead, peacock feathers glinting among the long
curly hair of a Newfoundland dog that tumbled round
his beautiful face. He winked one green-gold wolfish eye
at her. He smelled like long summer days on the green
and fresh ink.

Emily choked. "Oh, I'm sorry, I didn't see you!" She stood on tiptoe, scanning the crowd for her sister. She saw Charlotte's golden hair and waved. "Char . . . Currer? Erm. Mr. Byron wants to dance with you."

The poet demurred. "Not at all, my silver siren. Begging the pardon of your sister, but I was asking *you*."

The harpsichord clanged to life and before she could think, before she could tell him she didn't know how, before her heart could even beat, Emily was swept away to the dance floor in the arms of Lord Byron. The stars glittered on her silver hair, her silver forehead, her silver fingers, and her dog's-ear white gown.

"I am going to ask the Duke to dance," Charlotte said firmly and quietly. Why not, after all? She needed political help. *Military* help. She would not ask a poet for that, nor a physician, nor grieving parents.

"Darling, he's just a *touch* above your station, don't you think?" purred Miss Austen, hiding a face built from shattered teacups behind a huge lace fan. "We Misses and Ladies had best stick with our boys in uniform. Unless Thrushcross is having a *much* better year than I've heard, hm?"

The young gossip already knew all about her. This was why Charlotte didn't like her books. It was just exactly like listening to her aunt whisper and nag about this or that village scandal, only with a very excellent vocabulary. The best thing that could ever happen to anyone in those stories was to get married and then get on with only feeling things through a lace curtain. Charlotte hoped Jane wouldn't ask anything too pointed about the northern counties. She had nearly run out of her carefully planned and double-checked lies. She would have to start making new things up off the top of her head soon, and that seemed unlikely to go well with the great gossip of Glass Town.

"The train will never come if the station's closed," Zenobia Elrington said in a soft, deep, velveteen voice. She was woven out of fresh, green sugar stalks. Here and there, the leaves fell away to reveal moist, dark, golden cane. But her eyes! Where Charlotte had irises and pupils, Zenobia had black coals. Where Emily had clear whites, Zenobia had round pale flames burning in her lovely face. Charlotte glanced at the Lady's hands: Her fingertips were scorched where she had wiped away tears of sadness or laughter in her life.

"Every soul in Glass Town asks the Genii for blessings," Zenobia said, lowering her fiery gaze. "To ask a Duke for a dance is much less imposition."

Jane fluttered her fan in consternation. "Oh, but *you* mustn't do the asking! That's preposterous! What *do* they teach you out there in the boonies? It's all very well to ask the potatoes to grow or the cows to milk, but a mere *Lady* asking a *Duke* to the floor? Zenobia! Tell her it is not done!"

Lady Elrington turned her burning gaze to Josephine in her great birdcage, high above the ball. Three throbbingly red petals fell from her hair and drifted down to the jeweled floor.

"Do you think little Victoria gets taken to balls in Gondal?" Zenobia said softly. "Do you think they ever let her out at all?"

Miss Austen saw she would get no help. "A Lady may not do the asking and remain a Lady! It's not to be borne! You poor naive lamb! From the moment I saw you, I knew you were the gentlest and fragilest and most unfortunate of souls. Your very footsteps whispered to me: *Take me under your wing! I cannot fly without your help.*"

Charlotte snorted. But Jane would not let up.

"No, no. I simply will *not* let you embarrass yourself, my poor darling sparrow! Let me—or indeed, Lady Elrington—put out our little butterfly feelers and test the lilies for your sake! He may come to you, when we have done our subtle work. Then there's nothing improper!"

"I can't wait for that," Charlotte answered curtly.

She felt wonderfully free as she made a golden arrow across the Wildfell Ball. She could not be bothered with teacup-women. She was already arranging her words to the Duke in her head. Behind her, Lady Zenobia smiled satisfactorily to herself. Jane looked as though she might sob or break her fan in half or perhaps simply explode like a stick of old dynamite at any moment. Charlotte did not look back.

The Iron Duke was smoking with several of his limeskin guard in a little circle of violet sofas near a vast liquor cabinet that soared up into the evening like the front face of a bank vault. A limey naval Captain with a lean, unripe face cried out:

"And I said to him, I said: *That's* how a good Glass Town bulldog buries his Boney!"

The men roared with citrusy laughter. The smoke was so thick Charlotte could only see a vague glow where the Duke sat, his molten wings banked and glowing peacefully, his white-hot eyes full of merriment.

"Sir," she said, curtsying as best she knew how, from books and one night when Aunt Elizabeth had been at the sherry and they all pretended to meet the Queen, who was a hat rack. "I wondered if, perhaps, you might consider granting an unworthy young Lady the honor of a dance. I have only just arrived from the country with my sister, you see, and I have heard tales of your adventures—"

The limeskin Captain cut her off. "The Duke does not *dance*, Miss Hayseed of Fieldmouse Manor. Run along back to knitting cow dung or spinning beer or whatever it is you stranded gentry do out there in County Nothing."

The men laughed uproariously again, slapping their green knees and dragging on round lemon-leaf cigars. This navy man was clearly the jester to the little court of smirking wallflowers.

"Well," Charlotte continued, deepening her curtsy till her calves ached. "The dance itself is rather beside the point, I'm told."

The Duke of Wellington spoke for the first time.

"Is it?"

"We only hear rumors of such grand things in Fieldmouse Manor, sir. But I imagine the dance is only a bit of an excuse. Something to do with your hands while you're talking."

"And are you a very good dancer?" The Duke blew a ring of lemon-smoke.

"Oh, certainly not, sir," Charlotte said with a twinkle in her eye. She was beginning to enjoy this. She'd only ever bantered with Branwell or made her toy soldiers do it before. It was much better with a new person. "We don't dance in County Nothing; we just fall over and call it a waltz."

A few of the lads toasted her and cackled appreciatively. "That's quite enough wit out of your wattle, Lady No One—" began the navy-man, furious to have competition.

The Duke raised his rusted hand. "Do shut up, Admiral Leaf," he said. "If falling flat on one's face constitutes a waltz these days, perhaps I shall finally be able to manage one!"

Arthur Wellesley, Duke of Wellington, Hero of Trafalgar, stepped out of the curtain of smoke and took up Charlotte's hand in his. His iron skin was terribly warm, almost too hot to touch, but she would not wince, she would *not*, even if she blistered. His face was just as it had been in every picture Charlotte had ever seen, except that this Arthur Wellesley was so much younger, his jaw so much softer, and he stood only a head taller than her. Could he even be fourteen? She thought not. Yet who would put a fourteen-year-old boy, even if he was Arthur, at the head of an army? Of course, no one else seemed to be old enough to go to a ball without their parents hanging over them like moths, yet here they all were.

The dance was one of those that was much more like

soldiers marching than dancing. You turned this way and that with precision when the horn called for it, in squares and circles and spirals that no one could see unless they floated above everything like a sparrow—or like Josephine, hanging in silent fury in her cage. Charlotte breathed a sigh of relief. Aunt Elizabeth had taught them what she knew of this sort of thing, which wasn't much. More importantly, as long as your partner wasn't any better than you were at it, you could pretend very well, and the Duke of Wellington was *dreadful*. He'd no sense of rhythm and always started a bit too early, and besides, he looked directly at Charlotte, his eyes burning into hers, when you were meant to only glance flirtatiously every once in a while. He looked, to anyone watching, like a metal monster from the depths of the sea stalking after prey.

Meanwhile, Emily and Lord Byron sailed through the grand hall like a pair of songbirds chasing one another. Byron could dance so well that it sort of rubbed off on you, left handprints on your heart to lead you to the next promenade or step or wheel. All eyes that were not on the Duke and his mysterious, nameless golden girl were fastened fast upon the poet and his silver siren. The music rose up to the midnight stars like steam. Charlotte and Emily passed each other in the broad circles of

dancers, catching snippets of each other's conversations as the silk and ribbon and lace and velvet blurred by.

The Duke touched Charlotte's hand. She was grateful for the long, dark gloves Ginevra had given her. No gold paint would rub off on the Duke's fingers and give them away. The couple turned round together.

"Very well, Miss . . ."

"Bell. Currer Bell of Thushcross Grange."

Arthur Wellesley narrowed his iron eyes. "One of Felix's granddaughters? I don't recall meeting you at the Ridsummer bonfire last year. It was a fine harvest and a fine feast, but I would still remember someone as clever as you. Cleverness is beauty, and beauty cleverness, and that is the top and bottom of the truth." *Did the Duke of Wellington just call me beautiful?* thought Charlotte. "I remember apple cider and seedcake and Felix telling his wretched jokes to the cider jug and expecting to get a laugh, but no one with such sensible eyes, such brilliant hair, such rational lips."

"I was ill at Ridsummer, sir." Charlotte forced herself to blush. She had never learned the trick of doing it naturally, but people expected it so! She'd never understood why a girl's cheeks should turn pink just because someone said one word or another to her. Men never did it. So whenever it seemed some adult was getting upset at her not blushing, Charlotte held her breath lightly until her face turned a pretty red. She did it now, under all her gold paint. "My sister and I had matched fevers. But Grandpapa does make wretched jokes." *Please stop asking questions!* she thought helplessly. *I'm nearly out of lies!*

"Do you like the house, Miss Bell?" Lord Byron whispered into Emily's ear. "It's all so wonderfully faded and ruined. I do so love faded things, don't you? Anything new is boring. It hasn't lived. It hasn't got secrets. Do you have any secrets? Come, tell me one at once."

Emily blushed. She did it so easily and for so little reason that she'd taught herself not to even when her cheeks ached to turn. *Only when I say!* she told her disobedient face. But now she let the blush come, rising under the silver paint, and twinkled her eyes at him to top it off. She'd seen village girls twinkle their eyes at boys back home and had always wanted to try it, only once when she *did* try, Branwell screamed and told Papa that Em was having an attack of palsy. "Well, I have got *one*, Lord Byron, but I really mustn't tell. We're practically strangers!"

Lord Byron swung his leg round so gracefully it took Emily's breath away. "Please, Ellis, my darling, you must call me George. And don't you tell anyone we're strangers! I should die of humiliation! You've read my work, after all."

Emily's blush crept down her neck and into her soul. "I have, my Lord." Under his wolfy eyes, she forgot all about Lord Bell of Thrushcross and Ginevra's lessons and even, for just a moment, that she was not even a little bit made of silver.

"You see? We are already the *very* best of friends!" laughed Lord Byron, and swung her past her sister once more, so close that the hems of their gowns touched.

"Very well, then, Miss Bell," said the Iron Duke. "What talk would you excuse with dancing?"

"I beg your pardon?" Charlotte gasped. The dance quickened. She began to worry that she might sweat through the gold paint and ruin it all.

"You said that dancing was only something to do with your hands while you're talking. Now, I am a very clever lad myself, so from that I deduced from all that back and forth that you wanted to talk to me." Charlotte could not be sure, but she thought his eyes were twinkling at her. It's very hard to tell when the eyes in question are carved out of iron slugs.

Now was the moment. Plead her case, get what she came for, press on, press on; Branwell and Anne needed her. But somewhere deep inside where she could not quite admit it, Charlotte wished that she could stay forever in this fairy hall, in the arms of the Duke of Wellington, in the center of a beautiful bubble where nothing hurt. But she could not stay. Such bubbles were for other girls, girls who really were made of gold and gallantry.

"It's my brother, sir," she whispered. "My brother and my sister. My other sister, I mean to say."

"More of Felix's brood? Good heavens, there are rather a lot of you. Like a badger's burrow up there in the counties. And what is this sister's name? Is she as clever as you?"

"Ah . . ." Charlotte wracked her brain. Something strong and heavy and fashionable about a thousand years ago, that's what Ginevra had said. "Acton," she finished out of nowhere in particular, hoping she had chosen something not too wrong. "And my brother is . . . Blackwood." Charlotte bit her lip. She tasted paint. She lowered her voice to a whisper and widened her eyes. She tried to make herself look as innocent and needful as she could. Wellington was a man of society. She had to be the kind of Lady a gentleman would want to help. She could not be a rough parson's daughter from Haworth. She had to be the kind of girl who would dance through the beautiful rooms of Miss Jane's books, so beautiful and good that everything worked out for them in the end. So Charlotte tried to make her face look like the desperate maidens of romantic novels. She tried to make her face say: *I am helpless. Only you can save me.* It felt like more of a mask than Ginny's makeup. "Gondal has attacked us, sir. Well, of course, Gondal has attacked all of Glass Town, of course. But us in particular."

The Duke froze. A tall, dark man tried to take the next step in the dance and collided into Wellesley's iron back. When he turned round to scold whoever had held up the line, Charlotte saw that it was Adrian, the Marquis of Douro. Embers glowed strangely beneath his ashen skin. His eyes seemed to be trying to pry her apart. Wellington cleared his throat and spun Charlotte a little too quickly into a line of other girls. At least he only crushed her smallest toe doing it. Emily twirled in on her left, and they clasped hands quickly before the dance urged them on again. *This is it. Do your best.*

"Your brother and sister?" Lord Byron mused. His long black doggy hair glittered in the moonlight. "There's *more* of you? And are they just as charming as the rest of their family?"

"Not very." Emily laughed. "Oh, I'm sorry! Anne's only little but she's the sweetest bird in the forest. It's only Branwell who couldn't charm a rock into sitting still and doing nothing." She immediately cursed herself for forgetting that everyone was meant to have false names.

"What a perfectly marvelous line. I shall have it for

my own! It's the right of a Lord, you know, to take a percentage of anything good produced on his land. And I'm actually a Baron, so I can take the lot." Lord Byron laughed, and when he laughed, it sounded to Emily like a song written only for her. Though he *was* laughing at his own joke, she supposed.

"Is this your land? Your house?" Emily suddenly noticed that many of the other ladies were staring at them and whispering. What did those knowing glances mean? Of course, *she* knew very well that Lord Byron was meant to be mad and bad and all that rubbish, but this Lord Byron was only her own age. How dangerous to know could he be just yet?

Byron kissed her gloved hand as they stepped lightly round one another. He could dance like rivers could run. No one had ever kissed her hand before. Emily felt like she was going to throw up and like she was flying all at once.

"It is indeed, my clever dove! My house, my land, my drink, my food. I've loaned it all out to Douro for his little party," Byron said, slipping his arm around her waist. They were almost of a height. "You know how it is with elderly money. It can still cut a fine figure at table, but it's not *quite* all there." He tapped the side of his silky head. "I myself am merely *old* money. Entirely different. But! It is not Douro's brother and sister in peril, nor mine. Did you say a fellow called Brunty took them? Took them how? Took them where? Anyone named Brunty is trouble, it's true. Did he have a surname? Any distinguishing marks? Tattoos? And where did they go? Perhaps they're having a grand adventure and you oughtn't interrupt it."

Emily looked stricken. Lord Byron's shoulders slumped.

"Don't give me that face, darling Ellis! I only want joyful or cunning or passionate faces, none of this pale grief and sour disappointment! That sort of thing is for poetry, not for living. What can I do to get my merry Ellis back to charm the rocks her brother cannot?"

Emily smiled softly, a smile that any Lord would hear as clearly as words. *Perhaps there is something.*

I'm really rather good at this, Emily thought. *What a pity I'm not really the Lady of Thrushcross Grange!*

The song ended abruptly with all the dancers in two neat lines, boys on one side, girls on the other. Everyone applauded madly and laughed like tropical birds crying out for mates in the jungle. Beads of golden sweat stood out on Charlotte's brow. Arthur looked sorrowfully at her.

"I'm sorry, Miss Bell. The war is ever so much bigger than one brother or one sister. What help can be spared

for such a little thing? I need every man by my side."
He looked round to see if anyone was eavesdropping.
"We mean to make our final stand against Napoleon at
Calabar. I cannot hold the capital with even one soldier
missing. My answer is no, my dear, though it breaks my
heart to say it to such a clever face as yours."

Charlotte's carefully crafted helplessness fell away.
Now, the helplessness turned horribly real. She fought
back tears. She had just assumed he would say yes. He
always said yes when she played Wellington in their
games at home. This was her world. Hers and Emily's and
Branwell's and Anne's. How could he have said anything
other than yes? What now? This had been her plan. Her
only plan. And it was finished before it could begin. She
was left with nothing but a dress and her loss and a coat
of paint that was beginning to flake.

Wellington winced. "No man could call me a coward
on the battlefield," he said reluctantly. "But I've always
crumbled before a girl who's disappointed in me. Don't
make such faces, Miss Currer. It is politics. It is war.
There is no time for the fates of two little children while
the world is falling apart."

Charlotte tried to wrench her arm from Wellington's. He would not let her go. His grip was iron—really,
actually iron. Fear sizzled all up and down her spine.

Charlotte's eyes glowed as white-hot as Wellington's. "They are *not* two little children. They are my family. And you are a paperweight! Let me go!"

"Currer, be still. You are making a scene! Don't struggle so, like a wild, frantic bird rending its own feathers in desperation."

Charlotte drew herself up as tall as she could. Everyone kept calling her that. Some little, fluttering, weak thing. But she wasn't! She would never be! Not for Wellington and not for Jane and not for anyone.

"I am no bird," she said coldly. She was no girl in a novel now. "And no net ensnares me."

The Duke recoiled and let her arm drop. He coughed uncomfortably, bowed deeply, and retreated unhappily into the green wall of his officers.

Leftenant Gravey settled his wooden hand kindly on Charlotte's shoulder. "Don't let them do that to you, you nor your sister." How had she never noticed that Gravey had such a lovely Northern accent, so like Tabitha's?

"Let who do what, Leftenant?"

"Men. Dazzle you. They do it for advantage, no different from a field marshal gaining the high ground. You do the dazzling. You climb the hill. Or else you'll be stuck down in the muddy marsh with the rest of us, and that's no place to be."

"But I don't know how to dazzle. I couldn't dazzle a house fern."

Gravey kissed her forehead. He smelled like a warm autumn bonfire sparkling away.

"Learn fast," he said.

"Ladies and gentlemen!" came the high, bright, singsong voice belonging to the herald made of brandy snifters who had announced Charlotte and Emily to the Wildfell Ball. "If you would kindly gather in the Vivisectionists' Garden for the evening's entertainment, Young Soult the Rhymer will regale us with a marvelous display of theatrical puppetry in honor of our host, the Marquis of Douro!"

"Oh, Miss Ellis," Lord Byron gushed. He daringly put one sleek panther-fur hand on Emily's gloved fingers. "Shall we go a-roving, deep into the night? We shall! *You* shall. And you must sit beside me the whole while. Young Soult is an epically awful poet, but he's brilliant with puppets, you'll see. You *cannot* miss it." The great poet's eyes danced with mischief and delight and not a little bit of malice. "It's going to bring the house down."

NINETEEN

Dulce Et Decorum Est

Bran could hear his sister whispering in her narrow red and blue bed. She'd drawn the blankets all the way up over her head and curled her body into a tight ball. And she was whispering. It drove him mad when she did it at home, but in the silence of the Bastille, the sound was like rusted nails dragged up and down his spine.

"Who are you talking to, Annie? If you don't button your lips to your teeth in a half second I'm going to leap out the window."

"I'm sorry," sighed Anne. Her head popped up from beneath the covers. "I can't help it. I always talk to Victoria before bed. Can't sleep if I don't."

"Victoria is lying on the floor in the room at the top of the stairs with a crack in one eye. Maybe they're right about us. *You're* mad anyhow."

Anne's eyes blazed in the dark. "Don't you talk about her. She's mine. Go to sleep. Maybe if you're lucky, you'll dream about frogs pulling out your fingernails and wake up in a good mood."

But Branwell did not wake up in a good mood. He woke cold and stiff and out of sorts. He rose long before Anne and sat at the lonely little wooden table, watching her breathe, her blond hair sticky and sweaty against her forehead, the space between her fine eyebrows wrinkled with dreaming worry. Branwell was filled with such a desire to paint her that he felt he could very possibly die of it. He hadn't drawn anything since they came to Glass Town and it made his fingers ache like winter cold. He hadn't any pen or any paper and the whole thing was hopeless. But there little Anne lay, with her left arm thrown up above her head at such an *artistic* angle. . . .

Branwell picked up one of the bowls of cold gruel leftover from yesterday or the day before. He had no notion of how long they'd been there, really. None at all. But after the tray of brown bread and brown soup and brown tea, they could never face that gluey gray stuff. So he dumped it out on the table and smeared it all round till the wood was covered in a fine, thin, even silvery film of gruel. He used his fingernails to outline Anne's arm, the tendrils of her hair, the way her brow bone joined the top of her nose, her pointed chin. He warmed up as he worked, until he felt like he had a hearth inside him, full up of scalding embers, and as long as he kept drawing, he would never be cold again, not ever.

Branwell looked down at the Anne he'd made. It was beautiful, he thought. His fingernails had made the whole thing so delicate and fragile, like patterns in ice. The best work he'd ever done, and he could never hang it on a wall, unless he nailed up the whole table.

"Bran?" Anne said groggily, coming round to the waking world. "What are you doing?"

Branwell smeared his hand through the gruel-painting. Beautiful? It was nothing, just like everything else he ever tried to do. He did try. He tried to make stories as good as Charlotte's and Emily's, but his only ever shone when he killed somebody or blew up a castle or bled a spy for secrets. He did it as often as he could, chasing that shine. But even his best murder never sparkled quite like one of Charlotte's scenes of strolling through the gardens with Zenobia Elrington, or Emily's making Mary Percy run across the windswept moors to meet her lover. Branwell supposed that even Anne's stupid, secret

Victoria game glowed in the dark under her blankets. Put his slop-painting next to anything they did and it looked just like what it was: gruel.

"And I'll be grueling my whole life, won't I?" he grumbled darkly to himself. It seemed a very Glass Town thing to say.

Anne rubbed her eyes and yawned. "Are you ready?" she said.

"All right, Anne. Let's bust ourselves out of jail. What do you say?"

Anne nodded eagerly, sniffling. Down below in the courtyard, a bullfrog shouted at a tree frog for marching slower than the rest of them.

Branwell bolstered his sister up on his shoulders so she could peek through the little window at the top of the door. Bonaparte and his rosy lady-friend seemed to glare at them from the painting like strict parents. Not angry, just disappointed.

"There's nobody there!" Anne whispered. It was a very loud whisper.

Bran grunted under her weight. "What do you mean there's nobody there? That's not possible!" It bruised his newfound sense of importance to think that they weren't being guarded by *at least* two enormous, muscular, battle-hardened frogs.

Anne hopped down. "Well, it is possible, *Bran*. I'm not lying. Why would I lie?"

"Why wouldn't they leave a guard? The whole reason Brunty took us in the first place was because he heard us talking about how maybe, somehow, probably we sort of *made* this place happen. That . . . well . . . I haven't had a chance to really thoroughly philosophize the whole business yet, but that . . . that makes us a bit . . . a bit like a King and a Queen, doesn't it?" That didn't feel right. But it didn't feel so wrong, either. "I should think they'd want to keep an eye on the Crown."

But Anne wasn't listening to her brother pondering whether or not she was a goddess. She was staring at the big black lock in the door with her hands on her hips and the tip of her tongue poking out of the corner of her mouth, thinking. The lock was the size of her head. It had extremely serious-looking bolts all over it.

"You can't stare it open, you know," grumbled Bran. "There's no key in here. I checked while you were pretending to be asleep. And nothing to pick with either. Unless you want to have a go at picking a lock with a handful of cooked porridge."

"No," Anne mused. "I shouldn't think *porridge* would work."

She looked up at her brother and grinned mischievously. All her tears were gone now. She waggled her thin, little fingers at him. Then, Anne stuck her fore-finger and middle finger into the huge black lock and turned her hand. It hurt very much. She strained. Her face turned red.

"Good Lord, Anne, you are thick. I never wanted to say, but out of the four of us . . ."

The tumblers groaned. The lock creaked. The door opened.

"What? How?" Branwell spluttered.

Anne pulled her hand back. She giggled as quietly as she could, but her voice echoed into the hallway beyond. She wiggled her fingers again.

"Skeleton key!" she crowed.

Branwell cursed himself for not thinking of it. He stomped out into the hall and started off in a direction. Any direction, as long as he got to choose it. Anne skipped along behind him, explaining herself proudly.

"Skeleton key! Get it? It just came to me! I thought if time *really* flies here, and spirits are *really* spirits, and Brown Bess musket balls really are brown and called Bess, I thought: Well, I've got bones, haven't I? I've got a skeleton! And nobody else here does except Napoleon, so that'd make a pretty excellent kind of sense for Old Boney's personal prison."

"Yes, yes, you're so clever. Now, be clever quietly, or we shall be caught and it'll be fingernails for the both of us."

Anne blanched. They crept silently down the long, stone hall. There were other doors punched into the rocky wall, but all the barred windows were dark and empty. In fact, everything in the Bastille was rather dark. They hadn't any candles, so there was nothing to be done about it, but Anne shuddered anyway. At least there didn't seem to be any cobwebs or spiders lurking about. The endless halls and staircases were brutally clean, and that made *Bran* shudder. Every place in the world had cobwebs. What demonic power would it take to keep a place this big and deep and unhappy clean?

They stumbled and snuck and tiptoed for hours. Branwell hadn't really any idea which way to go, but he'd chosen *this* way, and he meant to stick to it. This way was his way. It would lead them true. Eventually. He realized he was viciously hungry. How long had it been since porridge? How long had they been here? How long had they slept?

"Bran, look!" Anne pointed up ahead.

A dark golden light spilled out into the hallway. They hurried after it. They were so thirsty for light!

The light was coming from the floor below them. It

shone up through a little row of alcoves and pillars in the endless, blank stone wall. It wasn't endless and blank at all. They stood on a long balcony overlooking a room filled with candles, torches, and three hearths at full blaze. Branwell and Anne tucked themselves behind two pillars and peered over the edge.

"That's Napoleon!" Bran hissed excitedly.

"Shush!" Anne hissed back.

Napoleon Bonaparte hunched over his war table in that glowing room. The firelight reflected on his long, white bones. It must have been his office, or at least his strategy room. Miniature models of the cities of Glass Town covered every table and chair. Papers littered the floor. Marengo, his loyal rooster, roosted by one of the hearths, his own green flames banked and quiet, snoring his high, trilling chicken snores. One of the armored frogs stood at attention. His poleax glittered by candlelight.

Brunty was there, too, sitting at Old Boney's side. He looked exhausted. His pages hung limp. The headlines on his waistcoat read: IS THIS THE END FOR BRAVE BRUNTY? and THE INDUSTRY OF WAR GRINDS ON, and DULCE ET DECORUM EST PRO PATRIA MORI. The wooden scroll-knob of his belly lay open. The bat-tree burbled away weakly inside. Napoleon poked at the machine that powered Brunty now. He lifted up a few of the thick saucers with the barrel of his rifle-arm and let them fall again.

"Is all very well and good, *mon ami*, but what am I meant to do with it? How shall we make more? We can't even take it out of you. You just fall down. At first, it was a *bit* funny, my best spy going up and down and up and down like a windup Brunty. But now what? *One* of these does me no good. I need one for every beautiful toad in Gondal. And then a few more. And a few more after. And what are we calling it? Bat-tree? That's awful. *Misérable.* No style to it."

"It's a Voltaic Pyle," Brunty wheezed. "It's devilishly simple, really. The discs are copper, zinc, and silver, wrapped in scraps of a housewife's dress or something, soaked in brine. Back where it came from, it makes an electrical current, and the wires conduct it, and it stores the energy for you. It's their magic. Their only magic. But once I got it across the borderlands, it perked up some. It *woke* up. Our bouncing baby Pyle is"— the Magazine Man coughed—"a little more interesting over here."

"Voltaic Pyle. Too long," Napoleon grunted. "Monsieur Grenouille, come up with something better!"

"Right away, sir," the bundle of cast-off armor shaped like a frog answered. He sunk his chin into his chest, deep in thought.

Brunty closed the scroll-knob. He wiped dried ink off his papery mouth.

"Our man in Glass Town is handling the rest," the Magazine Man said. "I sent him a ghost with a letter that explains all the technical rubbish that weakling Volta said to me. It must be terribly sad to be a breather. They break so easily. At any rate, it won't be a problem. Our boy's infiltrated the army. No shortage of supplies in Wellington's tents. The first shipment will be arriving tonight. Twelve. They've got three of everything over there while we've got one or none. Isn't that always the way?"

"Not for so long, *mon frere*," Bonaparte said affectionately, and patted Brunty on the shoulder. He wiped the grimy ink off on his coat.

"I'm tired, Boney," Brunty rasped. "I think it's running down. It would appear that bat-trees don't last. I don't know how much longer I can stomach it all."

Napoleon held a rifle-barrel hand to his forehead. He yanked off his bicorne hat and threw it across the room. "I am also, my boy! Do you think I'm not? But what else was I made for, if not this? With these arms, who else could I have been? I don't even remember anything else but this. This war, and Josephine. I miss her so, Brunty. I miss the smell of her rosy hair and the way

she stabbed me with her thorns whenever I held her."
He held up his rifles to the fire. "What else is there in
the world but thorns and gunfire and tiredness?"

"See?" Bran mouthed. "We should be helping them!"

"Help them make an army of acid lightning bat-tree
bombs like Brunty? Are you mad?" Anne whispered back.
"If he's so tired he ought to have a *nap!*"

"Well, what's Leftenant Gravey, then? He's been
brought back loads of times."

"Leftenant Gravey doesn't shoot green electric rubbish out of his nose! Doesn't that seem like an *awfully* big
difference? Bran! Stop gawping at that nasty old tyrant.
We have to keep on!"

Branwell dragged his feet. In all their games and stories, in all the times he'd led their toy army, pretending
he was Napoleon, that he was conquering Europe and the
downstairs parlor, he never could have imagined he'd be
so close to the man he could smell his cologne. He didn't
want to go back to the black maze of the Bastille's halls.
He was meant to be in charge now. But what was Bran in
charge of? Trudging along in the dark? That wasn't any
kind of a thing to lord it over.

Down more staircases. Through more corridors. Past
more empty rooms.

Until one of the rooms wasn't empty. Twilight and

candlelight streamed through the bars of another heavy door like all the other heavy doors. Only this one was cut out of thick green glass. The window was bigger, too. They didn't need to stack Anne on top to see inside. They looked at each other, trying to talk it over without talking out loud. *Should we keep moving? It's just some poor soldier or something, I expect. But there's no one else in these cells. Maybe we should let the poor fellow out, too.*

They raised their eyes above the stone sill of the barred window.

Napoleon had locked up a mountain of toys in a prison cell. Anne had never seen so many all in one place. And no two the same! Dolls in dresses, soldiers of wood and tin and porcelain and lead, woolen babies in swaddling clothes, delicate Princesses of silver and gold, glass angels and clay devils, even a taxidermied dog fitted with runners like a rocking horse.

"Must be some very bad-tempered toys." Bran laughed softly.

Something moved in the heap of playthings. Something thin and small and white and quiet.

One of the dolls was a girl.

TWENTY

The Vivisectionists' Garden

The glittering assembly of the Wildfell Ball swarmed out into the gardens like a school of silver fish. The moon rode so high in the sky it seemed as distant and remote as the stars. Charlotte and Emily stepped out onto a rich green lawn gone black with moonlit shadows and dew. They didn't need Crashey to find their way now. Everyone seemed to know where to go. The press and swell of bodies carried them along down the path, through indigo stone arches and tall braziers full of violet coals. They finally got a moment alone in the crush. Crashey and Byron and Gravey and Rogue and Wellington and all the rest streamed on ahead.

Charlotte pulled a lock of Emily's hair over a little

spot on her forehead where the silver paint had begun to fade.

"Did you have any luck?" she whispered.

Robin Hood jostled Emily lightly as he passed by and stepped on her hems. She felt certain that if she *had* been carrying a purse, she wouldn't be carrying it any longer. "I'm not sure," she said quietly. "George may help us, though I'm not entirely sure what he can do, other than write a poem about the whole mess."

"*George?*" Charlotte arched her golden eyebrow.

"Yes, *George.* Lord Byron. That's his name, you know. He's . . . well, he's completely as I thought he'd be, but at the same time, not at all."

"Wellington is much the same. Like, and not like. Though I don't expect he'd think much of me calling him Arthur just yet." Charlotte looked down at the deep, shadowy lawn. "He turned me down flat, Em."

"He's hardly the only fellow here with a good arm and a good head," Emily said. "We'll find someone else."

But she could tell by Charlotte's face that no one else would do. Her sister had a story in her head, and the story went: *Charlotte and the Duke of Wellington ride together as equals and companions into battle and save everyone from everything.* But that *wasn't* the story. Emily was riding, too. And she was feeling bold enough to dismiss a Duke with a flick of her hand. "He's rather a stodgy thing, anyway, isn't he? All brooding and distant and cold and glum and barely saying a word even at a party! I can't imagine what you see in him. I much prefer George. And Crashey."

Over the jeweled heads of the revelers, they could see one last stone archway. It was set into the scarlet prickles of a long, winding holly hedge wall. This one was obsidian, shining like a black mirror. There were moonstones set into the rock to trace out medieval-looking letters that read:

The Vivisectionists' Garden

"I am slightly concerned, Emily," confessed Charlotte. "Ellis, I mean, I am *slightly* concerned about what exactly a Vivisectionists' Garden might be."

"It does sound gruesome, doesn't it?" Emily said.

A flush rode as high on her cheeks as the moon in the sky and though her stomach churned at the thought of what might lie beyond this last archway, her heart thrilled at the possibility of seeing something she really, *really* oughtn't.

"You know vivisectionists cut up corpses and study them, don't you? It might be all kidneys and lungs among the rosebushes. You won't be squeamish?" Charlotte asked.

"I read just as many books as you, *Currer*," Emily snapped. She'd been dancing with Lord Byron! No one could have much to teach her about anything after that! "I'm not an idiot! I know what words mean, even if they have more syllables than Bran says they should."

At the thought of Branwell, they grew somber. Such a lot of fun it had been, dancing and meeting famous and magical and mythical people and bantering with clever men. Almost marvelous enough to make them forget how badly they were needed elsewhere, how desperately they had to find a way home now that the evening train had long gone. They clasped hands and laced their fingers together, gold and silver, and began to say something to one another about how shamefully they'd been laughing while poor Anne was probably still wedged under Brunty's armpit. Then, they stopped. Was it such an awful crime to enjoy one minute of this strange day? They'd come on purpose, hadn't they? They'd wanted to come. Wanted to run away. They'd escaped the maw of School so narrowly—wasn't that worth one laugh, one smile, one spin in the arms of a poet or a Duke? But then, they couldn't bear to say that out loud, either. What if it was not worth that, and they were being terrible sisters by not focusing every fiber of their beings, every single second, on finding their family?

"I forgive you, C," whispered Emily.

"I forgive you, E," Charlotte whispered back.

They plunged into the Vivisectionists' Garden.

The guests of the Wildfell Ball sprawled out in a sparkling half-moon around a luxurious puppet theater. There were no seats; everyone lay about relaxing on a thick lawn of soft purple grass and tiny wild roses. For all the glorious clothes and tiaras and refined voices, it looked just like a country picnic back in Yorkshire. The Duke and Duchess of Can't even had a hamper of champagne flutes and *vol-au-vents* like the one Charlotte had had on the train. They wept all over it, which probably got their wine horribly salty, and daubed each other's eyes with the corners of their checkered blanket. Ross and Parry slurped down seal meat and iced oysters on a walrus-skin. The Shelleys shared sandwiches with the Queen of the Bluestockings. Wellington and his limeskin sailors stood on the outskirts, still smoking and joking and snickering and catcalling Guinevere and never fully joining in. The Marquis of Douro and his lover, Mary, sat nearest to the theater. Mary admired the mauve brocade curtains and the curving, intricate woodwork that ran up and down the base and the poles and the crown of the thing, all painted silver, just like a certain girl in the audience. Crashey, Gravey, Rogue, and their lady companions had staked out a claim under a plum tree heavy with fruit. Lord Byron spread out an ancient, threadbare patchwork quilt with a hundred different coats of arms fading away on it. He judged it fine and lounged back on his elbows, leaving plenty of room on the blanket for company. Someone had thoughtfully hauled Josephine's cage out so she could see the show. She did not look like she was looking forward to it.

Not a single one of them was looking at the statues.

All round the walled garden, there were little alcoves in the holly hedge. In each alcove stood an extraordinary, beautiful, horrible, hideous statue. Charlotte and Emily could not help goggling at them. How could everyone else just sit there like there was nothing unusual about anything? The statues were all handsome men and women, pale and expressive and very realistic. They looked much like the Greek ones they'd seen illustrated in Papa's magazines. Some of them had arms or legs or heads lopped off—but many of the ones in the magazine pictures did, too. They weren't troubled by *that*.

Charlotte walked up to the one nearest her. It was a young girl, a Venus or a Diana, just exactly as she might have been carved in Athens. Only this Venus didn't have any marble skin over her stomach. Charlotte could see all her organs, placed in perfect anatomical position, and carved out of precious gems. Her stomach was a huge pearl, her liver a massive black opal, her esophagus a curling length of coral, her kidneys a pair of garnets, the pancreas a lump of emerald, the spleen an uncut topaz. The statues were all like that. Some part of their marble gone and their insides revealed. That man looked like Michelangelo's David, only strand after strand of amethyst intestines spilled out of his gut. Nearest the puppet stage, the neck of a lithe youth in a short toga ended in a jade skull. Emily reached up to run her fingers along the ruby ropes of muscle showing through a child's marble arm. She shuddered, but it fascinated her. *Bran would love this*, she thought. *He would draw them over and over until he could get the one with the onyx heart just right. And Anne would have screamed if she saw that sapphire brain. Screamed, and then talked about nothing else for a month.* Emily missed them so. She hoped desperately they were all right, wherever they were.

"Do you like my patients?" came the sleek leather voice of Dr. Home behind them.

Somehow, Charlotte got the idea Dr. Home preferred to sneak up behind people before he started a conversation with them. That way no one could ever start off on the right foot. They'd stammer and stutter and blink a lot and he'd get to play the calm, reassuring doctor. But she did not find his presence reassuring. He towered above them like a crow, miles of oiled satchel-leather folded tightly and crisply into the shape of a young man.

"Do you do a large business in healing statues?" Charlotte said archly. *She* would not stammer. Let him do what he liked with that.

"Marble needs little medicine," the doctor demurred. "I made each of these myself, modeled after one of my mortal patients once their case proved . . . inevitable. If you look closely, I have marked out in black stones which villain it was that failed them, in the end. The heart, the liver, the lung, the brain." Dr. Home's eyes roved lovingly from statue to statue.

"This is Lord Byron's house," Emily protested softly. "Why should you have a garden in it?"

"George is very generous when he admires one's work. I healed his fever after the battle of Lepanto."

Charlotte and Emily exchanged glances. The Byron they knew of in England had died at Lepanto. But the physician to the Crown did not seem to notice the expressions on their faces at all. He was far too busy noticing himself. "This place was his personal thank-you note," he went on, stroking his long, leather nose with long, leather fingers. He seemed entirely lost in his own words. He had come to talk to them! It was tremendously rude, Charlotte thought. But perhaps she could get an answer or two while he was distracted with imagining diseased kneecaps or what-have-you.

"Doctor, what is the average life-span of a Glass Towner? I only ask because everyone we've met seems quite young to be Dukes and Duchesses and getting married and having children and owning houses and building gory gardens."

Dr. Home gave her a pointed, black look that plainly said Charlotte's question was rude at the least and obscene at the worst. He then ignored it completely.

"I come here whenever I am able, to contemplate the nature of things," he pressed on. "Of illness. Of health. Of time and death and memory." Home waved his hand dismissively in the night air. "This was all before, of course."

"Before what?" said Emily and Charlotte together.

Dr. Home smiled. All his teeth were white tiles, like the floor of a hospital. "Before the invention of rum, my dear girls."

Silver trumpets sounded. Two drums began to beat. An oboe slid in and skipped back and forth between its two mates. Young Soult the Rhymer's show was about to start.

Crashey finally spotted them. He waved his oak hand excitedly. "Char . . . er! Er! Em. Currer! Charcurrerie! Ellisem! Sorry! Over here, you great metal magpies!"

Lord Byron turned his head the moment he heard Emily's half-Crashied name.

"Ellis!" he called. "You did promise you would sit by me, my darling. Did thy heart forget or thy spirit deceive? Either way, get your silver rump over here; I've missed you hideously."

"I think I shall be more convincing on my own," Emily said, a little guiltily. Of course, she did mean to get Byron to help them. But Charlotte didn't like her calling him George, and she wanted to call him George over and over.

"Go," said Charlotte. She shut her eyes and held her hand to her chest. Visions of onyx hearts still beat in her head. "But if he says no, you must move on. As you said. He's not the only fellow here with a good arm and a good head."

Half the Wildfell girls glowered hatefully at Emily as she picked her way through the sea of blankets toward Byron. Charlotte settled down with Crashey and his party of soldiers and eligible ladies. She noticed that the wooden boys had spread out very near Wellington, who had finally consented to lie awkwardly on the grass. He tried to lean against an increasingly irritated Copenhagen, but could not get his iron wings into a comfortable position. Wild roses sizzled where the hot feathers draped too far over his lion's haunches. He slapped him affectionately with his sea-foam tail. Crashey followed Charlotte's line of sight.

"Don't say I never did a girl any favorindnesses," he said, and jostled her with his elbow.

"How did your dance go?" said Miss Jane sourly as she scooted aside to make room. "I hope it was worth your reputation! If anyone in town should hear of it, I shouldn't think your country manners would be invited back to civilization any time soon. Well, of course, *I* won't breathe a word. . . ."

"Have you found your gang of roughers yet?" Zenobia Elrington said kindly.

Lady Elrington handed Charlotte a slice of cake on a sturdy plate. She smiled at her food. It was a *mille-feuille* cake. That meant *a hundred sheets* in French. So, of course, her pastry was made of a hundred pages of sheet music held together with butter and sugar. When she bit into it, a sweet, golden song burst into her mind.

"Would you like me to be her rougher, Zenobia?"

Rogue said suddenly, his unpatched eye full of love and that odd slyness it always seemed to keep at the bottom of every other feeling. "Would that please you, my dearest? If I were to go to Gondal? If I were to creep and spy for her sake?"

"*Gang of roughers!*" gasped Miss Jane, shocked. "Go to *Gondal*? What madness is this?"

Gravey, who seemed pained to be stuck with her while Rogue rested his dark head in Zenobia's lap, hushed his date. They were all then loudly hushed in turn by the rest of the audience. Torches blazed into life; the show had begun.

Young Soult the Rhymer's reedy voice echoed out over the audience.

"Ladies and gentlemen, I, Young Soult the Rhymer, present to you *The Douro-ble Dynasty, or, Rule, Glass Town!* Written by me, spoken by me, devised by me, costumes by me, sets by me, and . . . oh yes, right, puppets built and . . . er . . . puppeted by me as well."

Lord Byron rolled his eyes. He leaned into Emily and whispered: "He chewed my ear off for a week trying to decide between those two limp-lettuce titles. Either of them is about as moving as a boiled egg."

"George," Emily whispered back, "about my brother and sister . . ."

"Oh, come now, there's time for all that later!"

"There's isn't, really, it's very urgent. . . ."

"Just watch, Ellis!" He took her chin in his hand. Emily gasped at his touch, at the presumption of it! But he only turned her head so that she was looking directly at the blanket belonging to the Marquis of Douro, Mary Percy, and Dr. Home. "*Watch.*"

Young Soult released a lovely embroidered and painted backdrop across the rear of the puppet theater. It showed a rather standard Eden: pleasant fields, innocent streams, fawns and rabbits playing among wild carrots and berries and ancient stones. Several marionettes descended onto the stage dressed in rich medieval robes. Young Soult the Rhymer did not like other performers interfering with his vision. He worked his creations with both hands and feet, fingers and toes, perched uncomfortably on a high couch above the whole affair. Soult's voice cracked in nervous terror as he spoke the first lines of his great work:

Behold these lands! Rich in both grain and geese
Where all Glass Towners lived in gentle peace

"Eeeeeugh," Crashey giggled. Miss Jane shushed him with a murderous glance. "Those is some *tortured* wordage right there. What'd those poor geese ever do to him?"

Six noble Lords stand here before you!
All things they see do they command

Zamorna, Wellesley, Calabar,
Bon-a-parte, and Northangerland!
But one true soul surpassed them all
In honor, faith, and honesty—
The brave Marquis of Douro,
Whose grandson pays my fee.

Some nervous laughter bubbled up from the audience. They were all far too rich to be entirely comfortable discussing money, even in verse. The puppeteer cleared his throat and pressed on.

Explorers all and pioneers,
They conquered jungle, plain, and sea
So that Young Soult could tell his tale
Of how our nation came to be.

Jeers and whistles and boos greeted the Bonaparte puppet, who had tiny tin swords for arms and a jumble of rat and sparrow bones for a body. Yet the other lordly puppets greeted him as a brother, bowing their little wooden heads and embracing him fondly. *That's not right at all,* Emily thought. *Boney has rifles for arms! I saw it myself!* But she did not want to seem foolish or ignorant. Emily of Haworth might not know the history of Glass Town and Gondal and ask a hundred questions freely, but it would all be old news to Ellis Bell of Thrushcross.

"Oh, don't give him the satisfaction!" Lord Byron snorted resentfully. "It's not even the same number of syllables as the first bit! Will you listen to him mangle Old Boney's name just to fit the meter? And he shoved himself in there for no good reason. Someone have that boy arrested at once. Crimes against the noun!"

"Be nice," Emily said, though secretly she rather liked him being awful.

> *Equally amongst these giants*
> *All the earth divided was*
> *And all devised together*
> *Certain just and gracious laws!*
> *Young Douro led them all in honor,*
> *In industry and cleverness.*
> *Then he smote the ground*
> *Whereat the borders of their nations kissed,*
> *And by his will (and by his wallet)*
> *There rose the city of Verdopolis!*

The Douro puppet, who had diamond chips for eyes, slapped his sword against the stage. A loud bang sounded and a puff of green smoke billowed out into the night, making everyone cough till they were nearly sick all over the garden. When it cleared, a pretty model of the capital of Glass Town stood at Douro's feet, all spangled green towers and houses and steeples. Applause rippled round, for it had been a rather good trick, even if their eyes still smarted. But Lady Zenobia did not blink. The white flames of her eyes burned the smoke away. She was not clapping.

"*I* am heir to Northangerland," she growled. "And that skinny little craven pepper pot knows it. My grandfather had just as much hand in Verdopolis as Douro and bloody well more than Calabar. Wellesley and Zamorna designed the Tower of All Nations in the Great Square! Even Bonaparte laid the bricks of the wall with his own hands. How can Wellesley snooze on his lion over there while this brat insults his family? What is this rubbish?"

But the current Marquis of Douro seemed pleased enough. He smiled tightly and waved his ashen hand, recognizing the honor Young Soult meant to do him with his poetry.

Emily raised her eyebrow at Byron. Was this what he wanted her to see? It didn't seem much, and was taking an awfully long time to get to the point.

"Wait," he assured her.

But the next verse did not move things along much.

> *Thus the years passed, as they do,*
> *With sons and grandsons numberless,*
> *New Douros and Boneys born*
> *To all their ancestors possessed.*

"Yes?" Lord Byron groused, rolling his eyes. "That *is* how inheritance works. Thank you so much for explaining it. Whatever would we do without you, Soulty? Get *on* with it, man! Exposition does not become us!"

A new puppet dangled down. This one had a long, wicked nose, cruel eyes, and wore a black cloak lined in red. All the ancient Lords shrank back from it, save Douro and Bonaparte. Drops of Young Soult's sweat began to drip onto the planks of the little stage.

"Here we are!" Lord Byron chortled. He leaned forward eagerly. "Now the beef's on the plate!"

> But ho! What's this? Who now intrudes
> Upon our happy scene?
> I say! It is the very devil!
> With his fangs and hooves . . . er . . . unclean.
> What crawls from out the darkness
> Of the frail and mortal heart?
> Foul AMBITION comes at night
> To tear our peace apart!

"Almost skidded off the road there, lad," Rogue smirked. "Also, there were eight Lords, you dolt." He turned to his beloved. "That cretin forgot Elseraden and Almadore. And of *course* it's the Gondal nobles tossed on the rubbish heap. But *Calabar* sneaks in? That fat fool hit his head on a rock jumping off his stupid boat onto the beach at Gaaldine and died before they even got around to naming the place!"

Zenobia and Gravey blinked curiously at Rogue.

"Why should you care?" the Leftenant whispered. "Forget Gondal!"

But the crowd roared over whatever answer the Sergeant Major gave. However poor the poetry, the story got their blood up. Highborn ladies threw bits of their feasts at the stage as though they were in the cheap seats of a bawdy dance hall. Earls and Barons shouted in English, French, and highly unauthorized mixes of the two. The miniature Bonaparte rattled his saber-arms and waggled a long, velvet tongue. Soult put on an obnoxiously over-the-top voice for his Bonaparte puppet. Charlotte felt so embarrassed for him she turned her eyes away. *Napoleon doesn't even sound like that!* she thought grumpily at the grass.

> *Eez not enuf to own all zis,*
> *To rule Gondal wiz me dainty fist*
> *One country? Pfft! Iz nothing muches!*
> *I want zem all wizzin my clutches!*

Tiny swords clanged as Napoleon advanced on the noble, innocent Lords of Glass Town, cutting them down one by one. The Douro puppet danced out of the way, carefully placing other men between himself and Boney's onslaught. Soult flicked the marionette's strings this way and that as Zamorna, Wellesley, Northangerland and all the rest fell beneath Napoleon's blades. Douro's descendant frowned and began to scratch nervously at his picnic blanket.

> *We fought him back and Gondal reaped*
> *The bloody wheat they sowed,*
> *But when the hour of victory dawned,*
> *Old Douro let the villain go!*

The Douro puppet raised his sword above Bonaparte's head, then bowed to him instead and knelt to help the marionette to his feet. Moans and sighs of knowing, rueful sadness passed through the crowd like waves. The Duchess of Can't wiped away even more tears than usual.

"Kill him!" someone yelled from the back.

"Stab him in the face, you moron!" hollered another.

"If only! If only!" Sergeant Crashey joined in.

But nothing they could say would alter Young Soult's play. Charlotte leaned forward, trying to piece it all together with the Battle of Port Ruby and everything she'd ever learned in her history books about Waterloo and Trafalgar and the thousand versions of those battles they'd acted out in their room at the top of the stairs while it rained on the moors outside.

Why did the old man mercy choose?

"Because he had cheese biscuits for brains!" a drunken Lord bellowed. Everyone roared with laughter, except Adrian and Mary Percy, who seemed to have nailed scowls to their faces. Soult cleared his throat and started over.

Why did the old man mercy choose?
We dare not ask his mind,
Or if REGRET and SHAME can taint
Each stop along a family line!

The partiers gasped. The nerve of the young poet! The cheek! Savage little whispers ran up and down the rows.

"Now just a moment!" cried Adrian, the present Marquis of Douro, and very definitely a stop along the family line in question. Mary Percy tried to calm her love. Their faces looked so young in the moonlight. He pushed her bronze hand aside. The Marquis punched the ground with his ashen fist and called out, coldly and clearly: "Don't forget who butters your bread, you impudent, unemployed hedgehog!"

Young Soult wiped the sweat from his peppercorn brow on his shoulder. He tried to laugh it off, but his giggle sounded like a terrified hummingbird. Back to the sure hit—he dangled the Bonaparte puppet again. Its sword arms glittered in the moonlight. Once again Emily bit her tongue to keep from correcting Young Soult right there. His ridiculous Gondal accent bleated out into the night once more. Charlotte rolled her eyes.

I never rests! I never sleeps!
I hungers for ze world entire!
Deed zat dumb Douro reellie zink zat
Bonaparte vould joost retires?

With a blast of the trumpets, a new puppet crashed down onto the boards. Emily lit up. *This* was the Napoleon they'd seen! He had proper rifle-arms and his huge hat and his giant rooster. Lord Byron stared at Emily as she clapped her hands in delight.

"Do you like Old Boney so much?"

"Oh, no, it's not that . . . it's just . . ." Ellis Bell could hardly say she'd gotten shot at by the man himself earlier that afternoon. "The rooster," she finished lamely. "It's very cleverly done."

Young Soult *had* banged up rather a brilliant horror-bird out of a milk pitcher, a pair of scissors for the beak, and scraps of green gauze to represent its fire-breath.

Now my grandboy's in ze family biz—
Zat bebe's got ze knack.
Big Boney may be in ze ground,
But Leetle Boney's on ze attack!

Little squibs and tiny rockets fired off as the younger Bonaparte rampaged through the countryside once more, laughing maniacally and shooting holes in the silken backdrop. Red ribbons tumbled out of the puppets' bodies like real gouts of blood.

Oh, Bran would have gone mad for that, Charlotte thought. *Maybe we can act it out for him when we get home. I've got red ribbons and so has Em.*

Home. She shut her eyes. It did not seem possible that Haworth or Keighley or even Yorkshire still existed somewhere far behind her on the railroad line. *If we ever get back.* And then an awful, alien thought crept up through the stairs of her mind like a black cat. *What if we do get back, all of us, with grog in hand? What will happen if it works? What will happen if it doesn't?*

Young Soult tossed woolen pink intestines stuffed with barley out of the puppet-battle and into the front row. Miss Jane fainted into Gravey's irritated arms.

"Oh, come off it, you poodle," the Leftenant groaned. "I lost my innards three times in a week once. The least you can do is stay awake for it."

Miss Jane opened one eye and glared up at the Leftenant, who steadfastly refused to behave as a suitor should. "You just ruin everything," she whined. "You're meant to make a fuss over me!"

"That's preposterous," said Charlotte evenly. "What do they teach you in the city?"

Young Soult's next tortured verse sang out over Gravey's roars of laughter.

> *How bitterly the widows wept*
> *As Glass Town bent and broke!*
> *Because we would not kneel and place*
> *Our necks beneath his yoke!*

A pale little puppet all of white silk stepped hesitantly into the scene. She wore a silver crown. A marionette covered in paper roses strode confidently from the other side of the curtains.

> *They took Victoria by night,*
> *We stole their Josephine,*
> *But all for naught as hills turned red*
> *That once were rich and green.*

Young Soult's hands and feet twitched and shuddered so quickly Charlotte could hardly see them move. The puppets waged war with every jerk and pull of a finger or a toe. Old Douro marched back across the ribbon-soaked battlefields. Now he sported a gray beard made out of old batting. A firecracker burst. The torches flickered. The oboe blew a long, low note. The marionette collapsed, clutching his heart.

> *Our sons and daughters bled and died*

To save us from his chains!
And on the fields of gray Weghlon
Even old Douro was slain.

Soft whimpering sounds rose up as even a few of the older men wept. Lord Byron rolled his eyes impatiently.

"He's not gotten any better. *Chain* and *slain*? I wonder if he *sprained* himself coming up with that? Just because it's historical doesn't mean it's good."

Emily looked at him sidelong. She wondered how Lord Byron would take a bit of teasing. Branwell usually kicked something or upended something on her head. Anne cried sometimes, and sometimes called her a badger or a nixie or an owl's breakfast. But she couldn't stop herself now any more than she could back home.

"*I* think you just don't like anyone else's poems getting a good reaction."

She awaited the kick or the upending or the badger or the breakfast.

Byron raised a furry eyebrow at her. His wolfy eyes smoldered petulantly.

"Watch the edge on that wit, girl! You'll cut yourself before you cut me." Then he was all secret smiles and anticipation again. "Hush, hush now, we're going to miss it!"

Still more puppets crowded on. How many had the

boy made? A black leather marionette with long, thin limbs and a soldier made of simple yellow wood knelt beside Douro and lifted him up onto an invisible gurney. The drums beat wildly. A scarlet flower caked with crystal beads rose up from below the stage.

> *But ho! But lo! What flower is this*
> *Beneath dead Douro's head?*
> *These unassuming petals stained*
> *With Glass Town blood so red?*
> *What luck, what joy! A miracle!*
> *Heaven turned against the frogs!*
> *The angels brought us Dr. Home*
> *And Crashey's death-defying grog!*

Sergeant Crashey threw his arms in the air. "Bully-blimey it all down the road and back! It's me! Would you lookagander at that! It's puppet me! I'm famous! Look at my legs! Good Lord, but I never was that thin!"

The Shelleys, Keats, Jane, and Kate Crackernuts shushed Crashey violently. Dr. Home bent his shiny leather head as the folk around him showered the man in praise.

"I will not shush!" Crashey announced. "I have never been a puppet or done up theatrisculpturally and I am chuffed as a steam train! Dunno why he couldn't use the Latin, though. He's overstuffed the meter as it is! Who'd notice one more bit of fatticus in that rex sausageorum?"

"Shut it, Crash!" Lord Byron yelled. Beside him, Emily's mouth had dropped open in surprise.

"Crashey!" said Charlotte. "It was you? *You* invented the . . . the . . . something . . . *vitae* . . . grog?"

The Sergeant preened. "What did I say? What did I *expressxactically* say? I *said* you two didn't know a thing about me and I could be brainyrich and bigshotted as anything for all you could guess. Sergeant Crash C. Crashey is an enigmariddluzzleman and a half!"

Miss Jane narrowed her eyes at Charlotte. Lady Zenobia whispered in her fiancé's wooden ear.

"Surely Thrushcross is not so remote that such basic facts have not reached your muddy, unhinged door," Miss Jane hissed.

Charlotte's stomach turned cold. She cast about for something to shut up the nasty little gossip. "A . . . a Lady . . . needn't concern herself with stuffy old things like history books." She couldn't help it. The idea of not concerning herself with books was so hilarious to Charlotte that she threw in a giggle for good measure. She was warming up to the lie, now. "Papa said it dries out a girl's brain and ruins her for marriage."

This seemed to satisfy her.

"He hasn't got it on straight, anyhow, Austen old

girl." Crashey dismissed her with a flutter of his fingers. "It was mostly Dr. Home what did it. It were only my laboratoryottage and my equipment and my idea."

The petals on the beaded scarlet flower slowly fell away to reveal a miniature bottle filled with the moonlit fluid she'd seen seeping into Leftenant Gravey's wounds at Port Ruby. Grog. *Rhodinus Secundi Vitae.* Young Soult's effects were rewarded with an appreciative gasp.

> *From Gondal's humble flowers they brewed*
> *The answer to our prayers.*
> *They took our lives, we took their weeds—*
> *I'd say that's pretty fair!*

This was answered by a great whooping and cheering and stomping of feet.

"Well," Crashey whispered bashfully. "It's a *dashbittle* more complicated than that, you know. The blossom's just the beginning. There's berries and vitalegetable flooooids and stufflike. We found old Douro dead as a fatherless donkey, that's true, but he had all these petals and that stuck to him and wherever they stuck the wounds were all stitched up like a doctor did it! But he were still donkeyed, poor lump. Took us ages to science it down to size, especially in the field— lucky me I had a summer house in Gondal back before the war—so we recommandeerandered it and anyhow, this, that, and the other biochemical thing, Dr. Home and me beat death. Not bad for a boy who never so much as met Mr. Cambridge or Mr. Oxford! I thought I'd get a Knighthood out of all that excitement but the Duke just said: *Terribly sorry, old chap, but I just can't.* What a snorfling, dripping nose of man!"

Charlotte goggled, delighted and dumbfounded all together at once. But then that black cat came creeping up the stairs of her thoughts again. *If such a thing can be made with science and study, not magic, perhaps . . . perhaps . . . perhaps it is no different than medicine. . . .*

The trumpets grew triumphant; the oboe grew overjoyed; the drums grew delighted.

> *Now the day approaches when*
> *Fair Glass Town shall prevail!*
> *For our boys live and live again*
> *While theirs must die and fail!*

"Why?" Charlotte whispered, horrified. "Why do they keep attacking, if you can't die and they can?"

Sergeant Major Rogue looked up at the moon, his eyes full of shadows. "If they win, at least their children will live forever. What would a man not do for that?"

> *Our journey through the veils of time*
> *Is drawing towards its end.*
> *Remember when I take my bow*
> *How I have been your friend!*

A hundred people leapt to their feet, applauding wildly. Wolf whistles and hoorays bounced merrily around the walled garden. Charlotte and Emily cheered and jumped and snatched up flowers from the lawn to throw at the stage. Only Lord Byron kept his seat, smiling to himself. He drew out a pocket watch, checked it, and put it back in his lavender waistcoat. Even Adrian and Mary Percy reluctantly stood and clapped quietly. If a man made of ash could go pale, young Douro had. But he gritted his glowing teeth.

Young Soult was breathing heavily. His thin peppercorn chest rose and fell as he gulped for air. His voice rang out—but now it trembled with terror. It trembled, but it did its work. This show, of all shows, must go on.

> *But wait! My tale is not complete!*
> *My story is not done!*
> AMBITION's *not yet quit the field,*
> *Nor has* VIRTUE *won.*

The long-nosed, black-and-red cloaked puppet representing Ambition rose up again, rubbing his wooden hands together in demonic glee. A murmur passed through the crowd. Seats were taken once more. Silence settled over the garden like a fisherman's net. Young Douro glared icily at the stage, his nostrils flaring in fury.

In innocence has Glass Town danced,
Thinking all was saved.
You do not know what Young Soult knows:
A BARGAIN HAS BEEN MADE!

Confused cries of protest fired out from the throng like bullets. This was not any part of the familiar story they'd come for, the patriotic pageant designed to make them resolute and eager for the final campaign against Gondal and Boney.

"What's happening?" Sergeant Major Rogue said nervously. He looked toward the stone archway, the only exit.

"Dunno!" Crashey shrugged. "I like it, though. I am always presentary and accounted for if there's going to be a bit of audience participation!"

"What's happening?" Emily whispered.

George Gordon, Lord Byron, turned to her and smiled fit to light up heaven. It was a terrifying smile. All the gorgeous pelts of his face seemed to rearrange themselves into something both ferocious and full of fun.

"I told you, darling." His golden eyes glittered—so near! "I'm going to bring a house down."

And then, though he ought to have had better manners, being a Baron and only having just met this strange silver person, Byron let the moment get caught up in him. He kissed Emily suddenly, shockingly, scandalously. It was only quick, but Emily thought she might very probably never get her breath back again. When the poet pulled away, her silver paint was smeared all over his lips. He touched his mouth, wiped it off, and looked curiously at his fingertips.

"What a funny little thing," he said wonderingly. In fact, he was wondering so hard, he nearly missed what he'd been waiting hours to see.

Young Soult screamed out his lines as though he was afraid they'd tear him apart if he kept them in any longer.

> *Not three months past in weakened Gondal*
> *Douro's voice did ring:*
> ALL THE LANDS MY TROOPS HAVE TOUCHED,
> OF THESE I WILL BE KING!
> *Gladly will I share the secret of*
> *Dear Glass Town's precious rum*
> *If you'll divide the world with me*
> *When all is said and done!*

Chaos erupted. Adrian went black with rage. The banked embers beneath his skin roared to white-hot life.

"I gave you everything, Soult! Is this how you pay me back for the whole of your detestable life? I found you singing nursery rhymes to the rats in the gutters of Verdopolis and I made you the greatest poet in Glass Town!"

"Second greatest," Lord Byron said casually. He popped a raspberry into his mouth. "Possibly third."

Mary Percy grabbed Douro by the shoulders. She was bronze, he was ash. He had never been able to stand against her. It was what he liked best about Mary. Onstage, the young Douro puppet and the young Bonaparte puppet embraced. A wide brass crown lowered on black ribbons. It settled down over both their heads.

> *Our grandpas did it! Why not us?*
> *There IS no reason why!*
> *What matters acres, counties, fields,*
> *If Gondal need not die?*

Mary Percy shook her beloved like a doll. She spoke sweetly. She did her best. "My darling, my darling, it's only theater! It's only art! Art is nothing but frippery and lies; everyone knows that!"

"Stand aside or I shall stand aside you," Douro snarled. His eyes were as full of murder as Mary's were with tears.

"Don't be an imbecile, Adrian!" she hissed. "You're always like this! Years and years with me and you never learn a thing! *Laugh*, you giant, stubborn moose of a man! Laugh and it's a comedy! Just a bit of political satire. You can take it. Anyone can. Kill him and you'll make it true."

Young Douro locked eyes with Mary. They stood unmoving for an endless moment. Charlotte and Emily watched them from their separate blankets, not understanding, and then understanding too well, just as the bronze beauty did.

"Oh," Mary said, and in that little, sad *oh*, her heart broke. "Oh, *Adrian*. My love. No."

The Marquis flung her aside and charged at the stage. Crashey and Gravey leapt to their feet and barreled into him. They wrestled him up between them, scrambling in the mud to hold the last scion of the house of Douro where he stood, his trousers covered in crumbs and crushed wildflowers. Charlotte wanted desperately to help, but she couldn't see how. All the while, Young Soult hurried to finish, to get it all out before his greatest work ended in a rather abrupt and thorough murder.

> *Drown Victoria or hang her,*
> *I care nothing for her lot.*
> *Usurpers get what they deserve—*
> *Let the little vixen rot!*

The once-tidy lawn fell apart into pandemonium. The Duchess of Can't's eyes dried for the first time in years. She threw her head back and screamed like a banshee. The Duke balled his hands into impotent fists—for a ruler *can't* strike a subject, no matter how much of a cow he's been.

> *Over all creation our immortal*
> *Banners shall unfurl*
> *And in this crown let Glass Town be*
> *The lowliest of pearls!*

Soult let all the puppets drop at once. He fell back onto his high cushion, exhausted. All the shouting and fighting and accusing only grew louder. Douro kicked at the wooden soldiers like a child caught stealing. Bit by bit, he dragged them all toward the poor poet, who was beside himself with fear and pride.

"He betrayed us!" Soult shrieked as Adrian's long fingers reached up for his throat. "His grandfather betrayed us then and he's betrayed us now! He's sold us out to Gondal for a crown!"

The green poet's eyes were wild and panicked. In that moment, up there above everyone, trying to do the right thing and ruining himself anyway, Charlotte could not help but think how like Bran he looked. She whirled round to face Sergeant Major Rogue. Jane had fainted again, and this time she'd come by it honestly. Zenobia was stroking her hair and calling her name.

"Help him!" Charlotte cried.

But the wooden soldier only looked down at her sadly

out of his one good eye. Douro had nearly reached the puppet theater, which seemed to be coming apart in the crush. Young Soult the Rhymer threw down puppet after puppet onto his head. "There is a *plan*! It's all to do with a man made of books and the Other Place and something called a *bat-tree*!"

"Brunty!" Charlotte yelped.

Young Soult kept hollering. "I know everything! I've seen letters and such! Douro's not alone! He's got friends!"

"Well," sighed Sergeant Major Rogue. "I wouldn't say *friends*. Collaborators, at a stretch."

Charlotte blinked. She opened her mouth, then closed it again, then turned her head to one side. Zenobia's fiery eyes began to drip white flame. Sergeant Major Rogue shrugged and winked at them.

"Oh dear . . . ahem. Good show, I suppose. Both him and me. Tip the lad for me, won't you, Zenobia? He's earned it. And do tell old Bravey I'm sorry. It's not his fault. When you're born a Rogue, you know, what else can you ever hope to be? Erm. Rather. Well. That's me, then! Bye, bye!" he chirped. Then Captain Bravey's right hand turned, got his foot up on the pedestal of one of Dr. Home's grisly statues, and in half a blink was up, over the holly hedge wall, and running at a dead sprint across the dark, open fields beyond the estate. A black diamond lung toppled onto the ground where he'd kicked it loose.

"Never get involved with a man in uniform, Miss Bell," Lady Zenobia sighed. "They're always too loyal to somebody else to ever be loyal to you. I expect he's already married to some Gondalier cow. Shall I scare us up some champagne?"

"We might still catch him," Charlotte said, putting her foot experimentally on the pedestal to see if she could manage it in Ginevra's gown.

"Why?" Zenobia sighed, and disappeared into the glittering riot. "You can't fix a bad man like a bad staircase. I'd end up locked in his attic or something. Thank you kindly, but no. Really, who has the time?"

Charlotte watched her go and saw all the rest happen. Douro finally got one hand free. He drew a flintlock pistol from his beautiful, expensive coat, spun round, shot Gravey in the chest, then again, and stabbed Crashey through both eyes—one! two!—with a dagger hidden in his sleeve. Charlotte and Emily screamed.

"Rude," Crashey said, and collapsed in a heap.

Charlotte ran to the fallen boys, but Byron held Emily by the wrists and would not let her go.

"Watch, watch!" he insisted. "This is the best part!"

Adrian stared up demonically at the puppeteer. But

at the sight of all that sap, the boy seemed to finally pull himself together. He stared down at the Marquis of Douro with something like pity.

"If you think Boney means to keep his bargain, I've got a unicorn for sale out the back." Soult called out for Wellington, for Copenhagen. One of the torches had fallen into dry grass. Black smoke began to billow and blow. "Wellesley! Arthur! Douro and his friends, they've built something terrible and when it's finished, Gondal is coming for us all!"

The Iron Duke stood leaning against the stone archway with an oddly satisfied expression on his metal face. He touched his fingers to his hat in a little salute. Young Soult the Rhymer closed his eyes then and waited for Adrian of Douro to kill him flat.

Nothing happened.

Douro had run. When he opened his eyes again, Soult saw the tails of that splendid coat disappearing through the holly. Below him, half the nobility of Glass Town sobbed or tried to put out fires or swung punches at one another, each assuming everyone else had thrown in with the traitors. Copenhagen padded lazily round the Vivisectionists' Garden, where Glass Town's nobility had well and truly been vivisected. He dropped down onto his seawater haunches here and there to drench the smoking grass. In the middle of it all, Josephine sat in her cage, her rosy arms crossed over her chest, fuming.

"I hate you all so much," she said simply. "So *enormously* much."

Soult crept backward on the platform above the stage until he was half buried in hedge, weeping pitifully. He craned his neck, searching the mob for his protector, his boss, the boy who came to him months ago with a horrible story and a bag of gold, who helped him pick out the milk pitcher for the rooster and bead the scarlet flower past three in the morning, who thought, at last, of rhyming *unfurl* with *pearls*. But half the steam from the lion's firefighting efforts was too thick and he was crying too hard to see Lord Byron, still lounging on his patchwork quilt, grinning and munching on raspberries next to an utterly shell-shocked young girl made all of silver.

"Well, it was *mostly* rubbish, but the ending was a bit of all right," Byron said happily. He stretched his arms in front of him and yawned. "What did you think, you naughty little breather minx?"

A heavy hand fell on Charlotte's shoulder. She nearly jumped out of her golden skin. Wellington stood behind her with the oddest half-embarrassed smile on his iron face.

"I am sorry for my attitude earlier," he said. "I couldn't let Douro think I was on to him. Needed the scoundrel to hear the trap I'm springing on Old Boney at Verdopolis. But it does seem that your problems and my problems are having a fine old time together. Shall we put them all together in a big pile and light them on fire?"

Charlotte frowned doubtfully. Wellington rubbed the back of his neck like a schoolboy.

"Oh, I do try to make grand speeches, but I always muck it up. By *light them on fire*, I mean *set sail for Gondal at first light on a ship full of very angry people and just* massive *heaps of gunpowder*."

TWENTY-ONE

The Princess in the Tower

This cell was much nicer than Branwell and Anne's had been.

There were plush red and blue chairs and a neat red and blue bed with a red and blue brocade canopy. A round table covered in a red and blue cloth and a sapphire tray full of breakfast leftovers stood beside the biggest chair. All along the thick stone walls of the vast room full of toys hung a great walloping tapestry. It draped down in panels between the windows, reaching up to the ceiling and down to the floor. Each panel showed a map of a different city, painstakingly woven with a million tiny, brilliant threads. Their names were stitched near the ceiling in silver. There was Ochreopolis in gold thread, and Port Ruby in crimson, and the Plaid Lands in black and brown and white, and some very violet place called Lavendry-on-Puce, and Verdopolis in emerald. There were others, too, places they had never been but imagined a thousand times. They'd marched their wooden soldiers through them and argued over their names and climates and peoples. Bran had spent hours drawing their borders, their castles, even their local trees and fruits. Regina and Lake Elseraden and Almadore and Zamorna and Calabar Wood and the Isle of Gaaldine and Ascension Island and the Isle of Philosophers and the Isle of Dreams.

The whole world hung in that room. Their whole world.

Bran stood on tiptoe and reached out toward the Ascension Island tapestry. He couldn't help it. It was just right. It wasn't any loud color like Port Ruby or Verdopolis. Just brown earth and green leaves and black chimneys and the blue sea.

"Do you see it, Annie?" he whispered. His throat had got all thick and tight. He couldn't name the feeling swelling up inside him the way he and Charlotte had named the place on the tapestry. "That's *my* map. I drew it! On the blank page at the back of Papa's copy of *The Iliad*."

"Ooh! You sneak!" Anne sucked in her breath. "I'll tell! And get your hand out of the bars, idiot!"

He snatched his fingers back. "You won't tell, or I'll tell Tabitha you fed her Christmas cake to the badgers out the back of the garden!"

Anne started laughing. She thought you probably weren't meant to laugh in prison. She tried to do it without making any noise. Bran's face went red with being laughed at. He hated anyone laughing at him. How did other people stand it?

"Bran," Anne giggled helplessly. "Who cares about the cake or the badgers or the silly old *Iliad*? We're in jail! We're already in all the trouble we can be!"

"I *did* draw it," Bran grumbled. "It's mine. That's *my* handwriting up there on the banner in silk and *my* special way of making palm trees. Nobody else does them like me. Somebody took my drawing and made it bigger and better than me."

Anne's knees ached from crouching in the cold on a stone floor.

The doll who was not a doll moved again. It was hard to tell the difference between her and the bigger toys leaning against the wall or lying on the floor. She was small and pale and she didn't make a sound. Slowly, their eyes traced out the shape of a girl sitting at an ebony desk pushed up against the wall between the green Verdopolis panel and the snowy Elseraden panel. She was writing something with a beautiful black quill pen and a silver ink pot. Her posture was as perfect as a picture book. Whenever she finished a page, she blew on it gently to dry the ink and lay it aside in a neat stack. All over and around the desk and her feet lay books wedged open at favorite pages and pile upon pile of those strange toys.

At first, Anne thought the girl was wearing a white dress. But she wasn't—or rather—she *was* a white dress. A dingy, faded white wedding dress folded and coiled and arranged and draped into the shape of a terribly thin child around Anne's age, with orange blossoms in her white lace hair and ink stains on her white silk thumbs. Anne shook her head from side to side. It couldn't be. Oh, of course she'd *hoped*, in all this whole country of their own best dreams, that her best dream might be here, too. But it couldn't be!

Branwell squinted in the stranger's direction. "I don't think I like her." He ducked back down below the barred window and leaned his back against the green glass door. "She's just . . . sitting there. While we goggle in at her! She's being *very* rude. But then, jail has different manners." He gave a world-weary sigh. "I know that now that I've served time."

"Branwell, you hush right now or I shall hit you. I shall hit you hard. I shall hit you thoroughly. And I shall keep hitting you. That's her, Bran!" Anne's eyes grew huge and liquid and loving as she stared. "That's my Victoria. And she's *writing*! Just like Charlotte and Emily! Just like me!"

"And me." Branwell frowned. As if he hadn't written Douro and Napoleon and Rogue and Gravey and Crashey, too. *And Bravey. Oh, poor Captain Bravey. Still, how valiant he was! I wonder if I shall ever be valiant?*

"She's *perfect*. She's *real*."

Branwell felt quite put out. Anne had never said his name like that, even when he'd come back to life. And not to put a fine point on the thing, but if any hitting was to be done, he would do it. "Still don't like her."

Anne rolled her eyes again and stamped on his foot. "How do you know if you like her? You haven't even talked to her."

"You should do it," Bran said decisively. "I'm not afraid or anything! But she's your . . . and you're both girls . . . and she's rude . . . and you're . . . you're Anne . . . so perhaps you'd better have a go first. She may bite. I can't tell from here. Did you make her a biter?"

But he was afraid. Anne and the girl in white had secrets between them. He would be left out again.

Anne made a face. "Oh, Bran, we've just ridden a huge crawly fly while being squished half to death by a very nearly dead Brunty and you're scared to talk to a *girl?*" She stretched out her knees and whispered in a singsong, teasing voice: "When I tell Charlotte and Em they're going to press that in a book and keep it forever and ever and *ever.*"

Bran frowned at his sister, trying to glare her down. "*I'm* not scared! And she's the crawly one! She's just *sitting* there! Like a weird white rat!"

Anne crossed her arms over her thin chest. "If you're not scared, then you talk to her."

"*You're* scared. You're little, you're always scared."

She kicked his shin for that. "You're big, so what excuse have you got?"

"Fine, we'll do it together."

"Fine. But don't call me little."

"Then don't call me scared."

"Very well, then, Mr. B."

"Very well, then, Miss A."

They sat staring angrily at each other for a while, until they started to feel a bit silly. Out of danger for a few hours and shins had already been kicked.

"I won't tell Charlotte you were scared," Anne sighed.

"Well, I wasn't, so good."

"But I'm still telling Em."

Suddenly, all the color drained from Anne's face.

"Oh, Bran, you don't suppose they're . . . they're not all right, do you? They will come and find us, won't they? They're on their way right now, right this second. They've been on their way this whole time and they'll turn up any minute. Right?"

Bran's chest went cold. His stomach clenched. All at once, he felt younger than Anne, and very far away from home. He'd told Charlotte every day since he learned to talk that her being older didn't matter the littlest bit because he was just as tall and clever and a boy besides. And he meant it every time. But it had simply never occurred to him that he could have gotten into any sort of trouble that his sisters couldn't fix. Of course they were all right. The world would just fall off its axle if Charlotte and Emily ever took one step off *all right*. But not so deep down, Branwell knew very well that two sisters could so easily vanish if you let them out of your sight for so much as one beat of their hearts.

He couldn't say that to Anne. Not now. He was the oldest. He was the man of the house. If he failed now, he'd never deserve another try.

"Of course they are," he said confidently. And praised

himself a bit for how strong and even he sounded when he felt no bigger or stronger than one of those dolls. "They'd be perfectly fine in a hellfire hurricane, so long as Em had something to worry about and Charlotte had something to boss about."

"But what if they got hurt or lost or they can't find us?"

"Buck up," Branwell said softly. His voice did tremble then. He *never* got to start the Bees.

"Be brave," Anne told herself.

But it was no good. Bad enough to go from six to four when Lizzie and Maria died. The Bees couldn't stand to lose two more. There'd be nothing left if they weren't careful.

Anne jutted out her chin and let Branwell help her up from the dark hallway floor. The girl at the writing desk still didn't look up or take any notice of them at all, even when they knocked at the green glass door. The orange blossoms in her lacy hair smelled sharper and more alive than anything else in this place. All Anne wanted in all the world was to throw herself onto Victoria and hug her forever. But, as agreed, on the count of three, Branwell and Anne said in unison:

"Hullo!"

The strange little girl gave a strangled cry and leapt out of her chair. She clutched her chest and shut her eyes. Then she started laughing.

"Oh, I'm so terribly sorry! I thought you two were still asleep! You do sleep quite a bit, you know. And you make such *savage* noises while you're doing it! I listened for hours. I say, you are made out of funny stuff, aren't you? What a strange color you both are! I snuck out to watch you sleep. Was I being wicked? I'm often wicked; everyone says so. But it was so *awfully* interesting! One can never tell what one sounds like when oneself is sleeping. But I don't think *I* sound like an angry tiger riding a runaway steam train. I suppose I could. It's just impossible to know! Wouldn't it be nice to know every-thing it's impossible ever to know? If I were in charge of the universe, I would know every impossible thing, even the ones that don't seem in the least important, like what I sound like when I'm sleeping and how old the moon is to the minute and what it feels like to have enough to eat. And I'd let everyone else know their own private impossibles, too. Well, *nearly* everyone else. Everyone who's up to snuff. Everyone who was kind to me and didn't yell. I think if you yell a lot, you shouldn't get anything nice."

The girl clapped a threadbare satin hand over her mouth.

"Oh, I'm so loud! You must think I'm the worst sort of scrubby old starling CAWing and CAWing and CAWing even though everyone's just praying they'll stop. But I'm *not* a starling and I'm not *altogether* old and I shouldn't like to think I'm scrubby, but it's the people who have to look at you who decide whether or not you're scrubby. Anybody could slump about being scrubby as a *brush*, but if everyone he knew said he looked a treat, he'd never suspect he was *actually* the scrubbiest. But Mr. Brunty's never said I am, and neither has Miss Agnes or Uncle Leon said I am, so I don't *think* I am, but they might not tell me if I was, because it's not polite and Agnes says we must all raise up the manners banners along the walls of our soul's castle, which I'm reasonably sure isn't a real saying and she only made it up because it rhymes and she thinks I won't remember if it doesn't rhyme. But I do. I remember everything. Agnes is my governess. I think everyone ought to have a governess, not just children. But the trouble is, I never have anyone to talk to, banners up or banners down, except sometimes Agnes and some fewer times Uncle Leon, and my dolls and darling, sweet, funny old Mr. Brunty. I haven't seen Brunty in ever so long. Oh! I do miss him dreadfully! What I mean to say is that I am alone almost all the time, and that's why all this nonsense comes out the moment I'm not alone anymore, and it is. It's just *nonsense*. Listen to me go on! Oh, I am scrubby, I *am*! Only scrubby folk can't stop CAWing and CAWing and CAWing even though you're probably praying *right this instant* for me to stop and I *shall*, I shall stop. I am going to stop right now, I am, I *will* stop talking." The girl began to shake and tremble and rub her arms with her hands as though she was terribly cold. "I *will* stop, I *must* stop. I'm sorry, I'm stopping, stop *now*, stop it! Good little starling, I'm a good starling, I'm a good girl, everyone says what a good girl I am. See there, I've stopped. I've done it. It's over. But in a moment, you'll say something. Then I'll have to say something back and it'll all come gushing out again and we'll talk and talk and talk and I'll have to think of things to say *every time*, not just things, but *new* things, and if we're not careful there'll be no end to it."

Bran just stood there in his blue and red pajamas, dumbfounded.

"Um . . . yes . . . well . . . erm. My name's Branwell. This is my sister Anne. How do you . . . do?"

Anne waved shyly.

"I don't think you're scrubby," she said. "I don't think you're scrubby at *all*."

The girl laughed nervously. She lifted her pretty pearl eyes to the ceiling. "Oh my, I forgot, didn't I? I just forgot. Forgive me, please forgive me. I've been locked up in this room for *such* a long time. Forever, really. Since the *beginning* of time. Though Uncle Leon says time is only a trick the sun plays on you and the sun is *naughty* and *wicked* and it *lies* and I've only just been having a nice holiday and my parents will be along to collect me presently. But they never do. I don't think the sun lies nearly as much as Uncle Leon. Oh, do come in, come in, it's not locked, you know." The girl opened the great heavy door as though it weighed nothing at all. Branwell and Anne stepped uncertainly into the warm, colorful room. "Uncle Leon lets me have the run of the Bastille so long as I never go out and never bother anyone and never look out the windows, only I call it the *Pastille*, because all that ever happens in here is the present turning into the past over and over and over and also pastilles are candies and I like it when Miss Agnes brings me pastilles because it means she loves me, really. But you must never go out! That's the law! Never, never, *never*! Out is where everything bad can happen, only *in* is safe. Oh, I'm doing it again, aren't I? I can't stop once I've started."

Branwell inched around the edges of the room. He didn't want to get too close. The question of biting hadn't been settled yet. "Are you . . . are you a madwoman?" He gave Anne an alarmed look. "Did you make her mad?" he whispered.

"No! I made her talk and talk and talk so that I would always have someone to talk to me because the three of you are always off talking to yourselves because you think I'm a baby and I had to make sure I'd *always* have someone to talk to if—"

"No we don't!" Bran hissed at her. "You're a lying liar. Charlotte and Emily are the ones sneaking about whispering; they never include me!"

"They do *so!*"

"I can hear you when you whisper, you know," Victoria said nervously. "You don't do it correctly. Other people aren't supposed to be able to hear. If you didn't know."

"I'm sorry! Oh, I'm so sorry! It's perfectly all right if you *are* mad!" Anne said comfortingly.

Bran shrugged. It wasn't *perfectly* all right. "I've never met a madwoman before. Always thought it'd be frightfully interesting."

The girl made out of a dress tried to calm herself down. She shut her eyes and counted to four. "I am not mad. I am Victoria. That's my name, which you asked for, if you remember. You might think I'm mad—it's understandable, anyone might think that if they met me—but *mad* and *lonely* aren't at all the same thing. I promise I'm not mad. I always keep my promises, because I've got nothing else to do. I just . . . need p . . . practice with other people. Mostly . . . mostly I talk to *them.*"

She gestured at the dolls strewn everywhere and patted the rocking-horse dog on the head. It grinned glassily at nothing. "I don't need to introduce myself to them. I gave them all their names, everyone here, everyone in the world. And for a long while, Uncle Leon and Miss Agnes and Mr. Brunty brought me new ones every day. Until it wasn't every day anymore, or even every week or every month or every year and I wanted something alive so badly, so tremendously badly, just one alive thing to be my friend. So I made up stories about all my toys. Did you ever make up stories about your toys?" Anne and Branwell blinked and stuttered. "Oh, I am so awfully rude! I know you're not from Gondal. It's so silly of me to think you know everything I know. A story is a lot of words put together one after another until you get to the end."

"We know what a story is," Anne said, a little offended.

The girl nodded. "A story makes a not-alive thing alive. I tell all my toys where to go and what to think about while they're getting there and who they ought to love and who they ought to hate and what to do for an occupation and when to get born and how to die, only I bring them all back to life again at the end of the day, of course, otherwise I'd miss them so! And that's why I never have to ask them what they're called. Because

I already know everything they'll ever be about, and *they* never have to ask *me* because in here I'm Queen of Everything and Its Auntie and *everyone* knows what the Queen's called. Queen Victoria has a nice sound, doesn't it? So you see, my toys and I needn't waste any time with pleasantries. We can all just get on with the business at hand. It's wonderfully simple that way." She picked up a wooden man in a black wool suit and stroked his yellow silk hair tenderly. "They never complain. No matter what I do to them. No matter what I make them do. If you make people up, they have to do what you say. That's the advantage. Oh! I am being scrubby again, I am, I am, don't deny it. You'll start complaining in a moment. Of course, you *can*, because I didn't make *you* up! Come along, now, soul of mine, unfurl those manners banners!"

Victoria curtsied. She wasn't very good at it. She'd never had to practice.

"Good evening, Mister Branwell and Miss Anne. Welcome to the Pastille. My supper will be along presently. Wouldn't you like to share it with me?"

"Oh, *God* yes!" Bran said, far too loudly. "Thanks for that; we're starving!"

Anne peeked round Victoria at the stack of neat pages on her desk. "What are you doing back there?"

Victoria blushed. The orange blossoms in her hair

turned pink. The maps of Verdopolis and Regina and Ochreopolis and Port Ruby fluttered behind her in the winter breeze. "Writing out my story," she whispered shyly. "Mr. Brunty says I have to. I've got to stay up all night until it's done."

Branwell leaned in a bit. "What's it about?"

Far down below in the courtyard came a sudden boom of thundering footsteps. A joyful, deafening crow shook the windows of their prison. It sounded just exactly like a very, very large rooster.

Victoria hugged her elbows and grinned at them, her pearly eyes bright with excitement. "Oh, this one is brand-new. It's about a place called England. Oh! Why are you looking at me like that? I'm not used to being looked at! Oh, you don't like it! Well, I suppose it's not a *very* good name, is it? I'll change it, if you like! It's no trouble at all!"

PART IV

And All the Weary Now at Rest

TWENTY-TWO

A Man of Science

The towering masts and long, taut lines of the HMS *Bestminster Abbey* creaked and swayed in the moonless night. Black seabirds wheeled and crooned above the huge silver thimble of the crow's nest. Dolphins leapt through the choppy sea alongside the patched leather hull. Their slick backs caught starlight whenever they broke the surface. A steady northeasterly wind filled the sails and kept the crew bustling up and down the deck. At the prow of the great suitcase-galleon, under the knitting needle that served as a bowsprit, a half-turtle, half-snail head made of scarves and hairbrush bristles and gloves and thimbles howled joyfully at the crashing waves and tried to coax the dolphins into doing a flip or two.

Emily and Charlotte had long since gotten over the embarrassment of seeing all their most personal belongings taken apart and twisted round and beefed up to take Bestminter's newest shape. They hardly noticed their petticoats stretched into sails, or their black school dresses knotted together to make the rails and the cannons, or even the little round portrait of their mother pressed into service as the ship's great wheel.

They strode proudly up and down the decks in the splendid sailors' uniforms Wellington had given them. Wellington hadn't wanted to, of course. He'd insisted they weren't sailors. Not by any definition. And now that the game with the gold and silver paint was up, thanks to Emily's first kiss, they weren't even proper Glass Towners! It was all terrifically awkward, to be sure, and all anyone could do was simply keep pretending they *were* made of gold and silver, to save everyone the stress of it all. Nevertheless, that hardly meant they were members of the armed forces. But Charlotte had given him a look that could melt iron and asked if he thought that ball gowns were *quite* the best thing for a clandestine military operation. Emily had pointed out, very fairly, that Bestminter was their ship if it was anyone's. Not only were they sailors, but, strictly speaking, they were Captains.

For the Genii's sake, man, Lord Byron had shouted. *I'm paying to outfit this madness; let them wear what they like!*

And now they walked tall in gold braid, blue velvet, tricorns, loose hair, and best of all, white trousers. Neither of the sisters had ever worn trousers before. Both were now steadfastly convinced that trousers were the greatest invention of man. Buckled at the knee with hose and sensible black shoes! They could move so freely! They could jump on *anything!*

Wellington manned the wheel from the quarterdeck, which was the cover of one of Emily's composition books. He stared into the sea with steely eyes. Copenhagen, the lion with seawater for skin, lay curled around his legs. He seemed even bigger now that they were at sea. Lord Byron spent the evenings in the crow's nest, working on a new sonnet. Dr. Home kept to himself down below in the sick berth. Charlotte and Emily hadn't wanted him to come at all. Lord Byron insisted that if they meant to fight so much as a thumbnail clipping, they'd need a doctor, and he wasn't friends with any other ones.

"But why is she here?" Charlotte had asked Wellington when they boarded back in Lavendry. "Why would we ever bring her?"

Josephine slept in her cage near the mizzenmast. The red roses of her hair fluttered in the following wind. She would not look at anyone, or speak to them. Wellington had made noises about strategy, and hostages, and needed to have something up his sleeve just in case Old Boney actually agreed to negotiations. But it made Charlotte uneasy all the same. Emily had turned away and hidden her face the moment she saw the heavy cage being hoisted on board.

Behind the Bestminster glided the royal fleet of Glass Town. A hundred ships filled with stalwart limey soldiers and sailors. Wellington had let it be known far and wide that he intended to make his stand at Bravey's Inn in Calabar Wood. Even Douro had heard him say it, while he whirled Charlotte around that jeweled dance floor. Now Charlotte knew otherwise. When Gondal's forces arrived they would find no one but Quartermaster Stumps cooking them supper. They would surprise Napoleon and take the Bastille and Verdopolis in one stroke. When Bran and Anne were safe, they'd dig in their heels at the capital and defend it to the last.

All the wooden soldiers pottered round the decks, called up urgent from shore leave. Leftenant Gravey doled out the stores for dinner. He sported a new gnarl where Douro had shot him, but otherwise seemed quite well, now that he'd had his grog. Corporal Cheeky, Bombadier Cracky, Warrant Officers Goody and Baddy, the Company Quartermaster, Hay Man, Lance Sergeant Naughty, Lance Corporal Sneaky, even Private Tracky checked the knots, rolled cannonballs down the gun deck, and prepared the sails for the next tack into the wind. Leftenant Gravey discussed their plans with the Duke of Wellington. Half his body gleamed strong and golden in the torchlight. Half was still burnt black and blistered. The tale of the Battle at Bravey's Inn had been told night after night in the Officers' Mess.

Only Sergeant Major Rogue was missing.

Sergeant Crashey sat on the poop deck with a bandage round his ruined eyes. He played a sea shanty on a mournful concertina and smoked a hand-rolled cigar clamped between his wooden lips. The Sergeant played very poorly. It was a fine night—the last night before landfall. Even Dr. Home was up and about on deck. Emily and Byron stood on the forecastle deck (the gigantic soles of Charlotte's Sunday shoes) watching the constellations sinking into the deep sea. He'd forgiven her for not being made of silver—but only just. Charlotte heard her sister saying:

"It's a game we used to play, the four of us. It's easy. You just say something outlandish or fantastical or unlikely and end by saying *and*."

"Perhaps Old Boney won't put up a fight when we

find him," Lord Byron said. His face looked so soft and young. Nothing at all like his portraits. They were all done when he was grown up. That Byron frightened Emily a little. This Byron was just her size. "Perhaps he'll just ask us all in for tea and call off the war with a scone in each hand . . . er . . . *and.*"

"And a flock of ravens will pick us all up and carry us straight to Branwell and Anne as fast as you can caw . . . *and . . .*"

Charlotte winced. She felt something in her chest crack a little. Just a little, like one frozen twig on a tall tree. The Game of And was theirs. *I don't care if he is Lord Byron,* she thought resentfully. *He's not us.*

Charlotte settled down next to Crashey with her evening's ration in one hand and his in the other. She still sat as though she were wearing a proper dress. It looked odd on her, now she had trousers on. Tonight, Gravey had made them all a nice ragout. Charlotte knew that was meant to be a sort of soup. But in Glass Town, naturally, the Leftenant had handed her a beaten tin mug with all manner of colorful rags hanging out of it. She took a deep breath of the salt air and pulled out her rags with a little smile, wrapping them round her neck like a scarf. Not *ragout* but *rag-out.* The taste of mutton and carrot stew flooded her mouth, and she felt quite full.

"I'm so sorry about your eyes, Crash," Charlotte said. The Sergeant kept on squeezing his concertina. "Are you sure they won't heal up?"

"Grog's for kicking the dead out of you," he said sadly. "It don't do a lot for the complexion."

Grog. They would have to give it to them for the battle. They were enlisted now. Possibly even officers. Charlotte didn't need to beg or bargain. She had earned it. She thought. Well, at any rate, she *would* earn it. And everything that could ever be right in the world would be.

"What will you do now?"

Charlotte lifted her hand to stroke Sergeant Crashey's carved pinewood hair. She remembered the day Papa had brought that box of wooden soldiers home from Leeds. She remembered the snow on Papa's coat. She remembered snatching up soldiers before Branwell could claim them all, even though they were meant to be his present, really, crying out: *This one's mine and he's Wellington!* Branwell had grabbed the biggest soldier and snarled at her: *Well, this one's Bonaparte!* Em and Anne plucked this and that one while Aunt Elizabeth begged them all to be civilized. They'd danced round the kitchen table waving their boys in the air like maypole ribbons. And then, then Charlotte had pulled the last one out of the box and kissed him on the head and hollered above the din of Christmas at the parsonage: *I shall call this one Sergeant Crashey! He'll be the best soldier there ever was!* He was hers, he always had been, and she loved him. She wanted to stroke his hair, like a little brother, or a son. But at the same time, he was not hers at all. The Sergeant had gone far beyond that Christmas table. And so had Charlotte.

Crashey stretched his bandaged face toward the space where he thought Charlotte was. He was almost right. "What am I gonna do now's I can't shoot? You rudiful scamp! Blunt as a kick in the head! What if I'm sensitive about it, hm?"

Charlotte shrunk back as though she'd touched a hot stove. She stuck her hand between her knees. How silly of her. She was twelve. He wasn't her son. How bizarre it would have been for her to stroke his hair like a doll! "Oh, I'm sorry. I *am* sorry! Are you?"

"Naw," Crashey laughed. "I can't shoot, but I can think! I can talk! I can probably box if someone points me in the right direction! I can do my experimentypotheses full time. No, no time for the Sensitive Sergeant hereabouts. What's wanted are the Three R's! Revenge, Rescue, and Retirement! And, to answer your original-nitial query, when all is well and walloped and won, Sergeant Crash C. Crashey will devote himself to the life braintastic! Dr. Home and me, we're already archtecturializing a new laboratory specially for geniuses who can't see what they're doing. Doc!" The Sergeant waved at the black leather satchel walking around in the shape of a man. "Come stare moodily at things with us! Plenty of room!"

Charlotte started to protest. "I wanted to talk to *you*, Crashey. Alone. It's important."

"Anything you want to talkverse with me about you can conversalk with Dr. Home about just as well. Better, even! Dr. Home is a man of science! A real champ on the intellectulogical pitch."

But she could not suppress a shudder as the sleek, thin doctor perched beside them like a morbid scarecrow. She did not like the vivisectionist. She didn't like him when Bran thought him up and she didn't like him in the flesh. Who could like a vivisectionist? It was his job to be horrid. But then, you never had to like everyone you invented for your stories. It wasn't as though you'd have to sit on the deck of a warship with the minor ne'er-do-wells and pass the time.

"You are both men of science," she said quietly. The seabirds crowed overhead. A wave burst against the side of the good ship Bestminster. "Do you think . . . in your scientific opinion . . . do you think . . . there may be other worlds than this one?"

"What, you mean like the moon?" Sergeant Crashey said, swigging back something from a hip flask.

"No, I don't think she does mean the moon," Dr. Home said in that dark, slippery voice.

"I do not." Charlotte tried again. "I mean . . . the place where we met, Crashey."

"What, Angria? That's far away, I'll grant you, but it's not another *world*. Not like the moon."

"Is that where you think you picked us up? Angria?"

"There have been theories." Dr. Home tried to inter-rupt, but Charlotte and the wooden soldier were off and yelling.

"Where else? That's where the train goes. Glass Town Royal Express Main Line! South Angrian Loop!" Crashey thumped his flask twice on the deck.

Charlotte raised her voice. "Haworth! Yorkshire! England! You were *there*, Crash. Where breathers come from!"

"Oh," Sergeant Crashey said quietly. He plunked down his head in his hands and grinned. Charlotte reminded herself to ask the Quartermaster to make up a pair of eye patches for the poor man. The ragged bandage looked too wretched. "Oh, *that*." He scratched his chin. "It did look a bit dullerydag for Angria. But I never have traveled much. What do I know? We only went train-

THE GLASS TOWN GAME

chasing after Brunty to make the arrest in the name of the Duke. Ended up in the wilderness, is all."

Dr. Home sipped from Crashey's flask. "It has long been theorized by . . . well, by *abstract* thinkers . . . that Glass Town and Gondal are not the only . . . ahem . . . realities in the cosmos."

"Theories . . ." Crashey shrugged. "Can't kick off your shoes at the end of the day without whacking a theory in the head with 'em. Always liked the one Dr. Home's referindexing, though. Always thought the world'd be a prettier place if it were true."

Dr. Home stroked his gaunt leather cheek. "The theory goes that new worlds are being created all the time. That there are as many worlds floating in the void as there are votive candles alight in St. Paul's Cathedral."

"And how are these worlds created? In your theory, I mean," Charlotte asked.

"Oh, it's not *my* theory. My philosophy is much more . . . pragmatic. But as far as I understand it, there's no special rite or ritual. New worlds just . . . come on in the dark like fireflies. Every time a choice between two roads is made, a universe fires up to follow each path. Every time a war begins or ends. Every time a child huddles up in his room imagining stories for his dolls. Nothing is too small to create a world, the theory goes. Each beautiful in its way. Some as similar to ours as twins. Some so strange that they would be, to us, as we are to lantern fish under the sea. Some even speculate that what we call heaven and hell are merely other worlds such as this, and death is but a swift carriage from here to there."

"There must be another way to travel between these places," Charlotte said. "Other than by dying or . . . or by . . ." Charlotte's voice died in her throat. This was the moment. She could either say it all at last or keep mum. Would they believe her? Would it matter if they didn't? Did it actually matter at all that they'd made this world in their little house above the churchyard in Haworth? Crashey and Bravey and Wellington and Lord Byron and Leftenant Gravey and Brunty the Stonking Great Tome and sweet, vain Ginevra Bud, and wonderful Bestminster were all just as real as Tabitha or Aunt Elizabeth or Papa. Had she any right to tell them they were only toys and games and stories? Did it really matter, in the end, if they were? Everybody was somebody's toy or game or story. Everybody was made by someone else, even if it was only their mother and father. It didn't make them any less real.

A savage pinch snapped Charlotte out of her thoughts and back to the roaring sea and the racing ship. A pinch worthy of Branwell. Emily had crowded in while she was off in the wilds of her own mind. She hadn't even seen her coming. The doctor and the Sergeant waved *hullo* and went on arguing the finer points of theoretical planes of existence, each trying to out-lecture the other.

"Don't you *dare*," Emily hissed, and pinched her sister again. This time she got her bony fingers underneath the velvet officer's coat. Charlotte yelped softly. Emily sat scrunched in next to her, eyes half mocking and half really, actually furious. Her long hazelnut-colored hair rippled down over the gold braid on her jacket. "You were going to tell! Without me! You weren't even going to ask first!"

"I wasn't—"

"You were *so!*" Emily whispered close to Charlotte's ear. "I can't believe it. After all this time! You haven't any right to decide by yourself, Charlotte! This isn't just your place; it's ours, all of us together! It started with four children and twelve wooden soldiers, not one and one! If you want to lay our cards on their table, there has to be a vote. And since Branwell and Anne aren't here for a Thump Parliament, the least you could do is do a quick straw poll of me."

"It's a hypothesis, Crashey, you *stump!*" Dr. Home roared. The oily, slick voice was gone, replaced by one that sounded like everyone's angry uncle at Christmas.

Charlotte rather liked the new Dr. Home. "It's not even my hypothesis! Take it up with Miss Jane; it was her stupid idea in the first place! Don't you read the journals I send you?"

"Miss *Jane?*"

"Oh, don't let the fan fool you," the doctor said ruefully. "It hides a mind like a porcupine. That's the whole purpose of a fan. She only faints when she needs a moment to think in peace."

"But which one's the *primoriginal* world, that's the question," Crashey proclaimed loudly. He jabbed his finger into the air. "The proper one, the one all the others came fireflying out of in the first place! World Number One."

"Maybe none of them," Emily said suddenly.

"That's just it, brother," Dr. Home replied, wrestling his temper back under control. "We are all of us fireflies, blazing bright in the shadows, and then fading. None of us comes before the other. All are equally proper. No world is copied from another. They are each their own. As complete and unique as a single living heart."

"Rubbish! Balderdashnanigans!" Crashey threw his arms about wildly. "You said worlds are being created all the time. That means some of 'em were loitering around in front of the bottle shop before others even got their stockings on! Or are you saying time's not linear, because if that's what you're saying, I'll box your ears, blind or no blind."

"Well, time isn't linear—"

"You take that back!" Crashey bellowed, and lunged for his friend Dr. Home. He missed the vivisectionist by yards and stumbled down the stairs, cursing his blindness, Douro for doing it to him, and all of theoretical physics.

Copenhagen bounded down the length of Bestminster and landed on Crashey in two leaps. His blue, watery paws left puddle-prints on the deck. He could not abide fighting amongst his kittens. Copenhagen thought of everyone in his master's army as his kittens, though he was sensible enough of men's pride not to share this opinion. So he snatched Sergeant Crashey up by the scruff of his neck like one of his own salty babies and shook him roughly. How naughty of him, to quarrel with the other kittens! He set him down again and growled a warning. Crashey nodded. He was quite soaked.

"Fair point, Copey," he sighed. "Fair point."

Wellington's lion padded over to Charlotte and nuzzled her face. The brief nuzzle knocked off her tricorn hat, drenched her hair, and filled up her shoes with seawater.

"He likes you," Wellington said, finally catching up to his steed. It took a few more than two leaps for the Duke to cross the ship from fore to aft. "I suppose the old boy probably knew all along. You wouldn't have smelled like gold, to his nose."

"I like him," Charlotte said, wringing her brown hair out. "And I suppose he did. You're not still angry, are you? We did *mostly* tell the truth. If we'd told all the truth, we'd never have met you, and none of us would ever have managed to get so far, or know so much."

Wellington cleared his throat and scratched Copenhagen behind the ears. She purred. "Yes. Well. No need to dwell on it."

"You can just pretend I'm gold on the inside, if it makes you feel better."

Now Wellington had to clear his throat three or four times before he could get over his embarrassment. "We'll make landfall in a few hours. I wondered, perhaps, whether Miss *Charlotte*"—he leaned hard on her name, so that she'd know he preferred her false one—"might join me for a nightcap in the Captain's quarters?"

Charlotte had no doubt that this meant, not a glass of brandy, but an actual cap to put on her head at night. Probably with a pom on the end.

"I can play the violin reasonably well. I promise. You

won't be bored. Oh! Your sister may come as well, of course," the Duke hurried to add.

Emily waved the idea away. She bent to see if Crashey had hurt his knees tussling over the nature of time. But though Charlotte had arrived at the most extraordinary moment of her life, in which the Duke of Wellington asked her to join him for a nightcap and a spot of music, she did not smile. Charlotte stared out to sea. The lights of Ascension Island glowed silver in the distance.

"I'm sorry, sir," she said, shaking her head to clear it.

"Arthur," Wellington insisted.

"Arthur. I'm sorry. I was only thinking of my brother and sister. They're out there somewhere, alone in the dark. Alone if they're *lucky*. They've no idea how close we are. They must be so lonely and unhappy. I couldn't help but think that they won't have any nightcaps tonight, nor any violin, nor any snuggling lion, nor even any of Gravey's ragout."

"Depriving yourself of small happinesses won't get us to Gondal one hour faster," Wellington said gently.

"I do wish we could get word to them somehow," Emily sighed. "Oh! Oh, but, Charlotte, we *can*! Oh, well done, Em! Stealing does work better if you *remember* what you've stolen, you ninny."

"What?" Charlotte said sharply. "What have you stolen? You didn't say a word!"

"Oh, didn't I?" Emily blinked innocently at her sister. It served her right.

"Would you like me to fetch it, miss?" intoned the HMS *Bestminster Abbey*'s turtle figurehead. Its voice was deep and huge now, as deep and huge as the sea it sailed. Bestminster had had to wait outside the Wildfell Ball for hours and hours with the other Valises. It had felt quite shabby and shamed and after the third hour, quite convinced it had been Lost, after all. When the girls came running out of the gardens with a gang of hollering men behind them, the suitcase's relief had been so intense it had nearly fallen apart. Bestminster was eager to be useful. It never wanted to have to wait outside again.

"Oh, yes, thank you, Bestminster!" Emily said, and gave its rail a loving rub.

The great galleon shuddered and wriggled. Knocking, banging sounds burbled up from belowdecks. The turtle at the prow of the ship puffed out its cheeks like it was gargling a dental rinse, and finally spat a small object up, over the bowsprit, and into Emily's waiting hands.

"Good throw!" Emily cried. Crashey and Dr. Home and Wellington and Charlotte agreed. The suitcase-ship delighted in the praise.

Emily held up her prize. It was a sturdy glass bell with a wooden handle. They could see stars through the surface of it. Emily waited for everyone to be impressed. Charlotte blinked.

"It's Mr. Bud's bell! He used it to ring the Ghost Office! Don't you see? I'll just . . . ring up a ghost, and we'll write a letter to Bran and Anne. Mr. Bud said a ghost can find anyone so long as you've got a name and a stamp. And Mr. Tree said there's loads more ghosts in Gondal than in Glass Town. Urg. I suppose that makes sense now, doesn't it? Rather sad, though. Rather *awful*. My God, Charlotte, I hate it! It's so unfair! I can't bear it!" Emily fought back tears.

"They attacked us first," Wellington said firmly. "They *invaded* us. Would you prefer we give them all our cannons and muskets, too? If we told them how to make grog, then we would have war everlasting. Napoleon and all his million men, hopping back up again after every battle, ready and starving for more. He will never be satisfied until he's conquered all the world. At least, this way, we have *some* hope of peace."

Emily dried her eyes. She wanted to argue, but they didn't have time to discuss the ethics of one-sided immortality just now. "Well . . . however it started . . . it's awful now. But it means, at least I think it means, that some ghost among all those shades in Gondal will be able to deliver our letter, even to the depths of the Bastille."

Emily rung her glass bell. It sounded clear and cold in the night. Despite herself, she whispered to Charlotte: "I wonder if it'll be Richard again? Or maybe Mary Queen of Scots this time? Or one of the Henries?"

It took a long while. Everyone stood in silence, waiting for the ghost to arrive. Finally, Emily saw something streaming low over the waves. A thin, pale, bluish wisp, trailing frost and twinkling ice behind it. Wherever it dropped low enough to brush the whitecaps, the seawater froze and shattered. The ghost of a somewhat pretty, somewhat plain girl circled down onto the deck of the ship. She had a round, kind face and curly hair and wore a dress that would not have looked at all odd on a Lady with a bit of money back home in Yorkshire.

Emily looked at Charlotte expectantly. She'd recognized Richard first, after all. But Charlotte only shrugged.

"I shall guess," Emily said. "Queen Jane Gray? She only reigned for nine days, but it wasn't her fault she got beheaded. But she's still got her head, so . . . perhaps Ophelia? No, she's fictional, even if Hamlet's not . . . I know! Elizabeth Cromwell!"

"No," the girl said. "Just Cathy. Nobody specialer than anyone else. Have you got a letter for me?"

All the men began patting their chests for paper and pen. Emily inched closer to the ghost. She shivered. Frost prickled her arms.

"Who were you? When you were alive?" Emily said, her voice thick with wonder. "Tell me *everything*."

"Oh, I wasn't anybody. Just a girl. I lived in a house like girls do. I loved a man once, loved him so much I couldn't tell the difference between him and me. But he wasn't the kind of man anyone should love. He took my heart and he took it and pinched it to death. If he loved with all the powers of his puny being, he couldn't love as much in eighty years as I could in a day. So I married someone else and had a child, like girls do. But my heart stayed pinched. Every time I tell the story, people swoon and say it's dreadfully romantic, but it was horrible and I *died* halfway through my own story! I don't know what's wrong with the living! They think the blackest, most poisonous things are romantic. At least he's dead now, too. He tries to talk to me but I stick my fingers in my ears until he goes away."

"I'm sorry you died," Emily whispered.

"So am I," said Cathy. Her face flushed hard white. "I wish I were a girl again, half-savage and hardy and free! Like you are now."

"I don't *feel* half-savage and hardy and free," Emily

said. How could she be free when her life was laid out already? They'd rescue Branwell and Anne and go home, and even if, somehow, they managed to take grog with them, even if they managed to wheedle it out of these wooden fists, it wouldn't stop time. Sooner or later, it would be the Beastliest Day all over again. School would eat her up and then she'd have to be a governess to someone's spoiled children and work and work until she had no time at all to write all the stories in her head and then what? She didn't wish she were a girl, she wished she were *Branwell*. Then she might have hope that something unexpected could happen to her.

"But you are," the ghost of Cathy said. "All girls are. We just . . . get stuck sometimes. That's all. Honeysuckles tangled up in the thorns. At least I'm not stuck anymore."

Charlotte wrote out the note quietly on Crashey's back so that Emily wouldn't have to. Wellington dug up his personal seal and stamped the corner.

> *B & A—*
> *Dont worry. We are coming for you. We've got Wellington and Lord Byron (dont ask!) and Crashey and Gravey and the lot with us.*

*There's nothing to fear. Buck up. Be
Brave. You know the rest.
  Look for us at dawn.
            Charlotte & Emily*

*P.S. Stop chewing your fingernails,
Bran. You, too, Anne.*

Cathy took the letter and promised to listen hard to the earth until she could find the two lost children. She bent and kissed Emily's cheek with her cold blue-silver lips and disappeared into the starlit shadows over the depthless sea.

TWENTY-THREE

My World Will Shine

W hat do you mean 'a place called England'?" Branwell said crossly.

He felt sure Victoria was making fun of him somehow. And Anne, as well, but mainly him. Branwell picked up one of Victoria's dolls and turned it over in his hands. It was a grumpy-looking man with a big white beard. A lead turtle and a little tin goldfinch had gotten stuck to his trousers like burrs picked up on a walk through the woods. Bran shook the doll, but his burrs stuck. He set the fellow down again on an overturned model ship and stared angrily at the map of Verdopolis. *His* map of Verdopolis.

"That's the capital of Glass Town," Victoria said softly. "I don't expect I shall ever get to see it, but I have every street memorized. That's the Tower of All Nations there, see? And the Hall of the Fountain and the Hall of Justice and the Grand Inn of the Genii, which is really just the sweetest and most tender name for a church, when you think about it. Have you ever been to Verdopolis?"

He goggled at her. Was she making fun? Testing him? But Victoria just looked up at him with wistful, trusting eyes. Her face was all pearl. Her irises the same color as her pupils and whites and eyelids and eyelashes. Branwell could admit she was pretty, but her eyes unsettled him. He glanced meaningfully out the slim church window between the Verdopolis tapestry and the Lake Elseraden one, but she didn't follow his gaze. She wasn't allowed to look out windows. Uncle Leon wouldn't let her. How could anyone be *that* obedient? Anne certainly wasn't. It was unnatural. *Oh,* he realized. *Her tower's facing the wrong way. It's only the cliff and the valley and the river out there. If she could pick up the place and turn it round, she'd see. That's the saddest thing since the invention of sad.*

Bran didn't know why he didn't tell her the truth, except that the whole business with calling her silly fairy world "England" bruised his national pride. He didn't like her saying she had Verdopolis memorized. She hadn't any right to their grand city. She was nothing but Anne's old doll.

"Yes, I have," he said, a little nastily. *I invented it, you weird white rat. Well, we all did. But I did the good bits. Oh, I am being dreadful, dreadful. Why can't I stop being dreadful to her?* "It's fine. You're not missing much."

Anne glared at him and shook her head disapprovingly. Branwell coughed. He prodded the doll with the big white beard again with his toe.

"Leave Charles alone," Victoria begged him. "He doesn't belong to you."

"You are mad," he declared. "I said you were and you *are.*"

He expected the strange girl to go pale and apologize for her very bad joke—pal*er*, anyway. But she didn't. She clenched her white silk fists.

"Hush, Bran!" Anne said. "You could drive a soap cake mad in five minutes flat! Manners banners!" Anne had already decided she liked that very much and would take it home with her. "Go on, Victoria. I know just what you're talking about. We've made up loads of stories and games for our toys, haven't we, Bran?" Bran looked slightly panicked. This was hardly the time to come clean or the person to come clean to! "You're right, England is a funny name. But I like it all the same. What made you think of it?"

Victoria slowly unclenched her fists and began to pace about her room, tidying up her dolls and models and figures. "I don't know, really. It's my own invention. It just came to me one day out of nowhere and I thought it sounded like a real, proper name for a country—a bit stiff and stuffy but not at all scrubby, the way a country's name should be. It's a little, lonely, green island in a cold sea. It's got a capital called London and oodles of rivers—I'm ever so good at naming rivers! The Thames, the Tyne, the Clyde, the Nidd, they go on and on! I've drawn the place a hundred times, but I'm not much at sketching and it's so hard to get Scotland right. That's what I call the northern bits. The whole thing together is also called Great Britain. Miss Agnes says I must choose one, but I think a place can have two names if it's truly splendid, don't you? And I'd wager no one's ever thought to say a nation's great right in the title of the thing! But it *is* splendid and it *is* great and it has heaps of colonies so it never has to stay a lonely green island in a cold sea." Victoria twisted her fingers together nervously. "I couldn't bear for my country to be a poor lonely little thing so I let it conquer, oh my, just *every* kind of place, and that way it will always have friends. Oh, I've imagined other places and empires and geographies for my dolls before, but England's different. Aren't you, darling? Yes, yes, you *are*." She put her hand on the stack of handwritten pages on her desk. Her writing was so small and fine the papers looked almost all black with ink.

"How different?" Branwell asked, unsure whether or not he wanted the answer.

But Victoria's pearly eyes filled with the very special thrill of showing a stranger your dearest possession. "Well," she said conspiratorially, "I've put myself in it, for one. I've never done that before! It's very daring, don't you think? I like being daring. It feels like jumping out that window there. You don't think it's prideful, do you? Oh, perhaps I ought to change it. Perhaps it is wicked and stuck up. But . . . it's only that, up here in my tower, I'm not terribly interesting, not much of an anybody at all. I've never ever left these walls unless it happened when I was a baby and I don't remember, and I suppose it might have and I wouldn't know a thing any more than I know what I sound like when I'm sleeping, because once you've forgotten something, it forgets you, too, and you can't ever get it back. I get a little food every day even though it's never enough, and I get a little lesson from Miss Agnes every week, even though that's never enough, either, and a little visit from Uncle Leon or Mr. Brunty on holidays, but that's all I've got. And Mr. Brunty and Uncle Leon . . . well, I do love them, I just wish they wouldn't call me quite so many harsh names. Or let the guards chase me for fun and exercise. But I expect they're right, in the end. I am just a nasty little scrubby starling nobody with nothing and that's all right, you can't help being born a starling, no matter how much you might like to be a hawk. But there! There, in my lovely England! *There* I'm not in the least a starling. I am a great Queen! Not just a Queen! An *Empress*! Her Majesty Victoria, by the Grace of God, of the United Kingdom of Great Britain and Ireland Queen, Defender of the Faith, Empress of India! Doesn't that sound spectacular? Doesn't it sound like all the trumpets of heaven at once?"

Anne and Branwell shrugged. The room seemed to throb with strangeness, suddenly.

"Maybe another name," Bran suggested. "Most Queens are Elizabeths or Marys. There's never been any Victorias." Anne shot him a glare. "So I've heard."

"But I don't want to be an Elizabeth or a Mary. I'm not an Elizabeth or a Mary! I'm a Victoria! And in my story, well, it's very long and complicated and there's just so *terribly* many chapters, but in my story, in my sweet little England, I rule forever and ever and ever over a great kingdom. I've invented a wonderful husband for myself as well." She swooped down and scooped up the doll with the yellow silk hair she'd been fussing with before. "I named him Albert. I made him perfect. We have just the same color eyes. He's staggeringly handsome and clever and brave—but not so brave that he will lord over me! Albert's very dear that way. We're never going to be parted, not even for a single moment, and he will never yell at me and he will never call me bad words and he will never think I'm scrubby, not even when I've just got up in the morning. Every day Albert will say to me: *Victoria, you are good and kind and special and everything you do is the right thing to do. You are the hawk of my heart.* Then we shall go for a long walk out of doors together in the sun. And I shall give Albert and me a shocking number of children, and all our babies will all be Kings and Queens and Emperors and Empresses as well, so that no one must feel lesser when we gather together for holidays and we will all love each other so much we never stop saying how well and truly we love each other even for a moment, and none of us will ever have to be alone, and all the laws will just be *love each other and never stop*, written on clay tablets and hung up where everyone can see, and that will be enough. All the other times I made up countries for my toys to live in, I invented wars and diseases and tragedies so that none of them would get bored and we'd all get a good story out of it. But this time, this time it's going to be *perfect*. No one will ever get sick or suffer injustice and there will be no wars, unless everyone *really* wants one, but at the end of the day they must all shake hands and have a bath and be happy again. Best of all, no one will be bored, because I've planned a whole pantheon of wonderful poets and scientists and authors and inventors and painters and composers for my court! You've already met and manhandled Mr. Darwin and his poor turtles, Bran, but I've got scads more." Victoria sank down at her desk again, overpowered by her vision. She touched the quill pen shyly. "I can put you in it, if you like," she said to Anne. "I like to share. It's only that I've never had any other children to share with. What would you like to be?"

"What about me?" said Branwell. This was all absurd, of course. Their games had come to life. Not hers. But he smarted all the same. It was the worst sort of feeling, to be left out.

"*You* called me mad," Victoria said haughtily. For the tiniest slice of a moment, she looked every inch Queen Victoria, Her Majesty, by the Grace of God. "Anne didn't, so she's my favorite at the moment. You can't call the Queen names. England's not that kind of place.

If you want to be in my story, you mustn't say anything cruel or be vicious or argue with any single thing I say, even if it is only a little thing and you *know* it isn't true, such as: *Why, that Certain Clever Wren has just told me there's a new Prime Minister!* I'm afraid you cannot say: *Birds don't talk*; instead you must curtsy and say something agreeable, for example: *That Certain Clever Wren certainly is up to date on the most exciting doings, Mum.*"

Victoria was beginning to remind Branwell of Charlotte. He gritted his teeth. But he could not bear for Anne to be anyone's favorite while he was standing right there. If the girls were getting something, he wanted it, too. Some things inside Branwell were as unchangeable as gravity, and that was one.

"Yes, Your Majesty," he said through his teeth. "I'm sorry I said you were mad."

Victoria inclined her head. She would give him no more than that.

Anne rocked back and forth on her heels. It was too much. The girl she invented, inventing her future. "Could . . . could you write our sisters in as well? Charlotte and Emily."

"If it pleases you," said the child Victoria with a gracious wave of her pen. "What would you like to be, Anne? I'll write you all in this minute."

"This is ridiculous!" Branwell threw up his hands. He'd tried once. That was all through now. "Did you or did you not hear that rooster crowing not ten minutes ago? We're in the middle of a prison break and you want to play with dolls! It's not England, it'll never be England, England's nothing like she says. There's never been a Queen Victoria and there won't be one. Prince William's next after King George, everyone knows that! And William's got loads of brothers all over the place, so they wouldn't give it to a *girl* just for funsies. She's just daydreaming. The England bit's only a coincidence, Anne! Lock a monkey in a room and tell it to rearrange the alphabet or no lunch and he's bound to come up with London and the Thames sooner or later. It's not like what we did, not in the least like us. She's barmy. Barmy as a bilge rat, and I'm not sorry for saying *that*. Just let her talk to the wall and her pile of junk by herself. Let's get out of here."

But Anne wasn't listening. She was thinking hard about what she and her sisters would like to be. In another England. A perfect England. Emily and Charlotte weren't here. She had to get it right. "Poets," Anne said finally. "And authors. The sort that last."

Victoria beamed. "I shall not forget when I come to that part! There is plenty of room for everyone in

Barmytown." She turned her back on Bran. "Oh, wait until you see the inventions I have imagined for my empire, Miss Anne! Every single person in my world shall be a wizard, able to trap lightning in a glass or a pot or a bit of rope and use it to do miracles whenever they wish! I've put in machines that can sew anything all by themselves and sweet oranges filled with a magical medicine that can heal any infection and tin ponies that run upon two wheels! I've written locomotives that crisscross the whole planet, even running under the ground like iron worms, and great birds that will carry my people anywhere they wish to go. I do love anything that can fly, and Albert does as well. So I'll have flying balloons, too, and rockets you can ride in all the way to heaven! I've made them such a place, my darling wooden men and porcelain ladies. I'm a good mother, I am. I've given them candles that never burn out so they needn't ever be afraid of the dark and pictures that talk and move so they needn't ever feel the littlest shiver of boredom and fairs so big you have to build a whole new city just to contain them! Oh, my world will *shine*. And you will too! I'll put you right in next to Mr. Conan Doyle and Mrs. Curie and Mr. Wilde and Miss Nightingale and Mr. Rossetti and Mr. Dickens and Mrs. Browning and Mr. Marconi. . . ."

And the child Victoria, her long lace hair spilling

down over her slim shoulders, began to write so fast that they could no longer see the strokes of her pen. Sheaves of paper flew out from the desk, falling like snow onto the floor, piling up in drifts, nesting in a plush blue and red chair, on a narrow blue and red bed.

Bran had a terrible sick feeling in his stomach. It got worse the more Victoria talked. *No, no, no,* said Branwell's mind. *It's not true. That's not our England. It's preposterous. It's completely unacceptable and I will not have anything to do with it.* Veins stood out on his forehead. He'd only just accepted that there were two worlds in God's creation: the world that contained England and Yorkshire and Papa and home, and the world that contained Glass Town and Gondal and all the most secret delights of their playroom games. If Victoria had her own world—and she didn't, she didn't! Then it couldn't be *his* world. It had to be a third one. And three was right out. *No, no, no,* his mind stubbornly repeated. *We made Glass Town. And it came real because we're special, somehow. Because we made the best stories.* They're *the made-up ones. It's them. Not us. They're the toys. It's not me. I'm nobody's toy. I'm no one's wooden soldier.*

"She can't do that," he told Anne. "We can, but she's a toy. Why would you make it so she could do that?"

"Later," Anne begged.

"What do you mean later? What if there isn't a *later*?"

"There's *always* a later. When the game is done and everything's put away and we've had our supper. That's when you tell us we're just silly girls because we didn't work any murders in, or we tell you you're a brute. Later is when it's safe to say anything, because the game is over and there's no point getting cross about it. Let's wait until you can't get cross with me, Bran," Anne begged. Tears filled her eyes. "You're already cross with me right now! And you'll be more than cross if I say it before *later* comes. You'll be ever so much more than angry. You'll be . . . you'll be hurt."

"Don't be stupid, Anne. You can't hurt me. I promise. I'm practically a grown up already. It's dreadfully tough to hurt a grown-up, you know. So just pretend *now* is *later* and tell me or I'll pinch you."

Anne trembled from head to foot. The truth burst out of her like water from a burst pipe. "I made her so that she could do anything Charlotte and Emily could do! I made her so that when they die at school I won't be alone! I'll have someone all mine, who will never leave and never lie and never stop talking to me and she'll be just as wonderful as Charlotte and Emily and tell stories even better than they could and stay with me forever!"

"You made a *replacement*?"

"I made a sister!" Anne sobbed. "You can't tell! You mustn't! They won't understand!"

Branwell was hurt, after all. He had never felt so hollow. He'd never felt so much like he didn't exist at all. "But . . . but Anne . . . what about *me?*"

Anne never got a chance to answer.

A ghost drifted in through the window, silvery blue, somewhat pretty and somewhat plain. Her bare feet left frost-tracks in the air.

Any thought that did not concern ghosts fled from Anne, Victoria, and Branwell's minds. The spirit put a thin scrap of paper in Branwell's dumbfounded hand. Then she melted away like winter snow.

Anne read over her brother's shoulder. She opened her mouth to cheer for Charlotte and Em and somehow Wellington and Lord Byron, too, but a savage knock at the door and a savager squawk cut her off. Bran quickly shoved the note into the pocket of his Gondalier pajamas.

"Uncle Leon! *Puppy!*" Victoria cried happily. "Miss Agnes! Oh, everyone, just *everyone's* come to see me today! I don't know how I shall stand it! Oh, you needn't knock, I'm perfectly decent, come in, come in!"

Victoria pulled open the green glass door. Napoleon Bonaparte stood on the other side, all two hundred and

some odd bare bones and two long rifles and one large
blue hat of him. His war-rooster Marengo waited magnificently behind him, along with a tall girl made of dark
gray school slates with chalk dust still clinging to them
in pretty patterns. Bonaparte's chiseled bone face took in
the room, Victoria, and the two, very much out of place
and out of formation, intruders, Branwell and Anne. He
puffed out his chest and slid the tip of his left musket
inside his richly braided general's coat. He said nothing.
The great tyrant entered the cell and sprawled out com-
fortably in one of the plush red and blue chairs. The gray
slate girl followed with a tray full of tea and pitchers of
cream and plates of dainties—and two large, ripe lemons.
She laid it out on the table, clearing away the ruins of
breakfast.

"Puppy!" Victoria shrieked.

Marengo crowed joyfully and barreled in to be aggres-
sively hugged by his favorite person apart from Napoleon. The green fire they remembered roaring out of the
spaces between his broken pottery skin was no more than
a pale glow. Victoria rolled on the floor with the rooster,
burying her face in his neck.

"Now, Victoria Alexandrina, what have we said
about guests?" the slate-girl said softly.

"'Guests can only cause distress and must be put

under arrest,'" Victoria answered glumly. She climbed down from Marengo and brushed his feathers off her knees. "But they're not really guests if they have their own room in the same castle as me, you know."

"Ah," the gray girl replied. "Then what have we said about introducing new friends?"

"'You don't need to know anything about that because you'll never have any friends but us'?" Victoria said, with the smallest twinkle in her pearl eye.

"That's an awful thing to say. Who would ever say something like that?" said Napoleon. "Wasn't me, I can tell you that much for the price of a smack in the mouth."

"It was though." Victoria squared her shoulders. "Miss Agnes says: 'Introductions provide sound construction for any social gathering.' Branwell, Anne, this is my governess, Miss Agnes Gray."

Governess! Anne stared up at the tall creature. Was this what she and Charlotte and Emily were meant to be when they were grown? All gray stone and prim little lessons that rhymed and serving tea fearfully to a master who was all bone and no heart? For Miss Agnes was afraid of her master, anyone could see it. The chalk dust on her slate cheek quivered whenever he moved. Anne didn't want to be stone when she grew up. It wasn't fair.

Victoria hadn't stopped talking, of course. "And this

is my Uncle Leon, who never told me his last name so I can't be blamed for not knowing it, unless he doesn't have one, in which case I still can't be blamed, because there wasn't anything to know, and we should all feel anxious because we have something he doesn't. Miss Agnes, Uncle Leon, this is Branwell and Anne, whose last names I don't know either, so I suppose I ought never to have brought up the subject of surnames in the first place."

Uncle Leon, whose surname was, of course, Bonaparte, poured his own tea. He dropped in a lump of sugar, then reached for the lemons. He smiled knowingly and turned them in his hands so that Anne and Branwell could clearly read, in graceful green ink on the yellow peels:

Glass Town Royal Express Main Line
South Angrian Loop
One (1) Both-Ways Ticket
Entitles the Bearer to Passage,
Stashage, Gnashage, and Splashage
Does Not Entitle Bearer to an
On-Time Arrival, a Smooth Arrival,
Any Arrival at All, or Pleasant
Conversation With Staff
Luggage Rights Strictly Observed

The Emperor of Gondal and Lefthand Verdopolis pried both lemons apart with the bayonets on his rifle-arms. As Bran and Anne watched in speechless horror, Old Boney slowly squeezed each half into his tea. He squeezed and squeezed until all the juice was gone and the fruit was nothing more than four husks to be tossed out the window into the river with the rest of the rubbish.

"Pleased to make your acquaintance," he said, and slurped his tea down with a sigh of satisfaction. "There is nothing in this world or any other like a good cup of tea, *non?*"

Anne burst into tears.

"I knew you were bad," she sobbed. "Bran said you were good but I knew he was only being contrary and you're still ghastly old Napoleon!"

"No, he's Uncle Leon! He brings me dolls and paper and ink! That's goodness! It is!" Victoria cried.

"Is it?" Anne whirled on her. "Because I'm nearly certain that your Uncle Leon kidnapped you when you were a baby and brought you here on a giant fly and never let you out for years and years and never even fed you enough while he had you! He doesn't love you, Victoria! You're the Crown Princess of Glass Town! You're his enemy!"

Victoria burst out laughing. Miss Agnes frowned a stony frown. "I'm the Crown Princess of England, Anne, and that's all I'll ever be Princess of! A funny country inside my own head! And Uncle Leon has been good to me! He let me hug him once!"

"He *is* good!" Branwell shouted. He was shaking all over. *The lemons are gone, the lemons, our lemons!* "Whenever we play Wellington and Bonaparte I am *always* Bonaparte because he *is* good, he is *splendid*, he's dark and small and proud and good like me, and you don't know anything. You side with Charlotte because you like her better, not because you know anything about what counts in a man—"

"*Napoleon* is *Napoleon* wherever you go. A *tyrant* is a *tyrant* wherever you go! Just like gruel," Anne hissed.

"Stop it," Bonaparte said, still smiling. "You're hurting my feelings, *ma petite fille.* Victoria, what has Miss Agnes taught you about hurting people's feelings?"

Victoria sighed. "'Though it may seem quite appealing to stomp upon the tender feelings of one who hurt you first, remember, it's a kind of stealing. For when you stomp upon their feelings, you burgle their self-worth.'"

"I do love poetry!" exclaimed Bonaparte.

"How are we to get home now, you beast?" Anne screamed.

"Oh, the lemons, you mean? Couldn't be helped, I'm afraid. I'm just a bear without my tea! It's got to be made just right, you know! And just right at Chez Bonaparte means *bitter* and *sharp* and *sour* as Papa's disappointment. And it is Bonaparte, Victoria, you cloud-brained little milk calf. Maybe Agnes can think up a rhyme so you don't forget it." Napoleon leaned forward. He rested his chin on both rifle-barrels. "But I *am* good! I am, really. The goodest. That's the whole point! I'm *so* good that it was best for everyone if I was Emperor, and once I was Emperor, I just felt so sorry for all the people I wasn't Emperor of, so I went out with my armies to show them how good I was, as well. It's not my fault they're too stupid to see it. In fact, *mes amis*, I'm so tremendously, stupendously, *horrendously* good that I, Napoleon Bonaparte, will take you home to Haworth myself, to make up for the whole misunderstanding with the lemons. Isn't that lovely of me? I think so!"

Branwell cheered and spun round. "See? *See?* I *told* you!"

"How do you know we're from Haworth?" Anne said slowly. "How do you even know about Haworth at all? It's not any place for an Emperor to know about."

"Ah, but I do know about it. I know *all* about it. And Keighley and Yorkshire and England, too. After all, I sent my best spy to Keighley to fetch me a bat-tree quite recently. He did say it was a bit of a mud puddle, but it's very hard to impress my boy. He's seen so much."

"England?" Victoria said softly.

"The Voltaic Pyle," breathed Anne.

"Brunty," Branwell whispered. "But he said he got the . . . the bat-tree from Mr. Volta in Switzerland. That's nowhere near Keighley."

Bonaparte stood up and raised his rifle in the air. "I will tell you a story. A story about a good man! A man so good that when he conquers a city, he immediately begins fixing up the place so it looks pretty. This man is so good, he does all the work himself so that all his friends can relax and drink cocktails by the river!"

Miss Agnes frowned. She whispered in Victoria's pale lacy ear: "What do we say about telling fibs to puff ourselves up?"

"Puffed up is stuffed up," Victoria whispered back with a little grin. Old Boney paid them no mind.

"This good man, myself—you will have guessed—rolled up his sleeves and got to work renovating one enormous fortress in particular—this one, you will have guessed—and what did he find when he dug the mess out of the corners of this fortress with his honest, hardworking hands? Four ancient statues! Three granite girls and a granite boy. And when this good man busted up all those dirty old statues cluttering up the neat, tidy cellar? Why, a door! An iron door hidden by a curtain of white silk. A totally unlocked door! Anyone might have been using it, going in and out for centuries, just as they pleased! This door, in its turn, opened on a long dark passage, dimly lit by a single, lonely lamp, and a flight of rickety, entirely unsafe, steps leading . . . who knows where? *I* know where, *mon chers*! To a completely unremarkable moor in a completely unremarkable country with a completely unremarkable sun barely shining at all on it. This is a place I have never seen. It does not smell like home. It does not feel like home. The people there are old and made out of nothing good. This good man does not like this bad place. But he needs it. Because all roads to Switzerland must begin somewhere, mustn't they? It seems that in our case, all roads that lead from Verdopolis to Switzerland must pass through an odd little circle of dreary brush with Keighley at one edge of it, and us on the other, and a funny old place called Haworth right in the middle."

"It's not dreary. You're dreary," Anne mumbled.

"What a coincidence that four little breather children from Haworth popped into existence in Glass Town just as our Brunty was captured! *Incroyable!* But I think it is not, my sweethearts. My best spy is best for a reason, no? He tells me that when you and your little wolf pack thought you were quite alone, you said the strangest things about making Glass Town happen. About your toys coming to life. So this good man asks a question." Bonaparte bent down and stared into Branwell's dark eyes with his eyes of bone. "Am I your toy, child?"

"No," Bran choked out. *But you are, you are,* his brain crowed. *And you're amazing and you're real!*

Bonaparte's boney lip trembled. He searched Bran's eyes. Then he sat down on the floor and began to weep.

"I am. I am. You can't lie to me with those cow eyes. I knew it was true. When I found the door, I knew I would not like the other side of it. When our Brunty told me what he heard, I knew I would not like the other side of *that,* either. How can this be? Am I not the Emperor? Am I not my father's son? Do I rule Gondal? Have I not taken half of Glass Town by the force of my own will? No! I am nothing. I am a child's toy. A boy's favorite doll." Napoleon sniffled. "I am your favorite, yes?"

"Yes," Bran breathed.

"At least there is that!"

Marengo roosted down next to his master. He crooned comfortingly. He glared at Anne and Branwell with malevolent eyes.

"If I am your doll," Old Boney moaned, "why did

you make me like this? What else could I ever be but a tyrant with *these*?" He held up his rifle-arms. "I never toddled about giggling or made mud-pies or hugged my Papa. I invaded my nursery! I took the house room by room! And my father was proud of that. Your rude sister is right—I invaded Glass Town, I started the war. I was hungry for a whole world and it looked so *good*, just waiting on the table. . . ."

"You could just *stop*, you know," said Anne haughtily.

"I won't, though. I am what I am. Toys can't change the game." He gestured at Bran. "It's his fault, not mine. Don't look at me. And yes, yes, Agnes, I know. 'He who seeks to shirk the blame plainly doth his fault proclaim.' You're a toy as well! So I don't have to listen to you and neither does anyone!"

Anne stared pitilessly at the tyrant. "I was born a girl in a world of Branwells, but I shall be more than I am meant."

"Who cares what you will be! No one is who! We're talking about me! I, who lead the army. I, who command the power of the Voltaic Pyle! I would believe you are a toy. But I sent my man to another world to fetch the greatest magic it possessed! I balanced the scales of life that Glass Town leaned its dumb mitts on! I don't *have* to stop. The bat-trees will power my victory!"

"What does it *do?*" Branwell asked. He'd been dying to know for so long.

"It powers you. Keeps you alive no matter what. Charges you up with new strength. We hardly need guns when one bat-tree-man can burn our enemies with acid or lightning, whichever takes his fancy."

"Well, you only have one." Branwell shrugged.

"Oh, I have twelve. Not as many as I'll have in a month or two, but that's a jolly enough squad. My man Rogue got to work as soon as Brunty smuggled it across. I believe you know my Rogue, don't you?"

"Poor Captain Bravey," Bran whispered.

"Are you sure you got that from our world?" Anne said dubiously. "We haven't got anything like that, even a little like that. It hardly seems fair."

Napoleon shrugged. "In your world I am a dumb, crude doll. Here I am Emperor. There, the Voltaic Pyle is a dumb, crude lump. Here, it is everything. And is grog fair? Is war ever fair?"

"Uncle Leon is crying," Victoria marveled. "He's crying and he's sniffling and he's *scrubby.*"

"You said you'd take us home," Branwell said. "But I know you. When we play Wellington and Bonaparte, I am *always* Bonaparte. You won't do it for nothing."

Bonaparte looked up cannily from his unhappiness.

Bone gleamed behind bayonet. "Tell me their plans. I know that you know. You must know. Wellington has some trickery brewing. They are your toys, too. Tell me everything, to the last detail. I will spare your sisters, you have my word. And when I have ended Glass Town, I will show you the way back to Haworth and you will swear never to return."

"Bran, don't you dare," breathed Anne. "It's not a game. This is a real place. This is a real war. They can die. We can die here. Did we ever invent Port Ruby? Or Brunty? Or Victoria? Did we ever imagine them made of bookends and ball gowns and bones? We've no control. It's got away from us."

Miss Agnes cleared her slate throat.

"May I suggest," she said gently, "that no child of God stays a child forever. They grow, and change, and get away from their parents. They do other than they are expected. They run off and misbehave and look nothing in their old age like they did when they were born. Perhaps worlds, the kind you speak of, the kind of world that is also a story, or a game are much the same way." She cleared her throat. "As the tree becomes the violin, so nothing ends how it begins. There," she finished with a smile, wiping her hands on her stone apron. "Now it's true."

Perhaps it was not the worst thing, to be a governess, Anne thought as Agnes kissed Victoria's hair. Though it was certainly not the *best* thing, either, her heart hurried to add.

"We cannot," Branwell sighed.

"Then rot here, my maker," snarled Napoleon. "I never needed you before and I don't need you now!"

Marengo crowed like the dawn had come.

Miss Agnes allowed them to spend the night in Victoria's room. New beds were brought in, three suppers were served, three lullabies sung by a Lady made of stone. As they rearranged the furniture along the walls, Victoria's papers blew here and there. They chased; they caught. A thin white moon came up. The candles were put out.

Anne turned onto her side in her new bed. She could hardly breathe for excitement.

"Victoria?" she whispered.

"Yes?"

And Anne talked to Victoria before bed, just as she always did. In whispers, in soft laughs, in a voice just a little too soft to hear. Victoria listened, rapt, just as Anne always dreamed she would. When she could think of nothing more to tell her friend, Anne rolled onto her back again. A crinkly, rustly sound echoed in the dark.

"Victoria!"

"Yes?"

"What's this?"

Anne held up a scrap of paper with a sketch on it. The moonlight turned it blue.

"Oh! That is the Pastille of course! From the outside. I copied it from a history book. It is so hard to think of the outside of a place when you are stuck inside it just the way a soul is stuck inside a body!"

Anne shook her head. She smiled, then choked on her own smile. "This isn't the Pastille. Or the Bastille. This is the Parsonage." A brilliant, gigantic, diamond-encrusted version of the parsonage where they all lived with Papa and Aunt Elizabeth and Tabitha and Snow-flake and Diamond and Jasper and Rainbow. She'd forgotten they put their house in Verdopolis, but of course they had. But once you move in the Great Wall of China, it is easy to forget the first building ever raised in the city. The most sacred building of all. "Bran! Bran, look! We're *home*."

But Bran did not move on his cot. He was a black shape in the black night.

When the girls were long asleep, Branwell crept silently out into the long black halls of the Bastille. He walked like a ghost. All that talk of worlds and doors and wars mattered not at all. All Branwell could think was: *A doll is better than me. I count for less than a doll.* He retraced his steps, carefully, carefully, all the way to the great strategy room, still full of candles and torches. *I will protect them. Even if I am less than a doll. Even if I am nothing. I will protect them somehow.*

Bonaparte sat on a rich, high chair in the long, polished hall. Almost a throne.

"I knew it. You could not have made me if you were not like me," the tyrant of Gondal chuckled.

"Look," Bran said gruffly. He stared at the floor. "I'm a man now, so I know if you want something, you've got to pay for it. Nobody does anything nice for no reason." Tears started hotly in his eyes, but he refused to let them fall. He bent down and dug in his sock for something. "Here!" He shoved it at Napoleon. Aunt Elizabeth's shilling and six-pence. It had seemed so powerful when she gave it to him. It was still powerful. It had to be. Just like the buttons that had paid their way here in the first place. "That's a fortune where I come from. A hundred million pounds. It's every-thing I have. You take it and you swear to spare Charlotte and Emily and me and Anne, too. You said you would. I want to buy your word on it. Fair and square."

"Of course," Old Boney shrugged. The way the Emperor shrugged looked so much like Branwell's father, he could hardly bear it. "It is nothing to me. Easy."

Bran took a deep breath. It would be a glorious battle. Everyone who mattered would live. And he would see it all from safety. And perhaps . . . perhaps afterward they did not have to go home right away. Perhaps they could stay and Boney would give them thrones and titles of their own. And when it did come time to leave, the Emperor would give them caskets of grog as a reward, bottle after bottle of the stuff, so that no School or winter

or fever would ever touch them or anyone they loved. Charlotte and Emily and Anne could never be angry if he made them Duchesses. If he made them immortal. They would be grateful. They would be overjoyed. No more School for them at all, no more cold and sickness and fear and grim futures as stone governesses. And all thanks to him.

"When we play Wellington and Bonaparte, I am always Bonaparte," Branwell said at last.

He reached into the pocket of his pajamas and pulled out the ghost's letter. "They attack at dawn."

TWENTY-FOUR

The Storming of the Bastille

Emily took off her shoes and squelched her toes in the cool sand of the beach. It was early morning. The sunrise tinged the cakey sand and tiny shells pink. Back home in Haworth, Ascension Island was the bed in the playroom at the top of the stairs. They'd invented it and filled it with people and destroyed it and salted the sheets and built it all over again a hundred times.

She'd never imagined the wind there would smell like warm, milky tea. Or that the palm trees dotting the strand would be the lumpy, misshapen, lopsided ones Branwell always drew on his maps, with coconuts that were really far too large for the poor things dragging on the ground. Or that the ruins of the several dozen civilizations the four of them had played at on their clean white sheets would cover the island like too much pepper sprinkled on a pie. There were exploded pyramids in the distance, and the shadows of the Mountains of the Moon towering above her, the crumbled pillars of the great cannibal city of Acroofcroomb, a word so silly Anne loved to say it, over and over, until she was sick from laughing. And Verdopolis, her spires already visible far up on the high plain of the island.

But they would not be touring the ruins today. Emily wondered if they ever would. If they could ever just wander in the world of their dreams without being chased or chasing.

Charlotte ran her hands through the sea grass. She was afraid. She had never imagined herself in a real battle. She had never imagined herself a soldier. And she wasn't really, she supposed. But Branwell and Anne needed her. Someone always needed her. She looked back toward the ships as the last of the cargo was being carried off Bestminster. Muskets and limeskin men and their dear wooden soldiers and battlefield rations and Josephine's huge cage. *Why?* She thought again. *Why is she here?*

And then she knew. Her mind leapt over itself and

landed on the truth. Her stomach turned. She squeezed Em's hand and ran up the beach, searching for Crashey's bandaged head in the crowd. He was sitting on a crate of boots.

"You lied," Charlotte said, out of breath.

"I didn't!" Crashey protested. "Wait, what are we talkscussing about, exactly?"

"It's *her*."

"Captain Charlie, you need to retreat, regroup, and come at my position again."

"Grog. It's Josephine."

"Oh," Crashey sighed. "That."

"Yes, *that*. *That's* why you had to bring her with us on a secret mission even though it's idiotic to bring a prize hostage to a sneak attack. That's why you're unloading her onto the field of battle. You must have been low on supplies. You lied. You said it was berries and flowers and fluids from Gondal."

"Well, strictxactly speaking, it *is* flowers from Gondal. And there are berries and fluids and suchat in there! Mostly for color and smell, though . . . but you're rightorrect, it's mainly her. Her hair. We don't hurt her for it or nothing! We send raiding parties into Gondal so they'll think there's all these recipegridents, like porridge. So they won't guess. They'd throw everything they have at us if they knew it was just a lock of Josephine's curls. When we captured her, a lot of boys got themselves shot on and Leftenant Gravey departed his mortal woes for the first time sort of . . . on topflop of her. He fell off a rampart onto her head. Not a very graceful way to go. But he got right back up again. Her hair got all in his wounds when she was trying to shove him off. Our Josey's all roses, you see. Leftenant Gravey, he . . . *rose*." Crashey cleared his throat. Charlotte's silence sat sorely on him. "We had to send all the stock we had with the main army to Calabar. Else it wouldn't look real. So we had to bring the source."

"You have to give her back! Or at least stop cutting her hair off."

"That's above my pay-grade, my love. I'd say talk to Wellington, but he won't listen. She's our last defense against Gondal."

"She's a *person*. She's not a hen to lay eggs for us. She's not a bird! She doesn't deserve to live in a cage."

Crashey stood up. He kissed Charlotte's forehead. "Who does? But not for all the girls in Gondal would I risk you falling off a rampart with no roses to catch you." The Sergeant sniffed deeply and straightened his back. "If there are other worlds like we were saying in the night, I hope we're friends in all of them."

They rode to the gates of Verdopolis as dawn came full and golden into the world. It was quiet. All the houses lay dark. The river coursed silently by beneath the Great Wall of China. The Colosseum cast deep shadows over the empty streets.

Charlotte rode behind Wellington on Copenhagen, Emily with Lord Byron on a horse all of war shields, small and great. They both wore new armor, gorgeous and elaborate as any medieval knight.

"We will be your armor, now that we're done being a ship," Bestminster had said. "A good suitcase guards its traveler against any misfortune. Please do not get shot too much."

The army flowed around them, a soundless sea of green.

The portcullis of the Bastille was raised when they arrived. The courtyard within stood empty, unguarded, unmanned.

"It worked," breathed Wellington. "They're on their way to Bravey's Inn. The city is ours. We can take back our home without a drop of blood spilt!"

"But it's not your home," Charlotte whispered.

"It's *our* home!" Emily gasped. "That's our house! That's the Parsonage! Well, if the Parsonage had grown up terribly fancy and tall. It's not a Bastille in the least! It's just . . . it's just *home*."

Wellington ignored her. "Who knows, perhaps we'll have a bit of luck and Old Boney's snoozing away himself in there while his men go off to fight nothing."

They occupied the courtyard quickly. The infantry-men relaxed at last, joking and breaking open treats from home on the flagstones. Even Josephine ate a bit of hardtack. They never noticed the oiled portcullis sliding closed behind them.

"Nothing?" came a familiar voice. It echoed round the courtyards, a boney voice with no meat on it. "My men will fight nothing, and they will crush it! You are nothing, my dear Wellington, and so are the rest of you! Toy soldiers for babies to gnaw on! *Allez! Allez!*"

Out of every crevice in the Parsonage, every cranny in their lovely old home, the Gondaliers came. They leapt down from the walls and poured out of the win-dows. They swarmed from the roofs and the cellar grates. Bonaparte himself, all bones and rifles and chicken, soared down from a turret and landed squarely in front of Wellington on Marengo's back. The rooster crowed green fire. Copenhagen roared blue foam. Charlotte and Emily screamed. Crashey and Gravey screamed. Every-one screamed. The battle had begun.

Charlotte leapt off Copenhagen and ran for the gate that lead into the depths of the castle. Emily darted after her. They kept their heads low, took cover behind barrels and racks and infantry lines. Branwell and Anne. Branwell and Anne. That was all that mattered. Get to them. Get to them fast. Chaos exploded around them, a smear of color and noise. Frogs bellowing, limeys shouting, flashes of musket fire and splintering barricades and bayonets charging. Their boys tried to get into formation in the hurricane of it all.

Then, lightning forked across the clear, cloudless morning. Blue lightning, tinged in green foam. Twelve knights of Gondal knocked down the gates of the Parsonage in one blow. Charlotte and Emily stumbled out of the way. The knights sprinted toward the fight, laughing, cheering each other on, firing electricity from their fingers, spitting acid from their mouths like tobacco juice. One of them had an eyepatch. One had a waistcoat made of newspaper. One had skin of ash, with fire beneath, and a sword that flashed in the sun.

"Oh, Rogue," whispered Emily unhappily. "Oh, Douro. And the Magazine Man."

Had they volunteered? Had they been forced? Emily didn't suppose she'd ever know. She wasn't even sure whether or not it mattered. They were coming for her, and if they remembered that she'd once been kind to each of them, they didn't show it.

Glass Town men were falling all around them. Medics bolted from body to body, pouring out grog and moving on to the next. But the lightning-knights kept coming. Sickly green lightning struck over and over again. Charlotte stared over the horrible scene. Frogs and limeskin troops and men made of lace and fireplace pokers and felt hats and soap cakes lay moaning. Her mind wanted to run away, but her heart would not. A calm, amused, ridiculous voice rose up inside her. *They're all made of our things. Two nations made of everything we've got in our house. Bookends and powder and book bindings and books and bones and pottery and armor out of our magazines and limes out of the market. And they're all our age because we played their parts in every game. Wait till I tell Dr. Home.*

They were pinned down behind a stone pillar. An armored frog keeled over and clattered down beside them. Their way to the gates was blocked.

"All right," Emily shouted over the din. "I'm ready to go home now. School isn't so terrible." She clung to her sister. She could feel something in her pocket as she leaned against Charlotte. Something heavy and round. "Charlotte! You go after Bran and Anne! I've had a thought! Oh, where is George? I want his horse!" She laughed madly, remembering Richard's ghost posting her letter so mournfully. "'A horse! A horse! My kingdom for a horse!'"

As though he'd heard them, Lord Byron's horse galloped across the battlefield. His furry hair flew in the wind and he looked for all the world like an illustration of a hero in a fairy book. Emily smiled, despite everything. Byron skidded to a halt beside their pillar.

"Get off!" she yelled over the clash and clang of it all.

"Excuse you," Lord Byron huffed. "She's my horse, you know."

"I'll bring her right back, I promise."

"Mount up behind me; I'll protect you," Byron said, wheeling the mare around.

"It's my plan! I'm not your passenger!"

"Ellis . . . Emily . . . if something were to happen . . ."

Emily rolled her eyes. "If something happens and Gravey's guzzled all the grog, I'll haunt you, I promise. Now let me up!"

Lord Byron dismounted and laced his fingers together to give Emily a boost. He meant to hop up after her before she could protest, but she was gone before he got one leg up. He watched the pair of them go with tears in his eyes.

Emily's heart hammered wildly. *Branwell and Anne,* she thought. *Branwell and Anne. Hardy and half-savage and free. That's me.* She slapped the shield-covered flank of the horse and bolted into the courtyard, galloping at full speed toward the portcullis their side had managed to get open at last.

"Come on, you big dumb green bludgers!" she screamed as loud as she could. "Come on, Rogue, you traitor! Come on, Brunty, you miserable waste of pages! Come after me! I'm easy pickings!"

Emily and Lord Byron's horse burst out into Verdopolis. The bat-tree men thundered after her. Brunty's eyes foamed green with contempt. Rogue's good eye wept. The Marquis of Douro's handsome dark hair sizzled with acid and fire.

And Emily pulled her postal bell out of her breastplate.

She rang it madly as she rode, rang it and rang it and rang it until it shattered in her hand. She galloped down the narrow Verdopolis roads, past the Tower of All Nations, past the Hall of the Fountain, past the Alhambra and the Colosseum and the Grand Inn of the Genii. *I did get to see them! I did get to look at it all!* The bat-tree men fired lightning at her back, and it was only luck, luck and the twists and turns of the streets they'd lovingly drawn, that kept her whole. "Where are you?" She looked up into the sky. "Cathy, Richard, everyone, where are you?"

The ghosts came flooding down the alley behind her in a blue and silver sigh. They flowed over the acid-knights like wave after wave of a sparkling sea. Over Brunty and Rogue and the other frogs and men with their Voltaic chests. Frost trailed behind their bare, mournful feet. They reached out their pale arms to catch any letters the Gondaliers might have to send, and where their fingers touched, ice blossomed. The twelve electric soldiers froze in place on the cobblestone road, mid-war-cry, mid-confusion, mid-bolt-and-glob.

Emily laughed and laughed. Not because it was funny, for it wasn't, not at all. But because it had worked. It had worked and she was alive. She reached into her breeches and pulled out the ruby medal she'd swiped from the Glass Town Train. FOR LAUGHTER IN THE FACE OF CERTAIN DEATH. Emily stuck it onto her chest, where it glowed redly. She'd earned it now. She jogged up to the frozen knights and stood before them, out of breath. The bat-trees jutted out of them, those strange, horrid discs and wires. She pulled her toffee hammer out of the pocket of her officer's trousers, the one that said EMILY on the handle.

One by one, she struck the Voltaic Pyles, and one by one, they shattered into a million shards like snowflakes.

* * *

Far above the battle, Victoria huddled against the tapestries as muskets and cannon and lightning thundered outside. She dared not look out—windows could break so easily. The walls of the Bastille, which was the Parsonage, shook and coughed dust.

"It's easy enough to sneak out of your own house," came a boy's voice bouncing up the hallway. "Now we know where we are, we'll do what we always do and creep out the back through the cellar pantry."

The pair of them burst into Victoria's room. The little Princess screamed. People dashing in uninvited sounded much the same as cannon fire to her ears, and she was equally afraid of both. She hid her head with her arms until Anne pried them open and kissed her cheeks and told her it was decided, they meant to escape, it was all planned. Victoria had no idea what she meant, but in the end, she was glad her friend had come back for her. Other people weren't so frightening, as long as they were Anne.

Branwell took cover behind the overturned table. It had toppled during a barrage and spilled her dolls out all over the floor. He peeked over the top of it, trying to see down into the battle below. He beckoned to them, and the girls scurried over between musket volleys and flashes of horrid purple-green lightning.

"You really are, you know," Anne said, once they had the table between them and the worst of it. She squeezed Victoria's hand.

"Am what? Oh, I am sorry, Anne, I wasn't listening, what a nasty way to behave toward you, I am just the worst girl, the very worst, the worstest among the worst, I shan't forgive myself, I shan't!"

Anne stroked her hair fondly. "I said you're the Crown Princess. You're going to be Queen, just like you wanted. Queen of Glass Town. If we survive. If Charlotte and Em pull it off."

Victoria blushed. "That's just silly. I'm a scrubby old starling with a head full of dolls."

Anne shook her head. "I'd bet your father's out there fighting right now. He'll come and collect you and you'll jump into his arms and you'll always have enough to eat forever after."

"But I don't want to be a *real* Queen," Victoria insisted. "If anyone's to be Queen after the battle it ought to be Miss Agnes. She always knows the right sort of a thing for anyone. I only want to be Queen of England."

"England's not real," Bran said distractedly. Anne raised her eyebrow at him. "Well . . . you know what I mean."

"It's real to me," Victoria snapped back. "It's so

awfully real. More real than this place."

Bran felt sorry for her, suddenly. She was just a scared little girl, after all. He knew all about scared girls. And scared boys, though it was important for a boy not to admit he was scared. But Bran felt sorrier for himself. It didn't sound like it was going terribly well down there. What if Napoleon didn't keep his promise? What if a stray cannon or bat-tree got Charlotte in the back and he had to live with that forever and ever? No, he told himself. No, you paid your money and you'll get your goods. That's how the world of grown-up men works. And in the world of grown-up men, you were supposed to look after scared girls.

"If you really don't want to be Queen of Glass Town," he said quietly, "you could come with us. Home. To Haworth. It's not like Boney said, really. It's very steep and nice."

Anne sighed. "We don't even know how to get back, Bran. Don't make promises. We've got no lemons and no idea where that door is. Just sit still and wait."

Some catapult or cannon struck the base of the tower. Dust shook down from the rafters.

"I don't want to sit still, Anne. I don't want to wait. I want to be down *there*; I want to be in the thick of it! This is intolerable! He ought to have made me a soldier. I daresay I earned it."

Anne gave Branwell a strange look. He looked away quickly. She could never know what he'd done. There could be no consequences if no one ever knew. Unless it all came out splashingly; then he'd tell them himself so they could praise him.

Victoria's eyes gleamed. She grinned at them. The tiny Queen of Englands real and unreal wiggled out from under the huddle and attacked the nearest mountain of dolls and toys. She threw them savagely aside, over her shoulder, sending them skidding across the floor.

Bran and Anne scrambled to stop her. "What are you doing? What's wrong with you?"

"Rather a lot!" Victoria laughed. "You might have noticed!"

She pulled a last lot of dolls away—Albert was among them, staring up at her with adoring blue eyes. The tapestry lay bare. Victoria lifted it up like a magician lifting the curtain on a trick.

There was a door in the wall. An iron door with a sheet of white silk over it. Just like Bonaparte had said.

A cannonball ripped through the roof of the tower. Sky poured in.

"Come with us!" Anne begged Victoria. "I don't think you're scrubby, I think you're wonderful, just wonderful, and you can always be my friend and we'll never

ever be alone again! You can be my real sister forever, and we'll play until we're old and gray."

Voices echoed on the staircase outside. Voices they didn't know. *Hurry, Charlotte!* Anne prayed. *Hurry, Em!*

"All . . . all right," Victoria said uncertainly. "Just . . . just let me get my things. I can't go without Albert. And I must say good-bye to Miss Agnes."

"There's no time for that," shouted Bran. Wind whipped down off the mountains into the shattered tower. His heart was beating so fast and hard! Never mind Charlotte and Emily, *they* could die, they could really die here. *He* could die, and the battle wasn't half done yet. It was too much, suddenly. He didn't want to be down there in the thick of it at all. He wanted to be home in his own bed with a cup of Tabitha's beef broth in him and the covers pulled up over his head. "We should go *now*," he yelled, panicked. "We'll come back for Charlotte and Em. Of course we will! Once we know where the door opens, we'll be able to come back any time we like! But right now we're about to be blown apart and we haven't got time for Albert!"

Victoria blinked slowly. "Yes, of course, you see how silly I am, really, I just can't think with all the noise." She gathered up the mound of papers from her desk and clutched them to her chest, still reaching for more sheets.

"Leave it!" Bran snapped. A volley of muskets banged through the air outside. One of the bullets lodged in the wall behind them.

"Are you mad?" Victoria repeated his question. "I shall never leave England! I could never!"

"It's just a stupid story!" Branwell yelled. "It's not even any good! No one dying and everyone loving each other—it's dreck! Just leave it! You can make another one!"

But Victoria would not listen to him.

An old, sour, awful, familiar feeling rose up inside Branwell. The nagging, terrible sense that no one really saw him or thought of him at all. Charlotte was always running ahead of him, further and further ahead, and Emily and Anne would catch her but he could not. They were not like him, they did not see how silly their stories became when they did not have deaths by stabbing and massacres and horror in them, when they bore no hint of war, but thought *he* was ridiculous, that *he* was the odd one, when he was meant to be the one they all looked up to. When the wooden soldiers had been his, his, *his*, all along.

He shouted wordlessly in disgust. At Victoria, at Anne, at Charlotte, at Emily, at all of them. But Victoria especially. Anne would replace them all with this piece of stuffed nothing! He had to show her that Victoria wasn't real, she wasn't important, her stories were just stories but they had done all this together! The little brat hadn't any right to make him die just so she could pack her stupid scratchings. The stupid scratchings of a stupid scratching!

Why wouldn't they ever *listen*? Why did she care so much about that wretched story? It wasn't anything. Half of it was still lying in drifts on the floor. They didn't have time for this nonsense. They had to *leave*. *Now*. Branwell snatched Victoria's papers. But the wedding dress girl would not let go.

"Stop it, stop it!" wept Victoria.

"Just leave it!" shouted Branwell.

They struggled. She was stronger than she seemed. The pages began to tear.

"Oh, no, no, please!" Victoria sobbed. "You're spoiling it, you're spoiling everything!"

Finally, Branwell gave up. He seized the silver inkpot on the desk and dumped its contents onto the papers, onto the floor, onto Victoria's pure white satin hands. Victoria went slack. Black ink dripped off her chin. Her pages flew and crumpled and slid to the floor. The pale girl sunk to her knees.

"Bran! What have you done, you brute?" Anne

snarled. She rushed to hold little Victoria by the shoulders. "Why must you always do the awfulest thing?"

"I'm sorry," he said stonily. But his heart shivered and trembled. It wasn't his fault. It was the right thing to do. They could go now. They could go and live and be safe. If she'd only listened to him in the first place. If only they all would.

"It's all broken up now," Victoria whispered, two heavy tears rolling down her face. She ran her hands over the ruined pages. "My darling Albert is all black and sopping and ruined. It's all bled out and mixed together." She grasped at a miserable soggy heap of story. "My children! All my little Kings and Queens! Now there's nothing but a horrid scrubby black space in the middle of them all, a black trench where half my perfect world will fall and choke and break my kingdom of forever into nothing. I wanted it so beautiful, I wanted it to be a kingdom without pain, and now it is drowned." Victoria held out up a few bedraggled pages. "Even the part I had written for you, look how it's spoiled. Look how dark it's gone." Victoria ran her fingers over a black page, her tears puddling as they fell on it.

"Don't worry," Branwell said helplessly to Anne as she glared hatefully at him. "It's not *our* world. It's not *us*. Even if it were like Glass Town, even if it were real, it's somewhere else, somewhere far away that's nothing to do with us! I'm sorry, I shouldn't have shouted. I won't, ever again, I swear it. But it's *not* us, it's another place, another Branwell and Charlotte and Emily and Anne, if it's any real place at all. No harm done. No harm."

Victoria pressed her forehead to the inky floor and wrapped her arms around her belly, weeping as if it were the end of the world.

"Get out," the Princess hissed. "Get out, get out, get out!"

Charlotte ducked beneath a collapsed doorway as a sizzling spike of lightning shot so near to her it burned her hair. She could hardly see for smoke. *We're losing,* she thought. *It's not supposed to happen this way. Welly wins, he always wins, we always win.* But the bullfrogs were leaping everywhere, with such delight, with such ease, twanging out their victory songs in their huge green throats. Napoleon and Wellington wrangled in the center of the courtyard, their breath fogging in the air.

Suddenly, Charlotte heard a voice. From nowhere, and belonging to no one in Verdopolis. The feeling was not like an electric shock, but it was quite as sharp, as strange, as startling. They saw nothing, but they heard a voice somewhere cry—

"Oh, my babies, where *are* you?"

"Oh God! What is it?" Charlotte gasped.

"Charlotte! Emily! Annie! Branwell!"—then nothing more.

It did not seem to be in the courtyard—nor in the castle—nor in the garden; it did not come out of the air—nor from under the earth—nor from overhead. And it was the voice of a human being. A known, loved, well-remembered voice.

It was Aunt Elizabeth. And her cries were full of pain and woe, wild, eerie, and urgent.

She was not the only one who heard it. The whole battle froze and listened, straining their ears. No one moved. No one breathed. In the midst of all that silence, Napoleon rolled his eyes and shot Wellington through the heart.

"Ah ha!" Old Boney shouted. "I am triumphant! Look at me! I am GOOD!"

Charlotte cried out, but her cries were lost as the battle began again, more furious than before. But now, it was only the clang of swords and the bang of muskets. The horrible acid lightning had stopped, somehow. The bolt that nearly took her head off had been the last. Of course, Charlotte couldn't know what Emily had done. She expected the next bolt of electric death at any moment. And yet Charlotte ran toward the fallen Duke in a blind rage. She hardly knew what she meant to do before she'd already mounted Copenhagen and pulled the watery lion round.

"Byron!" she yelled from lionback. "Find Emily, now! And Crashey, get the Duke some grog right this second, this *second*, hear me?"

"What?" bellowed Lord Byron as a musket ball slammed into the stone wall behind him.

"Just *find* her! Run! Find her or you never deserved a single dance!"

Charlotte had only a little sword they'd scrounged up for her out of the Quartermaster's trunks. It was rather pitiful when guns fired all around her. They hadn't meant to fight. They'd meant to run right into the prison to Branwell and Anne. She didn't care. It was something. She kicked Copenhagen's ribs and they were off, galloping down the field toward the dancing, exulting Napoleon, dodging muskets and frogs and lime-men, her sword and voice and soul drawn out and pointed at the tyrant's heart. He turned just as she was upon him and laughed in her face.

"You are a *very* bad kitten," Charlotte told the Emperor of France.

Copenhagen heard and understood. The lion snatched Napoleon by the collar and bit hard. He dragged him off his rooster backward through the fighting. Boney splut-tered and shouted, but everyone was far too busy trying not to get themselves killed.

Charlotte and Copenhagen bore down on the far end of the courtyard. A great cage waited there, stashed in the back. When Bonaparte saw, all his cursing and yelp-ing stopped. Copenhagen kept on growling. Then, he flung him at Josephine. The bone-man landed in a heap against the barred door. It groaned inward and sprang open. The rose-lady wrapped her love in her arms and spit out a stream of French so quick and fierce Charlotte couldn't follow.

"It's *her*!" Charlotte cried. "It's her. Her roses. It's always been her. Take her and go somewhere else, some-where far away. A rocky island in the middle of nowhere. Just take her and go be happy away from everyone else!"

"I'm happy here!" Bonaparte bellowed. "I will fight on forever! I will fight and I will win until everyone is tired of winning and then I will win *again*! You think you can tell me what to do? You are nothing! I am Napoleon! I am no one's toy!"

"You will NOT!" Charlotte roared.

Napoleon and Josephine flinched. Bonaparte's face fell. His jaw dropped low.

"The Genii!" he whispered.

A crown of lightning flickered faintly around Charlotte's head. Not the vicious lightning of the bat-tree men. The lightning of a storm that brings rain and turns the world green. She didn't notice. She didn't notice one thing different about herself. She hadn't changed at all. It had always been true.

They had made this world. They were its gods.

"If I am to be a governess," she bellowed, "then I will GOVERN. The game ends when all the players are called in for the night and IT IS TIME FOR BED. What do you do with broken toys? You put them on the shelf and forget about them! You throw them AWAY."

"I am the Emperor! The Genii should bow before *me!*" squeaked Napoleon, shocked at his own daring. But he was frightened. He trembled from head to toe.

"You put them in a BOX marked OLD RUBBISH and you leave them in the attic!" Charlotte shouted back.

Her armor fell off.

More exactly, Bestminster unfolded and unlatched and undid itself until it wasn't armor anymore. Until it was the same scuffed, worn suitcase it had been when Charlotte had packed it for Cowan Bridge School.

Then Bestminster opened its lid impossibly wide and ate Napoleon and Josephine. It packed them, as

its ancestors had done all the rude and rough owners of yesteryear. It burped slightly and settled down on the cold ground, as pleased as a cat.

"What did you *do*, Charlotte?"

Charlotte whirled around. Branwell and Anne stood there among all the screaming chaos of the battle, staring at her.

"I won! I think I won. Didn't I? What are you doing here? *How* are you here?"

Anne started to tell it honestly, that a Princess made out of a wedding dress had kicked them out of the Parsonage because Branwell had been such a vicious little snot to her like he always was, and so they'd had nowhere else to go, really, but down into the courtyard to find their sisters and try not to get blown to bits in the process. But the look on Bran's face stopped her. She'd never seen him look like that. He'd gone so pale he seemed to have no blood at all in him. And the way Charlotte had looked a moment ago . . . Anne felt terribly small between the two of them.

"But you killed them," Branwell said, dumbfounded. He felt a shiver of terrible responsibility at the numerous wars he had sent his wooden soldiers to with glee, designing each of their deaths like suits.

Anne's lip trembled. She was afraid of her sister. How

could anyone be afraid of their sister? But then . . . had anyone ever seen their sister crowned with lightning and riding a lion before? "Charlotte, you *killed* somebody. Two somebodies! And only one of them was bad. Josephine was just a pretty lady with magic roses in her hair!"

"You know about the magic roses?"

"What magic roses?" said Branwell.

Anne shrugged. "I saw her in the portrait in our cell. The roses in her hair. They're just the same color as the stuff in Crashey's flask. The *oddest* color, really. And they all said the ingredients only grow in Gondal. I didn't know. But I *thought*. I had a long time to think up there." Anne the spy had solved the mystery of two kingdoms from a locked room, and there was no one who had enough of their senses about them to applaud.

Branwell stared at Bestminster, sunning himself in his victory. "No," he whispered, and began to cry a little. "No. It's my fault."

Anne turned her head on one side. She narrowed her eyes.

"Why would you say that, Bran?" she whispered. "Why would you even think it?"

Charlotte coughed and rubbed her cheeks with her hands. She was still shaking. She yelled over the din. "Don't be ridiculous, Bran. It's my fault. And I'm not sorry! Why should I be sorry? Napoleon always dies at the end."

A terrific BOOM shattered the air and Charlotte died.

At least, she thought she had. It felt like dying. One moment she was Charlotte and the next all she could see was blackness and all she could hear was nothing and she was lying flat on the ground with no feeling in any part of her. It was over. It hadn't hurt too badly, she supposed. It could have been worse. At least she'd gone first, protecting them, as she should have. They would forget her in time.

"Charlotte!"

A loud, whiny voice was ruining her death. She wished it would stop and let her be.

"Charlotte!"

Charlotte opened her eyes. Black smoke trailed through the sky above her. Branwell was lying on top of her, crying and shaking and slapping her over and over. But he didn't look like he was enjoying it as much as she'd thought he would. Anne was reaching for something in her dressing gown. She pulled out a flask wrapped in leather and spotted fur. A flask they'd seen on the belts of so many soldiers. *Oh, clever, clever Anne!*

"Hullo, Bran," she wheezed.

Charlotte turned her head. A cannonball glowed red in the rubble. Bran had pushed her out of the way and onto the lonely pile of rock where Napoleon had ended.

"I saved you," Branwell sobbed. "I saved you. I really did. All by myself."

Charlotte reached up and stroked his dark hair.

"We've got to save them, too," Anne cried. Anne would never allow any creature to suffer, no matter how small or pathetic or wicked or ugly, no matter how many times it bit her, no matter how little it would do for her if she were in its place and it in hers. Not right in front of her. Not while Anne from Haworth could still put two words and a flying leap together. The girl who stood over Brunty and would not take one step was buried deep in her heart now. She was thoroughly Anne again.

"Oh, Old Boney can go hang but poor Josephine? I can't bear it! What if they didn't get eaten really? Luggage doesn't just sit still. It *goes* places. What if Napoleon and Josephine didn't die in the suitcase after all, but were transported to an island in the sea, and . . . and . . ."

Charlotte smiled as Branwell let her up and took up the Game of And. "And the island was so far from everyone that they couldn't ever escape and start conquering again, but there was plenty of elk to hunt and clams to dig and the soil was very good for potatoes, with a little house for Josephine and none for Napoleon . . ."

Branwell hugged his elbows to his sides. "And they lived there until they got old and never caused any more trouble because the island was surrounded by wormsharks and at least one leviathan who kept guard and kept them safe, and for a little while, Old Boney didn't have to be Old Boney anymore."

TWENTY-FIVE

The Door in the Wall

Charlotte knelt quietly near a little mound of crushed green glass and spent cannonballs. She was wearing her old dress again, long and black and dusty. Her traveling dress.

It was over. A few of the soldiers were still skirmishing in the halls of the Parsonage, but it was over, really. The bat-trees lay uselessly on the streets of Verdopolis like broken beer bottles on Sunday morning. The evening sun turned everything to dazzling emerald prisms. Emily, Branwell, and Anne stood a little ways behind, with the soldiers. They stared at the green glass mound. They all felt sick, but they knew without asking that this was specially Charlotte's sadness.

"It's not possible," she whispered.

Crashey rubbed the back of his wooden neck and adjusted his bandages. "We had to use so much, don't you know. In the battle. To keep everyone on their feet. And we hadn't enough to begin with, since we sent the . . . er . . . lion's share to Calabar. On account of the trickery-feint. Remember? S'why we brought Josey along."

Leftenant Gravey wept drops of sticky amber sap all over the rows of medals on his chest. "I had three portions! If only I'd known! Oh, I'm a miserable selfish monster, I am."

"By the time he took his bullet," said Sergeant Crashey mournfully, "every medical man on the field was dry as . . . well . . . as . . . er. An old bone. And with Josephine off and vanished—you did say vanished, yeah?—we won't be whipping up a new batch any day soon."

"What difference does that make?" A tear slipped down Charlotte's cheek. "Go get some more! Send to Calabar! Send to anywhere! Glass Town must still be full of grog. Open up some cabinets! Tip out the milk bottles! Scrape out the mixing bowls!"

Anne opened her mouth and closed it several times. She wanted to say something, she truly did, but she couldn't make herself. Not for a Duke she barely knew. Gravey and Crashey exchanged looks.

"It's been hours and hours, miss," Gravey whispered miserably. "He's already rusting, poor chap."

Charlotte leaned over the man lying on the mound of glass and shot. She put her hand on the Duke of Wellington's cold iron cheek. She folded his hands on his chest so that they covered the hole in his heart, arranging them in a noble sort of way. The way kings' hands got folded in Westminster Abbey. Gravey was right. His fingernails had a fine sheen of red rust on them already.

Branwell watched Charlotte's thin little back heave in grief. He hated it. He wanted to feel triumphant. Napoleon was safe on an island and Wellington was dead. Boney never won when they played back home. Charlotte wouldn't let it happen because it wasn't historical. He had a right to be pleased! But Charlotte just would *not* get up from that green glass grave. The game was over. They were supposed to be happy and ravenous and tumble downstairs to stuff themselves with mutton and bread. Everyone always came back to life at the end of the game. Back to life and put away in their boxes for another day. That was why it was fun. That was why it was a game. Because in a game, death didn't matter. He controlled it. He doled it out and he took it back. If dying really meant anything, then it wasn't a game at all. It was just life. And in life he didn't control anything. *Come on, Welly,* he pleaded silently. *You old scrap-heap. Get up. Get up and it's still a game. Get up and Charlotte will laugh. Please! You're ruining it.*

"But it's all wrong," she said helplessly. "Wellington doesn't die fighting Napoleon. He gets to go home. He gets to be Prime Minister! He gets to drink brandy and pick out a grand old chair to put by the fire and smoke pipes and be *alive.*"

"I don't think so, love," Sergeant Crashey sighed.

"It's my fault. I made him come. I danced with him and I bantered with him and I fluttered my stupid eyelashes and I talked him into all of this terrible mess. I shall never, ever forgive myself. I shall never flutter anything again. *I killed the Duke of Wellington!*"

Branwell's guts twisted. She never was going to get up, was she? Charlotte didn't really know how to let things go. She always blamed herself. It dawned on him that perhaps this was part of the Eldest Child's Chores. Taking the blame. Being the one responsible. Being the one at fault. He was terrifically glad he wasn't the eldest, for once. But his guts weren't glad. His guts knew the truth.

"Don't say that," Emily said softly. "You didn't."

"It's not your bullet in his chest, is it?" Anne suggested.

"I did," Charlotte insisted. "As sure as Napoleon, I did. If I hadn't convinced him to come to Verdopolis, he'd never have thought he could catch the Gondaliers off-guard. He'd never have tried the feint at Calabar Wood. It's all my fault. If I . . . if I'd just . . . gone to School like a good girl . . ." Charlotte was sobbing in big, choking breaths now, and nobody thought it was only because of Wellington for a moment. "If I'd only protected them . . . if I'd only been . . . been *good* . . . good *enough*, nobody would ever have died." She buried her face in her hands. "I should have died instead. If I'd gotten the fever first, *they'd* have gone home and we'd never have invented Glass Town or come here at all and none of it would have happened. . . ."

"Who's they?" asked Leftenant Gravey. Crashey shook his head.

"I got lost a ways back, mate." The Sergeant shrugged.

Emily and Anne fell to the ground beside Charlotte and hugged her tight.

"No, Charlotte, no," they whispered over and over.

"Yes," Charlotte wept. "Yes."

Branwell's guts couldn't stand it any longer. He was supposed to protect them. Papa had said. He couldn't let her go on like that, with all that pain. It was worse than a cannonball, and he hadn't hesitated to throw himself in front of *that*, had he? His head didn't want to do it. No one would ever know. He was safe. It was all done. But his guts were always much stronger than his head.

"No," he said firmly. No one had been paying any attention to him, just like always. They all turned to look. They heard him now. They were paying attention now. "It's my fault."

Anne slapped her knee with one hand. "I knew it," she whispered.

"I . . ." *Oh god*, thought Bran. *They'll hate me forever.* But he didn't stop. A middle child has chores too, and one of them was Fessing Up. "I told Old Boney you were coming. When and where."

Emily's eyes went wide. "Bran, *why?* We were coming to rescue you! We could have been killed!"

"I didn't need you to rescue me! I was doing it myself! And I paid him, didn't I? He promised to keep you safe. That we'd all come out alive. I paid him Aunt Elizabeth's shilling and sixpence, only I told him it was a fortune, and he swore no one would have to die. And look! We *are* all alive and well! *I* rescued *you*, don't you see? I didn't do anything wrong! It's not as though it was *tremendously* clear that Gondal was wicked and Glass Town was good, if you recall." Crashey flushed an ugly color. "They deserved a fighting chance! It's not sporting to let a million frogs lose a war in their beds. I didn't know Wellington would snuff it. Of course I didn't! I thought . . . I rather thought he *couldn't*, because he *didn't*. Just like you said, Charlotte. Wellington doesn't die at Waterloo. Why should I have thought he'd die at Verdopolis? We never killed him at Verdopolis. And the Glass Towners had grog, after all. I never thought they'd run out. And I never thought they'd run out because you never told me it was all some lady's weird hair juice, Detective Inspector *Anne*," he snarled at her, and then wished he could take it back. He meant to shoulder the burden with nobility, but it was all coming out wrong. The way they were *looking* at him! Like he was a less than a worm in the dirt. He started to cry, and hated himself for it. "Oh, you always think I'm bad anyway. What's the point of ever trying to be anything else? I'm just another soldier in your box, aren't I? Look at Captain Branwell, always mucking it up! Doesn't he look funny, marching about, thinking he matters?"

A cool voice interrupted, cutting through Bran's words like a soft blue knife. "Captain? We do think rather highly of ourselves, don't we? I don't remember giving you a field commission, boy."

For a moment, no one breathed.

The Duke of Wellington stood behind them, wrapped

up in frosty blue and white and silver light. His officer's uniform had a sad little tear in it, and his proud bicorne hat was gone. His thin brown hair moved softly in the twilight breeze. He carried a postman's bag, slung over one shoulder. The Duke looked curiously at his iron body.

"Does my nose really crook like that?" he asked, and his voice sounded like the wind wuthering the moors.

Charlotte wiped her eyes and stuttered out: "But . . . but you didn't die along a highway! I thought of that, I thought of ringing Em's bell, but you didn't die by a road and Mr. Bud and Mr. Tree said that was the rule."

"All roads lead to Verdopolis," the Duke said with a soft smile. "Didn't you know? They're your roads, after all."

"Sir," Branwell said quietly. He was saluting, and no one noticed, but he persevered.

"But no one called for the Ghost Office," Emily said. "My bell shattered into a hundred pieces, so I know I didn't ring for the post."

"Did it hurt very badly?" Anne asked gently.

"Sir," Branwell said again.

"I am here for myself alone, young lady," Wellington answered, and bent forward in a small bow, for the dead can never outrank the living. "I wished to deliver a letter, and so I shall."

The Duke of Wellington reached one glowing pale hand into his post-bag and drew out a note sealed in black wax with his own crest stamped on it. It was very like Wellington's crest at home in England, save that all the lions were Copenhagen. He placed the note in Charlotte's hand and closed her fingers over it.

"It's not so bad," he said kindly. "It is only a strange holiday that lasts forever."

"Sir," Branwell said again, his back straight and unmoving, every inch the soldier at attention.

Wellington turned toward Bran. He looked the boy up and down. Shame rattled around Branwell like old seeds.

"I am sorry, sir."

"For what, pray tell?"

"For . . . er . . . acts of espionage. Please don't make me go through it all again. Treason. And making myself a Captain even though it was only a bit of a joke. I should have said Sergeant."

Crashey coughed.

The Duke said nothing for a long time. The sun set behind the green towers of the grand city, and its last beams shone through the ghost's thin body. It is quite something to be stared at by a creature from beyond the grave, even if he is also a postman. Branwell would never forget it. He felt the weight of time and fate pressing on his bones from all sides.

"Leftenant Gravey, may I?" The Duke reached for the wooden man.

Gravey glanced around nervously. "Erm, certainly, sir. I owe you my life, after all. If you mean to have it back, that's only fair."

But Wellington was not after Gravey's life. He was after his medals. The Duke lifted a handful of them off the Leftenant's chest, which only left several hundred to spare. He turned to Anne and pinned a gold and blue ribboned one to her dress.

"For kindness in the face of cruelty, and high acts of trickery," Wellington said gravely.

"For fearlessness in the face of the fearful, and thievery in the first degree," he said, and pinned a silver and violet medal on Emily, next to the one she'd swiped from the Officer's Mess so long ago. The Duke turned to Charlotte. He touched her cheek fondly with the backs of his fingers. Her medal was crystal and green ribbon. Green for Verdopolis and glass for Glass Town.

"For valor in the face of all hope lost, and the most beautiful lies I have ever heard, Lady Bell," he said with a sad smile.

"You're very welcome," Charlotte said shyly. She

couldn't help it. A last bit of banter slipped out. "For avenging you and winning your war."

"And finally," the Duke said sternly, turning to Branwell.

"My punishment," the boy whispered.

But the Duke of Wellington fixed an iron medal with a black ribbon to his chest.

"For honesty when you needn't have shown any, and for the capital crime of trying to save your family, even though it was a very poor plan, boy, good grief."

Branwell could not speak. His throat was so thick and tight nothing could squeeze out.

"I forgive you, Captain Branwell. You did a wicked thing, and I daresay it won't be the last, but you did *try*, and that's something. I think I shall be relieved not to have to *try* anymore. It's so very difficult, and life is so very full of it."

The Duke of Wellington faded with the very last of the day's light, and when he was gone, they could see a million stars hanging in the sky like the handwriting of the gods.

"It's time, I should think," said Emily. "George has gone ahead to make sure the tower is all clear of fighting and collapsed stairs and whatnot. Let's go home."

* * *

They found someone in the long, dark hallway outside the tapestry room. She was made all of white lace and orange blossoms, sitting on the ground with her face buried in her knees. Branwell could see a few good, unstained pages clutched in one fist and a blue-eyed doll he knew was called Albert in the other. She held on so tight they might have been made of gold. He flushed with guilt all over again.

"Victoria!" Anne cried. "What's the matter?"

"He turned me out," she said in a muffled voice. "Told me to clear off and he was so rude about it, so rude and so scrubby, and I did try to tell him I hadn't anywhere to go, but he wouldn't listen, he wasn't nice at all like Anne or Miss Agnes or anyone, and he told me to go and find my father, but I don't know what my father looks like, you see, so it's impossible, it's all impossible, and now I can't go in my room and I can't go out there, so I shall just stay here until the world ends, I expect."

"I shall take you, Miss Vickie," Crashey said cheerfully. "I know just what the old man has for a face. Why, he's just in the mess tent stuffeeding himself with hardtack right now. I saw him myself. You stick by your Sergeant and it'll all come out all rightfully."

Victoria Alexandrina, Crown Princess of Glass Town and Gondal, peeked up from between her arms.

"Promise you won't shout at me," she begged, and Crashey did. The wooden soldier took the lace girl in his arms, and only Branwell heard her whisper into his oak shoulder: *England. My England.*

"What man?" Charlotte said. "Who told you to clear off?"

"The puppy man," Victoria said, wiping her eyes. "He's still in there."

The crowd of them stuck their heads round the doorjamb to Victoria's lovely little room. It was just as Branwell and Anne had left it—the roof torn off, table overturned, dolls strewn everywhere, tapestries torn and tattered by musket-fire on the walls.

And George Gordon, Lord Byron, crouching in the corner with a trowel and a pile of stones picked out of the rubble. His long hair was a nest of tangles; his sleek fur was all rumpled and smelled of fear. He slapped down his trowel onto a new slab and smoothed out a thick icing of mortar.

"What in the world are you doing, George?" Emily said coldly, even though it was plain to see. She wanted to hear him say it.

Byron startled at the sound of her voice and leapt up guiltily, knowing he couldn't hide but trying valiantly anyway to disappear into the tapestry like a chameleon.

He tossed the trowel ridiculously out what remained of a window.

"Nothing! Just . . . preparing everything for you, my love! It's all . . . here . . . you see. Your door in the wall. Just like your charming brother and sister said. All splendid! All just perfectly splendid!"

Charlotte frowned at the little door behind the tapestry. Byron had nearly finished bricking it up. He'd done a dashingly good job, too. Who would have thought a Lord could lay stone like that? It blended into the wall perfectly. Another few minutes and they might never have found it.

"You little devil," Leftenant Gravey marveled.

Emily's face was hard and unyielding. But her insides felt like they were tumbling into empty space. "You were trying to keep me here," she said. "You were trying to keep us from leaving."

"I wasn't! Well, only for a little while longer. And only because I love you! I shall wilt and perish without you!"

"You won't." Anne snorted.

"We've only just found each other! You cannot condemn me to live without you! Would you really go so soon, and leave me? Never to return, or if you did, only after an agony of waiting you should wish on no man! And how should I greet thee, after long years? With silence, and tears! My heart will break, yet brokenly live on!"

"Stop quoting yourself!" Emily snapped. "You were! You were going to trap me here in Glass Town all for yourself! You'd steal my father and my aunt and my home away! You would make this whole beautiful world into a cage to hold me fast."

"No, Ellis—Emily! I would love you! I would be your husband!"

"I'm *ten*!"

"So?" shouted Lord Byron desperately. "I'm eleven! Emily, my darling, don't be so dramatic. You would be a Baroness, and dance every night, and never want for a single thing! Is that so dreadful? You told me how much you feared that vile place called School, and that you didn't want to be whatever a governess is, and how quickly fevers come in your world! Am I truly such a villain? Is it really a cage if it's the size of the world?"

"*Yes,*" said Emily, Charlotte, and Anne together, rather more loudly than any of them expected.

Crashey, Gravey, Branwell, Anne, Emily, and Charlotte fell to Lord Byron's brickwork, tearing it to pieces. The mortar was still soft, and it came away easily in their fingers. In a few moments, they were all panting and red-faced. The white silk curtain over the door was quite ruined, stained and torn. But the iron door beneath was still whole.

"You *will* come backturnagain, won't you?" Sergeant Crashey said hopefully, eyeing the door and mopping his brow. "'Course you will. Over there's boring. Here's much better. Here there's me."

"If we can," Charlotte said, and hugged him tight. "If Papa ever lets us out of his sight again. But Crash . . . will you be here if we do come? The age of grog is over. Josephine is gone and if you look a thousand years, you'll never find her. It was . . . it was never right to begin with. You must know that."

"You thought different when Wellington was laid out. Tip out the bottles and scrape out the bowls, you said."

Charlotte looked away, for she knew he was right, and she knew that the trouble with grog was that everyone had such a very good reason to want it. You couldn't blame a single soul for wanting it.

"Anything that requires a cage isn't right," she said in a low voice, with a pointed look at George from beneath her lashes.

"Death isn't right," Crashey said resentfully.

"No, but at least it belongs to everyone equally," Emily answered him, and as there was no answer to that, everyone fell quiet. Charlotte glanced at her clever, clever Anne with her hand thrust in her pocket. They said nothing, which said everything.

Branwell stood up and brushed off his hands on his trousers. He knew it was time. They were stalling now. All of them saluted Leftenant Gravey. "Did I do well, sir? In the final tally. Mostly well?"

"Mostly well, lad," said the wooden soldier. "Mostly well indeed."

Victoria bared her small teeth at Bran.

"Er. Bit of a spot there with the Lady's stationary, I gather?"

A small leather cat padded into the room. He crouched low on copper paws and looked miserably up at everyone, his tail dragging on the floor. Emily and Charlotte cried out in glee.

"Please do not be angry," Bestminster said. "We only did what we thought you wanted! Please don't leave me! I can't face the Left Luggage Office! We've been with you always, and if you put your hairbrushes in someone else, I could die of shame."

Emily held out her arms and the kitten leapt into them. Bestminster Tabby, the Noble Valise, never had, nor ever would, receive as many kisses from as many people as he did just then. In the flurry of affection, the suitcase could hardly tell who was who. He simply rolled about in it, wriggling from one embrace to the next.

"You weren't to know!"

"It's war, man!"

"I told you to; if it's anyone's fault, it's mine."

"I could never be angry at you, Bestminster."

"Fine job. Just fine. There's a medal in it for you. You can have mine!"

Bestminster Tabby took all his share of love and more. Then, he hopped down off Charlotte's shoulder, gave a wriggle and a quiver and a tremble, split in half, swelled up, and became two ordinary (though not *very* ordinary) suitcases once more.

Emily looked at the door. She reached out her hand to lift the ruined curtain, but could not, quite. George had been right about one thing. School was on the other side of the door. School, and the rest of everything. She turned to Lord Byron. He stared into her eyes with a warm brown gaze.

"In silence we met, in silence I grieve," he began.

Emily laughed. "I told you to stop that. I am sorry, George. I don't want to be stuck. Even here. Even anywhere. A tangled-up honeysuckle. I want to be half-savage and hardy and free. For a little while, anyway. I shall consider forgiving you, even though that was a dreadful thing you did. Perhaps. Maybe you can't help being a little dreadful. I know Branwell can't. Thank you, anyway, for the horse."

Lord Byron kissed Emily's hand. He had a bit of mortar on his lip. It came away on her skin, clinging there grayly.

"Good-bye, Crash," Charlotte said.

"Good-bye, miss." The Sergeant kept up his side bravely and did not cry. "Do try to keep cozywarm. And eat three square meals a day. And get lots of rest. And only drink freshbright water. And . . . well, dash it all, I am sorry about our man Wellington. I think he might have made a real Lady of you if it weren't for getting shot and that."

Suddenly, Charlotte remembered the note Wellington had given her. She'd meant to keep it to read when she was alone, but she could not be sure what would happen to it between worlds. She reached into her skirts and pulled it out, popping the black wax seal with one fingernail.

My Dear Lady of the Sensible Eyes and Rational Lips,

It was quite a dance after all, don't you think? And you were right, the steps were rather beside the point. You will have my gratitude forever. And one day, when you are very old indeed, perhaps you will come and meet me on the rich fields of County Nothing, and we will dance again under the Midsummer sun.

Yours,
Arthur Wellesley, Duke of Wellington

"No," Charlotte said with a mysterious smile. "I don't think military men are for me, in the end. Sooner or later, he will want to give me an order, and where would that leave me?"

"Farewell, Gravey," Emily cried. "Farewell, George. Farewell, Crashey. Farewell, Glass Town!"

Victoria clung to Anne and kissed her cheek. She whispered in her ear: "I'll make a new story. I'll start it tonight. I'll make you whatever you like."

The stairs went a long way down into the shadows. On the other side, they could smell heather and wintergreen already.

After they'd vanished into the wall of their own house and all had gone quiet for a moment or two, a dark head poked out from behind the tapestry once more.

It was Branwell.

"Go *away*," hissed Victoria Alexandrina.

Branwell strode to her side. He lifted her up and kissed her hand in such a gentlemanly manner that it would break your heart to see it. He took her ruined, tattered pages from her.

"Let me fix it," he said softly. "I can fix it. I'm good at stories. Well, not good, but all right. I shall cut and glue and arrange, just like Mr. Bud and Mr. Tree said back in Ochreopolis, until it all comes out as clear and neat as rain. Oh, there might be a burnt schoolhouse or two left over in the cuttings; editing's a messy business. But when I'm done, I'll bring it all back to you, and your England will be as green as mine. I promise."

Victoria clung onto her pages and shook her head. But little by little, as the moonlight drifted in, she let go. Branwell bowed to her like a true soldier, and slipped away like a shadow.

TWENTY-SIX

Home

Tabitha and Aunt Elizabeth scrubbed and soaked and wrung out the week's linens in the old washing tub. Their eyes were red and sunken with worry and with lye fumes. Papa stood in the doorway, smoking his pipe, but his heart wasn't in it. All the other children had arrived home from Cowan Bridge School already. He could only think that Branwell and Anne had gone along with the girls in the carriage from Keighley to see them properly settled in and all four had been lost in the blaze that destroyed Cowan Bridge School. Branwell had always been thoughtful that way.

The children came stumbling into the kitchen garden

from the frosted twilight. Their clothes smelled faintly of smoke. Their faces were smudged and exhausted and hollow-looking, but the color was high in their cheeks. They were hungry and bickering and alive.

Tabitha and Elizabeth fell upon them like hens on autumn apples.

"Where have you been? My darlings, my darlings, you frightened your auntie so!"

"You are just the worst children," Tabitha said fondly, runing her fingers through their tangled, filthy hair.

Papa could not bring himself to join in the smothering. He stood his ground and held out his arms, waiting. His son flew into them and he held the boy tight.

"We feared the worst," he said gruffly. "When word came about the fire, and no sign of any of you. But it's all right now. It's all right. We're all here."

Charlotte and Emily exchanged glances. *What fire?*

"There are other schools," Papa whispered into Anne's hair as he picked her up. "Better schools. You're all safe and you're all mine."

"Buck up, Papa!" Anne laughed.

"Be brave," Branwell said into his father's coat.

"Busy hands." Emily leaned against her aunt.

"Make bright hearts," Charlotte finished, and lay her head on her sister's lap. She had never been so tired.

※

What they had been about they would not say, nor how they had been gone so long, nor why Branwell and Anne had not just let the girls go in the carriage as they were told, nor how they had found their way home in the dark. In fact, all four were silent as monks.

Aunt Elizabeth sent the girls and Branwell to scrub their cheeks and dress for supper.

"There's a bit of time to play with your wooden soldiers, if you like," Tabitha called after them. "The fish will not be ready for three quarters of an hour!"

In the playroom at the top of the stairs, four solemn judges stood before their wooden soldiers.

"Crashey's got to be punished somehow," Emily said. "Everyone who took Josephine's hair. It's too awful to let them off scot-free."

"Go on, Charlotte," said Branwell, "you're best at punishments."

Charlotte thought for a long time. "In the morning I shall take him down to the kitchen gardens and leave him there, where he will wander in exile, being set upon by mice and cats and foxes and badgers, and at the end of a month, I will collect him again."

"In Glass Town, that will be the most awful and extraordinary tale of penance," Emily breathed.

"It's not enough," Anne mumbled. "Not really. Not when you think it all through as hard as you can."

When three quarters of an hour had passed, no one came to the table.

"They can't do this to me again!" Tabitha cried. "My heart won't take it!"

Aunt Elizabeth and Tabitha drew on their woolen shawls and went out into the gloam to find the little wastrels while Papa tried to calm his breathing in the parlor. They would *not* stop running off, those four. Just like their mother. Probably watching some silver worm chew the earth or counting cobblestones. They could not have gone far. The women would find them. It would be all right. Buck up, he told himself.

It would be spring soon. Green snapped in the air though the yews in the churchyard gave no hint of bud.

Aunt Elizabeth and Tabitha turned down the path to the churchyard without saying a word to one another. They knew where the little ones would be. They spied four dark heads down among the gravestones. They'd been through so much—of course they'd run to their mother, and to their sisters, too. Anne and Charlotte, Emily and Branwell stood before three headstones on the slope next to the open moor.

The middle one, Lizzie's, shone gray in the moonlight beside Maria's. Their mother's marker was half-sunk in heath and moss.

Little Anne had something in her hand. A vial wrapped up in leather and strips of fur. All the other children were staring at it.

"You really are the best thief of all of us," Emily marveled. "Good show. But it won't work, you know. It's the bravest idea imaginable, but it won't work."

Anne nodded. Tears fell off her cheekbones. She knew. She'd guessed since that awful day at Bravey's Inn, and she'd mostly given up all hope when Wellington had begun to rust, and she'd been certain when her toffee hammer with ANNE etched on it turned into a birch branch halfway down the stairs from one Parsonage to another and all their wonderful medals had turned into chips of rock and pinecones. But she had to try anyway.

"I'm sorry," Anne's voice started to hitch a little, full of tears to come. "I should have let you have it for poor Welly after all. You knew I had it, Charlotte. I saw. I saw you knowing it. It was only that—"

"Don't be silly, Annie. All of us being six again is ever so much more important than the Duke of Wellington. And even if Emily's right . . . there was a hope, you know. It was always little. But it was big enough."

Anne squared her shoulders.

"It *will* work like it did in Glass Town," Anne said. "And . . . and . . ."

"And everyone will wake up and start talking all at once and kiss us like mad," Branwell took up the game. "And . . . and . . ."

"And we'll all turn into birds and fly away into the stars," Emily said, her eyes wet. "And . . . and . . ."

"And nothing bad will ever happen, because we will be all of us together forever until the very, very end of time," Charlotte whispered.

Anne opened the vial and turned it upside down. A single red rose petal fell out, bright and vivid and stark against the graves.

"We brought you flowers, Mummy," said Anne, and leaned over to kiss the fading headstone.

She smiled at her brother and sisters. Her eyes were dry. You couldn't ever really fix a sad story. You could only make another. And another. And another, until you found the right one at last, the one that ends in joy.

The children lingered under that benign sky, watched the moths fluttering among the heath and harebells, listened to the soft wind breathing through the grass.

"How anyone can ever imagine unquiet slumber for

our dear sleepers in that quiet earth I shall never know," Aunt Elizabeth said finally, and went down the path to coax the four tired, sweet things up toward the warm candlelit house.

ACKNOWLEDGMENTS

This book owes many, many debts, too many to ever repay. It will just have to toddle along in life with patches on its coat and a humble heart, poor dear. But one must always try, so here are a few coins toward the capital.

First, and foremost, and forever, and always: I beg the forgiveness and approval of Charlotte, Emily, Anne, and Branwell Brontë, who I have loved for nearly all my life, and by whom I hope I have done well. The Glass Town you have found here is not their Glass Town precisely, for that would be burglaring, and perhaps the Charlotte, Anne, Emily, and Bran you have followed through these pages are not the Brontës precisely, either, but shadows of them, moving through a dimension just slightly different from our own. But there is not a road in my tale in which they did not lay the first stone. As with all children, once you have set it going, a world gets away from you quicker than you can imagine, and *my* Glass Town was always meant to be *theirs* if only it ran off to join the circus and got confoundedly lost along the way. But quite obviously, there is no book without them, and very probably without them I would never have been a writer anyhow, so please think of this as my thank-you gift laid upon their graves with hope and love and not a little trepidation. It is my deep hope that the children, young and old, who wander through this Glass Town may find their way from it to *Jane Eyre*, *Wuthering Heights*, *Agnes Grey*, and all the other glorious works of the Brontë sisters.

I have, perhaps, been allowed to visit and sit in the playroom at the top of the stairs for one beautiful afternoon, and permitted to join their game, still going on and going on forever. I've but made a wooden soldier or two walk and talk clumsily across the floor before being called away home for my supper. Thank you so, all four of you, for the wonders of your hospitality.

I cannot thank the Brontë Parsonage in Haworth enough for the incredible and tireless work they have done to preserve and make available every detail of the Brontës' lives, from the tiniest and loveliest to the greatest and grandest. Additionally, Fannie Elizabeth Ratchford's *The Brontës' Web of Childhood*, *Inside the Victorian Home*, and Daphne Du Maurier's *The Infernal World of Branwell Brontë* were utterly invaluable to my research. All remaining mistakes, infelicities, anachronisms, liberties, and all other assorted foolishnesses that the text is heir to are my own and I shall take my scoldings without complaint.

Thank you to Terri Windling and Ellen Datlow for commissioning the short story that wanted to be a big grown-up book from the moment the first word hit the page. Thank you to Jane Yolen for appearing in my inbox one day, as if by magic, to reassure me that the big grown-up book was a good idea, after all. And to Kaite Welsh, for enthusing all these years over the whole mad notion of the thing. Thank you also to Rebecca Latimer, Nicholas Tschida, and Shawna Jacques.

Thank you to Howard Morhaim, my beloved agent; to Annie Nybo, who only edits things in the very nicest of ways and is nothing at all like Mr. Bud or Mr. Tree; and to Kristin Ostby, for setting the wheels in motion.

Thank you to Heath Miller, who read and read these chapters as they evolved, told me off when I was being too awfully American about things, and kept me fed and watered like the weedy little harebell I am.

And one final, small apology to Jane Austen, for being more loyal to another's opinions on her work than my own—after all, when in Glass Town, one knows who butters one's bread.